THE CHOCOLATE BOX

ISABELLA MAY

"Life is like a box of chocolates."

— FORREST GUMP

For the following endlessly supportive and wonderful writing people. Happy and blessed to have you in my tribe. What you have achieved collectively is SO flipping inspiring...

Alphabetically:

Carrie and Cristina
Emma and Heidi
Kiltie and Lizzie
Natali and Taryn

ACKNOWLEDGMENTS

There are so many people to thank when it comes to showing my appreciation for the guidance I had along the way in the crafting of this book!

First and foremost, I must say a huge thank you to Lorraine Mace, who not only helped plant the seed for grown-up Ellie's opening chapter, but inspired me to lay the foundations for the entire story... over coffee and pancakes in our local Belgian café.

Next, Alice Cullerne Bown, a massive thank you for your patience and editing vision. The story transformed itself from Cinders to Cinderella.

Then it's another mammoth thank you to my family – close and extended - for their continuous support on this rollercoaster-stroke-waltzer-stroke-dodgem of a writing journey. Most days I swear they'd rather I set up my own bakery/ice cream parlour/cocktail bar. Chris, Carmen, William, Mum, Dad, Tina, Auntie Pat, Carolyn & Cousin Jo. From books 1-6, you have been amazing.

And a gigantic THANK YOU to Les Flitcroft, Namarta Gulraj, Preeti Samant Kirplani, Nichola Elliott, Vina Shah and everyone at the UK Institute of Pranic Healing, as well as Pranic Healing Gibraltar, and Pranic Healing Costa del Sol. Special thanks to Claire Skingley, Karen, Vince, Carina and Caroline. I'm not sure how I would have got through lockdown and the pandemic without you all helping me stay grounded, energised and chilled. Atma Namaste.

Back to the book world and I have a loooong list of people to thank for their unwavering cheers. In my last book I said something along the lines of 'thanking you all is easier!' but this time I will try to remember everyone who thoroughly deserves not just a pat on the back for constantly supporting (and inspiring) me, but a box of their very own handcrafted chocolates (preferably hex free). In no order of ranking, because you are all so wonderful, heartfelt thanks to:

All those brilliant female writers mentioned on the dedication page... also Rachel Gilbey (for her fabulous book blog tours and total commitment to her authors), Kel Mason, Sue Baker, Tessa Hastjarjanto, Hayley T, Lauren Rebecca, Maria Sinclair, Brenda Blair, Sarah Hill, Lyn Caro, Maiu Clark, Megan Mayfair, Rosie Travers, Katharine Johnson, Lynn Forth, Cathie Dunn, Nicola Slade, Emma Jackson, Jenni Keer, Ian Wilfred, Natalie Jane Smith, Cherry Karl, Chele Sugar Shell, Kayleigh Louise Brown, Kate Kenzie, Gary Bodley, Debra Jo Bright, Hannah Lopez, Helen Pryke, Katie Wells, Irene Rosenblatt, Nicola May, Portia Macintosh (our banter over a certain 'Dom' definitely inspired Barnaby Westwood's character!), Daisy James, Rachel Fowler, Leigh Richardson Hill, Penny-sue Wolfe, Priya Khajuria, Rebecca Lee, Shani Struthers, Rose McClelland, Sandy Barker, Belinda Missen, Tessa Sacramento-Menez, Zoe Fox, Lisa Parry, Collis Boucher, Peter Mitchelmore, Anita Faulkner and my friends from CC/DS,

A BIG shout out to The Fiction Café Book Club (especially Wendy Clarke), and TBC The Book Club (especially Helen Boyce)

Finally, thank you to Elizabeth Gilbert and Rebecca Campbell for your words of wisdom which have been gold dust this year.

Purlease tell me I haven't missed anyone...

*I*n a cobbled lane in the higgledy-piggledy mazes of the Georgian city of Bath, you will find a chocolate shop. Like Hotel Chocolat on steroids and thin as a rake, it is right out of Diagon Alley. Study it briefly, and you will salivate, whilst weeping tears of joy at its tenderly-crafted beauty. Let your gaze linger for a little longer and you will see the ghosts of a million handprints, their patina forming slowly, but indisputably, in front of your eyes.

Eleanor Finch had already felt the magnetic pull of the shop, and now she was edging toward its glittering display of shiny rainbow foils, their iridescent shimmers strategically placed in the corner of the window to capture the attention of every six-year-old child retracing Jane Austen's steps.

"I'm here for a hat, Eleanor, don't be getting any daft ideas." Her mother's piercing voice cruelly attempted to break the cocoa beans' spell, but wasn't quite enough to drag the child's eyes from the heavenly scene before her. "God dammit, if the nursery was open on a Saturday I could do this in peace and quiet. But no, and Glastonbury being Glastonbury, of course it wouldn't think to put a milliner's above a dozen blimming crystal and candle emporiums."

"Actually, Glastonbury does have a hat shop, Mummy," Eleanor enlightened Pamela Finch, absent-mindedly tugging at her mother's coat, her senses still enraptured by the delectable chocolatier and its mouth-watering wares. "There's a big shop at the end of the High Street, selling Tor paintings, fairy statues, and wooden drums... and one day I saw a witch's hat in its window... I really di—!" But Eleanor couldn't finish, dumbstruck anew by the spinning teacups, dangling on strings, their cups and saucers filled with pastel-coloured pralines and violet creams. *How did they stay on?* She covered her gaping mouth with her hand.

Pamela attempted a tug of her own to get her wandering daughter back onto her trajectory. "That's the kind of useless comment I'd expect from your father. Now come on, we need to be back at the bus stop in an hour. I swear there was a less snobby shop around here somewhere. That last place we tried was priced for the Royal Family and their cronies. Awful headpieces, especially that thing with the giant bow. Like something for flaming Ascot. Or... or... a chocolate box." She closed her eyes and shuddered. "All I want is a respectable, decently priced hat; something that doesn't make me look like a cheap thrill... yet stops that Auntie of yours thinking she's totally stolen the show in her puffball gown. Especially after she dared wear virgin white on *my* Big Day. Oh, it'll *so* be a puffball or a pavlova, mark my words, Eleanor. I'd go as far as putting a tenner on it... if your father's wages started to reflect his grandiose talk about that excuse for a company, anyway."

Eleanor thought the puffball pavlova dress sounded pretty, like something her Crystal Barbie would wear if she got married to Ken. She'd loved the Chocolate Box headpiece her mother had hated, too. Almost as much as she'd fallen

2

head over heels for this real chocolate paradise that was calling her name. Now she refused to budge a millimetre in this boring search for a hat. She imagined the soles of her feet boring into the ground like little drills, rooting her to the spot.

"But it's true, Mummy, I promise," her words tumbled out. "And if they have a witch's hat in the window, then just think... that means they are showing people because they want them to come inside and see *all the other hats* they have." She opened her arms out wide as an opera singer to back up her point. "They'll definitely have a pink one that's just perfect to go with your wedding outfit."

Eleanor's Auntie Nancy was getting married. Eleanor thought Nancy was her mum's sister, although maybe she was her mum's Auntie too? Or was she her cousin? She didn't get the whole grownup family thing. It all seemed so alien a notion when you didn't have any brothers or sisters of your own to measure such things against, and when you were only in Class 2 at school, and Miss Tessa, your teacher, had never tried to teach you about such concepts with her trusty, laminated flashcards.

Eleanor took a deep breath. She knew it was silly to be scared, especially in public, but sometimes her mum made her feel that way; like she was as unpredictable as a spinning top, and if Eleanor or her dad pushed her too hard, she'd get out of control and cross and scary, wheeling off to lock herself in the bedroom for hours until she emerged all panda-eyed and sad. So Eleanor half-whispered:

"Why don't we go in here instead, and buy ourselves a chocolate? Just one. Look, Mummy, look! They sell them all on their own and they weigh them on those scales, and everything." Eleanor pointed at the beautiful golden balance in the centre of the display, one of its pans cascading with the sort of pleasure that even Gwyneth Paltrow couldn't ignore.

"Oh, please, Mummy. We could just have a tiny one each, which would cost *waaaaaaaay* less money than getting a box. They're so pretty, aren't they? I know they would cheer you up, and I could pay you back from my piggybank when we get home…"

Pamela stopped tugging at her daughter then. For one sweet moment Eleanor tasted victory. She sucked in her cheeks, not daring to express her happiness until her mum had given the green light – as she surely would. In that blissful snapshot of time, Eleanor sensed she was suddenly grown up enough for her mum to be her best friend; grown up enough that Cadbury's Buttons might be allowed as an above-board occasional treat… instead of being rationed to her in secret by her dad.

"The only thing you need to *look at*, young lady is what happened to the girls and boys in Willy Wonka's factory."

Before Eleanor could even ask who this 'Willy' was, Pamela seized her daughter and shook her to attention as if she were but a tin soldier plucked out of a fairy tale; a tin soldier who'd enraged the Queen and was now on a very last warning.

"We are here to buy me a hat. And if you want to get married one day and wear a beautiful white dress, I suggest you give all ideas about that hideous stuff," she eye-rolled the decadent display without even looking at it, "a very wide berth."

Eleanor's heart sank. How could that be true? Auntie Nancy ate chocolate. Eleanor knew she did, because she'd seen her with a plate of those Jaffa Cake things at a family eightieth birthday party! She thought it was for Uncle Jack. But maybe he was a grand uncle or a great uncle or something. He was ancient, anyway.

"But…" Eleanor started to relay this titbit of information to her mum, then briskly changed her mind. Instead, she drank in as much of the scene before her as she could before the dream was over: the shopkeeper behind the counter wrapping something chunky and delicious, tying it with a bright red bow, and handing it back to the world's luckiest child (standing next to the world's kindest mum); the assortment of suede, bronze, dried leaf, and clay-brown chocolates in their orderly tiers in the window, like something out of a seaside amusement arcade. Perhaps she could will the little shelves to nudge the bottom row of snow-speckled white chocolate truffles into a hidden hatch beneath the pane of glass, as you would with a tuppenny slot machine, so she could furtively gather them up when her mum wasn't looking, feigning a cough and stuffing them quickly in her mouth to melt on her tongue?

She broke free from Pamela for a moment to try her luck, but it was futile. Weston-Super-Mare's pier this was not. Eleanor's fingers slid down the window as her mum yanked her away via the strings of her annoying mittens, stitched into the lining of her duffle coat.

Her fingers stayed splayed like a starfish for an hour on the bus, they stayed splayed like a starfish (under the table) at tea time, they stayed splayed like a starfish even when she was later rearranging the furniture in her dolls' house, her right hand furtively dotting Barbie and Sindy's miniature table with brightly coloured beads, each one representing the mini jewels whose images were printed in her mind. In fact, her rigid, defiant left digits remained outstretched until bedtime, when the heavy eyelids of slumber felt it would be kinder to erase the painful experience for the poor child.

Well, as much of it as they could...

ELLIE

$\mathcal{S}$he crossed her legs, she uncrossed her legs. How to perch seductively, sedately and successfully without portraying a tart? *Come on, Ellie!* She'd polished her body language to perfection a gazillion times in front of the full-length mirror in her bedroom. Probably best not to re-enact her Sharon Stone manoeuvre quite yet though, despite the fact she was also currently commando. Still, if Barney was interviewing her alone, she might be persuaded to reconsider.

Barnaby, *Barnaby*, **Barnaby**.

That's the way he was known nowadays, wasn't it? Well, according to that double page spread she'd devoured last year in *The Western Daily Press* it was. The posh hottie had only gone and grown himself up into a full-fledged phwoar of a businessman. She'd framed his pixelated features from the newspaper cutting and given them pride of place on her bedside table, completing the effect with a halo of orb-shaped fairy lights.

Ellie could tell you the precise angle of the crook of his arm as he shook hands with the Rotary Club's frumpy female president in the picture. Nineteen-point-five degrees. Yes, in his flawlessness, the object of her desire could almost position his anatomy in an aerodynamic twenty degree angle; a sentiment that made her giggle when she thought about the many ways his physique might also care to translate itself beneath the sheets.

Ellie could tell you where his shoes were made, too: Savile Row, whilst the glint of white that dazzled at his ankle strongly hinted at a pair of quality Pringle socks. She could even guess what he'd had for breakfast. Oh, all right. She didn't quite have X-ray vision into the cavities of his stomach, but his Instagram post that same date had dutifully informed her that he was 'running on empty save for the rescue remedy of my beloved **#americano** for the past 8 hrs **#famished**'.

So what?

Anyone who told you they didn't play Silent Witness on Insta and its cacophony of social media cousins was lying out their backside.

As she was saying, Barnaby Westwood was the last thing she saw before she went to bed at night and the first thing that greeted her as dawn's glow heralded a new day. At least for the past year and a bit. Prior to that, she'd furtively stashed all her relics of Barnaby's existence beneath *their* bed. The *he* in said pronoun had belonged to her thoroughly academic, thoroughly disappointing, and thoroughly ex-husband, who wouldn't even know how to switch on a vacuum cleaner, much less make up a bed with clean sheets if Mari Kondo had tutored him herself. And so there her secret had remained, safe as houses – and plush Bristol waterfront apartments.

Meanwhile she'd morphed from an Eleanor to an Ellie. From a no-frills Finch to a sultry Sanchez. And she couldn't wait for Barnaby to see it.

Keep your shit together. Stay professional, woman, for goodness sake! How many times have you gone over this already? And do not, under any circumstances, get so freaking nervous that you shorten him to 'Barn' – despite the fact this is Somerset. Got it?

Got it.

Ellie snapped herself back to her current surroundings and attempted to stir her uninspiring beverage to life, still miffed at the way the barista had written her name as 'Benny' on the side of the paper cup. What in the bloody hell? How could anybody interpret her BBC English 'Ellie' as a bloke's name?

It was annoying for sure, but she wouldn't let anything sour her upbeat mood today. Her job interview with Barnaby was finally happening. Ellie had dreamed of it for years. The visualisation board had only gone and made manifest. Many were those who sniped at the not-so-new-fangled notion of the Law of Attraction; the mind – and one's words and deeds – creating one's reality. But Ellie Sanchez was flesh and blood proof that pinning up collages, indulging in childish felt-tip pen sketches (and framing certain newspaper cuttings) of your heart's wildest desires flipping well delivered.

She took a hasty gulp at her dull flat white. *Arsehole.* The guy must have brewed it in a furnace. But Ellie refused to let the scald be anything more than a triviality. Hell, she even threw him a smile, ignoring the unappealing mop of Harry Potter-esque hair clinging to the sides of his face for dear life, which would have been put to far better use if you'd turned him upside down to mop the floor – because today was the day *her* life was going to change forever.

Tables turned. Dues paid. She was on the up.

She lifted her iPad from her extravagant pillar-box red Mulberry bag and ran immaculate nails over the tips of its keys. She'd opted for purple. Yes, it clashed hideously. But it was the colour of prestige, symbolic of all she was setting out to achieve.

A husband: She wouldn't settle for a lover.

A best friend: She wouldn't settle for fair-weather.

The minutes ticked by, every sip of coffee buoying her up for the body-language role play she'd also nailed, in every spare second of her recently monotonous existence.

Ellie nursed her almost-empty cup in her hands, pouring over the catalogue of scenarios she'd painstakingly rehearsed. She'd meticulously typed out every imaginable variation of interview patter on her laptop, but it was imperative she cram in a little last minute tuition. A girl with a goal as lofty as hers could never be over-prepared. She bit down seductively as she contemplated her Kindle.

Barnaby would ask her about her last position. She'd run her fingers enticingly through her hair, teasing out the blatant innuendo; the double entendre, leaving him breathless for more. At which point she'd grant him a barely-there flutter of the eyelids, sealing the deal with a pout like an 18-year-old on Insta. She'd only had to scour a cluster of fake eyelash and cartoonish eye-browed social media accounts and YouTube videos to master that move.

Her mobile vibrated, rudely interrupting the final part of her groundwork. She gritted her teeth. Ben. Impeccable timing, as ever. *Not.* She'd have slow hand-clapped the oik if he were in the same room. She knew she was being the world's most ungrateful cow, what with the groundwork *he'd* put in; the painstaking research he'd unflinchingly done, but shitting hell, there was such a thing as a time and a place.

'Don't forget to impress the company with your knowledge on the latest advances in HR practice, Els. It's important they sense your clout, that you relish the opportunity to tactfully dissolve conflict; that it's all one big breeze. Remember the bullet points I

tested you on last week, too. They're the key areas; the ones the interviewer is most likely to throw at you.'

Ellie could have tossed him a grenade then. What did he take her for, a complete fool? She'd put in the hard home-work yards, she'd barely left her apartment except to restock on salad, fruit and the occasional sushi fix from the Sains-bury's down the road, for crying out loud. That's what it took to rock the comfortable halfway house of a size nine these days; a status she adored, once she overlooked the dietary discipline part. As a nine, you could be smug either way, either squeezing into an eight... or, oh, heavens above, you always had an infuriating inch to spare around the waistband of a ten. He'd got her so riled she would just have to have that extra glass of wine later, dammit!

'Yeah, chill. I'm good, mate,' she speed-typed back before he could get above his station and send more. *"It's all going to pan out perfectly, you'll see. You've gone above and beyond, Benjamin. I owe you a takeaway. Now stop it! Go crunch some numbers... or whatever it is you do in that swanky bank all day.'*

Best add a friendly wink emoji or ten.

'I only want the best for you, Els.' He pinged her back instantly. *'You deserve it – after all you've been through.'*

Give her strength. Anyone would think the guy had a thing for her.

'XX' came his P.S.

Oh, FFS.

She almost fired it back as well.

Right. Now. Where was she?

Too many miles away from the erogenous zone, that's where...

Next Barnaby would grill her about her strengths and her weaknesses. She'd tip her head back just so, shake it at a precise angle – she'd be lying if she said she hadn't debated the merits of a token bust-shimmy as well – beam a tickled-pink smile, then fix him with expertly smoky eyes. Side note: thanks very much, House of Fraser's glamorous Chanel counter for the freebie first thing this morning. Side side note: the shop really did need to train its staff to recognise fake bridezillas who had no intention of either marrying, or purchasing a particle of primer.

Well, she needed at least a six month safety net to woo Barnaby into a wedding proposal first, *purlease*…

"I'm not going to waste your time or mine," she'd tell him. "I don't have a single fault. The darkest, most luxurious 85% Columbian cacao couldn't lead me astray. And really, you may as well quit while you're ahead. You're looking at your new Human Resources Manager, and you know it."

Ellie had um-ed and ah-ed about paperclipping a wink at the end of her declaration. Tempting, but probably taking things a little too far at this stage. There'd be plenty of time for fun and games with her soon-to-be beau once she'd got her new career in the bag and zipped it tightly with a self-assured smile.

Then a young mother plonked her coffee cup in front of her toddler at the table next to Ellie, and hoofed it back to the counter. Ellie didn't need a crystal ball to see what would happen next. An inquisitive hand made a grab for the coffee before Ellie could, and hundreds of mocha droplets cascaded through the air, dousing her opulent bag – and one tenth of Carlos's settlement – with it.

Why, the little…!

But Ellie could forgive the podgy cherub with her halo of golden curls instantly, for there was another child who couldn't seem to hold the attention of her parent. Ellie studied the girl's innocent features and felt a pang of regret. There was no excuse for such a slip-up. Just as there'd been no excuse for her own mother, carting her off to nursery at the tender age of seven months.

A voice from the past piped up from the filing cabinet in Ellie's head. The one that loved to fling itself open without warning.

*'Excuse me? Somebody had to **woman** the hotel reception desk, see to the bedrooms when the cleaners were faking sickies, restock the lobby bar, and basically run the entire show. And don't get me started on the month of flipping June and Glastonbury festival. Michael Eavis – sorry, his Highness **Sir Michael** – never had a bleedin' clue about the extra work he landed on little old me every summer for the past umpteen years with the town's increase in tourism. I doubt very much that any of that's changed now his daughter, Emily's in char—'*

Ellie blinked the voice away ferociously, seething that it, too, should infiltrate her pre-interview buzz.

The leggy blonde mum returned to the table, another tray of steaming hot drinks in hand, and a glut of chocolate cake to accompany it. Ellie's stomach groaned in protest. The quick glance she'd earlier allowed herself at the counter when she'd put in her caffeine order told her this was the deep brown, mirror-glazed, amber-sandwiched and thoroughly chunky Sachertorte she'd thought she'd successfully ignored. This young mother was either meeting friends, or she was one of those lucky cows whose super high metabolism could burn up an all-you-can-eat buffet and still leave room for dessert followed by cheese, biscuits and port.

Ellie frowned at the injustice of it all as she grappled with the serviette holder on her own table, yanking out as many paper towels as she could. She bent to pat at her bag before the same blast from the past voice could have its merry – and wordy – way with her again on this, its favourite of subjects: the cocoa bean and its dark side. Thank goodness her bag was of the highest quality leather, finished off with the best varnish. But that was hardly the point.

"Ava! Look what you've done. You naughty girl! I turn my

back for two seconds and you've completely wrecked the joint," the blonde screamed.

Ellie, continuing to sponge off her bag, waited to be acknowledged and showered with the avalanche of apologies she was irrefutably due. When she realised she'd be waiting until Doomsday she couldn't help herself. "Actually, I think you'll find you were gone and your child was left unsupervised for more like *fifty* seconds," she said, flapping a handful of soiled serviettes at the young woman to labour her point. No way was she letting this neglectful, poured-into-her-jeans, Ugg-booted excuse for a mother mouth off at her sweet little child like that. The mum was almost a child herself, couldn't have been a day over twenty-one.

"Did I ask for your opinion?"

Gawd. How mainstream-predictable a retort. It was enough for the *Flying Without Wings* ballad; Ant, Dec and sodding Simon Cowell to waltz into the café with a cluster of cameras and *Kleenex* boxes trailing in their wake.

"You didn't, this is true."

Ellie relished the way she was assuming the role of diplomatic HR Manager already. *Act as if, and you're halfway there!* And not even Ben could accuse her of being indiscreet and unethical in her current predicament. Many were those who'd have slapped this excuse for a mother across both cheeks by now.

"Then kindly keep your beak out, and kindly take your eyes off my kid."

"I'll happily do that, now you've remembered you have a role as her – *presumed* – caregiver," Ellie delighted in retaliating. Ah, the HR etiquette had gone out of the window already. But until she stepped into a certain gentleman's office, all of this was but a dress rehearsal anyway. She might as well let her acid tongue enjoy its freedom while it lasted.

"Not only could your child have given herself third

degree burns with that haphazardly positioned hot beverage, she's also drenched my designer bag."

"So call the filth," the woman retorted. "I'm sure they'll be happy to put a two-year-old in a cell. They'd be doing me an effing favour, that's for sure; I could finally let my hair down and have a night out with the girls. *Designer bag!* As if," She said, cocking a brow, tainting Ellie's carefully curated accessory as though it were a cheapjack from a market stall. "Whatever. You're a nobody."

Ellie sensed the flick of an inner switch.

But she wouldn't let it show. She packed up her belongings, straightened her back, splayed out her victory nails; the same talons that would later be clutching a well-earned, and thoroughly chilled glass of Bollinger – and definitely not the decadent and delicious Marc de Champagne truffles she was successfully ignoring, as they sat, testing her rock hard resolve, in the same goddamn fridge – and gathered up the soggy napkins, plonking them in the woman's lap. She hoped they damn well stained it and caused her untold hours of embarrassment. She proffered the little girl a wink.

What Ellie Sanchez did next was to turn her back on the fast and furious missiles of abuse streaming her way, click-clack in her sumptuous stiletto heels towards the door, and open it up on her new life, shutting it firmly behind her on the old.

3

ELLIE

*E*llie strutted to her Audi, quite possibly in the manner of a peahen. She wasn't yet accustomed to the height of her stilettos, but no way was she under-selling herself in half-arsed kitten heels or those hideous-yet-supposedly-stylish articles dubbed *brogues*.

It was all, or it was nothing.

Ellie had never been one to conform to the peanut gallery's opinion when it came to Audi drivers. She still fawned over her beautiful car. Who wouldn't, after years of being ferried from pillar to post in their parents' embarrassing, paint-peeling, bubbled, Kermit the Frog-green Volvo estate, complete with tacky furry di? All right, so this baby had eaten into almost a third of the Carlos pay-out. But an Audi made a statement and it was worth it.

Yes, there was a new colour-coded power theme going on in her life, thought Ellie, opening the pillar-box red passenger door, and she really shouldn't gloat, but so far it was aiding her swagger quite nicely. She hadn't expected to see a scratch on the paintwork. She grimaced at it. Did the humdrum motor parked next to her, with its teddy bear-strewn parcel shelf, belong to Bitter Bitch? But she batted another of today's trivialities away, reminding herself instead of the triumph of that napkin dump and cafe door slam – her metaphorical way of staking her claim on all things shiny and new.

It was only a twenty-minute drive from the insipid coffee shop to her destination, and yet she could have been travelling to John O'Groats, the journey dragging on forever with the incessant blink of red lights. Finally, the dorms of Monty's cheered her on, overlooking the main road from afar as they did; their public school haughtiness towering above all of Somerset on the brow of Primrose Hill. There, too, were the minion motorists completing their school runs to the lesser establishments that were Springhope and St. Ed's.

For all her qualms, Ellie had been lucky, for a short while anyway. *One of the chosen few.* Then again, sometimes it was better never to have had a taste of the finer things in life; things like Monty's. Appearances could be deceptive. The aforementioned di didn't always land in the right slot on the roulette wheel, especially if it was oversized and furry. Brand new Mercedes could be driven off the garage forecourt in sparkling silver one day, and traded in for fifteen-year-old, door-to-door salesman-style, Kermit the Frog-green antiquities on wheels the next.

She shivered at the recollection, eternally grateful to Lassie, her unoriginally-named pet Collie dog, who'd flanked the giant window of said vehicle's boot to protect the teenage Eleanor from the prying eyes of the High Street. All of which was slightly ridiculous, since Eleanor Finch had never exactly cast a fluttering of mystique on her classmates or year group – neither at Monty's nor at the local state school, stale old St. Ed's, where her secondary studies had started and finished devoid of the aplomb they deserved. Nobody's eyes would have been eagerly documenting her automobile or scholarly downgrade. Sometimes, she reluctantly conceded, being the wallflower had its unexpected perks.

How convenient, though, that The Really Bad Photo Company's head office should be located so close to Monty's. Barnaby and his slightly younger sister, Clementine, had only to sail through their A levels (with the turbo boost of much extra tuition), scrape through uni for the token gesture of a degree scroll and beaming mortar board-clad grin, join Daddy's company, get bored with that, accept Daddy's investment, and set up a venture of their very own. Westwood Senior undoubtedly got to stick his fingers and thumbs in the peachy pie as time and mood dictated, but he was a minor inconvenience to tolerate for world domination in their niche business.

Ellie had to hand it to the siblings. That lengthy piece in the newspaper suggested pacey growth and monumental success for their gimmick-churning tourist souvenir company. Ellie had even stifled a giggle when she'd picked up a RBPC passport holder on her way back from one of her last holidays with *him*, her ex, when she'd still been completely oblivious to the way he'd already been shagging *her*. The kitsch-on-the-borderline-of-tacky merchandise showcasing dodgy travel pictures had been plastered all over Ibiza's largest airport shop, with some eye-watering prices to match. Little had she known, a few summers ago, that any of these frolics were the brainchild of Barnaby and Clementine; that their duckling-turned-swan company was going places, shrugging off some serious competition to do it in style.

But now that she'd caught up on current affairs, she totally planned to cash in on them, too.

"Make hay while the sun's shining, babe."

Ellie turned off the B-road to navigate the narrow, hairpin bends of the stony, potholed track that would lead her to her destiny, following the curvaceous font and camera logo on the wooden signposts dotted among the berry-studded hedgerows and bracken. Finally, tantalisingly, the track gave way to the tip of a tower, and then, rounding one last bend, Ellie's view opened out onto one humdinger of an edifice, causing her to hold her breath in awe, almost stalling the car. Remembering her monumental slam of the café door, and her current commitment to bravado, she put the temptation to leg it to one side and drove slowly on, taking note of another series of wooden signs instructing her to pay heed to hedgehogs, deer and rabbits. Random but undeniably quaint.

She glanced at her sleek black bob in the mirror, nodding her head in reverent approval, before sandwiching her Audi between a gleaming jet black Land Rover and an Alfa Romeo Spider. As if she had always belonged there. Though she gritted her teeth at the latter car. It was cherry red.

She turned off the ignition and glanced at her Cartier watch, swallowing down her guilt that with this recent purchase she'd whittled her way through fifty per cent of the settlement. Again, it was worth it. You couldn't put a price on keeping up appearances. Like she said, they could be deceptive. That weekend shopping spree to Bond Street's finest boutiques might have seemed beyond frivolous to an outsider, but it had been an investment, really.

Speculate to accumulate.

As calculated as putting the money into shares. If she pulled off today, she'd not only see her salary soar but the first inch of the red carpet to one of her many future Westwood abodes would lay itself obediently at her feet. Recognition on this level was worth the wait. Barnaby couldn't fail to fall for her. She'd done all her homework. The timing was perfect. His frequently updated social media accounts didn't as much as hint at a permanent girlfriend or spouse.

Ellie pressed her lips together again, ensuring maximum distribution of Chanel's finest Rouge Allure Velvet, and stole a final glimpse of herself in the mirror. She wasn't vain, and yet she'd never looked more captivating; the Moroccan argan oil she'd sprayed her hair with that morning set her swishy, cropped mane off with a fabulous inky-black glow.

'You've got hair like the tail covering a donkey's arse,' another voice from the past deemed it timely to remind her, embellishing its words with a wicked snigger.

Ellie could almost feel the spiteful yank at her ponytail all over again; punishment for causing her house, Tintagel, to lose the school mixed rounders match. Clementine had finally taken a chance on Ellie, sifting her from the straggle of losers, third from last to be picked for her carefully constructed team. But then Ellie had failed to reach first base with her bat, right at the nail-biting match's decider.

Huh. Well, she wouldn't be caught short any more, thank you, sweetheart. The only picking going down in this century would be for Clementine's bridesmaid's dress, and at Ellie's leisurely pace.

Ellie slammed shut another poison arrow-filled drawer of the filing cabinet in her head.

She was going inside this magnificent building standing proudly before her right now. And she was going to re-write history in style.

History and his story. Ellie giggled at her play on words.

Then she screwed her eyes tightly shut and determined to imagine herself giving the blasted elephant-grey filing cabinet a massive kick for once and for all. She watched on – inside her mind's eye – as it shuddered violently; the drawers recomposing themselves obediently, the locks clicking in sync, the exterior flush and flipping well closed. That was more like it. There was only one way present-day Barney would be looking at her now.

Barnaby, *Barnaby*, **Barnaby!**

She was early for her catwalk appearance, though. Too damned early. Gingerly, she scanned the windows of the imposing building in front of her. Nobody was about. She couldn't detect any nosey CCTV either. She was back in the genteel Somerset countryside after all; a place where the biggest threat was the invasion of a band of badgers. They probably only switched the cameras on here at night.

All righty. Time for a little snoop then.

Ellie gracefully alighted from the car, pulled her bag onto her shoulder and began to pick her way along the path that led to the main building, mindful of toning down her recently acquired avian strut.

Still, there wasn't a Barnaby or any other soul to be seen. Perhaps everyone was in a meeting? Perhaps they were planning a surprise party, stoked at her arrival? Barnaby was going to be pretty floored when he made the connection; that was for sure. Most people were. Well, great aunts and pervy great uncles who'd not seen Ellie in years were, anyway.

The silence felt a little eerie. She checked in with her glittery wrist. Was twenty minutes early a little keen? There was eagerness, and there was desperation. It was important that she didn't signal the latter.

Poking her head furtively through the ivy-clad window, she clocked a row of men in perfect succession. It was as if somebody had measured the distance between them with a metre stick, so that somehow, even with their short backs and sides, they mimicked that rather hilarious meme that had been doing the rounds on Facebook; the one with the old men on the bus, whose bald and shiny heads aligned to such a degree that they resembled a row of planets. She gulped down a nervous chortle. They really didn't look like they ever moved an inch. Maybe they were due the same fate as the bus men and would grow old and grey in this place?

But why weren't they facing the natural daylight? Blimey. Talk about bad feng shui. She'd sort out the office layout right away. Barnaby might well be seeing a string of interviewees, but none of them fused talent with looks *and* knew how to harvest the ancient laws of the universe like Ellie did. Well, sort of. She was a bit rusty, but it would all come back to her after a couple of weeks. She'd written up everything Connie had passed on to her during their short but intense friendship, hefting that manual – okay, shoving it under her bed – from abode to abode.

*'Don't forget **my** notes!' her mother's words rang out in exasperation.*

Ellie sighed in resignation: Time to padlock the filing cabinet now too.

She frowned momentarily, for it was true: the manual had been the only place she could think of to stash her mother's bizarre, and ultimately shocking, memos, away from her father. Ellie had spent the early part of the nineties retrieving the litany of PostIt notes from their weird and wonderful hiding places around the house: behind the carriage clock, wedged between the hinges of the cupboard beneath the stairs (Hogwarts really should have tried that with Harry's mail, it would've made things so much simpler), inserted between the tracing paper Rice Krispies bag and its cardboard box – even once jumping out of her pencil case when she got out her compass one morning during Maths.

She'd stabbed that particular note repeatedly until the words were dead, as empty as their threat.

What Keith Finch didn't know couldn't hurt him. It was only more of the same hammed-up lies, anyway. Her dad had been her good cop for so long. No way would she let her mum's poison pull the rug from beneath her feet; especially not when she'd abandoned them both for the marble flooring and hot sandy beaches of foreign shores.

Except Ellie had somehow, and inadvertently, let the words of the endless exposés become a mantra for her own life; reeling from their sensationalism, yet reading and re-reading them, hoping they'd change shape, language or place within the sentence. Anything to erase the things that had supposedly been said and done. But the message was always as loud as it was clear, and stubbornly so.

No: non, nein, nee, HeT, ei...

It mattered not a jot which language she said it in. The PostIts' warning had such a deep-seated hold on her that she didn't dare to cross them.

She gritted her teeth, determined to leave the past in the past for as long as it took to sweep Barnaby up in her charisma and be offered the job on the spot.

What a sensible girl Ellie had been, on her own note-taking front, unbeknownst to her parents, who'd barely tooted a trumpet at any of her adult achievements. That much she would pat herself on the teenage back for. Well, then of course there'd been the stuff she'd learnt from Gloria. But that was a whole other story and the present demanded her attention if she was ever to improve her future.

Ellie snapped herself back to it before her mind took off like a runaway train again. She skirted the building's edge to admire the view of endless fields and rolling green hills in the dappled late morning sun, squinting to take in the panorama of her new surroundings, until her eyes settled on something quite unexpected.

No shit!

There was a bloody giant swimming pool out back, and everything! She edged herself closer, pupils now saucer-wide at the sublime turquoise water offset perfectly by those intricate mosaic tiles. Who in God's name had a swimming pool in the workplace? This set-up had to be part-business premises, part family home, surely? It was so much more than she had bargained for.

A coquettish grin worked its way across her face as she imagined the sort of after-work parties she would naturally need to suggest, solely for team building purposes, of course. The recently purchased red and white polka dot bikini coming in very useful indeed (and making seriously overdue amends for that hideous Speedo one-piece and the revolting rubber swimming cap all the girls had sucked themselves into during Monty's swimming galas past), not to mention the enticing faux diamond that was her belly piercing. Especially during a game of champagne-infused Lilo wars, when she and Barnaby would find themselves stranded, up close and very personal, on their miniature 'love boat', although she might need to order a few of those bust fillers online, give her pancakes a little boost.

"Can I help you there?"

Holy smoke? Where did *she* come from?

"Oh." Ellie straightened up immediately, acknowledging the thirty-something woman standing before her, praying to an imaginary god she had not clocked her drooling over the pool. "I was... er... just making a quick recce... before my interview... not assuming at all that I'll get the job or anything like that, but you know." She offered a cute laugh, hoping it would mask her nerves as she took in the unmistakable hint of accusation in the inky-blue eyes giving her the once-over. They were framed with the most fabulous lashes.

Ellie thought fast, offering her hand for a shake. "I'm Ellie. Ellie Sanchez." Mercifully, the attractive, caramel-locked and doe-eyed woman accepted it.

You could tell a lot by a handshake, so they said, and this one was laced with grounding and sincerity; coming from a person so genuine they could seriously scupper your plans.

She'd need to keep this family hanger-on at arm's length, for sure.

"Ah yes, Clementine mentioned she was holding interviews today." The woman threw her a conspiratorial wink. "The solitary dowdy geek of a male candidate has been and gone. Clementine is certain to give you the false impression that you're just one of many remaining hopefuls, a cog in the interrogative wheel – but don't you dare buy it… And don't you dare say I said, but the job's pretty much yours." She whispered the last bit, adding a friendly smile, and Ellie's stomach somersaulted at the ease with which this was all shaping up. "I'll walk you to reception. I'm heading that way myself."

"Thanks very much. That's really kind of you."

And it was. Ellie couldn't help but immediately warm to the girl. Well, that was that, then. It had to be a no-brainer. She'd be sitting at her very own RBPC desk by this time next week, meaning she'd better get swotting up on all the fundamental firsts an HR pro does (aka another yawn-inducing dinner with Ben) when they're sworn in as Captain to run, and steer, a very tight ship. She let out a gasp as the realisation hit her.

Then she swiftly recomposed herself. It would be a piece of proverbial piss. She'd got herself this far, after all. She'd toe that very steep learning curve for some things. She'd completely wing it for others. She'd get the job done.

"Sorry. I just realised I haven't introduced myself," the woman said, with a slightly giddy laugh. "God, it's been one of those days where not even a caffeine drip can fix the fatigue. And heaven help me, it's not even the dreaded three p.m. slump yet. I'm Brooke, by the way. Brooke Westwood."

Oh.

So this was the infamous older sister who'd missed out on Daddy's fortune by all of three years; at least when it came to the posh education part. Ellie suspected they'd probably been ships that had passed in the night; Brooke could well have been in her final years at the same local state high school that Ellie had stopped, and then re-started at; the latter action carried out with her tail between her legs and a monumental amount of paranoia.

"It's great to meet you, Brooke. I appreciate you pointing me in the right direction. It's quite a sprawl," she coughed, "I mean a, er... special property."

Ellie followed Brooke to an identical path to the right of the building that had previously been hidden behind a pink rosebush. She berated herself for tripping over her words. This would not do at all in front of Barnaby. And the caramel-tressed woman in front of her must have got that rather important detail wrong.

She was here to see *him*.

Not that Clementine didn't feature in her plans. It was always wise to be BFFs with a future sister-in-law, and she was certainly owed the woman's companionship to compensate for the way she'd been so cruelly treated at school. But Ellie was croupier now. She would deal their cards in the correct order. And soon they'd all know it.

"So, here we are, anyway," said Brooke, in such a way that Ellie cringed she might have voiced those last thoughts aloud.

The eldest Westwood child pushed open the stubborn, chunky racing-green door with her shoulder, ushering Ellie inside, gesturing at the waiting area and its stark white table stocked with a gigantic fan of statement *Vogues* – eek, they needed to be nudged further to the left – along with a rather forlorn-looking spider plant; a miserable artefact that would soon be feeling the sharp end of Ellie's chop so that a cactus could thrive in its place. Hmm, and she wasn't convinced about the positioning of the receptionist's desk either. Ellie would have to switch on her mobile phone's feng shui App when nobody was looking. It was crucial that she made a start on her next piece of homework, because talking of pieces, just about every piece of the flipping furniture here would need re-orienting, and at lightning speed. Time was of the essence.

"Good luck, Ellie."

Her hostess brought her back to the first hurdle with a jolt and a smile so wide it could rival Julia Roberts' finest.

What a sweet touch. She'd take it, thank you very much, Benevolent Brooke Westwood. But with the tricks she had up her sleeve, Enigmatic Ellie Sanchez knew she wouldn't need it.

One is never enough...

Mum X

4

BROOKE

*T*here was something familiar about the woman peering a little presumptuously – it had to be said – into the design studio window. Maybe their paths had previously crossed in a clothes shop or at a cocktail bar?

She was a willowy waif of a thing, but undeniably alluring with it, putting Brooke in mind of Alan Rickman's necklace-hogging mistress in *Love Actually*. Now what was her name? She'd always been useless at remembering. But, like that fictional adulteress, this Ellie Sanchez girl could indisputably work the red lippy. Whilst Brooke was thrilled at the no-holds-barred aura she seemed to effortlessly exude, she wasn't entirely sure the brash war paint was a job interview look. Still, somebody needed to bring order to the ranks. Barnaby had pushed one too many buttons this week. And don't even get started on blimming Clementine and that hasty decision of hers to pull out of the Texas Travel Expo.

Brooke's unwavering tenacity had finally got them a stand at the highly rated American exhibition. It had only taken years of bloodshed, sweat and some very late nights begging and pleading on the phone to bend the will of the authorities and their ambitious criteria. None of which the RPBC exactly met. She bet Clementine's withdrawal had something to do with 'inadequate loo facilities' – translation: absence of *Dior* hand soap in the washrooms; 'inadequate veggie options' – translation: fatty diner-style hamburgers, fries and Coke; 'inadequate coffee options' – translation: complete and utter lack of skinny soya white, and 'inadequate lighting' – translation: harsh electric violet rays that highlighted every pore and unwaxed facial hair.

Not for the first time, Brooke was truly grateful for the perspective of a Duke of Edinburgh expedition or two. There was nothing like a hike through the unyielding moors of Bodmin in a pea soup fog to get your priorities in order. It made Brooke wonder how, *just how*, she could possibly be born into the same family as her sister.

Who was she kidding? She didn't understand how she could have been born into the same family as any of them.

She'd followed the beguiling stranger at a distance, marvelling at the way she could rearrange her face so quickly, as if she were one of the aforementioned movie stars – taking in her 'curious', 'awestruck', and then 'rumbled' expressions in quick succession.

Ellie was definitely a little bit rabbit-in-the-headlights when Brooke finally made her presence known. She was probably just lost, overwhelmed by the property's twists and turns. Brooke swore there were nooks and crannies that she herself hadn't even uncovered and explored yet; secret passageways added on by her father in the height of his empire-building excitement. In fact, just that very morning she was on a mission to track down marketing banners; rumour had it they were lurking in the male pool changing rooms. Ha, that wouldn't have anything to do with the fact that one of them was showcasing a bevy of Brazilian beauties in thongs on Ipanema beach now, would it? Brooke might be the eldest of the Westwood offspring but she was also the savviest. The wisdom of a few extra years on planet Earth, and a good old fashioned education, had certainly kitted her out with that handy piece of street-wise armour.

Which was how she just knew that Ellie was the very woman they'd all been waiting for.

It had been highly unprofessional to dish the dirt on the previous hopeful like that, but he really had been unappetisingly vanilla – and he'd driven away in a Mr. Bean Mini to boot. The exact same shade of lime-bogey-green and everything. Whereas something gave Brooke a sixth sense that the highly polished, and recent vision that was Ellie, would be just the tonic to shake things up. She had an inner take-no-shit vibe about her. And that handshake was firm and assured. Then there were the nails – in Brooke's favourite colour, too. Purple meant business. No pathetic pastels about this candidate.

Besides which, Brooke was peeved that she'd picked up the key to the female changing rooms. She swore her brother had done that on purpose, switching them around on the hooks so as to buy himself time to find a new hidey-hole for his treasures, sporting a face like a slapped arse, as Barnaby was today. Hell, yes. This was the everyday tomfoolery, the everyday sexism, that needed to be nipped in the bud, along with the many goalposts that needed to be super-glued to the spot. Not because Brooke didn't have a sense of humour, but because it had never been funny in the first place.

None of it.

If she was honest, the novelty had worn off their family-run business at the end of week one of trading: In other words, the precise moment that her brother and sister had bagsied the biggest offices and comfiest thrones. But she'd committed herself to the selling and marketing of their Far Eastern-produced novelties by that point. In ink. Signed and sealed. At least for seven years, as per the terms of the rather lengthy contract and its myriad stipulations. There was no turning back.

Brooke had been instantly, yet quietly transfixed by their sudden and exotic HR hopeful, surveying her from afar, until (too late!) Ellie must have felt Brooke's eyes boring into her skull. Brooke knew her sudden shyness was a bit of a contradiction when she'd personally just taken centre stage herself, giving the TED-style talk of her life at a rally of spiritual conventions in Glastonbury, Dublin and Amsterdam; gatherings of the high and the mighty of the juju world featuring every Hay House author you could visualise with your third eye and a guided meditation; gatherings which had left her seriously star struck. So much so that she'd had to smuggle one of those travel matcha mug thingies into her bag – filling hers with vodka and Coke instead of the vile-tasting green tea doing the convivial rounds – just so she could secretly snatch sneaky tots of Dutch courage. She'd only recently opened her mind to all things mainstream unconventional, and although she wasn't about to drink tree bark tea, hug giant oaks, or turn vegan, she was a sucker for horoscopes and pretty crystals. Then again, times were changing and even the likes of Victoria Beckham was supposedly getting into the latter.

"Here's to abandoning perfection with relish, ditching the airbrushing tools of high-tech gadgetry and embracing our true nature – wonderful warts and all," she'd cried, amidst whoops and cheers at the finale of her spiel.

Subtext: we have a funky retro Volkswagen campervan (aka an extortionately-priced merchandise stall) parked conveniently outside flogging a vast array of imperfectly perfect festival pictures printed across T-shirts, BPA-free drinks bottles, jute bags, hemp purses, 3D posters (made from recycled paper, of course), rucksacks and tents. Yes, tents. The very latest invention in our weird and wonderful range of paraphernalia that you really didn't know you needed in your life... which would be because you don't.

She was morphing into one of them.

And sadly she didn't mean the gurus.

She was turning into her blasted family!

Of course the RBPC's products were nothing more than cherry-on-the-cake extras. The wise shopper knew that. There'd really been no need for her to tarnish her talk like some kind of modern day Pied Piper attempting to lure all and spiritual sundry into a Diderot-effect trance of crass consumerism. The French seventeenth century philosopher wasn't wrong when he'd coined the term for the spontaneous amassing of personal belongings. *It was a thing.* And it was a thing that had lined the Westwoods' designer label wallets and purses beautifully.

But time was running out.

Slowly and imperceptibly, those sticky family tendrils had crept up on her, wrapping themselves around her like poison ivy until they threatened to destroy her last remaining shred of dignity. She was Luke Skywalker battling a three-pronged Darth Vader, whilst Jar Jar Binks (her darling mother), poked and prodded at her from the side-lines with her ridiculously elongated fuchsia talons. Out on that infamous ledge, and with a light sabre in hand.

All of which meant the last thing that she'd wanted was to distort destiny by coming across as a negative Nellie to a potential new recruit. Jesus, Mary *and* Joseph – Ellie would run a mile if she knew the real state of affairs the company was in: if she knew how many had faltered before her.

If she clocked the increasing stack of empty wine bottles in Barnaby's office bin.

If she heard the way Clementine spoke to the puppy dog junior designers. Oh, yes, she picked them specifically for the gooiest, most loyal eyes – and for how many centimetres she could wrap them around her privileged little signet-ring finger.

If she saw the way Daddy ground the workforce to a halt with one of his impromptu Golf Fun Days. Which were anything but entertaining. More like something out of a super-warped fairy tale with a wannabe king lording it over his subjects, picking their swing apart whilst he quaffed the champers and guffawed at their lack of prowess. Of course, the local golf club was in its element, totting up the funds Daddio had thought nothing of syphoning – *from where exactly?* – to hire the prestigious eighteen-hole course.

It was selfish not to spare another the heartache, and Brooke knew it. But despite the immediate affinity she felt with Ellie Sanchez, she had already started to see her as her way out of this place.

Somehow she sensed that Ellie was the bowling ball which, depending on how lovingly it was handled, would either fool them all by falling into the gutter, then achieve a last-minute curve and strike… or steamroll dead centre, blasting stubborn, unwavering pins – her brother, her sister, and her father – to smithereens.

ELLIE

"*T*ake a seat, please. I'm Clementine Westwood. And you are? Gosh, excuse me. I'm nursing the hangover from hell this morning and you're like… my twelfth interview this week. Not all for the same role though. No need to look so petrified."

Ellie went to open her mouth, only to find her lips had cemented themselves together. This was categorically not the way she'd rehearsed things. She was madder than mad at herself for not having prepared a Plan B, to deal with the letter C – and the spanner being thrown into the works by the infuriating woman who embodied that initial.

It was certainly surreal, though, and from a psychological point of view, very revealing, the way Clementine had avoided all eye contact, except for a quick glance at Ellie's fancy watch, as she'd gabbled that last bit out. Brooke's assessment had been right, then. Still, any moment now the ellipses would join up for her interviewer, surely? Ellie sensed the *'don't I know you from somewhere?'* which would trip off Clementine's tongue, so they could both 'ooh' and 'ahh' at her glorious transformation, reminisce about their mutual hatred of algebraic equations, and clink glasses to their company comradeship; the start of a very beautiful new adventure.

But Clementine simply scurried back to her desk, flipping frantically through a messy pile of paperwork – tut tut, her organisational skills hadn't changed a bit since school. Ellie had zero idea how this company had shot into the stratosphere. Her previously perfected script flew right out the quaint country window of the office and into a fly-encrusted cowpat.

Just as well, in one sense of the word. She suspected that the minxy middle-school maestro of the hair twist, Clementine Westwood, was as obsessed with the opposite sex as she'd always been; Ellie's risqué foreplay would have had her running a mile.

What a bitch not to have committed her next candidate's details to short-term memory. What a bitch not to have revved up that very decadent-looking coffee maker sitting on the bureau behind her. And what an even bigger bitch not to have looked her in the eye; not to have done the aforementioned math; the very same subject in which she'd hastily snatched Eleanor's exercise book and copied down her answers the moment the teacher's back was turned; the very same subject for which they'd shared the same actual desk!

"Sit down, I insist."

Clementine's posh intonation rose, consuming the room, just as it had always done. She made a grab for the mug balancing precariously on the edge of her desk and took a swig of her drink.

Ellie, seriously miffed at the complete lack of manners and memory, but hiding it admirably, did as she was told.

But this was wrong. Ellie had assumed Barnaby would be the decision-maker; the big cheese who called the shots, hired and fired. Not that she was sexist. Far from it. But…

"So, then, Ellie," Clementine finally relinquished her mug and took to shuffling her papers like a newsreader about to announce something monumentally serious, causing Ellie to involuntarily twitch. Her revision skills on HR, the subject she knew only superficially, were about to be put to brutal test. It was horribly like the half-arsed teenage cram-style-revision attempts of her GCSEs. "Sanchez, yes. You do look a bit Hispanic, don't you?"

Ellie smiled politely. Inwardly, she was astounded. How little impact one classmate could make on another! Fair dos, if she had been sixty, seventy, or eighty, and school had been a whole, and very literal lifetime ago. But c'mon… they were only just over a decade down the track! Speechless at the un-PC guestimate as to her nationality, she silently prayed for the invisible Barnaby to jump out of the over-stuffed cupboard behind his sister, and take over this 'interview' immediately.

The cupboard had a Canon camera strap poking through its hinges, leaving Ellie seriously *unhinged*. Jeez. The clutter in this room was something else. She made a mental note of more changes she would make once she sailed through this interview, adding a vase of luxurious peonies to the list. They should be an interior design staple in any office, and would signal both her arrival – and a sudden increase in company turnover, which would turn heads.

"Things have been going very well for us," Clementine continued and then stopped abruptly, so that Ellie was unsure if this was a statement, or the point at which she was meant to fill in the blanks. "Nice watch, by the way. Couple of seasons old, now, though." Clementine stroked her own Ballon Bleu model from the same brand. It looked so effort-lessly sophisticated on her wrist.

"Y-yes," Ellie ventured, thrown by the woman's nerve to unnerve her by spotting her second-hand purchase. "I've read extensively about your successes. Naturally that draws me to the company."

Get. A. Grip.

But Clementine smiled politely enough at her pathetic response and carried on with a magnanimous volley of words, most of which Ellie could recite by heart herself, having sufficient knowledge of the company to compete on *Mastermind*. She nodded in all the right places anyway, until they got to the first question:

"So, tell me, Ellie: how do you deal with the many grey areas when it comes to the classic issues of HR in the twenty-first century workplace?"

Bleugh. She'd inserted quotation marks in the air with her fingers, too. Barnaby would never do that.

Just one small problem, relieved as she was that the inter-view had finally got under way: Ellie hadn't *exactly* worked in Human Resources before. And this question wasn't one on her series of sample interviews, extensive though her research had been. All right, Ben's research. She shuddered at the thought of her doctored C.V. It was only a little white lie. Everyone exaggerated on their C.V.s, right? She'd granted herself a First instead of a 2:2 at her last successful interview, for the University library. Well, that had landed her the Assistant Manager-stroke-part-time-Curator role, which had admittedly gone belly up by leading her to Carlos. But still. Nobody had died. Her colleagues had been beside them-selves when she'd handed in her notice, too. Which had to be a sign of a job well done, if ever there was one. As well as a nod to her supreme confidence in pipping any and every contender to the post. Although it'd definitely taken every ounce of her will not to scowl at their parting gift; those blessed mouth-watering Marc de Champagne truffles, which continued to taunt her from the fridge.

But never mind her old job. The endless and deafening

silence reverberating around the room was in serious danger of costing her *this* job. She had to pluck some words from somewhere, and fast.

"I… er… well, I find it helps tremendously to throw a rainbow at it," she heard herself reply, wondering if her hippy-dippy friend from the past, Gloria had rigged her up with a headset and was hiding outside, undercover in her caravan, drip-feeding Ellie the answers on a mic. She gazed briefly out the window at the row of oak trees fringing the field to buy herself time, unable to repress the sudden memory that flew into her head unbidden: Barney and Clem initiating the Great Autumn Conker Fight on the school playing fields. Eleanor Finch had been too shy to join in, as usual, sitting on the side-lines munching at plastic-tasting string cheese with one hand; the other clutching at blades of dewy grass in frustration, wishing she had Clem's bravado, and the guts to chat to her brother. Not to mention her fashionable swishy bob.

Words, not drivel.

*And it's **Clementine**, brother of **Barnaby**!*

Ellie silently dragged herself back to her half-constructed answer, refusing to let anxiety appear on her face. She upturned her lips into a watery smile.

"Go on," Clementine's brows knitted together, she folded her arms defiantly, and pushed herself back dramatically from the desk on her wheelie chair with her feet as if she were a swimmer hell bent on swiping the gold medal in a race. She still had a bob to die for, and her sudden movement had it swishing quite fabulously anew. Nowadays, though, she doubtlessly coloured it with more than a little platinum, to disguise the monotony of her true mousey-brown. And nowadays, she had some serious bob competition. The realisation had Ellie plumping her own hair-do up reassuringly.

The thought was fuel to what remained of Ellie's dwindling fire. Clementine Westwood just didn't recognise her at all. And she hadn't changed a bit.

Bullshit it. You've got this.

"Of course I realise that probably sounds like quite a bold statement," Ellie injected some volume to her spiel now, determined to come across as the voice of authority on all matters of humanity within the workplace, as well as to bridge the physical distance between them. "But to elaborate, once we put grey under the spotlight, throw some colour on the discrimination issue or the harassment case," she tucked an errant wedge of hair behind her ear to buy herself a few more seconds, "once we unravel the layers to get to the root of the problem, the issue at hand is usually far closer to black and white."

Clementine offered her the strangest smile, a grin whose sentiment was impossible to decipher.

"Did you study poetry at college or something?"

Ellie dug her heel into the carpet, twisting it this way and that. Did her interrogator have some kind of inside information? Was there a hidden camera trailing behind her, following her through the poetry section to the tome on HR management in the business section; the one she'd not quite finished digesting in her last minute flap once she'd learned of the Somerset company's rather juicy vacancy? Three times a week it was Ellie who was left to shut up shop and flick frayed Bristol students out on their ears and into the Union bar; a transition most were quite happy with.

Why hadn't she lined up *all* her ducks, though? Barnaby could be off sick, on holiday or away on business. There had always been every chance that Clementine would be her first port of call to the series of mansions and performance cars waiting for her. Clementine or, worse still, Daddy West-wood. She'd got off lightly with his youngest daughter, she realised. She geared herself up. She would exceed Clementine's expectations in the grilling that followed.

"Well, I finished my education at the University of…"

But that was as far as she got, for the door flew open with a colossal bang, startling the pair of them. Ellie physically jumped at least an inch out of her seat. Embarrassing. Humiliating. Not part of the script. Clementine just let her scowl do the talking.

Ellie bent to swipe the water bottle poking out of her bag, furious with her hand for yet another involuntary twitch. Thank God she'd packed the perfect distraction. Thank God for this excuse to redirect her composure. Her breath hitched in her throat.

Barnaby.

Here he freaking well was, in the flesh, standing before her. Definitely not a mirage, much less a cardboard cut-out. Barnaby Beauteous Westwood was larger than life, as jaw-droppingly good-looking as he had ever been. As unphased as ever.

And yet… what an obnoxious prick, to waltz in without even knocking on the door. Much as Ellie wanted to put her student flicking skills into practice with his sister, so she could lock said door and jump on top of him; much as she wanted all of that and a whole lot more, another side of her kicked in. A side that had matured over the years, on the journey from Eleanor to Ellie.

But then she started to make excuses for him. Maybe, just maybe, he hadn't realised his sister was interviewing this afternoon – although grown-up Ellie could have sworn there was an exam board-style notice on the door, its puerile marker pen scrawl reappearing now before her eyes.

Gingerly, and then more determinedly, she raised her head, taking a sip of her water. His mesmerising, chocolate-brown eyes connected with hers.

This is it. The moment you've been waiting for. Just don't spurt out the contents of your mouth, for crying out loud!

She kept it together, mercifully managing to swallow her glug of H2O; holding her breath in sweet anticipation of the Eureka moment. Any second now, and he'd greet her...

But the seconds passed like short, sharp slaps to the face, and Barnaby looked right through her, as if she were but a pane of glass. Ellie's dizziness subsided, her pulse down-grading itself from a canter to a trot. Disappointment seared through her. Furiously, she erased the sex scene that had already started to play out in her head, shoving the handcuffs and the whipped cream back in the drawer.

Oh, he was still the spit of a young – and ironically, given the activities of his enterprise – airbrushed, trim Dom Joly. Although you'd probably never see Barnaby don a snail outfit as the *Trigger Happy* comedian had in his TV prime. Ellie suspected you wouldn't catch Barnaby Westwood in anything less than *French Connection.*

He still possessed the comic's brazen and ballsy nature, too. Kind of essential, Ellie imagined when you had to direct a Really Bad Photo Company shoot. Well, that was as maybe. It was also a very quick way to get Ellie Sanchez's back up.

He didn't even bleeping recognise her.

How many years of her life had she spent imagining a reunion like this? How many hours had she spent poring over the many faces of Barnaby Westwood, courtesy of his free-for-all settings on Facebook, Twitter and Instagram?

Reality bit hard. Nothing had changed at all.

"These Sydney actors," he slapped a pile of glossy photographs on top of his sister's desk, causing Ellie's posture to immediately re-align. "Which agency did you use this time? I don't like any of them. The brunette's profile is too pointy, and her legs should be leggier. I want shorter shorts. Denim preferably. A few strategically placed holes would be nice. A flash of the butt is *essential*. What do you call them? Hot pants?"

"God, you are so derogatory." Clementine turned to her brother, eyes half-closed, head shaking from side to side as if she were warding off the start of a bad migraine. "They're from the Rosebud Agency and, as I recall, you had no complaints with the female models I hired from there last time for the Bondi Beach party shoot. Polite aside," she stuck the most bejewelled of her sparkling fingers in the air as if checking for the wind direction. "Do I, or do I not, have a notice on the door instructing my staff that interviews are currently in process?"

"I'm not your staff, sweetie," Barnaby shrugged. "Rosebud? Pfft. I've seen more bloom on a dead dandelion."

"Sorry." Clementine offered Ellie a weak smile this time, as if she'd suddenly remembered she was also there. "Please bear with me. I'll deal with him as quickly as I can."

Ellie looked on, incredulous, her eyes adopting a fast and unwelcome blinking impediment. Was this the way they conducted business with their clients, too? Barnaby still couldn't find the decency to even acknowledge her. That impetuous, yet utterly adorable smile tugged at the left side of his mouth, just begging it to break into a curl. His eyes danced, measuring up his sister's retaliation, as if this were all part of some family point-scoring game. And yes, there it was now, in all its glory: his customary Bruce Willis smirk, the one that used to leave his entourage sitting on the edge of their seats. Will he or won't he break out into spontaneous laughter?

Nothing had changed.

"Australasian shoots have been your domain for the past year," Clementine hissed. "If only you hadn't pulled so many sickies, which might better be phrased as dirty little lie-ins, you could have cast your eagle eye over everything before the contracts were signed. It's too late to make changes now."

"Need I remind you that it was *you* who pulled my last Sydney-based photographer, the one with the solid working relationship with Oz's top agency!" Barnaby spat.

Clementine's cheeks flushed decidedly crimson.

"Because he was over-doing the bloody Bokeh effect, to the extent that the harbour bridge looked like a string of sodding fairy lights on a Christmas tree!" she barked back.

Oh. Oh. Oh.

All definitely wasn't shiny, happy – or twinkly – in paradise.

Barnaby let out a delayed, and thoroughly masculine, snort.

"When I said pulled, I did, of course, mean it in both senses of the word," he added.

And now he lost his eyebrows somewhere in the roots of his hair. Meanwhile Ellie picked her jaw up off the floor at their hideous display.

"It's not rocket science," Barnaby continued. "Sex sells, Clementine. And gentlemen prefer hot women. Like it or not, that's a fact. Lord knows, you've had more than enough experience." He paused for breath; his attention resting momentarily on what Ellie assumed was those majestic oaks in the distance, as if he might extract some of their timeless wisdom – or bound outside for a spontaneous conker fight to relive his youth.

"So here's what's going to happen." He scratched his forehead, suddenly back in play. "You'll upgrade these models immediately... like within sixty seconds of me exiting this room... find whatever loophole you can and get it done. Or I'll fly south, sever all ties with your latest fancy-pants Lothario behind the lens, and pursue my old tog, regardless of how *totally awks* it makes life for my little sister." Ellie took a stab in the dark that 'tog' was industry slang for photographer. "Oh, I'll soon win him over with some of the finest wining and dining Sydders has to offer, you needn't worry about that, sis. Kerchiiiing."

In that moment, Ellie's mind was like a camera; saturation point maxed. There was nothing left to flick, or indeed snap. She, Ellie Marie Sanchez, was still invisible.

Classroom or interview. Finch or Sanchez.

The spare wheel. The lemon.

Or was it the gooseberry?

Barnaby stormed out of the room, leaving two women buffeted in the wake of their own very personal views of his typhoon.

"Right, well, thank you very much for your time, er, Helen."

"It's actually… ahem… Ellie."

Clementine brushed Ellie's protest away with the imaginary crumbs she was also brushing from her shift dress, as if that was all it would take to cleanse herself of her brother's ugly tirade.

Okay, Ellie got that Barnaby's stunt had been the height of embarrassment, but Clementine had only asked her a solitary question! She couldn't wind things up already; this was beyond absurd.

"But we haven't even—"

"I have a few more people to interview." Yeah right, thought Ellie. "And then I'll be in touch later this week – one way or the other."

'You're a nobody.'

The words from the callous bitch in the coffee shop rebounded like a shiny silver pinball around the room; palpably chipping away at Ellie's carefully constructed chainmail armour. All she could think about were the unwelcome truffles in her kitchen, as she reached out to try and shake

Clementine's discourteous right hand. It rested resolutely in her lap, whilst with the left the woman knocked back the dregs of her coffee.

And that was twice. Twice in not even twenty-four hours that she'd been called the wrong name.

Letting herself out of the office without a backward glance, she slunk back to her car, started the ignition and lifted the handbrake to reverse as gently as she could, before white rage engulfed all five of her senses and had her tyres smouldering past the speed limit signs of the main road. Her sixth sense had evidently failed her.

But then something told her to look at the last car in the row where she'd parked: a pathetic and practical little hump-backed-grey whale of a Fiat. More twee you couldn't get, and how very in keeping with the countryside... Then out hopped a Mary Poppins-lookalike; all neat and trim and prim and proper in her belted suit with her matching brief-case and (eugh) sturdy brogues. And about to rock into the RBPC HQ and steal Ellie's job from under her very nose.

"Oh, I don't think so, lady," Ellie muttered under her breath.

Her nemesis was zooming towards reception – not getting herself lost like Ellie. She had to do something. She scoured her immediate field of vision for a lightning bolt of inspiration.

Nothing.

Unless...?

But no: there was low and there was lower than low; lower than lower than low, even. A scraping the bottom of the barrel-style low that even a limbo dancer would walk away from.

How much do you want this? You know damn well she's going to wipe the floor with you if you don't resort to drastic measures, and FAST.

Ellie Sanchez didn't need to be told twice.

"Hi there!" She jumped out the car and adopted her very best la-di-da accent, as if she'd been woven into the fabric of the company for years; a queen's consort, an unwavering support. "You're here about the HR job, right?"

Mary Poppins stopped in her tracks, eyes all endearing yet confident, face blink-and-you'd-miss-it forgettable, without the bonny beauty of Julie Andrews – which made Ellie feel even nastier for the stunt she was about to pull.

The silence stretched on between them for what felt like an eternity, until Ellie could take it no longer.

"Well, I'm Barnaby Westwood's wife," Ellie melded her smile with a tinkle of laughter, as though this fact should have been obvious. "It's a pleasure." She extended her hand for a shake.

"I see," her victim replied. "Hello, I'm Martha." She placed her limp hand in Ellie's and it was all Ellie could do not to stab it with her purple talons.

Hello, you're Dreary.

"Barnaby's actually running a little late at the moment. Why don't you come sit with me for a while in my car whilst you wait? I can run through any last minute questions you might have about the job. I get the gut feeling you're practically perfect in every way for it, though."

Cringeworthy, but Ellie just couldn't resist.

Unbelievably, neither could Martha. She followed her without a protest to the passenger side of Ellie's car, and Ellie opened the door to help her in like a chauffeur, scuttling quickly to the driver's side before Brooke – or anybody else – appeared to call the next candidate.

Ellie turned to Martha, wondering what on earth to say next. But oh, what wonderful timing! Ellie's phone beeped with a 'message' from her 'hubby'. She stole a glance at the screen. It was a notification from a delivery company. The clueless idiots had deemed it appropriate to leave her parcel (more clothes shopping) with that git of a neighbour downstairs; the one who played his hideous rock ballads too loud every Sunday morning without fail, intensifying Ellie's weekend hangover.

Now she really was furious.

"Yes, as I suspected, Barnaby has just asked me to find you and take you out for a coffee… he's so very sorry but he's had to take an important call, meaning the interview will be delayed for an hour or so," she read, amazed with herself for pulling this off so convincingly. "I'm so embarrassed on his behalf, Martha. I mean this never, ever happens, let me assure you… what a terrible first impression of the company he must be giving you. But I'm free right now. I was popping out to do some stationery errands for reception, in any case, and I'm more than happy to treat you to an espresso or a latte at this *fabulous* little place down the road I know. On the company, of course."

"Oh, right, of course. That's… well, that would be fine. Thank you… very much."

Martha digested Ellie's words painfully slowly. But they had to be true, when Barnaby Westwood's wife looked every inch the part; drove every inch the automobile; wore every inch the watch (see, the investment had paid off already), talked every inch the talk. Who was this little madam to protest?

And so Ellie, Martha and the red Audi wended their way back through the narrow winding track and onto the main road, Ellie humming somewhat ominously, somewhat hauntingly – if she did say so herself – all the way to the layby that had miraculously pinged into her memory. Funny how landmarks could do that. She parked up adjacent to a rust and lichen-speckled farmyard gate.

"That's most odd," Ellie declared. "Usually there's a cute

little coffee van here... you know the type: olde-worlde but trying in vain to jazz itself up with fairy lights, assuming it can quench the thirst of a businessman with its mutton-dressed-as-lamb coffees... and *tarts*."

Martha's expression was puzzled. But Ellie was on a roll now, too late for second thoughts and kindness.

"Er, perhaps we should go back? I'm quite happy to wait in reception. I've had a coffee already, I can read my book. It was very good of you but I'd rather be early, I—"

Ellie's eyes narrowed, her pulse raced. Here was her window of opportunity. "You think I don't know that?" she hissed, turning her head in slow and chilling motion to take in the petrified blue eyes of her passenger.

"I beg your pardon? I think perhaps we've got our wires crossed..."

"The only thing that's staying crossed is your filthy legs. And as for your desire to play early bird, to think you're bedding my husband just like the last HR hooker, and the one before that... and the one before that. Not a chance, darling. I spotted your antics a mile off and here is where it ends."

Ellie reached calmly across Martha's body to the handle of her door in a move that felt, and must have looked, spookily polished. Martha visibly attempted to meld herself into the passenger seat. Ellie smirked at her pointless effort at self-defence and stretched further across the girl's bony lap to open the door wide; she unfastened Martha's seatbelt, and she pushed her out onto the hard grey tarmac.

Martha let out a delayed reaction scream, landing, most fetchingly, on her back.

"You can make your own way back to your prissy car... and then off my property before I finish *you* off."

Ellie contemplated signalling the imaginary slit to the throat that would be Martha's fate if she dared to cross that pink rosebush-studded path to the RBPC reception, but the scant remains of her conscience refused to let her fingers uncurl themselves from the steering wheel.

Driving on autopilot back to her Bristol pad, Ellie would never know how she later managed to resist the buttery cocoa and fizz-fuelled temptation of those chocolates. They would assuage her guilt, cocoon her despair – but there in the fridge they stayed. The proof of her discipline was always in the untouched pudding.

'That's a good girl,' her mother's voice chirruped from the bowels of the lousy filing cabinet, echoing over and over in her head. 'Look but don't touch.'

Ellie mentally parcelled up her mother's four words of warning, sending them out into the cosmos after any remnants of her souped-up, bells and whistles career competition. She rubbed her hands together and allowed herself a coy grin.

Now there wasn't an HR interviewee in the land who would bloody dare swipe Ellie's trophy.

One becomes two, two doubles to four, four to eight, eight to sixteen...

One chocolate leads to another, in a formula so scientific, so precise that the only way nature can cope is for the dress size to BALLOON.

Mum X

6

BROOKE

*S*ix months later...

"I am very sorry, Madam." Pfft, the receptionist of one of Stuttgart's top hotels really didn't look it. "It's definitely not an error. This is the fourth time I've tried your card and it's stating that you have insufficient funds."

He whispered the latter, sloping an eyebrow in some supposed move of discretion, as he turned the credit card terminal towards Brooke yet again.

"But that can't be right." She laughed nervously, tugging at her earlobe as if it, and the delicate gold hoop she was wearing today, might erase this situation so she could be on her merry way. "It just can't be!"

And it couldn't.

She was a Westwood, and these things happened to other people. Not even in the family's pre-nouveau riche days would they have been slapdash enough to exceed their overdraft. Brooke's pulse began to race at the implications, scenes from a plethora of Netflix crime series flashing through her mind.

"Well now, your bank declining the payment seems to be

rather a strong sign that it is, in fact, the current status quo. Maybe you have another card we could try?" the receptionist pursed his lips, nudging his avant-garde, pointy-framed specs further up his snout with a scrupulously clean index finger.

Really though… who on earth threw *status quo* into conversation these days?

The bill was astronomical, no thanks to the cast and crew of umpteen photo shoots strewn across the city, and beyond; the Black Forest's quaint chocolate-box twists and turns providing twee backdrops for a medley of RBPC (read thoroughly cheesy and unnecessary) merchandise. Brooke cringed again at the memory of the braided milkmaids in their low-cut outfits and the photo-bombing male yodellers (weren't they supposed to be from a whole different country next door called Austria?) with eyes wide as flying saucers, unable to contain their apparent 'luck'. It was as screwed up as it got, and she could hardly disguise her crestfallen expression as she stood behind the photographer – dishy as he was – thinking of her Travel and Tourism degree. All that sacrifice and study, for this?

She knew they were making the biggest balls-up pursuing the 'Regional Markets' idea, the moment the alarming words had spilled from her brother's lips. But Barnaby and her father had outnumbered and overpowered her that day at lunch, as was increasingly becoming the norm. Clementine had been directing a series of shoots in California at the time. Backed into a corner, Brooke had grudgingly agreed, sure that the idea would never take off. She'd also been desperate to clock off early so she could spend some much-needed quality time with Ruben, after a particularly fraught five days at work; the heady dessert wine only making her cave in all the faster.

"I'm not saying it's a *bad* idea."

"That's because it isn't, sis!"

Barnaby had tittered at her audacity, questioning his testosterone-fuelled business plan.

"It just feels a bit too soon; a bit too ambitious to be undertaking this from afar," Brooke had countered, already feeling the weight of her words begin to wane. "Shouldn't we be building up local teams in each country to take care of this sort of thing? We hardly have the intimate knowledge needed and we don't want to risk stereotyping and mis-representing these markets. I mean, we're stretched enough as it is when it comes to our own UK-based resources."

Her gut instinct had told her they were growing too fast, attempting to run before they could walk. Yes, there was no denying they had created ripples through the tourism indus-try; breaking into some of the High Street giants, budget airlines' in-flight magazines, and even one or two of the posher supermarkets. But it could never be sustained.

"Darling, you really do worry too much," said her father, his expression laced with sarcasm, as was often the way when he felt the need to resort to mansplaining. "Business is all about carpe-diem-ing the moment. After all, we wouldn't be where we are today, would we? One of Somerset's wealth-iest families," he mouthed, as there were other mega-minted diners within earshot. "Were it not for a little buccaneering spirit."

Harry Westwood tipped his head back to sink the remainder of his pricey Portuguese wine, immediately clicking his fingers at the waiter for a refill. How he loved the theatre of being served from a St. Louis crystal decanter!

At times like this, Brooke yearned to see her parents knock back the baby pink Matteus Rosé in its iconic oval bottle. It was noble enough for them not so long ago. Just like the rest of the good old days before their fortunes had changed, when a meal out had consisted of a family quintet of spag Bols, followed by banana splits topped with aerosol cream, glacé cherries, and rainbow sprinkles at their home-town's one and only Italian restaurant. A sparkler on top if it was your birthday. But her mother was just as bad as her incorrigible father – and probably concurrently racking up a similar bill at the country club with her girlfriends, after her usual Friday morning shopping spree in the ritzy boutiques of Bath.

The impatient male client queuing behind Brooke reached around her to slam-dunk the hotel reception bell, presumably to call for extra staff. It roused her from her daydream to her current life pickle. She began to panic that she was creating a check-out traffic jam, not daring to look behind her, fumbling her way through her mega purse and its multitude of compartments. There were cards for this and that; her gym membership, supermarket loyalty, her driving licence, even her National Insurance number, but none of these would save her from disgrace this morning. For Brooke was disciplined when it came to her personal account cards. Work trips were work trips, and The Really Bad Photo Company footed the bill for everything they entailed. Her other cards stayed at home.

"I… uh… I don't appear to have anything else with me, I'm afraid."

Bollocks. This was not looking good. And pulling a stunt like this in Germany could likely lead to hotel arrest!

Think, Brooke. Think.

One word, and one word only, sprang to mind: Ellie.

She had to get the receptionist to call Ellie. It was her only shot. Yes, they'd got to know each other since Clemen-tine had hired her, but then a token lunch together here and there hardly made them the best of friends. She was way too mortified to recount the pitiful situation directly. Let Verbal Diarrhoea Dude do it instead. After all, he had to be heavily trained in such scenarios and would relay things faster than Brooke ever could. Plus, unlike her, he did get paid for this.

And Ellie would know what to do. She'd square it with accounts, shift some funds about, juggle some numbers, wave a magic wand in her Fairy Godmother way. Fitting for the pathetic panto Brooke had inadvertently woken up to this morning. Not that dealing with any of this crap was even remotely part of an HR Manager's job description, and not that Ellie had had quite the impact Brooke had initially hoped for. Her father, Barnaby and Clementine always seemed to be one frustrating step ahead when it came to bending the rules. As the maxed-out credit card for this week's jaunt, and the sneaky way she'd been cornered over that blasted (and sinfully delicious) gold leaf-encrusted blueberry panna cotta that lunchtime, clearly demonstrated. She'd put money on it – well, she would if she had any in her purse. This shortage of funds had one, or all, of the aforementioned trio's names on it.

"Here." She frantically scribbled down Ellie's number, praying she was already in the office, preferably tanked up with conundrum-solving caffeine. "This is my company's number. Somebody there will have a card that can cover this, you'll see."

"Fine," the receptionist's teeth put Brooke in mind of a ventriloquist's dummy. "But I really must insist you stand to one side so I can deal with Herr Scheuermann first."

Whatever.

She'd gladly let the arrogant idiot barge in if it gave Ellie more minutes to get to her desk. Not that she was anything but an early bird. Evidently the plonker who'd now completely barrelled his way in front of her was a regular here. Probably keen to pay up his porno bill separately and far away from the beady eyes of his company. Ha – *yes, he was.* Brooke knew enough German to eavesdrop on their conversation, and two separate bills were now very definitely being generated.

Eight minutes and forty-five seconds later and she felt like she was having a déjà-vu, her life in the receptionist's fat liver-spotted hands all over again.

Brooke watched on, brimming with anxiety, as the receptionist called Ellie. He coiled the telephone's wire just as her large intestine was wrapping itself around her stomach. Thankfully she'd only eaten a few spoonfuls of muesli and yoghurt for breakfast.

Satisfied that her unfathomably disorganised English company was attempting to do everything it could to rectify the situation, Hartmut – whose name suddenly jumped out at her from his mock gold badge with a mighty thwack to the solar plexus – gestured to the seating area so she could await her fate. Brooke pulled her handbag straps up over her shoulder, shunted her sample case of mocked-up marketing wares in front of her – for this trip had also served as a sales scurry to the headquarters of any number of German consumer giants – and lugged her suitcase behind her. She fell into a seat and waited and waited.

And waited…

It took the best part of the morning for Hartmut to play the multi-tasking role of international trouble-shooter-cum-hotelier, and her heart sagged at the realisation that she had now missed her flight. It was torture to see the minute hand of her watch pass the cut-off point for check-in, and beyond. Ruben had wanted to take her out for dinner that evening as well. As a side note, he'd suggested she invite Clementine and her new(ish) squeeze, Archie.

Again.

Yeah, it was no wonder Clementine had swiped the U.S. from Brooke with that toddler tantrum earlier in the year. A city break to Chicago had turned into the ultimate meet-cute on the verdant banks of Lake Shore Drive, when her sister had twisted her ankle on her morning jog *read cunningly spotted a shapely male butt up ahead, girlie screamed, and bagged herself a hero and a hot chocolate date in one fell swoop*. Naturally, long-distance romance just begged for a deft change of sales markets.

Curiously, Ruben had struck up a 'bromance' of sorts with Archibald the American, leading to a string of double dates that were beginning to get just a little long in the tooth, especially when one wanted to get flirty and initiate foreplay during dessert. Footsie beneath the table in a foursome could lead to some eye-opening consequences.

Yet seemingly only Brooke was getting bored of this arrangement. Even Clementine was remarkably unbothered about the waste of her quality time with her boyfriend. Equally curious was the fact that Ruben never thought to invite Barnaby and his current Plus One. For again, in Brooke's humble opinion, Clementine was no less annoying than her brother.

That said, something did feel just a little off kilter with Ruben lately – even when they were alone.

He'd cancelled on Brooke twice in a row, citing heavy work issues. It wasn't enough to throw her thoughts into a tailspin, yet it didn't make her think she could rest on her laurels either.

She sensed she'd been getting a tad broody for his liking. The birth of her nephew had reduced her vocab to a glut of goo-goo-ga-ga-ing, as cousin Becca forwarded Brooke a flurry of WhatsApp videos of baby Hugo. He was blithely unaware he was clad in Prada's haute couture infants range as he filled his nappies with poo and dribbled his milk. For some reason, Rubes would never comment on Hugo's chubby-cheeked grins, changing the subject with lightning speed whenever Brooke brought him into the conversation. Which was often.

She couldn't help it. Thirty-three was approaching, after all. Mother Nature's call was getting ever louder. She'd read too many articles in too many magazines about women putting things off, trying to slot children into their thirty-ninth year as if life were as simple as a one-hundred piece jigsaw puzzle. Sadly, it didn't always work out like that and their stories made her well up in sympathy. The years flew fast. That was the truth of it. And when you worked for the RBPC, your personal life revolving around its frenetic pace – which was always at least three seasons ahead – the years were akin to clockwork toys. On acid.

She'd be lying if she said that her boyfriend's dismissal hadn't pricked her antennae. Not that Brooke had felt the tug of maternity before Hugo's birth. Likely she'd just momentarily scared her boyfriend of two years. Time would help him warm to the idea. That was all. She still fancied him like mad, and he her. The sex was great, wasn't it?

Wasn't it!

Why, the weekend before this trip they'd even done it in the car. Just like they used to in the early days when spontaneity had its wicked way with them. That had been quite a thrill, quite the surprise! She felt the creep of scarlet flush her cheeks. Yes, he possessed every quality to make a good husband – and father. Ticked all the prerequisite boxes. *And* he worked in Canary Wharf doing something high up with a jargon-studded title. She couldn't have gotten better if she'd picked him from a *Joules* catalogue. Now she just had to wait until his grand gesture of commitment unveiled itself.

It was all she could do to look after her pooch at the moment, ensuring the walker arrived on time and that her regular dog sitter was as stocked up as her pedigree Bichon Frise in food and luxuries. She loved Bambi to bits, much as she'd initially refused to offer her refuge, much as she'd tried in vain to get her to answer to a different name – *any name than that of a cartoon fawn whose fur was a completely different hue.* But when Clementine had unceremoniously dumped her unwanted pet on Brooke's doorstep with her highly-strung and highly-polished "I'm-appealing-to-your-better-nature-Big-Sis… I've-made-a-humungous-mistake-and-realised-dogs-really-aren't-just-for-Christmas-but-well-*you*-couldn't-possibly-let-her-go-to-a-rescue-centre-*could-you?*", she'd quickly given up and given in.

All well and good with a fur baby. You could pay for Team Toy Dog to rally around with 24/7 support for your curly lap pup with its white fluffy clouds of hair. But you could hardly mirror that with a human baby. She'd have to put her clucking on the backburner; at least until the company finances were ruler-straight.

And wasn't that whole pitiful episode with Bambi yet another classic example – a metaphor, in fact – for the way that every one of her nearest, and supposedly dearest, treated her like a doormat?

Brooke necked her on-the-house Turkish rose water. Admittedly, it was delicious, but it was also probably her lot. She'd never felt more like a criminal. The various members of staff slipping behind the reception desk seemed to be snickering at her predicament, talking in feverish whispers; one of them always ensuring Brooke was under their steely gaze. Oh, she knew she was the subject of their hilarity. And now she was ready to commit murder.

She extracted her phone from her bag, sending a stream of heated WhatsApp messages to her dad, Clementine and Barnaby. No use involving her mum. Nothing other than the opportunity to go boutique shoe-shopping would have a snowflake's chance in hell of interrupting Mum's cham-pagne-with-everything spa break in the Cotswolds anyway.

Nobody replied.

She curled up her toes in a bid to transfer her fury to the marble floor.

Just when she thought it was never going to happen, Hartmut beckoned her. Then he gave a tiny nod of his head. He passed her a mountain of paperwork to check and sign – so much for the perpetual recycling efficiency of his nation – just as a lengthy message pinged onto Brooke's phone.

Ellie's name popped onto her screen like a virtual hug. Brooke swallowed down the sudden and unexpected lump in her throat, determined not to cry.

"Sorry to hear about your embarrassing situation. It took a fair bit of juggling and negotiating with Frank in accounts, but everything is sorted. I have NO IDEA what's going on this month but some SUBSTANTIAL chunks of money have been moved around... although 'fiddled with' would probably be closer to the mark."

Despite the alarm bells ringing in her head, Brooke couldn't help but be impressed with Ellie's texting skills. This was effectively an essay, with not a typo in sight. *"Listen, Brooke: we need an emergency meeting when you get back. There's enough on the card now for a taxi to the airport. I've booked you on the next flight to Heathrow. Oh, and lunch with a glass of red. Sounds like you need it! But we're effectively short of cash flow thereafter until the end of the week when the Americans' payment hits. It's not good."*

"I can't thank you enough, E… and OMG, yes, that's absolutely SHIT!"

Brooke texted back all fingers and thumbs. A fit of blubbering had snuck up on her, so goodness knows what came out in predictive text – no time to think about that now.

She reacquainted herself with her paraphernalia, swiping a plethora of printouts from beneath Hartmut's sneering nose, and stuffed them into her bag whilst ferreting around for a scrappy remnant of tissue to dab at her tears. The world's greatest HR Manager would know what she meant in any case.

But how could they be short of money?

She wasn't sure Ellie was right. She seemed to think that once the colossal sum came in from their U.S customers, all would conveniently be smoothed over, until the next time, and the next.

Things just had to be nipped in the bud somehow. It was now or never. This wasn't the first time money had gone walkies. The past six months had been littered with examples of loot vanishing overnight. And it wasn't only cold hard cash. The most recent disappearing act had involved a bank of computers...

Her phone trilled and she somehow managed to answer it, sobbing as soon as she recognised Ellie's soothing voice.

"Your message said, *'I can't escape them... it's absolutely SHIT!'* What the hell's going on there, Brooke?"

"It's okay. It's all right! I'm perfectly safe. Honestly." Brooke just about stifled a whimper.

"Oh, thank goodness for that. I thought for a moment you'd been dragged into a broom cupboard and taken hostage, and I'd have to call the British Embassy or something."

Brooke could refrain from expressing herself no longer.

"Brooke: stop it. I can't handle tears." Eerily, the calm in Ellie's voice never faltered. "I know, *I know.* Not the smartest thing to confess as HR Manager, but I just don't do them. We'll sort this mess out once and for all when you get back. I promise, okay?"

"I curse the day I ever instig—"

But Brooke couldn't continue, and the backstory to the company's creation would take as long as her flight back to London to relay to Ellie anyway.

"Just get yourself out into the fresh air and wait for that cab."

Brooke marvelled at the way Ellie could imagine her so accurately; reluctant to leave the gilt-edged, royal-red sofa behind, in case this was a dream and the *Polizei* were waiting to handcuff her outside the hotel, casting her back into her nightmare. It was the first time she'd had such a close brush with the law. She was no Goody Two-Shoes, she had her moments of mischief, but this was plain unacceptable, especially after all the new orders she'd secured for the RBPC this week.

Suddenly – and perhaps, ironically, thanks to Hartmut – she could see the manipulation by the men of the family for what it was, at last. It was ridiculous to think that she, the eldest sibling, had fallen for so much nonsense hook, line and sinker. If only Clementine wasn't so aloof, so wrapped up in herself, and occasionally, Archie, then there'd be strength in numbers. Or at the very least equality. Her mother, having never lifted a finger in her life, would never join forces so they could outnumber the males.

Brooke couldn't help but glower, as she imagined Suzie insisting, *'I did once work in an exclusive department store beauty concession, handing out their most expensive perfume swatches, don't you know?'*

It was true but, upper crust or not, it was a position she'd held down for all of a fortnight; the young salesman Harry – and his quest for Parisian aftershave – netting him a buy one, get one free offer he simply couldn't refuse: high-end cologne and an even higher-maintenance wife. Brooke's parents had married within six months.

She brought herself back to the present moment, banishing her tears in a bid to reassure Ellie on the end of the line; childishly glaring over her shoulder at the cast of critics behind her. "Okay, no more tears and I'm moving outside, I promise. Away from reception. I'm trying to ignore their holier-than-thou faces. A right row of wannabe talent show panellists, the lot of them," she yelled.

Tragic behaviour. The kind of thing she expected on occasion from Clementine, and more frequently Barnaby. But damn, it felt good.

"You're painting quite the picture," Ellie giggled. "For once I'm feeling blessed to be stuck in the office."

Brooke pushed the revolving door, wedged herself in and kept shunting herself and her luggage forward as fast as she could – quite the multi-tasking skill – so as not to re-enact her Budapest airport debacle. She shuddered at the painful memory, unsure whether humiliation or a crushed arm had wounded her the most, when she'd got trapped in that bitch of an unyielding door.

She burst out onto the pavement and hauled her case behind her; the doorman, who'd evidently been kept abreast of her downfall, eyed her with suspicion, lifting not a finger to help lighten her load.

"Brooke? Are you still there?" Ellie probed across the miles.

"Alive and kicking," she responded, slightly out of breath.

"Can you think of any recent events that might have led to… ahem, well, how else can I put this other than to come right out with it… family members splashing out on anything unusual, or acting untowardly? Strictly between you and me, of course."

Brooke broke off as Stuttgart's speediest taxi driver corralled her case and her sample bag and put them in the boot, simultaneously opening the door for her with his foot – funky! She stepped inside his Mercedes, ready to disappear from the disdain of the stuck-up hotel staff.

"*Zum Flughafen?*" he asked her and she confirmed her destination with a fervent nod.

"Ah, I'm airport-bound, at last," she said to Ellie, letting out an elongated sigh, sticking her finger up with relish at the git of a doorman, then unable to refrain from poking her tongue out at him too.

Why couldn't she be more like that with her own flesh and blood, hey? They all deserved a flipped bird. Once the façade of it all was deconstructed, block by block, so that the RBPC's HQ was no more than a family home with its (admittedly) vast plot of land, when had they ever really had her best interests at heart?

She already knew the answer.

"Anything at all?" Ellie asked her again, a slight insistency to her tone. "Far be it from me to suggest family fraud, your father borrowing money for a new yacht, or other things of that ilk but, as you're probably aware, nobody else has access to this particular credit card account."

"Hmm. There's got to be something fishy I've let slip by, these past few weeks." Brooke frowned as they hit the Autobahn. She skimmed through the recent days and weeks. She was as sure as she could be that her dad had just the one boat, for now. "Tell you what: give me the flight to think it over. I'm sure it will come to me… especially after the wine."

"Perfect. And make it two glasses. You're not driving back, remember. I don't know about you, but I always find my short and long-term memory resurfaces after that second glass of vino."

See, she'd been right about Ellie from the outset.

She loved her quirks, and, despite the fact Ellie was younger than Brooke, she loved that big-sisterly feeling she seemed so naturally to exude. It neatly took the edge off the authority of her role so that any decision she came up with – huh, even the occasional cringeworthy corporate team building event – was perfectly justifiable. Ellie really was always putting the company first. That's why she'd earned

Brooke's respect. You could smell the girl's dedication a mile off. Brooke only hoped Ellie had somebody special to share that with, in a relationship. She hadn't yet managed to find out. But one thing was sure: Ellie deserved fulfilment in her private life. Even if Brooke herself was straining to hear the peal of wedding bells when it came to her own.

"I'll see you tomorrow morning in your office. And Ellie… thank you for everything today. You totally saved my bacon there."

"Oh, it's nothing compared to the way you'll be thanking me for my next idea. Like I said, company meeting tomorrow."

7

JOCK, JULES AND JOURNALIST

French Homes, Dreams and Disasters magazine,
August 2020 edition:

**Jock and Jules, owners of Les Nuages, tell our reporter,
Joanna how nice turned to nasty in Normandy**

Jock: "Never in my wildest dreams could I have imagined it."

Jules: "Never in our wildest nightmares!"

Jock: "I'd worked my balls off."

Jules: "He really had *worked*. Eight-and-three-quarter years
with a reality TV production company, filming mind-
numbing shit about delusional, stargazy wannabes at all
angles and all hours of the day and night. The show was
years past its prime. 'Leave on a high, Jock,' I'd say to him.
Would he listen?"

Joanna the Journalist: "Ahem, loath as I am to interrupt before we've even got started, I'm er… not sure that's a particularly kind way to express the ambitions of reality TV stars in this day and age. They are, after all, human beings, albeit they've chosen to temporarily dwell in a goldfish b—"

Jock: "You're quite right. Makes me sound like I didn't have a scrap of integrity. But to be fair, love, I had no choice but to carry on. It was a means to an end to help us finance this place, manna in the middle of nowhere, Glastonbury in France, Sedona in the fruit orchards. A shabby chic *gîte*. An escape from reality. A vegan, organic retreat for writers, artists, yogis, musicians, wand-makers, and faeries – anyone unconventional who wanted to come here and meditate on mandalas, forget about the madness of society. We opened our rustic doors to them all."

Jules: "Well, that was the original idea – to be selective about whom we let in – but it didn't quite pan out like that, did it? There were bills to pay."

Jock: "A lot of bills. A lot of money. A lot of previously unde-tected damp."

Jules: "Pfft. In fungi and human form. Sometimes we had to take a chance on the riffraff, and then look at what happened with the last group of guests."

Joanna: *There follows a brief interlude while Jules studies her bitten-to-the-quick fingernails. Jock and I sup our kale and logan-berry smoothies and wait for a sign to continue (at this point, it's also worth noting I vow never to imbibe either fruit or vegetable again, solo or in tandem). Jules nods her head, indicating I may proceed.*

Joanna: "According to reports, the Westwood party and Ms. Sanchez weren't – *aren't* – quite what you'd class as riff-raff. But yes, I'm on a tight schedule, so if we could please get back to the subject of the fire that would be most help—"

Jock: "Can I just make it clear: all those years of being untrue to myself might appear to an outsider as if I was selling my soul. I wasn't. Not really. I mean, I always kept the greater good at the forefront of my mind when I was zooming in on a will-they-won't-they couple in the sack… or heavily editing a confessional, or wondering which filter would best capture a Z-list celeb, hell-bent on reigniting their career prospects with a spot of karaoke in the hot tub. We'd get a hefty bonus if the producer deemed our footage successful enough to elevate them to a C-stroke-D-lister. That's what covered the barn conversion. Not that we ever got that far."

Joanna: "You really don't need to explain yourself to—"

Jules: "Oh, but he does. We do. It bothers us immensely to think we could give the good folk out there a false impression of our vision."

Joanna: "It's really none of my business. I'm just here for the exclusive."

Jock: "We'd like all of our backstory kept in. It's only right that readers get the Full Monty *vis à vis* our *mauvais quart d'heure*. That's the term the French use for a shitty five minutes of fame, in case you weren't fluent in the lingo."

Joanna: "Well, I am."

Jock: "Oh, right. Anyway, er… I know you have a word

count. I sort of worked in the media. I'm not into payment in kind, though, 'cos we're not one of those free-loving swinging couples."

Jules: "Although we know more than a few who are."

Jock: "Would one of the wife's raw cacao and beetroot layer cakes do it for you? She'll throw in a rosemary and stevia drizzle.

Jules: "It's an aphrodisiac."

Joanna: "That's most thoughtful… but I've only just eaten my morning croissant, and root vegetables tend to… you know," *I wink and whisper, lowering my eyelids to drop what I hope might be a convincing hint toward my ever-growing spare tyre.* "They…" aggravate my IBS." *Surely a more polite way of saying your idea of a smoothie has rather put me off anything else coming from your 'kitchen' for the foreseeable future. The couple wince in unison. Result.*

"I'll definitely make sure everybody knows the unabridged version of your story, though," *Oh, hell, yes.* "In the meantime, shall we… ahem… *revenons à nos moutons,* as they also say in these parts, and talk about the complete and utter destruction of '*Les Nuages de Normandie,*' your holiday home, sometime this decade, or what?"

8

ELLIE

*W*ell that was it. The call from Germany was the very last straw in a kick-to-the-stomach of a day. Cliché or not, there was no other way Ellie could describe it.

Although she supposed it allowed her to momentarily park the hideous image of Barnaby, his latest dollybird, and their flushed and hideously breathless lunchtime kissing (which spoke of oh, so much more than tongues) to one side. Ellie really hadn't been spying, either. He and Saffy-what's-her-face had had no business pulling up next to her car like that, carrying on with that sickening display while she nibbled on her sushi; an exhibition which really, Ellie knew deep down, was just Barnaby's roundabout way of trying to make her jealous since both of them secretly couldn't wait to get their paws on each other.

Later she'd mentally enjoy the process of kicking that bitch to the curb where she belonged, climbing into his Land Rover and showing him the way it was really done. It would be a ritual thoroughly deserving of a candle-lit, sensually oiled bath. And a sniff. Just for a nanosecond and no more.

The briefest of inhalations of a square of dark and bitter Colombian chocolate; its brooding qualities perfectly matching her current mood.

Not that she hadn't tried her best to usurp the woman already.

Ellie'd spat in the hussy's drink while making the afternoon tea on a day when Saffron had totally outstayed her welcome, loitering around Barnaby's office in her skin-tight catsuit. Even Clementine had been furious, over the wandering eyes of her junior designer underlings.

Ellie had also stolen Saffy's Lancôme Oud Bouquet perfume (and a couple of token twenty pound notes while she was at it) from her handbag; the handbag that lay disregarded in the staff kitchen, whilst the super-serviceable strumpet and Barnaby had pulled down his office blinds.

So what? Saffy could totally absorb the loss.

On the other hand, Ellie couldn't stay mad at her beloved for long. The power was all hers Nobody else decided her destiny, not Saffy, not even Barnaby himself; the man who'd soon be her better half. Ellie just needed to crank up the visualisations of the two of them together as a couple. That was all.

Barnaby stalling their future happiness with the wrong woman was a minor problem, in any case. Ellie had, she realised with that godawful incredulity that comes with the increasingly imminent threat of middle age, reached a company milestone this week. She had officially been employed by the RBPC for half a year. And yet those six whole months had got her nowhere very fast; forcing her to forge an alternative pathway to romance. Nope, all the monotonous weeks and days had simply added up, like the thicket of brambles Prince Charming met in *Sleeping Beauty*. Except in this modern-day version of the story, it was Ellie who had the task of chopping down the thorns (company bullshit); of clearing her own exit, so she could become the princess she was always meant to be – Barnaby waking up at last, with a burning desire to sweep her up in his arms, and the pair of them cantering off into the sunset.

Fantasies to one side, and as thoughtful as she'd been earlier this morning, the chances of Brooke unearthing a deeply-buried clue as to her family's financial shenanigans was as likely as Clementine appearing at Ellie's office door with a bunch of flowers and a bottle of bubbly on her birthday.

Whoever was behind this was at the top of their game. Whoever was behind this thought they had all their bases covered. Whoever was behind this was in for a rude awakening. Nobody got in the way of Ellie's plans. She'd have to book another coma-inducing dinner with Ben. He'd have plenty of ideas on how to get to the bottom of it.

Maybe she was being a little hard on herself in her mental job appraisal, though? Ellie had ticked the boxes of the HR textbooks, after all. She upheld the façade of a 'typical' HR day rather admirably; nursing personal staff issues in the morning, dealing with annual leave questions and recruitment in the afternoon, answering foreign employees' endless tax queries come evening. The company hired a number of overseas social media graduates for peanuts, making sorting out the latter almost a job in itself.

When she wasn't doing that, she was keeping her files orderly, and she was eternally mindful of the importance of exemplary time management skills. Then there was her own blessed social media to keep on top of; the tedium of wages and hours, engagement and retention besides. She convinced, she 'cared', and – most importantly – she seemed to come across as credible. At this point, she couldn't deny she had Ben to thank for all of that; the mature student dork who'd incessantly tried to date her at Uni. For a guy six years her senior, his ploys were ridiculously kindergarten. Still, he was a handy occasional lunch date; especially pre-Carlos, when he'd often sub her sushi and salads. And speaking of guys, wasn't this one the fountain of relevant knowledge?

That's why Ellie had always kept him on the perimeters of her life, and yet arm's length enough for him not to develop too much of a romantic notion. That's why she'd continued to tap him up for advice the moment she'd been offered the job with the RBPC. Ben worked in a massive financial institution nowadays and knew everything there was to know about the corporate world – and then some. It was comforting to know he was on the end of the phone if she couldn't get to the bottom of this mystery by herself.

And okay, Ellie would even concede to a minor victory of her own here and there. Like the moment she'd found herself rather surprisingly voted onto the board of directors. She knew it was Brooke's doing, and of course she wouldn't bite the hand that fed her, but it was all rather laughable when 'they' (Barnaby, Clementine and the Old Man) wouldn't so much as give her an assistant. A skivvy who could be doing at least half of her aforementioned tasks.

And still none of them recognised her. She'd even played The Power of Love on repeat in the staff kitchen for the entire month of July. Would Barnaby care to cast himself back to the Monty's end-of-year party? Her in a hideous ra-ra skirt and paisley top combo. Him rocking the latest hoodie craze, paired with Levi's and the world's most expensive trainers. Frankie Goes to Hollywood's sweet lyrics willing Barnaby to take the shy girl by the hand after a teacher had paired them up for a twirl; Barnaby muttering something under his breath that sounded like the dreaded donkey-tail-hair-slight his sister had earlier thrown at Ellie, and then promptly making a grab for any other girl in the vicinity. Eleanor Finch's world falling apart at the seams, never to be stitched back together.

Still, it hadn't triggered a single guilt trip memory, not even when she'd turned up for the RPBC summer party in an adult version of said outfit; tastefully made, sexy in all the right places, by a dressmaker in Clifton who'd once worked with none other than Zandra Rhodes!

And her attempts at feng shui had been dismal at best. For every inch she'd succeeded in surreptitiously re-positioning desks, tables and chairs; staying behind later and later to do so, by the end of the week, the crafty cleaners would have everything back in its original place, as if they'd taken up dusting and vacuuming with a National Geographic map. Declaring her energy flow theories to all and sundry would have backfired badly. Subtlety was the only way. Yet, despite racking her brains for another indestructible in-road, time after time, all Ellie came up with was a big fat nothing.

Then one miserable Monday morning, Harry had appeared from nowhere; his expression sullen, his sulky demeanour rapidly spreading like mildew. He'd poked his head around a succession of doors, before storming the building in a breathless frenzy, gathering up every single stem of Ellie's beloved peonies and binning their beauty in his wake.

Actually *binning* them.

In full bloom and everything.

Without a clue as to the symbolism of his very act! "If I see these hideous things within the four walls of this building again, heads will roll. Is this some kind of sick joke? I do not wish to be reminded of the harrowing days following my mother's tragic death! The house was full of those flowers then. Do I make myself clear?"

That had left Ellie seething all right, and on the verge of flying to China to track down Connie, who'd be able to reel off feng shui plans B through to Z. Ellie expelled a frustrated breath at the hideous memory of Harry's outburst.

She'd worked so hard to position those flowers just so, the energy of rank and wealth greeting everyone at the doorway, helping all and sundry with their dream, and not just herself, as she was so fully entitled to do. Why hadn't he clocked them before, anyway? It'd taken every ounce of Ellie's will to bite her tongue for the greater good of her future family relations. Had he no idea how much he was sabotaging his company's performance?

She'd later discovered from some of the junior staff members that Rene Westwood, Harry's mother, had tumbled from Brighton pier in the nineties; her body mysteriously never recovered.

Tumbled or pushed?

Whatever. Ellie wouldn't be defeated that easily. Least of all by her almost father-in-law. He too needed to learn the rules of the game.

Speaking of which, that vision of Rene's plummet – and what Ellie supposed might have actually happened to action it – reminded her of Jenga; and the rather giant version of the game she was involuntarily playing with this excuse for a company. For every new plank of wood she stacked; for every layer she added to what could be a fortress, somebody else was pushing, pulling, and teasing away all her efforts – for what felt like the sheer hell of it. She'd gone from working in one of the most orderly and serene places in the world – all right, overlooking the austere academia pay cheque – to working for a bunch of clowns.

Clowns who paid her handsomely, admittedly.

But still. Her pride came before the pounds, and as every circus-goer knew, when you had clowns in the tent (or company) there was always the potential to get a custard pie in the face.

Well, now their shenanigans were going to stop. And Ellie's were going to begin.

Dual Focus.

The Goody-Two-Shoes jargon relished its brief moment in the spotlight, dancing a merry jig in Ellie's mind. She knew the drill. Yes, she ought to be dual-focussed about this. For there are times in HR (according to the oft and uber-parroted phrases she'd memorised from the books, and Ben's own pneumatic prattle) when one must make decisions to protect the individual.

The Ellie.

She'd skim neatly over the fact that someone in her lofty position should be protecting the organisation, its culture, and its values, too.

Where was the fun in that?

Exactly.

And since 'they' didn't have any of the latter values anyway, that was easy…

P.S. It would take a task force to disband this hierarchy. Ellie Sanchez neither had the time nor the inclination.

P.P.S. Charity begins at home.

P.P.P.S. Ellie was going soft in her old age. That was way too much justification for one day.

And now that she'd consciously made the decision to up the ante, she was sure something big was about to reveal itself; something so out-of-this-world incredible and Eureka that the two issues she was currently stewing on would dissipate in a puff of smoke:

1. A way to furtively plant a fresh batch of opulent peonies around the borders of the RBPC HQ to neutralise the mysterious movement of money; and

2. Distracting *her* quarry from his current money-grabbing girl, ignoring the slightly troublesome fact that this one had lasted a record-breaking three months.

Ellie was solution-oriented. Always had been. She decided to do something she hadn't done for a long time, even if it was breaking the supposed 'golden rule' of HR, possibly paving the way to her downfall. *'Human Resources are more than an island. Integrate, integrate, integrate!'* She mock-paraphrased one of the aspirational quotes from her latest HR management Bible as she locked her office door, cutting herself off from the mainland.

She extracted the pack of emergency cigars that sat in her drawer waiting for such a predicament, and sparked up, toking greedily, enjoying the hit of the dense, slate-grey smoke as it filled her lungs. Wondering if the very act of creating a real puff of smoke would somehow work its way backwards into that Eureka idea she so craved; the one that would finally get Barnaby to notice her.

Ellie exhaled at her leisure, waiting for the great billow of smoke to reveal her next move. She was more than a dark horse. She was a knight in a strategic game of chess. The King (Daddy Westwood) was going down. But to get to the King, would she need to take out the Queen (Who was she kidding? The elusive Mrs Westwood never brought her Jimmy Choos within a metre of her husband's part of the building), the Bishop (Baffling Barnaby), or the Rook (Contriving Clementine)?

That was the million dollar question. On and on she puffed; hoping the answer would reveal itself.

But nothing.

Ellie tapped out another of the slim Cuban cigars onto her desk and lit up, revelling in her rebellion.

She was also adamant this wouldn't become a habit. Carlos had once told her he found her 'intellectually stimulating' when she sparked up an after-dinner cigar, but she wouldn't give him the satisfaction of getting hooked. It had been exciting at the time. Steak and red wine – Argentinian, of course – at some high-end, over-priced place on the waterfront, then a taxi back to the uni: blinds down, library security cameras switched defiantly off (or masked by a strategically flung shirt/skirt/bra), Kama Sutra out; the Argentinian professor-in-residence caressing every inch of the librarian's body beneath the soft lights of the communal study table, whilst casually glancing over his naked shoulder at his guidebook to perfect his technique. His subject complying, moaning in pleasure as the table wobbled. They'd had insatiable appetites for nailing every sketch in the book.

Hell, Carlos was good. He was better than good.

But he was also Barnaby; the only man she ever really wanted to make love to. Ellie closed her eyes whenever she and her lover were face to face, imagining a very different head and shoulders on that torso. Though Carlos was fit enough for a sedentary geek.

Who'd have thought he'd march her down the aisle six months later? But Ellie was always going to fleece him one way or another. She might have been a fool to fall for his pre-climax prose, but she'd been astute enough only to switch one library CCTV camera off. The other was resolutely on. Once their daring deeds were done, she'd swapped tapes for good measure, keeping the shady evidence of their 'educational' encounters under lock and key. Once he moved her into his fancy-pants penthouse by the trendy docks, once that key had been added to her ring, she'd quickly turned into a bore; half the thrill was in the chase, and he'd well and truly caught her. She knew his type well, having read about wandering professorial eyes in many books. He needed art in all its forms, not just the literary. Small wonder then that he was soon *rueda*-ing around the vivacious Veronica; a Buenos Aires-based tango dancer extraordinaire.

Astoundingly, Ellie's soon-to-be-ex-husband didn't seem to mind about the emergence of the blackmail sex tape. He'd rubbed at his stubble, he'd huffed on his thick black-framed glasses and polished them attentively; he'd double clicked his pen as if he were filling in nothing more taxing than a questionnaire. He'd even thanked Ellie profusely for the *bibliobonking* – his exact words – as she'd watched him sign on the dotted line of the hasty divorce settlement, pinching herself under the table, because surely she'd wake up soon from the dream?

Ellie took the last drag of her second cigar and then went all out, lighting up a third. It was despicable behaviour but it was kind of essential today. All the Westwoods were out anyway. Marketing had an away day – arranged by hers truly – and would currently be team-building and all that jazz (bollocks), pummelling themselves senseless with paintballs in the Forest of Dean. Besides, there were no smoke detectors in her room.

Besides, there was no smoke without a fire...

Ellie rearranged the paraphernalia on her desk, grinning; a thoroughly delicious and wicked idea taking shape in her head.

She couldn't.

She bloody well could.

It was too much, taking things way too far.

Only nice guys finish last.

She lacked the finesse. It might get out of hand.

All part of the fun!

She made a heart shape with the stray paperclips in a bid to convince herself of her innate goodness before it was too late; smiling in the realisation that this wasn't the first time she'd locked her office door. Barney (from this moment on, she categorically refused to grant him the extra syllable that was his prerogative) was blissfully unaware that each and every time he pissed her off, she'd extract something else from her desk, pleasuring herself as she conjured up an array of saucy montages.

Dammit, she was just going to say it.

She'd get out her vibrator.

Usually, in her mind's eye, she'd be clad in black leather fused with a little pulse-racing red lace, teasing him with an erotic parade before straddling him on his office chair – although sometimes she had a penchant for the rough and ready of the carpet too. Especially when she needed a quickie. And never was there a better scenario conjured than when he was on a VIP call, so she could enjoy the pathetic waver in his voice as she took him to the edge, and then slowed her thrusting right back down, until his fingers were kneading at her buttocks for more. There truly was no better revenge for the way he incessantly ignored her. Afterwards she always felt so very empowered, especially when they passed each other in the corridor in the real world; her superior smile across her lips. All she had to do was keep these fantasies up for long enough, so that they became a reality. He couldn't go on denying their mutual attraction forever, and he must know it.

"If you can picture it in your mind, you'll soon be holding it in your hand," she reminded herself.

Wasn't that a saying from one of the self-help greats?

A bit too literal in this case, Ellie!

She let out a large plume of smoke and cackled, almost hacking up her lungs then at the image of Barney's balls in her palm.

It was time to get back to business. She wiped the smile from her face. In truth, that jobsworthy German git on the phone had done her a favour earlier; reconfirming her suspicions that everything had been going seriously pear-shaped for weeks. It wasn't just the unexpected chunks of missing money. Behaviour had shifted, too. Barney was cagier than cagey. Clem (yes, she got the same name-shortening treatment as of today) was sporting dark circles to rival a panda. And old Westwood Senior was suddenly popping in and out like a yo-yo, and a little too curiously for Ellie's liking. Okay, the guy might live next door to the business, but he'd left his kids and their more than capable staff to it, during her early days. Something was definitely, and increasingly, afoot.

"I'm calling a board meeting," she began the round robin email. "The Oval Office at three p.m. On the dot. Be there or be square," she typed – and then snickered at her lame joke, thinking better of it and erasing the last bit.

That's right. Her current workplace was so enormous that the meeting room that housed their round table, where Harry Westwood loved to hold court in the manner of King bloody Arthur, was dubbed the Oval Office. Go figure.

She stubbed out her half-finished cigar in the ashtray, head dizzy from the continuous hit; she poured herself a large glass of water, knocked it back, and walked to the window. Maybe the lime-green pastures behind her office would give her perspective, and stop her following through on her potentially lethal impulse.

She didn't have to dwell on that thought for long before something rather concrete *did* occur.

No way!

She zipped back to her desk and frantically flipped open her diary, rifling the pages to her bookmark. Just as she'd thought, today was only the freaking day.

September 21st.

The anniversary of Carlos's infidelity. Well, the discovery thereof. Who knew how long Carlos had actually been going to bed with Veronica? His trips back to Argentina had become so frequent that Ellie could quite believe the Humanities department would offer him another permanent job.

She returned to the window, fingers drilling at her temples; willing every sordid detail to resurface. She adopted the supernova position in the wide, cushioned windowsill; the irony not lost on her that this was, indeed, the very last stance she'd taken, the very last time they'd made love.

Yes, the commemoration of Carlos's affair with Veronica had shifted something all right; turning the screw suddenly. Ellie perched on the magnolia-glossed window sill, throwing the pile of dumb scatter cushions to the floor. She took in the panoramic landscape of shabby-chic hedgerows, unruly cows and the village's ubiquitous procession of distant tractors, as every memory proceeded to unravel in a series of detailed twists and turns. How very apt given that floozie's dancing profession.

Every past inadequacy in Ellie's life proceeded to lay itself bare, step by step, like a tango, or a screwed-up board game in reverse. Every subconscious thought floating beneath the surface now begged for a different kind of reflection.

Like the rowing-crew gaggle of Old Cheltenham Ladies College besties who hadn't made it to Oxbridge, descending on second-best Brizzle Uni instead. They'd been a steadfast annoyance in Ellie's daily academic library life. Hidden messages distilled to pointed looks as she checked out their piles of books. Those Hooray Henriettas stripped her bare of everything, their elegant, cynicism-filled eyes peering down on her above their up-turned collars and pearls. Sartorial aside: Ellie could never understand why that rendered one posh. More like a piss-poor imitation of Count Dracula, if you asked her.

Even if their scant acknowledgement meant she had *finally* been seen by the Public School Posse, it was only because they'd sussed her. Her ears whirred with the whispers of their inner dialogue:

'We know you don't have the connections... or the money. Better

luck next time. Try being born to virtual aristocracy like one of us. Perhaps then you won't end up in a university library stacking shelves and playing skivvy to us. A step up from balancing tins of beans in a supermarket pyramid – but only a slight one. Of course, none of us have to do either.'

In Ellie's mind's eye, they'd break out the jazz hands at this point; single-celled organism that they were. *'Daddy will always find us a super role with a title to match in the company we'll ultimately inherit. Even a 2.2 looks good on a rich girl's C.V. The equivalent of an extracurricular activity, Brownie points for rolling our sleeves up and mucking in with the masses. We don't even need to falsify our academic credentials, unlike some people. Mwhaha!'*

Round two would come in the car park. The Henriettas would scooch together in Izzy's sky-blue Audi or Ginnie's hip and trendy Citroen Dolly CV (because this was Gin, darling, and she had the sort of expensive face which made everything look like it was out of Harper's). They'd clock Ellie, caught out in the bus queue with the students who rented in Functional Filton. It was all she could afford. *She had a career, FFS, and they still had one over on her.* She'd watch the toffee-nosed-snobs saunter back to Classy Clifton and their Waitrose-laden fridges, grimacing at the thought of the microwave meal-for-one that lay in wait in her bedsit, all too often washed down with cheap vinegary wine whilst those bitches quaffed Napa Valley Cabernet Sauvignon and its upmarket counterparts.

Pray tell her who, in her life predicament, wouldn't fall into Professor Sanchez's arms, after a little steamy flirtation at the library photocopier? He was just about good-looking enough for a guy nearing middle-age; his intellect pushing Ellie over the threshold that was her dating norm. Frankly, it had been a while; and he was an improvement on her last fling, Dismal Dominic, who still lived at home at the age of thirty.

Yeah, that'd given the Henriettas something to put in their pipes. And their lacrosse sticks.

Still, it was never enough. The present could never quite erase what Ellie saw as the inadequacies of her past. Izzy, Ginnie and co. had long since graduated and pissed off back to their lives of polo and privilege, and yet Ellie still felt their scorn.

Shortly before the scrutiny of the students, had come the reading of her father's will. Keith Finch had left the bloody lot – *not that there was a whole lot of bloody* – to a sheep sanctuary in Devon. Anything would have been better than this nothing; a deposit on a starter home to get her out of her one-bedroom flat, at least. Sheep were her mother's least favourite animals. Like that was payback for her exodus and reversion to her maiden name, like Pamela Jeffers-was-Finch could even be bothered nowadays.

And three years prior to Keith's untimely heart attack, Pamela (then Finch) had fled to Spain with a parkour artist, keen to spread the word about his hare-brained hobby in and around the beaches, sunbeds, and bars of Torremolinos. As one did.

'You'll understand when you get to my age, Keith,' the post-card with the castanet-toting flamenco dancers had informed her all-of-six-months-younger father. *'My regards to Eleanor. See to it that she's **correctly fed**, watered and clothed, preferably in some other colour besides Gothic black.'* In hindsight, that was laughable. Her father could barely make toast, although Ellie couldn't deny possession of myriad moccasins and a hideous sheepskin coat, courtesy indeed of her dad. *'Fabien's not only the fittest athlete known to woman, he's also gifted me with the... well, there's no other applicable noun for it really: THE GIFT. Yeah, that's right. I'm living in the moment and*

enjoying the kaleidoscopic colours of the Med, after way too many years of ironing your uninspiring navy blue checked shirts, and listening to your fake-promises of the moon and the stars to the backdrop of the whingeing British soaps. It was us living in the soap opera. That's the irony! I'll never forgive you for getting me to give up 'playing maid' at the Hotel Guinevere – conveniently forgetting the fact that I was actually General Manager. All so I could be a lady of leisure for five whole minutes; the predictable timeframe it took for your big ideas, and our marriage, to finally crumble to dust. Just like a Cadbury's Flake, hey...'

Ellie's mother had been talked into quitting her role at Glastonbury's swishest hotel; the job which – along with Keith's redundancy from his not-too-shabby Sheepskin Export Sales Manager role at a local company whose garments had long gone out of fashion – had afforded their daughter a whole year and a bit at Monty's. That's how long it took for the money to run out. That's how long it took for Keith to realise he would never EVER match a sheepskin export sales manager's salary – and a fortnight in Corfu-style bonus – attempting to flog hand-stitched sheepskin boots from an oversized briefcase. Australia, their small Somerset town was not, *Ugg* much less.

... I would say hasta luego,' The postcard continued. *'But it's no use trying to persuade me to come back, so this is more like* adios.'

And there Ellie was. Reduced to a regard. By her own mother.

From that recollection it was a hop, skip and jump back in time to a very different distribution of paperwork: Clem handing out the invites for her thirteenth birthday party sleepover during French class.

Eleanor and the freckled Fitzgerald twins, Kit and Kat, hadn't made the list. *Quelle bloody surprise.* And no, the twins' names didn't make them popular with chocolate wafer-loving teenage girls. Not when it came to Monty's, where to be cool you needed a moniker like Fuji or Pink Lady. Eleanor could have strangled those girls for the way they further diluted her presence; the three of them lumbered together like some sort of Misfit Musketeers.

"There were only eighteen cards and envelopes in the pack." Clem had shrugged, snout in the air, as if her lack of tact was the fault of Hallmark. But you didn't need an abacus to tally up the females in the classroom. They totalled twelve.

The school trip to Lyme Regis to study fossils had certainly cheered Eleanor up. Run by a group of the most fossil-like public school teachers themselves, it was compulsory; the type of outing she dreaded, and not just because of the predictable autumnal soakings from lashings of rain and her squashed, miserable, and thoroughly under-buttered Soreen Malt Loaf 'sandwiches.' Connie hadn't started Monty's at that point, and Kit and Kat sat together on the bus as usual, so the invisible Eleanor would find herself playing Billy No Mates; her rucksack her imaginary friend as the tangled strands of her split-ended ponytail stuck to the coach window's condensation, and she feigned indifference.

Except this school trip was different, magically so; for it was two year groups venturing out together. Barney Westwood only went and bounded down the coach with vigour, stopping mid-aisle instead of heading for the customary back seats with his friends. Eleanor's breath hitched in her throat; his fresh, punchy CK One aftershave preceding him, stirring her every nerve ending to life. Ellie might recall it as a dream, now. Then, it felt as if she'd fallen down a rabbit hole into a world where anything was possible – including the heart throb of the year above falling for the underwhelming underdog.

"May I sit here, or is this seat already taken?'

Ellie blushed at his suave enquiry. Gosh, he was so

perfect, so polite. She plumped up her bag on her lap, arms wrapped around it, fingers gripping its rope handles, begging and pleading that this heaven-sent moment would last forever.

The rational part of Present Ellie's brain knew it had all been nothing more than an elaborate joke; a cruel bet fuelled by Barney's smarmy gang of pimpled hangers-on, their bellows of laughter reverberating up and down the aisle until they hit the A303 down to Dorset and the oldest of their dinosaur teachers reprimanded them. The nostalgic nooks of her memory still refused to listen, though.

Shyly, she told Barney all about her favourite things, waxing lyrical over her favourite indie pop group, Elastica. How she hoped to one day see them in concert, but being thirteen with naff-all pocket money totally sucked.

"I can get us tickets for their next London gig. I think they're dope too. I've got some older friends who can pull some strings. Piece of cake. We'll run away from home together if you like."

"Really? You'd do that for *me*?"

Her heart lurched at the assortment of implications put out there by this Boy Who Smelled like Endless Summer French Kisses (plus pineapple, nutmeg and sandalwood).

"Course. I wouldn't say it if I didn't mean it, would I?" Barney had even made a point of looking her in the eye when he said that bit. "You're the coolest girl in this school by miles, Emily."

She didn't have the heart to correct him. He'd remembered the first letter of her name. She was on his radar. Nothing else mattered!

Eleanor smiled serenely all the way to the beach, unphased that she was the only unpaired pupil clutching a bucket and hammer on this vast stretch of the Jurassic coastline. She filled up her receptacle with broken belemnites and shells; she even devoured her Malt Loaf sandwiches, embellished, as they were, with real sand, in spite of the metre of cling film that her dad had mummified them in. She climbed the steps of the coach at two p.m on the dot as Head Fossil had instructed them not to be late for the return to school. Her heart was already in her mouth at the thought of Barney sitting so close again. She would feel the warmth of his body. Maybe their legs would touch, and everything? Should she offer him the window seat this time? Oh, she hoped he would want to sit with her; they'd made gig plans and all, which surely had to mean that this was the official prelude to being boyfriend and girlfriend. What if he dove in and kissed her on the bus in front of everyone? Where should she put her tongue? She hoped he'd take the lead. *Of course he'd take the lead.* He'd probably kissed, like, a dozen girls already. What if she had bits of raisin stuck in her teeth? Her head swarmed with infatuation and unanswered questions, her heart hammered.

"Encore with wifey on the way back, Barney?" a semi-broken voice grated, somewhere at the end of the queue.

"It's not like I've got anywhere else to sit, after you lot decided to pay me back for my latest prank, and offer my seat to McDonald. Arse-wipes."

McDonald being the ultimate boy misfit of their year group.

"Them's the rules. Don't shoot the messenger, or Big Mac. He's quite a larf as it turns out. Correct me if I'm wrong, anyway, but it was you that started all of this."

Cue behemoth boyish snickers.

"Thanks for the reminder, shithead. Yay me! I've already given up my coach throne; let me resume my all-round-good-egg character while I'm at it. Tell you what, I might as well get started already and help that old dear over there cross the road with her shopping."

Guffaws galore enveloped the tail-end of the queue at that sentiment.

Eleanor tentatively panned the horizon for a zebra crossing but couldn't spot any black and white lines or doddery elderly women.

"Mate, you really are in a league of your own. You ought to be an actor."

"The only league I'm in is a thousand above *hers*, that hideous creature I'm stuck with for the next two hours. And that's twenty quid you owe me now, mate… ten on the way, and ten on the way back, as I recall. God, I must be desperate. Why couldn't my old man just pay for the effing PlayStation instead of making me save up and resort to this desperate shit? It's not like he's skint."

Eleanor's face sank, tears pricked her eyes. She pretended to wipe the sea air away with a tissue. She pretended to sleep on the never-ending journey back to school.

And then, a few months later, came the whimsical whammy.

Barney running towards the young Eleanor, after the end of term hockey match, with a giant beam on his flushed face. They'd been exchanging furtive glances all autumn and winter, hadn't they? Ever since their coach affair. Sucked into a vortex of glazed-eye trances that both of them were powerless to snap out of; that overheard school trip bus queue conversation must have been about somebody else, or perhaps just a part of the return journey's dream.

Spring was getting closer. Elastica would be playing at Wembley. Failing that, they were rumoured to be included in Glastonbury Festival's June line-up. Barney must have news/secured tickets/hatched out their joint escape route by now. That's why he was sprinting towards her with the look of love etched all over his beautiful face.

Butterflies made the pubescent Eleanor's stomach go all

squishy and topsy-turvy. She closed her eyes, puckering up in sweet anticipation of his imminent kiss. Thank God she'd had a crisp apple today for break, no mushed-up Malt Loaf to fret about. It was Valentine's Day next week, too. Ohemgee! She'd be getting her first card now for sure.

But, like a scene extracted from some god-awful American teen movie, the flirtatious giggles that accompanied Barney's jock-ish jog to the side-lines, emanated from none other than the French-plaited, blonde cheerleader jiggling right behind her. Which was how Barney came to enfold Amelia Garland, the emerald-eyed Canadian from Year 10, with an embrace that turned borderline raunchy, and a snog that lingered so long Eleanor could feel her own eyes turning a brilliant jade green.

The penny had then dropped. That was the moment her teenage life changed forever. She was nothing to him, as worthless as a bead of his post-hockey match perspiration.

And *now* the pound coin dropped in the present. With one almighty splash. As if it'd been launched from Niagara Falls itself.

Everything that had gone wrong in her life after her thirteenth year on planet Earth was *all their faults*: that bitch and her bastard of a brother. She only had to retrace her footsteps. It couldn't have been clearer. Monty's is where it had started. But even if she'd been mostly devoid of second-class citizen friends, she couldn't pin the blame on a single one of her innocuous classmates. Not even Amelia the Airhead. For each and every one of them had been civil enough. They'd rubbed along. Neither friends nor foes.

No.

Everything that transpired after her hopes-banked-up spell at that exclusive establishment was testament to the toxicity of two people: Clem and Barney Westwood. They'd spurned her adoration. They'd magnified her lack of meaning to her parents. Unwittingly or not, they'd planted the seed that had turned her into the background woodchip wallpaper.

And soon they were going to pay with their pennies and with their pounds, because now Ellie really did have a plan, and she was ready to execute it.

9

JOCK, JULES AND JOURNALIST

**_French Homes, Dreams and Disasters_ magazine,
August 2020 edition:**

Joanna the Journalist: "Just off the record. We won't publish this bit, of course… but tell me, I'm curious. Why would you choose to call your holiday home 'The Clouds of Normandy'? Isn't that a little, how to put this without offending, inauspicious from the outset? Why not something upbeat and cheery like '_Le Soleil de Normandie?_'"

Jock: "We don't like to be sheep and do the thing standard folk find most obvious."

Jules: "Clouds can be beautiful, you know."

Jules' eyes pan from left to right across the remains of their estate, readers. It's clear that our female intuition is in sync and she's considering my point.

Joanna: "So let's just get this straight. The only time you saw

the Westwood party was when you laid the welcome gift –
the decadent box of chocolates – on the dining table?"

Jules: "We prefer to let our guests get on with things. Usually,
that would be their art. So, no. We didn't feel the need to
check up on them after we'd dropped the chocolates – and
their dinner that first night. We do our thing, they do theirs.
Normally we'd only see them again at check-out time." *Jules
scratches her chin for several seconds as if in contemplation of
many things. Jock avoids all eye contact.* "I handled the booking
with Ms. Sanchez so I feel like *that* was the first time I
encountered the group, so to speak. She insisted everything
was done over the phone. I liked that about her. She was the
old-fashioned sort. Nothing worse than that lack of personal
contact from guests who insist on doing everything by email,
or the even less personal and soul-sucking WhatsApp."

Joanna: "Couldn't that insistence be so you had no trace of
the booking in writing?"

Jock: "You got good vibes off her, Ju. I remember you saying
when you put the phone down and went back to the tie-dye
weaving on your loom. As I also recall, we were chilling over
a pot of Rooibos; the white sage was smoking away nicely to
purify the surroundings, and the Cocteau Twins were playing. *Little Spacey*, methinks."

Jules: "Yeah, I guess I did get positive vibes. She seemed
kosher, you know? Good energy to her voice. Then again, it's
easy for the ethereal Scottish background atmospherics of
the Cocteau Twins to sugar-coat your perception, isn't it?
Maybe you've got a point. Maybe I should have insisted we
put her booking in writing."

Jock: "I'll never understand why they don't say honey-coat, or stevia… or orange blossom. What's so rosy about the white poison?"

Joanna: "Could we… can we perhaps try to not go off at any more tangents? I have a meeting with the mayor of Pruneau this afternoon.

Jock: "Ooh, tra-la-la!"

Jules: "I'm sorry. Yes, of course. Jock?"

Jock nods his head in semi-defeat, but the twinkle in his eye tells us this won't last long, readers.

Joanna: "So you didn't *physically* see your guests prior to setting the handcrafted chocolates, and their evening meal, on the table?"

Jules: "I'm sorry. No, I didn't. We were out when they arrived, and, as arranged, we left their key in the little red post box next to reception. In my mind's eye I did see them before they physically showed up here… but I know that won't be validation. Yours is a mainstream publication. It's… we're… still trying to process it all, to be honest. How our hopes and dreams could shift so suddenly from the tangible to mere ash. Listen: do you mind if I roll up?" *Jules places an eye-opening amount of paraphernalia upon her denim-clad thigh and proceeds to craft something rather aromatic without waiting for an answer. There are indisputable tears welling in her eyes… or it could just be the overwhelming smell of onions coming from the portable camp stove in the corner where Jock has 'something' simmering.* "Like I said, we ended up playing chef on the first night. It was a Sunday. Changeover day's on a Saturday." *Jules* *takes a long drag of her 'cigarette' and goes slightly starry-eyed, traces of tears long gone*. "But Ms. Sanchez was absolutely adamant her party had to arrive on the Sunday, which was hell for us as it meant finding cleaners prepared to work while the local church bells did toll."

Jock: "Impossible. This is a very Catholic village, you know."

Joanna: "As are many. Of course."

Jock: "In the end, even I was togged up in a pinny."

Jules: "It's called equality, Mr. But yeah, he was. It was rather a lot of work as you can imagine, getting this place squeaky-clean and whipping up a three-course gourmet, vegan, organic meal."

Jock: "You know I'm only having a giraffe, my sweet."

The air is suddenly thick with sexual innuendos.

Joanna: "Ahem."

Jules: "I left them their welcome gift on the dining table so I didn't see anybody's reaction. It wasn't the easiest task to track the things down in the first place. But the woman, Ms. Sanchez, made it clear that she wanted a specific box of artisan chocolates, from a place called *Chez Chocolat* in Honfleur, to be ready and waiting for them on Sunday night."

Joanna: "Did that not strike you as a tad peculiar, as if it was somehow all slotting in with a plan?"

Jules: "Not really. We get this from time to time with artists.

They can't bring all their materials over for their stay… can we secure them a stash of acrylics, watercolours, chalks, yarn, twigs, leaves, et cetera?"

Jock: "A bit of a trek all the same… expecting the apple of my eye to drive all the way to the pigging coast at short notice. I mean, c'mon! She could have asked us to make a batch of raw cacao truffles which would've tasted infinitely better, as well as nourishing her group with a higher antioxidant content. Jules did offer."

Jules nods her head vigorously in agreement.

Jock: "But no. They had to come from this *expert in Honfleur." As you can probably guess from the italics, my scant few readers, Jock is inserting annoying fake quotation marks in the air to emphasise his point.* "The geezer fills them with all these fancy-schmancy saccharine centres. No two the same, apparently. A beast of a box with twenty-two individual choco-lates." *I'd make short work of those in an evening.* "Mind you, I suppose that was only a five and a half per person. Or one-ish a night. If they refrained from scarfing them all on Sunday."

Joanna: "Who refrains from eating chocolate on a Sunday?"

Jock and Jules exchange a worried glance, and at this point, it's fair to say that I, like you, dear French Property Seekers, raise an eyebrow at their ideological, spiritual and religious beliefs, which seem to chop and change like the Normandy weather forecast.

Jules: "Anyway, I turned a blind eye to the amount of non-organics, picked the chocolates up in their admittedly beau-tiful box, and brought them back to the *gîte*. I left them on the kitchen table on Sunday, where it was cool and dark. Other than that, we gave the three Westwoods and Ms. Sanchez a quick pre-dinner tour around the main rooms of the house and pointed each in the general direction of their bedrooms. Guests are grown-ups, after all. Perfectly capable of working out where the light switches and spare complimentary herbal tea bags are, and so on and so forth."

Jock: *Digs into his pocket and symbolically (one can only guess) holds a lighter aloft as if at a gig, staring deeply into the vortex of its flame.* "Except when they burn your place to cinders."

Joanna: "I understand the Westwood party and Ms. Sanchez dined here every night. Were they cooking for themselves? Could they have forgotten to turn off a chip pan by any chance? These things are, after all, quite easily done, especially after a glass or two of red."

Jock: "Ms. Sanchez requested just a quarter-carafe of wine, organic, *bien sur*, to accompany each evening meal. As for your first suggestion, we categorically ban those unrepeatable items from the property. Hasselback sweet potatoes scattered with herbs in a wood-fired oven are the closest you'll get to the French fry in this house."

Jules: "Hasselbacks look a bit like hedgehogs. Just for your ref."

Joanna: "Yes, I am familiar with them."

Jules: "Really? Oh, right. Well, we normally offer private organic, vegan catering via our live-in/live-out/live-wherever-the-wind-takes-him chef, Thierry Faubourg. He's the guy who served the party on the other nights of the week, but we have to grant him one night off. I'd so do him if I wasn't happily married to Jock. Thierry's the food whisperer who spins all the plates *and* delivers them. I can't vouch for the guests' behaviour then. All I know is they seemed fine when I brought out the French onion soup that Sunday evening; a little apprehensive perhaps about the homemade croutons. I guess they're used to less rustic, more refined fare. Ms. Sanchez seemed to be the focal point. That much was clear."

Jock: "Oh, make no bones about it: that woman was definitely wearing the trousers. I'm not saying I blame her for the… er… the fire though. There are two sides to every story, we need to remember that – and in this case we're talking multiple points of view. I'm sure she had her reasons for bringing that lot here for the corporate bonding crap. Although one of them needs to take responsibility for the aftermath. Of course they do." *Curiously, Jock stops dead in his tracks, as if pondering a never-before entertained thought before declaring:* "Yeah, Ju. If I batted for the other side, I'd quite see your point there about Thierry. He is kind of fit."

Joanna: *Note to self: track down this Thierry bloke and find out if he's single because I bloody well am.* "Well, the village grapevine is certainly working on overdrive, what with various sightings of strangers… and their 'stranger still' attire, in and around the immediate area now being reported from that tragic week. Do you not mingle with the residents here?"

Silence. One must deduce our interviewees do not mix with local people. Jules offers me a drag of her spliff and I quickly nip that idea in the bud with a fast and furious headshake. She passes it to Jock instead.

Joanna: "Right. The thing is: I'm trying to establish if you sensed anything was up? Did anything set the Westwoods, and Ms. Sanchez, apart from your usual guests? Overlooking their evident privilege, of course?"

Jules: "We had no idea they were the toffs running that capitalist and hideously gimmicky travel company, if that's what you're getting at. I wouldn't have let them in had I known the truth. I certainly wouldn't have gone to such lengths to secure those chocolates."

Jock: "That makes two of us. Bloody upstarts, those Westwoods, with their stuck-up surname. And that kind of money-spinning machine goes against the very grain of our principles. Of everything we set out to achieve here... *there*."

Jock looks wistfully behind him at the rubble that was the gîte. In hindsight, readers, I should have mentioned that we convened for this 'interview' in the charred remains of the half-built barn conversion. Speaking of which, our reader numbers are falling. Only slightly! No need to panic! But if you'd care to recommend a friend for annual membership, we'll send you a set of coasters featuring the Bayeux tapestry. They're very lifelike. I sourced them myself. So dig deep and help us stay in circulation, s'il vous plaît... I mean, er... do take advantage of our offer, that's a saving of ten euros and forty cents in total. Bargain!

Jules: "Again," *Jules coughs, and I am back in the room, well, what's left of it.* "Jock knows he sounds hypocritical, having worked on one of the UK's prime reality TV shows, but it was all for this end goal; to inspire the dreamers, the right kind of folk making the right kind of worldwide ripples with their creativity; the guys who came to us not so long ago on retreat. Sometimes you do have to sell half your soul for the greater good."

Jock makes a spontaneous grab for the didgeridoo propped against the door behind him and begins to blow a melancholy note.

Joanna: "I'll um… I think perhaps I'll come back tomorrow."

BROOKE

*N*one of it had been Brooke's idea. She wasn't a violent person – per se – but she'd have given away the pink Himalayan rock salt lamp *and* the Dead Sea mud and organic camel's milk face pack, soap, shower gel and body mousse adorning her miniature en-suite to get her hands around Ellie Sanchez's neck right now.

She promised me atmosphere, ambience, art, amazing food, and awesome wine!

Alas, the Normandy village of Pruneau was sadly lacking in all these departments, and as dried up as its literal English translation: prune. In fact, it had little more to offer than one tired bar, in desperate need of a facelift and constantly closed. Its solitary café tried its best to take up the slack with the simplest of apricot tarts served up on a red and white checked tablecloth straight out of Red Riding Hood's picnic hamper – but it was the perpetual hang-out of the over-eighties males of the village, complete with cider and dominoes. They'd been here a whole day and night, yet a takeaway slice of that tart, shortly after arrival, was the single culinary highlight. This was a joke. They were in the supposed gastronomic playground of the world.

Six more days to go. One-hundred-and-forty-four freaking hours.

Already the walls were closing in. And they hadn't even got down to resolving their plethora of issues yet. At least if they'd had access to a decent wine cellar they could have had a drink. But Ellie had restricted their joint alcoholic rations to a quarter of a carafe. It was hardly worth the bother. Brooke preferred a fruit-infused gin and tonic or a cocktail given half the chance. But the thimble shot glasses of red were an absolute piss-take. They were a bunch of nursery kids treated to watered-down Ribena.

Then again, perhaps that was just as well. The St. Emilion and its bottled buddies would hardly help Barnaby's increasingly worrying lunchtime drinking habit.

The owners of the *gîte* were friendly enough, Brooke had to concede. But they were the living embodiment of eccentric; the woman dressed head to toe in concentric rainbow circles, interspersed with flying phoenixes and a gold 'banana' clip to scrape back her hair into the severest of ponytails, which in itself contained an inner posy of dreadlocks, with so many ribbons it reminded her of a blimming maypole. Meanwhile, the man sported a braided goatee that just begged to be snipped off and tossed onto a bonfire while he was asleep. And their homemade French onion soup was already beginning to repeat on Brooke; those cardboard 'croutons' really had been quite an unnecessary and tough garnish to work the incisors through.

Then came what Jock had announced as the *pièce de résistance*: aubergine, truffle and pecan loaf with an alfalfa sprout pesto volcano and honey *jus*. It smelt of old socks, and was endowed with a crusty charcoaled edge. This was swiftly followed by a pudding, of sorts, dubbed 'Calvados sorbet'.

Jules said it could also be used as a 'palate cleanser' but that was up for debate. It was basically a serving of uber-alcoholic, sugar-free, apple mush, the exact consistency of baby food.

All of which only made the exquisite box of chocolates, resting at its leisure in the middle of the elongated dining table, practically scream out Brooke's name. It was all she could do to restrain her fingers from walking across the table to stroke it; to peek inside, to smell the perfume of its tasty treasures. But it was a Westwood unwritten rule that only Clementine and Barnaby got to fight over the chocolates… and then Brooke might wind up with the toffee penny. If she was lucky. Completely overlooking the fact she was the oldest. Westwood regs rarely made a scrap of sense. Mind you, neither had her nonchalant decision to blindly go along with them.

But anyway, the point was, when Ellie had called them all into the Oval Office that day, this outlandish set-up was pretty much the last thing Brooke had in mind.

"Things categorically cannot continue in this vein," Ellie had announced to her startled audience, and Brooke had somehow refrained from breaking out in a solitary round of gusto-filled applause. "Whether your father graces us with his presence today or…"

"You're wasting your breath there," Barnaby chimed in, although gonged, bellowed and trumpeted would probably be closer to the mark. "Dad flat out refused to cancel today's yacht race, said it was important prep for his imminent biggie when I spoke with him last night. So that pretty much proves what a waste of everyone's time this is."

Ellie visibly blanched at that, shifting from foot to foot; fingering the opaque crystal strapped tightly on its black velvet band around her elegant neck. With embarrassment, Brooke could only guess. Had it been Brooke herself, she'd have turned puce (clashing dreadfully with Ellie's hair-do). But alas, Harry Westwood was *her* father, not the HR Manager's.

"As I was saying," Ellie continued. "The dynamics of this company are rapidly crumbling. Whilst it's for accounts to investigate the financial mess, if things carry on like this there won't be anything left for anybody to squabble over."

Clementine pulled out a nail file. Barnaby silently whistled and studied the piped coving of the ornate ceiling. In fairness, the interior could do with a lick of paint.

"You're a family business, for heaven's sakes," Ellie reminded them, brows arching north.

"Yup. I think we could figure that one out for ourselves," piped Barnaby eastward, out the corner of his belligerent mouth.

"Let her speak! Can you not see how much better she is than all the others?"

Oops. Cat well and truly out the bag now...

"So where's the rapport you should have built up over the years?" Ellie picked up, clicking her pen rapidly in her right hand. "Oh, and thank you, Brooke, for that revealing snippet of information… at least, I think."

Aha, now Ellie was colouring. This felt healthier.

"At the present moment, all of the intimate details, all of the many surface reasons why the business is taking an apparent and unfathomable nosedive, are neither here nor there. We're going to get back to basics and re-build rapport." Ellie's words held fast, and yet Brooke swore she detected a slight beam cross her face, possibly aided by the sudden garnering of priceless statistics on her predecessors. "Cancel everything in your diaries from this Sunday to the next: the four of us are taking a *bon voyage* to France," she announced.

Firecrackers danced in Brooke's stomach. Whilst she'd no idea what this impromptu and totally unexpected cross-

Channel trip entailed, the very notion sounded full of *ooh la la*!

"Y… you what? Say that again. Am I in some kind of screwed-up dream here?"

Her sister began to pinch at her non-existent bingo wings in a pathetic attempt to stand her ground whilst simultaneously showcasing her lean limbs.

"You heard me the first time, Clem." Hang about. Did Ellie just call her sister what Brooke thought she'd called her? No way. No. She must have been imagining it. Nobody 'Clemmed' Clementine these days. Clementine would have been the first one to grimace had she dared. "And I can confirm that you are very much conscious," Ellie continued. "The ferry is booked, as is the accommodation, and I'll be driving us."

"But that's absurd. And as a side note, I don't do ferries, anyway… I've always suffered terribly from seasickness. Tell her, Barnaby!" Clementine screeched. "So that's that. We'll simply have to fly," she added, screwing up her face in the exact manner she'd used since childhood to get her own way. She held her nail file aloft in a move that made her look like one of those bolshy city tour guides with a garish umbrella, waiting for her entourage.

It seemed to do little to deter Ellie. "Afraid not. The ferry's *simply* been paid for," she said to Clementine. "We're not shelling out on non-essentials any more than we have to. I have your father's backing, and that's that."

Good on Ellie. Brooke's father had evidently upped his game, too, and actually replied to an email, but he was on his stupid boat so fortunately wouldn't be able to put in a flesh and blood appearance. Brooke breathed a sigh of relief at that, impressed with Ellie's impeccable timing. It was so much easier when her father was out of the picture on his yacht. Which was no exaggeration from an orientation point of view. No matter how many lessons he'd had over the years; no matter how much money he'd thrown at them, he was only ever allowed to play a minor role lest he sent his crew to the far reaches of the Azores and they got eaten by sharks.

But it seemed Ellie had made him aware of the agenda and he must have agreed with every one of her proposals. This was an excellent and most fortuitous start.

Brooke's imagination began to run riot with images of Cannes by night, a stream of autumnal sunsets bleeding into starry-skied dates with Ruben – after shoptalk hours, of course. The weather would be warmer than here, that far south at this time of year. All of it was leading beautifully to an inescapable proposal on the beach. Why, the boat-bobbing, palm-swaying, cicada-chirruping, cocktail-studded backdrops alone would call for it!

"Normandy is the perfect place. The *gîte* is well-appointed, convenient to get to and, more importantly, well-hidden from other halves."

Oh, perhaps not.

Barnaby groaned. It didn't take much imagination for Brooke to interpret that protest as his plans to bonk his latest bit of stuff going belly up. And Brooke couldn't have been gladder that Ellie was unwittingly sparing them all from the orgasmic echoes rebounding around the *gîte* day and night. She wasn't remotely keen on Saffron, who, much like those who'd trod the tightrope to her brother's (supposed) heart before her, had the words Money Grabbing Bitch etched across her unlined forehead. Whilst that might've been nothing new, the relationship was seemingly flourishing, taking Barnaby into brand new territory that harked of pre-nups and confetti. No way was her little brother waltzing down the aisle before Rubes had popped Brooke the question. And if that wasn't to happen on a French Riviera beach, well, she'd just have to whisk him away to a Cornish cove when she got back, dropping several hundred hints as they packed.

"I take immediate issue with that," announced Clementine, intruding upon Brooke's future plans.

Too late to regret employing Ellie Sanchez now, sis. Brooke stifled a snigger.

Ellie remained stoically silent.

"It's just that... A... Archie intends to fly over for a zip trip from NYC this weekend," Clementine swallowed hard before adding: "Clearly none of you have any compassion when it comes to long distance relationships."

Was it Brooke's imagination or did her sister avert her gaze from her when she made this statement, time standing momentarily still? Clementine's words sounded bizarrely unconvincing, too, too, as if she'd tossed them all in the air, snatched them back again and haphazardly glued them together. Something about her sister's declaration was askew.

"Your relationship will *probably* survive," said Ellie in matter-of-fact tones, a welcome distraction from the whirring sensation in Brooke's ears. "I've been there," she tagged on a funny little chuckle. "You're hardly the first."

Wait, had Ellie actually dared to eye-roll Clementine Westwood? Then that earlier name shortening really couldn't have been a figment of Brooke's imagination.

Clementine arranged her features into a sulk and returned to attacking her immaculate midnight blue nails with the giant emery board.

"We will stay there, in said *gîte*, in remotest rural France, until no stone has been left unturned and we've got to the bottom of this," Ellie continued to instruct them. "You have no choice. Whereas, much as I love you all to bits," she smiled a sickeningly sweet smile. "I can wholeheartedly promise you I will hand in my notice," and now Ellie paused for dramatic effect. "If this circus carries on any longer. Taking my five-star services elsewhere, and taking you back to the ineptitude of your previous HR management."

Touché. And, oh. That was probably that, then.

Matron had spoken, and, despite Barnaby's blatantly pig-headed body language; despite Clementine's preference for her nails, despite it all, perhaps Ellie hadn't noticed yet, but Brooke certainly had. Her siblings' respect for the HR Manager was mounting.

Only in centimetre increments, mind you. But they were visible enough to Brooke, injecting her with much-needed hope. Yes, Ellie's board meeting had been a surprise and a half, and then again it hadn't. If Brooke were Ellie, she'd inject a little fun and games into this shiny new working week too.

"Why are you only pointing the finger at us directors? What about the managers?" quizzed Barnaby. "They should be on trial too."

"Hear, hear," Clementine added her two penn'orth. "And don't forget the interns. I wouldn't put it past any of them to hack into the system. Some of these uni newbies are so far up themselves, expecting to command instant London-style salaries and golden handshakes. They're also very clued up when it comes to the latest code breaking skills. Never underestimate the jealous, and seriously skint, postgrad designer."

"Clementine! How could you insinuate such a thing?" Brooke finally broke her silence. What a way for her sister to refer to the hardworking staff she had mostly hired herself.

"It is what it is, and I echo your concerns." Barnaby sided with his younger sister. "Naivety gets you nowhere when you're running a lucrative business."

Ellie raised her head slowly to appraise his remark. She looked like she'd swallowed a lemon wedge. Brooke cringed.

"That very 'them and us' sentiment explains why it's the upper tiers of staff whose deep-seated issues need to be dissected and resolved," Ellie retorted. "No social media or technology either. We're talking back to absolute basics."

"Els…Ell… Ellie," Barnaby began to flutter his eyelids now in sheer desperation, his boyhood mechanism during a bollocking, or when losing badly at a board game. "That's just not realistic now, is it? I have some *major* campaigns going on across Hong Kong next week, first-class flights, five star hotels and VIP meetings booked. When I say major, I do mean *like major-major*," he let out a nervous laugh. "I can't just swan off to France to munch on Brie and baguettes for a week, idyllic as all of this sounds, especially paired up with a case of Bordeaux's finest."

Ellie snorted his concerns away as if he were but a pesky child after cookie dough.

"Tough. Let others oversee them locally. Because I'm going to tell you something for nothing, Barney." She what? Oh dear God, *nobody* called him that anymore either. No-one! He hated it. The last time she and Clementine had done it in unison, he'd belted them. Brooke chewed hard on her lip in a bid to quell her giant fit of giggles. This was too funny. Never mind the Brie. It was like she'd gorged on Stilton and found herself cast in a Lewis Caroll dream. Which surely begged the question: what had Ellie been eating, or, indeed, drinking? "If you *don't* join us, you won't have a cat's whisker of a market share left in Asia or anywhere else for that matter." She paused again, and Brooke could tell she was revelling inwardly at something.

"And I'll tell you something else while we're at it. There may well be bread and there may well be cheese, but alcohol will be severely curtailed. Soberly and strategically is the only way to deal with the *sobering state* that this company is in."

Barnaby could have caught a swarm of flies at that bomb-shell. Their interactions during Ellie's time at the RBPC had always been brief yet courteous, although Brooke sometimes thought she sensed a certain *je ne sais quoi* of temptation from Ellie, radiating straight towards her brother. Always fleeting. As if it disappeared before Brooke could really assess it, stuffed back deep down into Ellie's pocket, with its awkward rumbles kept at bay. But this get-up? This was Ellie Sanchez Version 2:0, and Brooke liked it.

Oh, Ellie'd stuck to her guns all right and seemed to have frightened both of Brooke's self-entitled siblings into oblivion. In truth, it had actually left Brooke a little star struck. Even now, hundreds of miles away in France. Ellie's most assertive performance to date would go down in company history, regardless of whether the RPBC ceased trading, or not.

And, in keeping with all things gutsy, no sooner had the functional Renault Espace's wheels crunched on the gravel of the sweeping French hollyhock-fringed driveway, than Ellie announced her agenda for the coming week. With her recently platinum-dyed hair and long blunt-cut fringe, she'd taken on an undeniable Sia look, challenging Clementine's sassy blonde mop. It was nothing if not fetching – and a vast improvement on her previous hue. Brooke could only hope it meant Ellie would be channelling her inner pop diva for the week ahead.

"There'll be no paintball, Quidditch or Escape Rooms, you'll be relieved to hear," Ellie informed them as they each – some more willingly than others – stepped out of the car and took in the outside of the *gîte* and its rustic gardens; their home for the week. "But we'll start off with some standard team building all the same. Seeing as it's practically autumn, who knows, I might even throw in a conker fight," Ellie stopped, looked pointedly at Clementine and Barnaby, whose faces bore the blankest of expressions, and then continued with a massive sigh: "Unpack, freshen up, then we'll reconvene in the lounge for a good old-fashioned story time."

"Sounds as riveting as *Jackanory*," snubbed Barnaby, expelling a massive yawn.

"This is so... yesterday... so bloody, so totally and so utterly pathetic," Clementine tutted aloud.

Which was when quite the strangest thing happened – as if things hadn't already gotten strange enough.

Ellie pivoted. In slow motion, admittedly, but she literally swivelled right there on the spot; just a little over one-hundred-and-eighty-degrees, like a netball player in slow-mo. It looked uncomfortable. Her steely gaze rested on Clementine and, for a moment, they were a duo in a Spaghetti Western. Brooke and Barnaby watched in awe. Who would pull the trigger first?

"This is anything but yesterday. Don't make the mistake of thinking any of this is about the past. The power is in the present moment. All of it. *Yesterday is gone. Yesterday is history.* Now is where it changes. Is that clear?"

Clementine fell silent, head bowed to the floor. Everybody else followed suit. Mercifully, a distant cockerel punctuated the void with its warble.

"Absoluuuuutely cuckoo, as I was saying," Clementine finally muttered under her breath as soon as Ellie's heels crunched the gravel, spinning her back to face the *gîte*'s front door.

"Our key is in the *red* post box, it says here on the notice," Ellie had snapped back to less scary mode, clutching a piece of paper in her hand. "How very auspicious indeed."

Brooke watched on, slack-jawed, as Ellie tottered to the

panel of small square boxes at the far end of the wall to track down the key.

Clementine shrugged and walked back to the car. She made a grab for her collection of designer cases; correcting her high-heeled wobble, wrapping her arms around her belly and then diving, slightly more measuredly, into the Renault's boot again. "I just can't believe I've signed myself up to this idiocy. It's never going to work!"

Brooke didn't think she'd ever seen her sister so silently seething. And yet her complexion was less red and more green at the gills. Oops! Perhaps Brooke should have fought Clementine's corner on the flying front; evidently she'd filed away those long-lost family memories of Brittany camp trips and long ferry journeys with their grandparents (whilst mama and papa buggered off to the Dom Rep for a little mass-market luxury at an exclusive adults-only club).

"Oh, I think you'll find it will work. In the end," said Ellie loudly. How had she heard those distant whispers of protest? "Team building leads to trust... and honesty. Once we have that flowing freely between you all, I'm fairly confident we can work toward a most satisfying happily-ever-after end goal."

It was all a bit of a conundrum, but it had brought Brooke out in goosebumps all the same. As had that guy in the back-ground who'd just sauntered past the stone wall with a curious dash of a wave. *Ooh la la* indeed. Maybe this wouldn't be such a dull *sojourn*. And then she berated herself for even window shopping, when she was so smitten with her Ruben.

Brooke couldn't wait to get started in the end; to see what exactly Ellie had up her sleeve. She was the first one waiting in the *gite*'s open-plan mezzanine lounge and took the opportunity to poke about its peculiar perimeters. Why had Ellie brought them to this place? It hardly fit the bill. The walls were adorned with strange batik drapes in garish colours; there were Buddhas in all shapes, sizes and poses, and cross-sections of giant amethysts. Okay, Brooke had started getting into crystals and the more mainstream hippy-dippy stuff. The pretty accessories, the infinitely positive angel cards.

But she wasn't much of a fan of the stinky incense sticks strategically positioned in every nook and every cranny; not to mention the crooked and totally-not-of-the-Jo-Malone-collection candles randomly scattered across every available surface, just begging to be lit and inhaled out of curiosity before you covered your nose and your mouth and opened every window for a welcome gust of fresh air. Where was the charming *brocante* flea market decor and the plates of chunky, buttery Normandy biscuits?

The place felt anything but authentically French. Surely Ellie would have vetted the interior on its website?

Nevertheless, eventually the chimes of four p.m. gonged from some invisible timepiece and everyone gathered around in the shabby chic armchairs in a circle enforced by Ellie – Clementine and Barnaby begrudgingly so. Ellie proceeded to issue the three of them with an unremarkable piece of paper and a pen. Here we go, thought Brooke. It'll be one of those old-hat, long in the tooth, 'list your strengths and weaknesses' time-wasters of an exercise... or, don't tell her, a psychology test, so Ellie could – *what exactly?* – change their markets; shuffle around their individual team members; ensure the siblings only communicated with each other at set times of day that are well known in HR circles to extract optimum performance from extroverts?

But, no.

Ellie didn't embark on any of those classic tactics. Since nothing about this woman had ever hinted at ordinary – oh, Brooke had clocked Ellie's many failed attempts at feng shui over the past few months; her penchant for a crafty, and thoroughly pungent, cigar besides – she berated herself for pigeon-holing the HR manager's ideas so quickly.

Give her the benefit of the doubt. Ellie obviously had some kind of scheme in mind. She'd hardly go to all these lengths to rescue the company otherwise.

And then it was all Brooke could do not to visibly scoff.

The very first thing the inscrutable woman had them do was to play paper consequences!

That's right. She'd plonked them on a ferry, and driven them all the way to a Norman sodding *gite*, accompanied by the excruciating warble of an Elastica CD on repeat, just to play a daft word game. The very same daft word game that'd got Brooke in detention at least twice during English lessons at St. Ed's.

Take a piece of A4 paper, scribble down two hilarious lines of randomly made up shit (tip: throw in an unlikely couple from your class making out or having full on sex in the first line for extra comedy value); fold said first line back on itself so that only the second line enticingly remains, pass it to the person on your left, look to your right and collect your brand new offering from your neighbour. And repeat, until pages are filled, each of you is holding a concertinaed paper fan, and all of your words are thoroughly mixed together and baked into one giant cake of silliness. Read out the hotchpotch of stories while still warm... and collapse in stitches, clutching your bellies helplessly.

Consequences were swiftly abandoned, followed up instead by a game which involved rolling a collection of curious-looking dice with cartoonish pictures on them. The point of this little number was to invent a story based on the images that landed upright. Equally cringeworthy. So embarrassingly amateur. It was at this point that Brooke began to feel more than a little sorry for Ellie, wondering what the hell had happened to the ballsy woman who'd delivered that epic Oval Office speech? They'd get nowhere very fast horsing around like this all week. The company had fundamental problems to solve. How could make-believe stories possibly hope to change any of that?

"Possibility," said Ellie, as if reading her mind, "is exactly what this afternoon has taught us. Anything can happen when we open our minds. We can literally re-write the story."

All right then.

What choice did anybody have but to resign themselves to current circumstances and plough on with the nonsense? Even Monday had been spent in much the same way. But for a relative change of scene, Ellie had them seated around the dining table. Trying to avoid all eye contact with that opulent box of chocolates, the question of 'who will cave in first?' hanging heavily in the air, she'd set the eighties card game, Tell Me Quiz, in front of them. After half an hour of Barnaby's predictable Smart Alec responses and excessive wheel spins, which had sent the cheap plastic spinner careering off the table more than a handful of times, Ellie had sent them back to their quarters for 'reflection' while she made figure of eights, pacing around the room, as if deep in thought and assessing their performance.

Brooke knew this because she'd crept back downstairs and peeked through the keyhole of the door.

Table, game, bedroom; table, game, bedroom; table, game, bedroom.

All any of this had achieved was to make Brooke feel like a yo-yo in limbo. Meanwhile her brother and sister were reduced to a couple of puppets sucked into a trance.

She could only hope that some delicious Norman fare

would improve the mood in camp tonight. It could hardly decline. And rumour had it that Jock and Jules had only catered for their group yesterday because it was a Sunday; their regular chef's day of rest. That just had to mean things were looking up, right?

ELLIE

*I*t couldn't have been simpler. How laughable it all was, every drop of this juicily elongated performance. From her Oval Office oration, Ellie had followed up on the theatrics by driving them all to a drab little village in Normandy in a rented MPV – no way was she tainting her Audi's allure with a roof rack.

Here they were in France, obeying her military commands beautifully. Her trio of toy soldiers had marched back to their rooms for a little introspection. *Ad infinitum,* and remarkably, *sans questions.* Barney and Clem still hadn't managed to erase their panic-stricken expressions. At this rate maybe she wouldn't need to take things as far as she'd originally planned, the brainwashing alone easing things along nicely.

What was she like?

There was no fun in playing safe. She'd brought them this far, no going back now.

Definitely not after overhearing that jumped-up little shit, Barney branding her new hair-do a cross between a pudding basin and a dishcloth; Clem laughing along with him in the back seat, behind Ellie's indisputably sleek – and to commemorate this monumental trip, blonde –bombshell of a bob.

Like brother, like sister. The pair of them had never grown up, incessantly deflecting their own inadequacies by taking the mickey out of others. That was okay. Three could play at that game. And there would only be one winner.

Barney would fall under Ellie's spell, in more ways than one. She'd give him the best ride of his life. He'd get down on one knee after a fortnight; they'd tie the knot. Clem would soften her stance, realising there was little point in being at loggerheads with her future sis-in-law… and then… *ha, and then*… Ellie would swiftly divorce him, netting herself the lot.

Still, unable to focus on the end game for long, Ellie had seen salsa-red, just about keeping her own shit together during Elastica's 'Car Song'. Barney clearly couldn't even name an Elastica song, despite what he'd said long ago. Ellie was never more certain of this than when she made eye contact with him through the rear view mirror, silently imploring him to recall the pledge he had made on the coach. But she received nothing but his customary stare. How he still hadn't worked it out, she'd never know. She'd even resorted to furtively lining the staff kitchen windowsill with the treasured conkers he'd fought with at Monty's. One last try, before she resorted to the desperate measures of France. He'd carelessly abandoned them, way back when, and she'd rescued them from the school playing field, just as he'd left behind the largest of the Lyme Regis fossils in the coach that fateful day. So much privilege, he literally didn't know how to look after his mounting belongings.

Ellie had snapped herself back to the task of tackling her first foreign roundabout from the right, pent-up fury rising in her chest when a French motorist honked his horn at her for hesitating. Barney tutted at her dithering, adding ever more fuel to her fire.

Brooke, on the other hand, good old stalwart and reliable Brooke, had tapped at her thighs in the front of the car. Credit where credit was due: her co-pilot had good taste in music. Seems she'd underestimated this one.

Of course none of the things Ellie verbally threatened fell remotely under the umbrella of Human Resources. But that was the beauty, indeed, of working for a company where everybody, Brooke aside, was too bird-brained to know any better. And yet, even the savviest of the Westwood clan hadn't raised either eyebrow at her actions.

The mind boggled, but she couldn't complain at the ease with which these people were handing her everything on a silver platter.

Needless to say, she'd never bothered to call Harry Westwood. Of course she hadn't. They had zero rapport – at the moment, anyway. Things would change, well... just as soon as things changed. Streets ahead of Barney, Ellie had made certain her father-in-law-to-be was indeed all at sea on the day of the meeting. Still, there was no time to dwell on that particular scenario right now. Well-versed and rehearsed were those taking care of Old Harry.

Even Frank from accounts had been blithely unaware of his best friend's whereabouts as he circled his pool on a Lilo and lapped up the Caribbean sun. And that gave Ellie more than enough hidden clout. Frank was one of those deeply entrenched parts of the company furniture, having only ever worked alongside Westwood Senior in the days when HR barely existed, so that he hadn't a clue as to the bullet point basics of Ellie's job either. Moreover, Harry trusted Frank with his life. Which was ironic given Harry's current coordinates.

See, it was laughable. Ellie'd said it before and she'd say it again: she was working for an actual circus. But she'd play along and come out of this victorious, and now all her safety nets were properly in place. Not that she intended to fall.

She forced her mouth into a staunch line to erase the lingering simper.

Why, then, Normandy?

Oh, she had just fancied indulging in one last little bout of nostalgia. And why not? For this was the final trip Ellie had made with her parents before their acrimonious divorce.

This underdog part of France – and let's face it, compared to the glitz and glamour of Cannes or La Rochelle or the ever-obvious Paris, it was – this backend part of France felt a little like Ellie's geographical twin. They had history. Nothing much was ever expected of them. Yeah, if Normandy was a girl at a private school, likely she'd have been Eleanor Finch with split ends, whilst her Cannes, La Rochelle and Paris counterparts dazzled centre stage with coiffured Clem and her cronies.

And talking of Clem, talking of Honfleur, Ellie sensed she wouldn't be able to resist the temptation of those locally handcrafted chocolates for much longer. Curiously, for one so obsessed with clean eating, when it came to chocolate, Clem had no off switch. But only posh chocs, no Roses or Quality Street, mind you. Curiouser still, fizz-loving Clem had turned down the cider which accompanied their meal last night (knowing how much Barney hated the stuff, Ellie had swiftly, and uncharacteristically for this trip, approved a pint per person). She could only guess that Clem was saving her prescribed calorific intake for a sweet treat. Or eight. Well, that's how things should divvy themselves up between the Westwoods, as long as Barney didn't get too greedy and corral all the best chocs.

Ellie chuckled again. It really made no difference either way.

She couldn't wait for them to snaffle the entire box down in all its unctuousness, parking her own salivation to one side because, goddammit, she *knew* from teenage memory, and the solitary sample whose corner she'd nibbled, that they tasted good. Neither could she wait to witness the eye-opening *Consequences*. See, she was being cryptically clever. There was method to her 'madness'. Hidden meanings to everything, Witless Westwoods!

But Ellie couldn't afford to get ahead of herself. Why, she hadn't even added her special ingredient yet! Let them be lured *au naturel*... and then... one melt-in-the-mouth moment at a time.

Look what happened to the kids in Willy Wonka's factory.
Love Mum X

PS. Yes, I know we have had that conversation before, but I feel it's
my duty to remind you...

BROOKE

*I*ntrospection, hey?

Brooke supposed she ought to at least try to take some of this week seriously. Maybe there was a mysterious grand finale they were building up to, here? She seriously doubted it at the moment, though. Even a flipping jigsaw, a game of snap, or a spot of potholing would be more riveting. The only thing keeping her sane was the thought of those luxurious-looking chocolates. These were the depths she had sunk to after day one. Mealtimes in this place were already too far apart for her liking. She made a mental note to be one of those really bad tourists who smuggled napkin-cloaked *pains aux chocolat* and bananas from the breakfast buffet next time. Well, she did work for the *Really Bad* Photo Company, after all.

But it was no good trying to convince herself that the bowls of raw vegetables, the pots of cashew nut butter dip, and the linseed and apricot muesli with unsweetened almond milk had the same appeal. They could stay on the table.

She shook her head in disbelief at the vast journey they'd

been on, recalling the farcical way it had all started. It was an epic dinner party spiel that would have any guest extinguishing the centrepiece candle with a giant spray from their mouthful of wine. Chance would be a fine thing around this dining-table.

The Really Bad Photo Company's self-deprecating seed was sown during an unassuming family Christmas get-together. The bottle of Sheridan's had made its reassuring five p.m. appearance during the annual game of Monopoly when Barnaby had frittered away everything to secure himself the Dairy Milk-purple rental incomes of Mayfair and Park Lane. As ever.

But then that year, for some strange reason – and God only knew how many times Brooke had tried to grasp the fraying conversational thread that instigated it all – the dratted photo albums wended their way down from the loft. Her mum had drunk too much brandy to think it a pointless idea. And her dad, though he would usually be the first to protest, was kitchen-bound on a mission to polish off the remains of the M&S Christmas pud. So Suzie Westwood had miraculously scaled a stepladder in her sparkly Yuletide heels, without even a teeter, whilst the blissfully ignorant Harry chowed down his umpteenth dessert.

Suzie balanced the deluge of albums on her ridiculously trim, Pilates-toned hip. She'd fished out the Christmas fancy-dress bag while she was at it, tossing it over her left shoulder like an atypically helpful Mamma Claus, as she descended the steps to plonk her haul on the dining table with a pleased as punch 'ta-dah' for her darling children. It was the most work she'd done around the house all year.

Before they reached Brooke's early teenage attempts at Athena-esque poster Polaroids, it had been a rather pleasant meander down memory lane for them all. The Great British holidays to Torquay, in modest rented caravans with striped token awnings and dodgy pegs that refused to be hammered into stony ground. The quintessential baby years: Barnaby careering around the avocado-carpeted lounge in his baby walker, clutching a mushy Farley's rusk. Clementine throwing her toys out of the cot. Brooke modelling her neon pink Jelly Bean bag on one arm, spinning her siblings 'faster and faster' with the other on the playground roundabout; each of them wearing matching denim dungarees and stained glass window-effect souvenir sun visors from Weston-Super-Mare.

But then a certain long-forgotten, bubble-gum pink photo album had reared its ugly head too; the can of worms opened, never to be sealed again.

How they'd chortled at Brooke's beloved mishaps with her cheap and cheerful Kodak camera. She could never bring herself to throw away the montage of French exchange trip snaps of the Eiffel Tower featuring half of her best friend's blurred face… nor the shot of Tenerife's Mount Teidi with its procession of undulating cable cars making their way to the summit like a giant pearl necklace – with a thumb smack bang in the middle. And who wouldn't have securely Blu-tacked those over-exposed prints of their first family outing to London; the Queen's soldiers obliterated in a flood of brilliant white light? These were her childhood memories, pre-airbrushing. Imperfectly perfect, every single one of them.

The more they leafed through the pages, the more they laughed their heads off at her amateur errors, and the bigger – the more heart-thudding and worrying – Barnaby's grin.

"What? What is it?" asked Suzie. "You've got to remember, love; these were our Brooke's first real photographic attempts. I'd never even let her loose on my antiquated Nikon, not with the price of film back then. We forked out a small fortune at the time for that Polaroid camera of hers… well then, of course, she decided she wanted one of those cheap, slim rectangular things that were all the rage instead, so she could be like her friends."

But Barnaby held up his hand; quite the rudest of barriers to wind up his mother's musings.

"Now this is going to sound absolutely bonkers," he said, looking Brooke (and increasingly worryingly, Brooke only) in the eye; as if he were already trying to swindle her out of her destiny. A look long practised, ever since he'd pilfered her beloved Stickle Bricks to build his castles. "Brooke, my favourite sister in the whole wide world," he declared, now throwing in an eyelash flutter which was totally wasted on her, since she didn't remotely fancy her brother. "You've only been and given me the best bloody business idea, old girl!"

"Don't tell me: a photography school," said Clementine, shrugging shoulders and rolling eyes, her signature move when it came to most things Barnaby said.

"Nope. Way, WAY better than that," he practically screeched, wriggling so much in his seat, she'd swear he had ants in his pants.

"A self-correcting camera company, something to save worldwide consumers billions on their annual film purchases?" Harry Westwood's ears had pricked up at the mention of money, mid-figgy pudding digestion behind the shield of The Radio Times. He briskly rolled up his magazine to join in with the banter.

"You're getting warmer," said Barnaby, whose beam began to rival the fairy lights' golden glow. "It most certainly *has* got the word company in it."

And so it began.

By Easter they were on it. The very first RBPC shoot had taken place in Paris, aptly inspired by Brooke's errant thumb. They reconstructed her very picture in front of the Eiffel Tower, with a family friend, who just happened to be a part-time hand model for the QVC channel, happily standing in

Brooke's former bestie's place. Then a digital digit spree went on all over the French capital. By the end of the jaunt, butterfingers and thumbs, arms, legs, red eyes and bobbing heads, had taken centre stage outside the Ladurée patisserie with its pastel-hued backgammon sets of majestic macarons; the Champs Elysées (and its terrifying outer rings of traffic), infinite numbers of bistros and cafes, where their hired extras were made to don a stereotypical selection of berets, nautical navy-blue stripes, baguettes, and onion strings; and last but by no means least, the infamous Moulin Rouge. Barnaby particularly enjoyed the latter.

The behemoth grin on Harry Westwood's face said it all, when they'd dumped the glossy square images on the breakfast bar on their return. He'd sipped at his black coffee, pondering the official launch of their flagship collection. This was a far better display than any nine-letter *Countdown* moment on the box!

"Good Lord. You've actually got something here, lad," he belly-laughed, then he was up on his feet, jumping and punching at the air in the most embarrassing jig. Finally he seized his son by the shoulders and pulled him into a rugby headlock.

Clementine had simply reverted to the quadruple eye-roll whilst Brooke felt as if she'd been punched in the gut. Because technically she was the creative force here; the one her father should be kowtowing to (*merci beaucoup*), including in his warped bonding session, at the very least. But technicalities didn't apply to Harry Westwood's porthole on the world – not if you were a woman.

And yet at the same time, Brooke yearned to return to those simple days. Once her father's investment (he'd had a brilliant year with his shares) had got them started, the twists and turns of the journey gave her butterflies on a daily basis. Good butterflies. Overlooking the fact she'd landed herself the dinkiest office and desk. But then again, the extension to their family home was on a small scale at the outset; Harry pressing ahead with knocking down the south-facing walls, and sensibly building the first floor of the company HQ pro rata with turnover and outside investment.

They'd still qualified for the humble student rail card in those early days. In fact, in just about every aspect of their lives, they'd totally focused on the moment, appreciating the privilege of it all, minute by minute as the project unfolded, whilst some of their unluckier friends had to scattergun their CVs across the UK and the rest of the globe; crossing fingers and other body parts for entry level jobs. Brooke – late to university after backpacking around Asia and Australia – never went back to complete her travel and tourism degree in London the following September. Their many family weekends together, hatching out their business plans, and those long holidays of putting the shoots into practice, were so much fun. And her father had gone to great lengths to explain to her – no, that was being too economical with the truth: to mansplain – how crucial this next twelve months would be. Her decision to stay or go would have made or broken them, way back when. Her own heart broke in two when she thought of all the study, all the commitment, all the time she'd lost. But how could she let down her family? Besides, in theory, it was too exciting an opportunity to resist.

Even Barnaby seemed to radiate regular smatterings of gratitude over his great fortune in those good old early noughties days. Sometimes Clementine did, too. They spent that first summer of 2004 covering the length and breadth of Europe, working as a team to ruin perfectly good photographic opportunities everywhere. Pisa and Venice, Amsterdam and Berlin, tulip fields and Spanish fiestas, ski resorts and gothic castles, surviving on a hotchpotch of

McDonalds, Subway, tapas, freshly baked homemade pizza slices, and cheap boxed wine. Wine that was a gazillion times removed from the pricey St. Emilion that Clementine and Barnaby no doubt wished they could quaff here and now with Archie and Saffron in tow, like there was no tomorrow.

A fitting reminder, perhaps, of the fact that they couldn't go on like this.

Brooke sighed, admiring the view from her bedroom window. If only she'd thrown those dumb photos away, instead of childishly keeping them in an album. Who even had albums anymore, in this age of the Cloud and Google Drive? Why did she have to go and get herself so melancholic about the past, so ridiculously wistful for times and people and places long gone? She could have saved herself a whole lot of bother. When she unravelled the layers, all of this was self-inflicted! It was enough to reduce her to tears. Barnaby and Clementine would have undoubtedly paired up on a venture of some kind, magnetically drawn as they were to the fireworks of their exceptional style of office debate. And Brooke might well have gone on to finish her degree – the one her father hadn't stopped downplaying over the years as a waste of time, when the rungs of the 'biz ladder' were waiting to be scaled and there were thousands who'd take her place.

Travel. The word *and* the world had her expelling an even lengthier breath of CO2. Jumping on a plane at short notice was just about the only aspect of her company role that she relished. She never tired of seeing new places and making friends in far-off lands, while her siblings had long taken it for granted.

"I do so tire of Paris." If Brooke had a euro cent for every time those six words had issued from Clementine's nude lip-glossed pout, she'd be living by the *Quai* in the fourth bloody arrondissement of her favourite city by now. And her sister would always flounce about as she said it, too, à la Daisy from *The Great Gatsby*.

Okay, Brooke couldn't deny that *she* herself was taking *this place* for granted. But it really did have so little going for it. And she was holed up with a bunch of domineering personalities who were fast becoming her least favourite people on planet Earth. With the exception of Ellie, of course. Although she certainly had her kookier moments.

Probably just as well that Ruben wasn't here. Somehow she couldn't quite picture him down on one knee amidst the clutch of barren pear trees; the jagged, moss-encrusted stone of the questionable 'swimming pool' to their right, hardly enticed romance to bloom either.

Brooke's miniature bedroom kettle blew its top, somehow in sync with her thoughts. Because now she was quietly raging. Livid for the dreams she'd given up on; for the family business she'd let each and every one of them persuade her to put first. In essence, they might just as well have been saying 'ME, ME, ME'; Barnaby, Clementine and her father all gaining most magnificently from her novel ideas and her work ethic.

They'd all pressured her into it. Even her mum. Suzie was nothing if savvy. Superficial, but savvy to boot.

Brooke selected a peppermint tea. She was tanked up to the hilt after all these daft introspection breaks and the endless flurry of organic dandelion, chai and flipping rooibos their HR Manager would insist on pressing upon them – evidently Ellie couldn't cope with too much of a caffeine buzz when she was out of the office – but the ritual was kind of soothing.

"Whatever happens after the end of this week, it's time to make some drastic life changes."

Brooke raised her cup to herself in the mirror, meaning

every word of it. If things carried on the way she hoped and planned with Ruben, then starting a family couldn't be far off, and when she returned to work after maternity leave, did she really want to come back to this malarkey? She'd already given her family the best part of her twenties; they'd swiped her early thirties too. Now it was time to make her own plans.

Even if Ellie worked a miracle this week, it wouldn't take long before they were back at civil war all over again. Success had gone to everyone's heads; Brooke's seedling of an idea growing too big too soon. That was fine if you'd put in the hard yards. But their novelty enterprise stretched out prickly branches, spitefully knocking down every ambitious start-up that dared to grow an inch around it.

Barnaby wanted infinite levels of prestige. The more he got, the less the Universe seemed able to satisfy his taste buds.

Clementine wanted to feel more and more, *and more* entitled.

Harry just wanted ever-increasing piles of money to count.

And Suzie had no problem multiplying her spending budget to adjust to their income.

But what about Brooke? What did she want?

From a career point of view, she knew that already: Brooke wanted to tell them all to piss off. For she was OVER AND OUT with it.

God, she wished Ellie wasn't staying in the annexe. She needed to talk to her. Now would have been the perfect time to co-conspire. Surely she could switch from HR work mode to be her half-hour sounding board? They had way more in common than Brooke had ever thought.

But park that thought just a minute... or sixty!

There he was again. Brooke edged to the right of her

reflection in the mirror, offering herself a bird's eye view of… oh, wow; he'd only gone and taken his shirt off.

That tan! And would you just look at the abs.

The thoroughly gorgeous image of the gardener/handyman/who-cared-exactly-what-he-did-for-a-living flashed onto the glass before her as she continued to sip at her tea, in deep perusal of his many attributes. She clocked her own reflection then, two decidedly ballerina-pink cheeks and embarrassingly dilated pupils.

Well yes, but she was drinking a hot brew.

Nice try, Brooke. The tea was stone cold… and even heat wouldn't account for the puppy dog eyes.

No, no, no. This was all so wrong. She was loyal, honest, trustworthy; reliable in a relationship. The very antithesis of her sister!

She loved Ruben.

Didn't she?

The high-pitched peals of Ellie's hand bell rang out, signalling the end of the break.

Brooke mentally pulled back the moon and stars duvet of her double bed, where she'd been enjoying a steamy imaginary romp with the mysterious Frenchman, and made her way to the stairs.

Don't try to insist that Charlie won all the chocolate his heart
*desired, **and the factory, and the money.***
Charlie was a boy.

We are Violet Beauregard and Verruca Salt.
Unless we fancy a sex change.

Alas, the sooner we accept our fate surrounding the demon that is
cocoa; the sooner we stop falling for the serenade of serotonin, the
sooner we kick all those endorphins to the kerb...
the sooner we reclaim the remnants of our life.

Discipline is everything.

Love Mum X

ELLIE

"*T*ake a sheet of A1 card. No bickering over the colours." Ellie looked pointedly in Clem and Barney's direction. "Think of this as a giant board game. Snakes and ladders."

She paused to fiddle with the pendant on her cat collar (a striking red star today, whose points were most uncomfortable when she let her chin sag – so she didn't); the trace of a smile on her matching rouged lips. Down the slippery tail of the serpent was where some of the people sitting at this table were definitely heading, and much sooner than they realised.

Barney twitched. Ellie suspected his caffeine withdrawal symptoms were properly kicking in. Jock and Jules' home-ground dandelion brew would hardly be hitting the spot like Barney's regular blend. Too bad! Ellie totally planned to cash in on his weakness.

She almost bleated a string of giggles, thinking back to the delicious, rich, aromatic coffee that'd she'd lovingly brewed herself from the small, but perfectly satisfactory, barista-style appliance in her annexe this morning, prepping herself wonderfully for the long day ahead.

"I want you to flesh out the journey from the birth of the company to the present day. Now, it doesn't have to include the obvious steps. What's important here is that you record the incidents that feel significant to *you*; the milestones when things changed for better or for worse. Half an hour to do that," Ellie threw everybody a coloured marker pen, launching a succession of mini javelins into the air. "Then we'll lay your efforts out on the table and see what we make of the overall picture."

Her last surprise of the day was the timeline exercise. Utterly pointless, but it would fill the final hour before dinner rather nicely.

Barney stubbornly refused to release a drop of emotion, his red marker pen etching 1066-esque facts.

Clem was stuck, pointlessly shading the edges of square five. She had only written an indecipherable squiggle in her first two boxes. She was also beginning to grate on Ellie's nerves. How many times had she bunked off for a loo break today?

Only Brooke had bothered to take the task seriously; a quite fascinating story arc emerged, had Ellie been taking any of these silly games remotely seriously herself, that was.

And then, well, well, well...

Talking of serious, a seriously cute guy – but not a patch on Barney (not that he'd be getting his chance with Ellie for more time than was required to annul a marriage anyway) stood enticingly in the doorway. Chestnut hair, ruffled in a just-got-out-of-bed manner, did not go unnoticed.

"Ahem," he cleared his throat. "May I serve you dinner in ten minutes?" his impeccable English was furnished with the most glorious French accent.

"You may indeed. Today's team building exercises have left us quite famished." Ellie patted her washboard stomach, whose rumbles she couldn't deny.

Barney flexed his arms behind his head, sensing a challenge to his good looks. Ha – the boy would be whimpering in Ellie's pocket soon enough. "I'm not sure where you learnt any of these ridiculous games, Ellie. But can I just say... I fail to see how they are bringing us closer together?"

Oh, but they would. So much so, they'd have him down on both knees. The very fact that Barney was subconsciously asking for her permission to offer his opinion was testament to that.

"If you'd bothered to read my C.V, you'd know how my HR leadership helped a number of companies, including one or two FTSEs, to improve their ways," Ellie delighted in telling him.

"Thank you," said the French chef. He had evidently cast Barney as a spare part, bless his cotton socks; she couldn't have loved him more than in that moment, eyes only for Ellie as he responded to her cue to serve. "Although," he continued. "I should warn you, you must think of this place as an Italian *trattoria*. What's cooking *aujourd'hui* is what there is." His eyes danced. "In any case, I do 'ope you'll find a *plat* that takes your fancy." Then this sexy stranger panned the room, with not a hint of self-consciousness, his eyes resting just a fraction of a second longer on Brooke.

Aw. Cute. And what the infamous Ruben didn't know wouldn't hurt him.

"I doubt it could possibly be any worse than last night's culinary effort," sniped Clem. *"Merci beau cul* all the same."

"Ah, oui?" The chef cocked a brow at Clem's inadvertent appraisal of his arse, and somehow, Ellie suppressed an explosive guffaw. "I 'eard from Jock that you weren't too impressed with ze croutons; ze 'ens out back turned their beaks up too. Still, he wasn't too cross about the wastage, it all helps ze compost 'eap, non?"

"Croutons? Is that what he calls them?" Barney flicked his

hair as if to rid himself of the memory. "Corrugated iron, more like."

"So what's your name, anyway?" Ellie used her huskiest voice, in a bid to cut the siblings off. "We'll be seeing you every night this week, so the owners have informed me. Don't be a stranger now," she winked. She didn't fancy him. But when in character.

"I'm Thierry." He did something Roger Moore with his right brow, before beginning to recite the menu. "Tonight I'll be serving you French onion soup—"

"Oh, how bloody yesterday," yelled Barney.

"Literally. Do you not swap notes with the owners?" Clem was outraged. "I suppose you're microwaving the leftovers and throwing in a few sly 'erbs."

What had she told them about all and any references to yesterday? Ellie's hackles went up.

"Els?" Barney turned to her. Ellie fumed. How very dare he saddle her with a pet name? "Are we sure there are no pizza joints around here? A takeaway would be most welcome…"

"Noooo way. Too many carbs." Clem chopped her hand through the air. "I'd need a colonic with all the hours we're going to be spending sitting on our backsides this week. Some of us have Ashtanga yoga classes we should be attending."

And then she turned quite magnolia, as if a thought had suddenly washed over her.

Christ. They hadn't even started on the wine rations yet.

"*L'appétit vient en mangeant… pfft… ce n'est pas la mer à boire.*" Thierry spouted on about appetite coming once food filled bellies… and said he wasn't trying to make them drink the sea – or something like that. "Next, we 'ave duck five ways…"

"I think you'll find that we won't be having duck *any* way.

This is supposed to be a vegan *gîte,* for crying out loud!" Clem was now bordering on ivory.

"*Oui, c'est vrai*… but Jules is at book club *ce soir* and whenever that happens I 'ave *carte blanche* to... ow do you say? Tell a *petit* white lie… smuggle in ze goodies. He likes a little meat from time to time, does Jock."

"I'll bet he does, dirty bugger," muttered Barney.

"*Et puis,* to finish off, I 'ave prepared a rhubarb, cinnamon and thyme *pain perdu.*"

"Lost bread?" Clem scowled, remembering her GCSE French. "Sounds utterly revolting… and hello… *salut, mon ami*… carbs all over again…*glu*-bloody-*cides...* please tell me it's at least *sans preservatifs!*"

Thierry's eyes momentarily morphed into Andy's from Toy Story. Well, it probably wasn't every day somebody asked him if his cooking came without contraceptives. Ellie suddenly caught the flicker of a ruby glow emanating from Barney's general direction. Hell yes! She was back in the intuitive game. It was years since she'd practised scanning for colours in auras, but she'd definitely not lost her supernatural touch. Tonight was the night, all right.

"It all sounds scrumptious," Ellie said firmly. Thierry gave a perfunctory bow, seeming unperturbed that half his audience were miffed at the menu, and disappeared to plate up. The tea-towel hanging from his belt made her sure he was fun to have a cloth-flicking fight with, in the kitchen… or the *boudoir*).

Ellie now eyed the chocolate box blatantly, so that the others at the table couldn't help but follow her lead, all thoughts of carbs a distant memory.

A thousand unspoken words were in the room, hovering in the air.

Clem licked her lips in a move that mirrored everyone's

thoughts. Miraculously, she was now positively glowing, sporting a pair of perfectly circled and candied cheeks to rival Aunt Sally's. Ellie smiled.

Oh, don't you worry, Mademoiselle Westwood. It won't be long before you get your just desserts.

It's tempting to put the blame at your father's stinky, size twelve feet, but in truth, as with most troubles in this life: the media started it all...

Love Mum X

BROOKE

*B*rooke was restless. Okay, more to the point, she was boiling hot. No, she hadn't started early menopause – at least she hoped not. And no, she wasn't burning up at the thought of Tempting Thierry, and his electrically-charged fingers brushing hers accidentally on purpose every time he laid his fantastical foodie wares before her. Oh, all right… maybe just a little bit.

She quickly blinked his luscious image away, as well as the way his gaze had lingered between them for what felt like an eternity. How embarrassing, in front of all the others. Not that she had a clue if any of them had noticed. And yet, how divine, at the very same time! Like a thwack to the solar plexus, those eyes, well, *those eyes*; they'd not so much melted as scorched her core, setting off Catherine wheels in every direction. Some she had never seen on a compass.

She was incorrigible. As superficial as her mother. A jackdaw, that's what she was.

Served her right that Rubes hadn't stepped up his game yet, when her eyes were already wandering off to foreign shores.

Still, hot flushes to one side, for early October these night temperatures were stifling, for northern France – more like Nevada than Normandy. Tossing and turning in her celestial print duvet was getting her no closer to the land of nod, and besides, it was only ten-thirty. Brooke yanked her hair back into a messy bun, slipped into her sneakers, spritzed her face with a little water, and decided to go for a stroll in her pyjamas. Except her feet weren't the only things wandering; why had Thierry been topless in the garden earlier, if he was this culinary maestro? Maybe even the locals were struggling in this heatwave.

Taking her mind off tonight's chef and waiter for the millionth time, she forced herself to think back on the last exercise of the day. The timeline idea had proven futile and frustrating. She'd just about written an essay highlighting every pinpoint over the past few years; every moment when things had started to go downhill within the company... and then never even got as far as reading it out. Surely that alone would have given Ellie, and all of them, something tangible to work with and build upon.

It had started with the crude background graffiti:

"We need to give our scenes more of a backstory," Barnaby had announced during the monthly management meeting, way back when, laying his explicit print-outs all over the Oval Office's round table.

"I one-hundred-and-ten per cent concur with you," Harry had agreed with all the enthusiasm of a sleepy parliament backbencher.

Brooke's heart had set off on an Irish jig. She couldn't be hearing this, she refused to acknowledge the raw and edgy images vying for her attention.

"But the market for our stationery range is made up of a significant percentage of tweens and early teens," she couldn't help but shout. "I really don't think we should be going down the road of emblazoning our pencil cases and school bags with the F-word."

"Nonsense," Harry furrowed his brow and ploughed through the mock-ups that Barnaby's glamour puss of an assistant was now shuffling across the table, as if the obnoxious samples were nothing more than innocent playing cards in a game of snap. "They're only words. Tweens are teens. And teens are practically adults. Wake up, Brooke! We're not living in Enid Blyton times anymore."

"Well maybe not, but we can't go soiling our reputation…"

"Just what is it with you? Why do you have to be the eternal yeah-butter every time we ramp things up a gear to stay ahead of our competition? Clementine doesn't have any objections. She's a woman too," jeered Barnaby.

Brooke had been furious. Clementine had simply shrugged and raised a palm with an extended pinkie. It was all money in the bank to her. Never had she shown the end product a scrap of concern, never had she shown their customers – the very people who kept her in McCartney and McQueen – an ounce of integrity. Why change the habit of a lifetime?

Indeed, Barnaby, indeed: *why* had it taken Brooke so very long to wake up and smell the coffee – and the milk that had long since soured? She'd lived the past few years in a trance, being mansplained the whole blimming way.

Oh, look at that. All this reminiscing on autopilot and she'd somehow ended up outside Ellie's door, unable to even recall the *gîte*'s twists and turns; the floors and the corridors she'd travelled to get here. Brooke knew it was only polite to knock, but there was no harm in wandering in with a polite 'cooey' to announce her arrival. Ellie couldn't have been doing anything too private, with her door ajar.

The annexe was definitely the jewel in the *gîte*'s crown,

Brooke realised as she stepped inside and took stock. It was as if Jock and Jules' magical DIY wands hadn't reached this end of the property yet. All remained blissfully untarnished by tie-dye, eco-warrior wallpaper paste, and the general chaos of psychedelia.

"Blimey!" Brooke mouthed.

An ice blue chaise longue, an antique harp, a gargantuan crystal jug of pink water (rose-infused?), a wooden box (tut tut… it looked suspiciously like the home from home for somebody's clandestine cigars), and Ellie's signature peonies greeted her. Except there had to be almost a hundred of the things in opulent vases dotted liberally about the spacious living-room.

Okay, Brooke was used to refinement, extravagance besides, but compared to her own small guest room over-looking the dried-up fruit orchard – and what she'd seen of her brother and sister's quarters for the week – the HR Manager certainly wasn't slumming it.

Yet bizarrely, Ellie was nowhere to be seen. Curiouser and curiouser, as Alice might say.

Brooke loitered a while in the entrance, uncertain of herself and her bearings; willing Ellie to appear, not wanting to come across as a trespasser, much less a Peeping Thomasina, when she heard the strangest thing. Sort of halfway between singing and chanting, the noise appeared to be coming from a distant hallway. Gingerly, she tiptoed in and along a passageway, which gradually revealed a massive open-plan kitchen where candles were lit in a circle – side note, this place was a flipping tardis! A familiar-looking woman stood hunched over a familiar-looking box in the middle of the candlelight; arms stretched out wide as if conducting a secret orchestra.

"Ellie…? Erm, may I ask what the hell you are doing?"

Ellie let out a squeal in response, quickly slamming the

elaborate lid of the box down, spinning on her heel to face her unexpected guest, arms stretched out behind her; fingers splayed to safeguard her dirty little secret – whatever in God's name it could be. She bit down on her lip as if that might help her concoct a plausible story.

"I… I… it's all good, Brooke, honest. I can explain everything."

"Ohh, well, that's OK then. It's just that for a moment there," Brooke pursed her lips and put her hand to them, puzzled. She cleared her throat. "For a split second there, I could have sworn you were singing to a box of chocolates?" She paused, eyes growing so wide they were glassy and stinging; a nervous eruption of laughter ready to spill from her lips. She needed to walk away from this.

Like yesterday.

"Actually, noooo… it's not OK… but um… no need to fill me in on the details. I'm er… I'm not sure I really want to know. I think I'll… just be off then." She pivoted herself to make a run for it, willing her dithering Scooby Doo legs into more efficient Road Runner action. "I shouldn't have burst in on you like that, I'm sorry, my bad… although probably best you get a lock fitted, you know, just to keep private things… er… private," she said over her shoulder, scudding back toward the hallway.

"Brooke, no! It's not how it looks. I promise you, it's not how it looks at all!"

"What you get up to in your spare time is none of my business. Thank God!" Brooke volleyed back on the verge of hysterics, at a decibel that must have unnerved every dog in Pruneau. She couldn't help it. This was too weird to process. Okay, she hadn't walked in on a clandestine affair. And yet, it had been akin to some kind of warped foodie séance. Well, Ellie would be eating those chocolates all on her tod now. Ellie followed her. "I'm happy to include you, to fill you in. I know it looks mad, but there's method behind it all. Please stay. At least give me a chance to explain myself."

Brooke froze. This was the last place she wanted to be; Somerset was calling to her like never before. But she was intrigued by this supernatural scenario; a scene which felt more in keeping with the other half of the property and its runes, Reiki and rainbows.

"I can't think why anyone in their right mind would agree," she said, her nervous sing-song inadvertently mimicking Ellie's recent style.

"I know, *I know*. I thought the same when I was first introduced to all this. But I hope I might convince you, all the same?"

There was something about the way Ellie said it that made Brooke wonder if she were trying to convince herself. "But I saw you just then. You were *singing* to the chocolates, Ellie." Brooke fumbled with the cuffs on her pyjama top. She let slip an anxious giggle. "Wh… what was that all about? Why would anyone serenade a box of flipping candy? I… I knew you were a little different from the rest, and I'm as open-minded as people come, but you have to admit, that's just a little bit bonkers."

"It's an incantation," Ellie sighed. Brooke had never seen her look so defeated. "I was just helping things along, instigating a few improvements… and then I was going to put them back in their rightful place ready for tomorrow night. I swear."

"What the hell? Like… like *witchcraft* or something?" Brooke murmured under her breath, casting her eyes this way and that in case somebody overheard them.

Oh, heck. This was trouble. And how had she not seen it before? The goth-style clothes. The blacks and purples. The blood-reds. Then there was the cat collar. Ellie was only attempting to hex them! Actually, 'oh heck' was too mild for this. There was no other expression for it but 'OH, FUCK!'

As well as RUN FOR THE FUCKING HILLS! While you still have your life.

"Look. I know it's a really tall order but I need you to trust me; that's all," Ellie began to inch forward, causing Brooke to slide back; a dance taking shape between them. "*I'm doing this for you.* I'm doing it for the company too, of course I am, I'm HR Manager," she expelled a skittish laugh, "but mainly I'm doing it for you. I just want to get you a bit of equality, a bit of justice."

Brooke shook her head and screwed her eyes tightly shut, like that might make the weirdo standing before her dissipate into thin air. Alas, no. When she peeped through her lashes again, Ellie was still very much there, although mercifully she hadn't moved any closer. Brooke guessed she had the chocolates to protect, after all.

"Don't you start dragging *me* into all of this! Nothing about this spooky shit has anything to do with *me*!" She shook her head fervently again at the ridiculousness of it all. "*What the actual fuck* are you doing, Ellie?" Brooke loathed this amount of swearing, really she did, but her words had a stubborn agenda of their own, and these were somewhat extenuating circumstances. "No more riddles. No more conundrums. Tell me straight... before I... before I call in reinforcements and get you flipping well sacked, not to mention arrested."

"Come," Ellie gestured, beckoning Brooke with one of her piano player's fingers.

Brooke slowly retraced her steps, questioning her sanity all the way.

"I must be officially losing the plot," she muttered. The closer she got to the worktop and the intricately patterned chocolate box, whose lid remained resolutely shut, the more determinedly she shook her head. Ellie's hand hovered over the chocolates now in a worrying way. Any sensible person would have pegged it long ago.

"What's this chanting stuff all about, then?" she could hear herself inquire, whilst the other, more sensible, part seemed to be watching this whole debacle on a movie screen far, far away on a distant planet. "You're trying to poison them? Is that it? Or is this an attempt at brainwashing? I know more than most just how annoying my siblings are, don't get me wrong. But playing the witch from Hansel and Gretel? I'm not sure even I would take things that far, not even over some of the most spectacularly stupid things they've done to date."

"It's an incantation," Ellie reiterated.

"So you said." It told Brooke nothing.

"It's steeped in positivity... ultimately," said Ellie.

"The only thing is, it sounds positively evil."

Ellie sighed, her hovering hand guarding the lid: "Look, it's really not. I learned this stuff as a kid, all right... but it's like riding a bike, you never truly forget." If Ellie had bothered to offer Brooke a glass of red wine, from the bottle on the farthest kitchen worktop, she'd have sprayed it everywhere at this point. "I've used the words a handful of times over the years, but only in a good way. You really do have *my word* on that," Ellie finished.

This was over-the-top, out of this world surreal. More sensational than a flurry of Daily Mail headlines put together. "So what's all this going to do to my brother and sister?" Brooke ventured. "I'm guessing you're decent enough to omit me from your sick and twisted game. You know I want change in the company. You know you really need me on side. Or were you planning on taking me down while you were at it?" Brooke could not believe she was even having this warped conversation. She pinched herself hard on the arm. Ellie's eyes missed nothing.

"Take a seat. This won't be a five minute conversation… and no, of course I'm not planning on messing with you, so please refrain from self-harming."

Huh, thought Brooke. That felt like an after-thought if ever there was one. Her heart hammered as she shuffled her bottom onto a kitchen stool, never letting her eyes leave Ellie's face; the edges of it had begun to look eerily like a Hallowe'en mask in the candles' fierce glow.

"And what if it backfires, all this new-age shit? You hardly sound like a pro if you've only done it a handful of times and liken it to cycling." Aha, now she could see why Ellie had brought them all to Hippyville, to set the scene, get into the roleplay. "Where's your contingency plan?"

Ellie tucked wedges of hair back behind her ears with her free hand. "All the spell does is bring about the truth, bring the ego-inflated down a peg or two… that sort of thing." Now she looked like a DJ, spinning an imaginary disc with her hand. Even the average translator of body language would interpret said move as a definite dither.

"Well, what if they take *my* chocolate, instead of the ones with the spell?" said Brooke, gulping at the vagueness of Ellie's reply.

"Only two ways around that, I'm afraid: you either claim you're on a diet… in which case your sister might follow suit…"

They exchanged a look and fell about laughing. That would never happen. Chocolates were Clementine's nemesis. Despite her Draconian regime when it came to any and every other food, woe betide anyone who was foolish enough to leave a celebratory box of the things in the communal office kitchen. She'd have them hoovered up, or stashed away in her drawer, by 9:05 a.m. sharp.

"Or …you play Russian roulette and hope for the best. I have the list of centres here." Ellie continued.

Now Brooke berated herself for letting down her guard. She pinched herself again on the arm. Surely she was sleep-walking? It was the only plausible explanation. Ellie pointed to an indecipherable, handwritten list that looked like a spider had crawled across it.

"You'll just have to make your very best guess as to which centres your sister and Barney will go for, and hope like hell that luck is on your side."

...taunting average girls like you, and women like me, with unachievable fantasies about sexy, devoted, heroic men in black polo necks jumping through windows with boxes of chocolates and roses between their teeth. As bloody *if...*

Love Mum X

ELLIE

*E*llie hadn't factored nosey-parkering into her plans.

Still, try as she might, she couldn't help but warm to Brooke a little more every day. She wouldn't go as far as to say this was another friendship of Connie or Gloria proportions, but she and Brooke had become allies of sorts. As much as she wanted to deny it, a feeling that they were both after the same roundabout end goal was hitting her harder, with more clarity, as the week sped by.

She was mortified with herself for absent-mindedly leaving the door ajar in her haste to, yep... fair enough... to conduct a little hexing was as accurate a term as any – and hopefully it would also lead to a roughly accurate result. Like she said, it'd been a while.

Regardless of the fact she had a soft spot for her colleague, Ellie knew Brooke might decide to call her bluff when she least expected it. Edge of the seat drama was some-thing Ellie categorically did not need in the preparation of her delicate strategy. She cursed herself again for being an idiot. Then she quickly thought better of that sentiment, for Barney and Clem were the only ones deserving of a curse.

It would be OK. It had to be OK.

Besides, there was far too much for Brooke to gain from this personally now. No way would she spill the proverbial cocoa beans about the hexing. And so it was that Brooke made educated guesses over which centres and shapes Barney and Clem would be unable to resist, Although it would probably be more accurate to describe the selection process as an intuitive stab in the dark, for these were the finest Chez Chocolat creations direct from the hands of the artisan himself, Robert Robert (*oui*, that really was his name) of Honfleur. Concoctions that even Clementine, with her chocolate obsession, would probably never yet have experienced. Then Ellie let Brooke play voyeur as she resumed the incantation.

When Harry Potter spoke in Parseltongue, he was unaware of doing so. Ellie Sanchez (and her former incarnation, Miss Eleanor Finch) was much the same. What Ellie said to those chocolates, she couldn't – ironically – have said. It was a time and a place and a moment. It was flow. An immeasurable in-the-now act of being. When she attuned to it, it just happened. She hadn't even had time to get narky about her uninvited audience. In a strange way, Brooke's presence had somehow even helped, egging her on.

Ellie had Connie to thank for laying the foundations of this unconventional path. All of it had started with Connie; the feng shui, the incantations, the vision board. One of Monty's growing numbers of Chinese boarders, young Connie had befriended Eleanor Finch during a routine PE lesson when both were relegated to the gymnasium sidelines. Not vindictively. They were sports wallflowers, that was all. Heck, they were *everything* wallflowers. Small wonder their friendship blossomed. Connie was different from the other geeks. She taught Eleanor the art of origami, whose Japanese influence had long been present in Chinese culture. And Connie passed on her knowledge of sweet, sour, bitter, spicy, and salty, when it came to the intricate balance and fusion of flavours. She also passed Eleanor many bundles of surprisingly edible green tea-based chocolate products – well, according to Keith Finch they were, anyway. Haunted by the increasing volume and intensity of the strange notes from her absent mum that peppered her upbringing, Eleanor was far too petrified to take any culinary chances on the cocoa bean. Connie's parents, Chinese medicine entrepreneurs who had successfully infiltrated the great cities of the West with their trendy hot chocolate bars, created and sold their 'healthy' brand of chocolate and wintery antioxidant-packed beverages for millions. But, despite the vast wealth she'd one day inherit, there was no snobbery about Connie. She was as grounded as root ginger.

Connie opened Eleanor Finch's caterpillar mind, paving the way for her cocoon and gradual emergence as Ellie Sanchez, *apatura iris*, the purple emperor butterfly.

That's why later, once her sadness over Connie's return to Beijing had subsided; once her anger at being frog-marched back to state education had mounted, Eleanor had been all too persuadable and easily led outside those main-stream school gates.

One tended to meet all manner of folk as one ambled down the back lane and onto the main roads, dragging one's heels because one knew one would be returning home to Mr Brain's faggots, packet mash, peas and gravy. And that was if one made them oneself, when one's abode was 13, Tor View Parade. It was a uniform red brick house in a snail-like coil of narrow, new-build semis. The only view of the iconic Glastonbury Tor, on her luscious pea-green mound, was if you moved the bottle of bleach and crochet-covered loo roll, and craned your neck out the bathroom window, where you could just about peek at her turrets over the rooftops.

One tended to meet all manner of folk, like, for instance, the purple-caped, multiple-braided, British racing green Doc Martin-toting, sixty-something Gloria van Gaia.

"Call me Gloria, for short," she'd said. "Oh, and don't you think it's time you shortened yourself to Ellie? At least when you're not around those conventional parents of yours," she'd winked.

Longer hours for Keith, touting sheepskin further afield in Devon and Dorset, and later nights for Pamela at the Hotel Guinevere, had made Eleanor – or *Ellie* – the classic latchkey kid.

Gloria was part of the tribe who'd set up home in an old playing field, accessed through a gap in the hedge at the far end of the arching Parade. And, after several acquaintance-level conversations, mostly driven by the then Eleanor's curiosity at the woman's alternative lifestyle, there was a bust key episode. The teenager and her teeth chattered on Gloria's doorstep in a November downpour. It didn't take long for her newfound friend's sympathy, and her Romany caravan, to feel like a cosier option than 13, Tor View Parade.

Perfect timing, with the heart-breaking passing of Lassie, Ellie's ageing Collie dog.

Gloria would often throw chips and mushy peas into their arrangement, too, since they passed the award-winning Knight's fish and chip shop on their weekday afternoon stroll. Unusual for one so unconventional herself, but maybe Gloria conceded she needed a gateway to her apprentice. For some unknown reason, she was hell-bent on quietly passing Ellie her many skills.

That's when Ellie's interest in the occult began. She would rush through her homework at Gloria's ramshackle table so she could watch her friend rustle up thick, hearty broths in a contraption that would put most in mind of a cauldron. Ellie would attempt to memorise the incantations her teacher chanted, then she'd peer through the window in awe as Gloria pranced around her small travellers' community, dishing out evening meals empowered with... who only knew what?

Once Gloria felt she had earned Ellie's trust, she imparted her knowledge via a variety of spells, even letting her mix ingredients together, eyes shut tightly, as Gloria expelled her strange words.

Often the recipes were medicinal; concoctions of twigs and herbs you wouldn't want to eat; potions and lotions to be rubbed onto the body. And then, one day, those thick lentil and vegetable stews morphed into huge vats of the darkest chocolate, in the most surprising turn of events.

Gloria's cocoa was as far from the sweet and sugary Dairy Milk variety as you could get, but it wasn't as if Ellie would ever truly come to know it, what with Pamela's words of warning constantly overpowering her tastebuds. Ever the alchemist, Gloria infused her chocolate with cinnamon, cloves and star anise, as well as her words. Sometimes she enhanced its flavour with liquid ginger and rose oil (side note: sparingly and responsibly and never at the same time). Gloria doused many 'special' bars with generous quantities of roasted hemp nuts, too. She taught Ellie about cacao's chemistry and attributes; the importance of the snap, the pros and cons of dull versus shiny, and that Holy Grail of the true chocolatier: *mouth-feel*. A concept Ellie could only ever really imagine and drool over. Then, as now.

Gloria even showed her the way to temper the stuff. All from her humble little caravan. The perfume was incredible, something that even now, Ellie could bring to memory at will. Indeed, an outsider would never have known the latent magic going on in that unassuming little hut on wheels.

But one day, Gloria did what every nomad eventually does. Once the last echoes of Fatboy Slim had dissipated into the limestone of the Mendip Hills, once the custard and navy Glastonbury festival tent was dismantled and packed away for another year of rest, whilst Fatboy Slim himself fled to Ibiza to rave up the final verse of his summer on the beach, Gloria also disappeared, without a trace.

Well, save for the note she'd posted through Ellie's letter box:

"It's been a blast but for now it's time to relegate our friendship to the past.

The present is a gate, for the future we must wait.

Until we meet again... should that be our sweet fate.

*Use it (the you-know-what that I've taught you the past couple of years) or lose it, my dear. Wiccan greetings, Ex-**Goddess** Gloria van Gaia.*

Blimey. Who'd have thought it? And why, more to the point, had she never said? Then again, random notes seemed to be the story of Ellie's life – at least when it came to revelations.

And so Ellie had pinned those words to her vision board, certain their future meaning would unveil itself, as rightly it did.

Well, okay, she'd dabbled with chocolates and incantations on two whole occasions to date, anyway:

1: Honfleur 2004

Anything to make Kermit the car break down (again), and get her parents to love each other again, after the cancellation of the bumper Greek island cruise. Keith's endless apologies were followed by the booking of the 'Better Than Bournemouth' French camping trip. Sadly, Keith's solo sheepskin enterprise had already gotten far too ahead of itself. And Pamela and Keith had never really been that smitten with one another in the first place.

Still, surely Ellie's spontaneous plan to have a go at hexing couldn't fail, if it extended their hols? She was adamant she could make a difference; that they could patch up their differences with a little daughterly divine intervention. It was only a few weeks after Gloria's departure; the knowledge still fresh in her head, her confidence semi-high. Heck, maybe Gloria had a sixth sense and had instigated it this way all along?

Cosmopolitan Honfleur whispered its promises to Ellie on its romantic breeze, cajoling her into giving her hare-brained idea a go. The gorgeous harbour-side town was one-hundred-and-eighty degrees removed from the drab Normandy campsite of their holiday. If you could call it that. Her mother and father had bickered liked *chat* and *chien* the entire week, in the paper-thin static caravan; Pamela disappearing to ze club 'ouse (in the accent of the *gîte*'s Thierry) to drown her sorrows in another kind of house: house red.

Ellie had spotted the pretty artisan chocolates in the window of the charming chocolatier's shop on her day trip to the popular Normandy resort with her father. These would be the ones that would convert her mum from hating chocolate to loving it... and her father at the same time. They were French, they were classy, they were elegant, and they were everything that a box of Milk Tray wasn't. She'd add a little extra to the magic to make certain of it.

Oh, how she'd whinged at Keith to part with his euros. A more perfect specimen of chocolate you couldn't imagine, when attempting to recreate Gloria's alchemy. Back then, the legendary and local Monsieur Robert, chocolatier extraordinaire, hadn't experimented fearless Frances Quinn-style with his creations; he stuck to what he knew instead. And that was the most sublime dark and milk chocolate salted caramels in the world, laced with next door's Breton sea salt. The very chocolates that today were his national emblem and trademark; one always to be found in every box.

Ellie could hardly believe it when Keith caved in so

quickly, buying a small, sweet package topped with a red satin bow, despite its hefty price tag. She guessed he sensed it too; that these chocolates were different enough to be more than the sticking plaster to the deep-seated issue; the one Ellie was relentlessly in pursuit of. All of which was ever so slightly overlooking the fact that Pamela was currently lounging at the campsite pool to catch a few last rays (translation: to chat up the lifeguard both Keith and Ellie were pretending she hadn't played eye sex with all week) so was unlikely to protest that, for the same price, she could have bought actual perfume in the ferry's Duty Free.

'Not *eau de toilette! Parfum,*' Present Day Ellie could hear her mother's determined whispery shriek from the stubborn filing cabinet in her head.

Later that evening Ellie waited until almost midnight, when her parents were tucked up in their double airbed; her father snoring as loudly as the P&O ferry foghorn they wouldn't be hearing the next day... if Ellie's idea went to plan. She snuck the chocolates out of the miniature fridge whence Keith had somehow hidden them (Gloria would have had a fit; artisan cacao should always be kept at room temperature!) and quietly set about her work.

Suzie Westwood and her youngest sprog might currently rival the Kardashians when it came to travel baggage, but fortysomething Pamela Finch could weigh a car down in her day. Both the boot and the roof rack were practically buckling beneath her suitcases the next morning, full of clothes for all eventualities, plus her heated rollers and her make-up tool boxes besides.

'One has to look presentable when one is the face of Glastonbury's most popular hotel. One never knows when a Royal will grace us with a visit.'

That was Pamela's automated response when Ellie grilled her over the slicking of the cyan eye-shadow and frosted pink Avon lipstick at the kitchen window, where she could best capture the daylight.

And that was as maybe at home, but it was unlikely that even Prince Andrew would be revelling in any of this camp-site's paltry clubhouse bingo party nights. Clearly, with the amount of kit she had on board, her mother had an ulterior motive.

Pamela had watched on, hands on hips, her lifeguard 'friend' doing the same a few metres behind, as Keith secured her final load with a questionable piece of rope, gritting his teeth at the impending weather forecast of severe winds and unseasonable hailstorms.

Faking stomach ache as they finally set off in Kermit, Ellie had initially ignored Keith's pleading eyebrows, and their non-verbal invitation to rip open the box.

"Please tell me that isn't what I think it is?"

Pamela had emerged from her undoubtedly sex-replay filled doze and sniffed the air. They both snapped out of a false sense of security, as she let out a desperate and painful howl, quite unlike any sound Ellie had ever heard before or wished to again.

"They're gourmet, darling. Less sugar, more cocoa. All the good stuff," said Keith, tacking on an equally desperate laugh.

It was a nail in the coffin of a mistake. Not the beginning of the end, no, but the tail-end of the middle; the precursor to the point of no return.

"I can't believe you'd do this to me, spending good money on those things. It's beyond humiliating. You never change."

Pamela dabbed at her eyes before deciding to force herself into sleep of the comatose kind.

Meanwhile, Keith's earlier blood, sweat and tears in front of the young French lifeguard poseur – coupled with the snail's pace of a twenty-kilometre-per-hour car journey in the buffeting winds – meant he could ignore the lure of sero-tonin no longer. So he tossed a salted caramel to Ellie – thankfully it was the one at the bottom right hand corner that she'd kept spell-free – and devoured the rest of the box en route to Calais. Ellie nibbled the tiniest corner of her treasure whilst her mother snoozed on, then shoved the rest of it up her sleeve, later flicking it out of the window for a lucky bird.

The self-hatred, the guilt from even that morsel was inde-scribable; something she couldn't begin to unpick and put right until they got home. But above all that, it seemed she could never win this game she hadn't wanted to play in the first place. This had been Pamela's golden opportunity to make it all right for Ellie to eat chocolate like any other teenager. She'd also ruined her daughter's spell, which had been meant to be shared between parents, half and half.

The furthest they got was Lisieux, before the car started to sputter, as if it too had just gorged on a double-tiered box of France's finest confections. Three and a half hours (and many arguments) later, the reassuring headlights of the breakdown service finally appeared.

"Le seul mécanicien qui peut la réparér est à Honfleur."

It had to be more than coincidence, that the only mechanic who could fit them in was back in Honfleur. Sadly, the week they'd just spent there didn't warrant repeating. This latest episode only pushed Ellie's parents further ahead on the pathway to divorce.

She would never really know if the car broke down because it was a) a remnant of the Neolithic period, b) over-loaded with Pamela's tacky crap, or c) genuinely hexed by hers truly.

For the purpose of self-confidence, at this the most crucial moment in her life to date, she'd go with the latter.

2: The old man at the caravan park

This was a controversial example of her dabbling with the destiny of others, and yet she needed to recount it.

It was that very same year. Summer melded into autumn; the chill on the wind promising chestnuts, fireworks and sleigh bells ahead. September arrived and the local, much anticipated Tor fair hefted the traveling community, Gloria's former friends, from their homes in the playing field where the tradition took place. They were dumped ungracefully into a future unknown. The travellers began to cluster on the wasteland outside the town's largest allotment.

Which was when Glastonbury's controversy reached fever pitch.

Traveling folk were accused of pilfering prize-winning everything: from marrows to mushrooms (magic and otherwise), sweet potatoes to edible sweet peas. Ellie was sure it was nothing but a ploy; a strategic and unfair bid to rid the town of its unwanted 'eyesore'. The irony being this was supposedly one of the most inclusive places on the planet; a haven of hedonism where nobody questioned your lifestyle.

Ellie was incandescent, desperately seeking an outlet for her anger.

She couldn't help but perceive Gloria's community as her own personal, very kindred spirits. All right, she had the stability of bricks and mortar versus a home on wheels; regular food on the table, nearly-new clothes on her back and an education. And yet she felt as invisible to her peers and her parents as these people were to the town.

And then there was her bottled-up wrath towards those who'd blatantly shunned her good friend Gloria until she'd left town.

On and on the debacle went, growing so much in scale and scandal that the allotment was under twenty-four-seven surveillance, courtesy of a bunch of burly security guards. Even the town's soup kitchen was forced to close its doors.

Ellie couldn't watch for a moment longer, particularly not when she saw the near-skeletal frame of one of Gloria's eldest patrons; a ninety-something Romany man with a dandelion shock of hair, who had previously thrived on her teacher's brews.

Knowing of his particular penchant for chocolate, she'd racked her brains and consulted her notebooks, dragging them out from under her bed, dusting them off and letting her inspiration run wild. But in the end, even the best translation would have gone awry.

The trouble was that Ellie's books weren't accurate. Gloria hadn't told her quantities and weights, Ellie had guessed at the number of drops of oil, she'd written down the words she *thought* she'd heard Gloria use whilst gorging on video-taped Aussie tea-time soaps on the telly. Now she threw everything together in a blinding fury she hadn't known she was capable of.

Two days after Ellie had deposited her version of Gloria's dark cacao brew on the doorstep of the frail man's caravan, he had not only plumped up admirably, but had been caught on CCTV attempting not to only thieve from a handful of local shops, but to chat up umpteen local ladies in a persistent, and not particularly pleasant style, prompting a nationwide appeal for his children to get in touch and reassume their responsibilities.

They did, and one might go as far as to say that moving him into a quaint residential home meant that Ellie's intentions had mostly come good. On the other hand, she'd inadvertently unnerved any number of the town's female shoppers in the process, their complaints and articles about the man's shenanigans filling the pages of the Somerset rags for weeks.

Gloria had never officially announced to Ellie that she was a white witch, in any case. It was only years later, when

Ellie recalled her parting line, that very last afternoon they'd spent together in the caravan that summer of 2004, that the realisation hit her:

'And it harm none, do what ye will.'

Shit, had been her immediate thought, for in her hurry to be victorious, she'd inadvertently overlooked what had to be the single most important piece of Wiccan wisdom. Later, unable to make any link between playing God on those two separate occasions and any obvious boomerangs of negativity walloping her personally on the backside, she remained convinced that in both past scenarios, she'd strayed the right side of the line.

Just about.

But this time the decision had become a wrestle. Was she using her craft in the pursuit of her own happiness; was she simply evening out the score card of the past? Or were her actions steeped in evil? Whatever she sent out would come back to her threefold. She had to be sure her motive crossed that threshold of fifty-one percent purity of thought.

But then, after much introspection whilst the Westwood siblings were upstairs mulling over the company's downfall for the umpteenth time that week, she reasoned she really was doing this to help Brooke – just as she'd said. In a round-about way, yes. But Brooke truly did need someone to come to her rescue; she'd become a friend of sorts.

Besides which, nothing else had worked.

And hadn't she already had this inner dialogue with herself a hundred times? If only someone or something could give her a sign. Just a small hint that she was going in the right direction.

A shadow whipped past the crack of the annexe doorway then; the kind of blur that the RPBC loved to feature in its festival and clubbing range. It appeared to make its way down the hallway to the main *gîte*. Perhaps it was a ghost?

Ellie wasn't sure exactly what that meant, with reference to her request. But then she heard the 'apparition' slow to a halt. Before she could fly to shut and lock the door securely, it had turned back, tentatively peeping its braided goatee around the doorframe.

"Hey up! Sorry, I really ought to have knocked," said Jock. "It's just I saw your non-verbal sign for communication," he ran his fingers along the edges of the door as if it were a prize in a TV game show. "And I wanted to check that our Thierry's cooking was up to scratch for you all."

Talk about bad timing.

"Yeah, delicious, thanks. Really good," she replied with more than a hint of a head tilt at the passageway she'd much prefer the guy was pacing again.

"Oh, oh, oh… methinks something's up, no? May I?"

Jock inched himself around the doorframe and gestured at the chaise longue without waiting for her say-so. It was technically his, making it hard for Ellie to refuse. But what the actual fuck? This was hardly professional, worming your way into your guests' rooms and taking it upon yourself to probe at their head space.

"Erm, yes, of course," Ellie heard herself squeak like a pathetic French field mouse.

Surely this could not be the sign she had just asked for?

Whatever. It didn't seem she had much choice but to let the freak park his arse for a few beats. Seriously, if she'd known Jules' other half was this oddball, she wouldn't have chosen this place.

"You're trying to sort out the company dynamics," Jock informed her. "Am I right?"

Ellie nodded in slow motion, wondering exactly how intuitive the man sitting before her was.

"Want me to budge up, so you can sit at the other end? I'm no guru when it comes to this stuff but sometimes it's good to chew the cud with an outsider. Helps you gain perspective, cleans the lens."

Ellie nodded her head even more slowly this time. All right then. But please, let him not make a move on her while wifey was at – where did Thierry say she was again? – book group?

"Jules would spit feathers if she knew I was in here," Jock threw another cliché into the mix.

Fook.

"Sit, sit."

Ellie sat as instructed, right leg folded over left, hands clasped in her lap, hoping and praying that her body language would fend off any sudden impulse to pounce.

"They're too wrapped up in themselves to notice you. That's the issue. Now and then," Jock began, looking earnestly into her eyes, so that goosebumps – but not of the romantic kind, *phew* – dotted her arms.

"Uh-huh," she found herself replying. Now she could imagine just how surreal her dialogue with Brooke must have been.

"As the years roll by, even though you're not middle-aged yet… though I sadly am… and some," Jock sniffed. Ellie did her best not to notice. "The chances of any recollection of your existence in the sepia film reel of their former years becomes, well, it's harsh to say so, but… it becomes virtually non-existent. If they didn't register you then, they sure as hell ain't gonna bother seeing you now."

He paused to tut, tipping his head to the ceiling.

"It piques," Ellie croaked.

Where in the hell had that come from? Her tongue, yes. Her throat, which she now cleared, undeniably. But how had he made her say it? How embarrassing.

Jock nodded, the snake-thin line of his mouth turning itself upward into a miniature grin.

"It piques. I like that."

They sat there a while in silence, and yet somehow it was companionable, if a little surreal. Ellie had no idea the direction any of this code-like conversation was going, but it felt as if the guy somehow got her. At the very least, as if he had her back.

"We're the voyeurs, watching through the cracked glass of our lens... which can be tangible or proverbial, by the way."

It was Ellie's turn to nod now. He knew. She had no idea how he knew, but he definitely understood.

"We pin everything on these people, become infatuated with them," Jock knitted his brow as if repulsed by admitting it. "Even if we ultimately grow to loathe the buggers, the tragic fact is: at one point they were our role models. Our idols."

"Yes," was all Ellie could say to that.

"We're the wallpaper to their chandelier. That's the best analogy I've been able to find. Made it up myself, actually."

"It's pretty accurate," Ellie smiled shyly at him.

"We're attracted to their light, when we haven't yet learnt how to shine our own. Often that's because our parents have attempted to snuff it out to a dim glow, but not always..."

Okay, enough with the poetry. She got it now, thanks.

"Jock?"

"Shit on a stick! I've gotta go. Jules is back earlier than usual tonight! Doesn't like me mingling with the clientele. Been lovely talking to you. Good luck with it all."

And with that he fled, leaving Ellie to wonder if she hadn't just imagined the whole deranged thing.

But no, there was the indent in the chaise, the faint odour of hashish fused with onion. He'd been here. More to the point, he'd made everything she was planning seem natural, normal even.

So that was that, then. No turning back.

Ellie inhaled deeply, for what lay ahead was still big. She couldn't pretend she didn't feel a little out of practice. She might have packed the spell book for this trip, but those pencil scribbles from her teens now looked even more hopelessly childish than ever before, hardly helped by the fact they'd been overlaid by doodles and those ridiculous love percentage games everyone used to play at school – yep, even the misfits like her – their rough books for mathematical workings transformed into pages of statistics on who was most suited to who in the class for a kiss, fondle or marriage. Shipped would be the term teens used nowadays.

Soon enough she'd be licking her lips, a voyeur indeed, as Barney savoured the velvety shapes of his choice. It really would be quite operatic to watch.

How she longed to capture the pair of them – Barney and Clem – in 'burst' mode, taking frames in quick succession, with those chocolates. What better way to document the Jumanji-style antics which would unfold?

Not that she expected stampedes of rhino to head-butt the *gite,* as had happened in the over-the-top film about the legendary board game.

And yet, there was no real telling exactly how the magic would catch either; sometimes it spread like wildfire, sometimes it was all a bit of a damp squib.

One thing *was* certain. Forget Netflix, Barney and Clem. Tomorrow night, Ellie Sanchez would be showing the world some real entertainment.

That's not the way the cookie – or the Cadbury's Flake – crumbles.

Love Mum X

BROOKE

*B*rooke had encountered many thorny issues in her working life. Crooked images, the cutting off of objects; ill-timed poses, unbelievably un-photogenic people with bulbous noses and pointed chins; tourist attractions that were too small, even awkward pets – you wouldn't believe how common it was for pugs to pull faces right before the flash went off.

But never before had she encountered this. Whatever *this* even was?

Truth be told, she was still debating what she should do with the screwed-up situation. The temptation to go along with it was huge. She was desperate with a capital D. Nothing else had worked; nor did she have any better ideas.

And day two's exercises had hardly instilled faith in Ellie's team building talents; carrying on aimlessly with the activities mapped out before them would certainly not bring any kind of resolution by the weekend.

Indeed *martes* only set the unconventional tone for what threatened to remain of *miercoles, jueves* and co. There were hardly enough human beings to take part in this morning's task in the fashion Ellie was hoping (and had failed) to pull off, but not even that would deter her from bulldozing on with her claptrap to try and make a lame point. Yes, today had been the day of the ultimate exercise in bullshit; the Lean on Me Challenge. Brooke was sure that in swanky corporate circles, it had a different name. And in her experience this morning, that would be If-Somebody-Told-You-To-Jump-Off-A-Cliff-You-Wouldn't-Do-It-Well-These-Pesky-Shenanigans-Are-No-Different-And-It'll-Only-End-In-Tears.

They weren't members of a rock band with a sea of loyal fans whose outstretched arms were waiting to pass their lithe bodies and guitars through the air, for goodness sake.

They were siblings at loggerheads. Engaged in a brutal civil war.

Three people who categorically could not be trusted to catch one another in a real life drama. In other words, Brooke had volunteered to lean backwards first, into the arms of her brother, who sniggered as she reached tipping point… and, true to form, sidestepped briskly away.

No, this morning had reconfirmed only that elbows bruised easily when bashed against the mushroom wallpaper adorning the *gite*'s dining-room walls.

Ellie had stopped immediately, but then decided to surprise them all with a giant box of Lego instead, which she'd flung at the floor, causing even Barnaby to jump out of his skin.

"This isn't Lego building as you know it, guys. This is Lego building *without instructions*," she'd said, in the dulcet tones of a Marks and Spencer's food ad, a coquettish beam working its way across her face.

And so they'd spent the rest of the day (apart from the flaming Introspection Break) building brightly coloured mansions (Barnaby), pink shopping malls (Clementine), and yellow, sandy, palm-fringed remote desert island paradises, to escape from all of this idiocy and cry oneself to oblivion on, with a Rum-based cocktail in hand (Brooke).

"Well, that sums up your three very different creative visions nicely," Ellie enlightened them at the end of the session.

It was a fact that couldn't be disputed, but they'd hardly needed to travel to deepest, darkest France to unearth it. A trip to Toys R Us would have told them as much.

Still, buoyed up by the promise of some eye-opening evening entertainment, Brooke had gone along with it all; not even protesting at her injuries. If nothing else, today had reconfirmed that the chocolate spell probably was her last hope when it came to her siblings and any kind of restructuring of the company. As utterly ridiculous as it seemed.

She retreated to her quarters with her freshly-brewed herbal cuppa, gnawed at the complimentary organic gluten-and-everything-else-free biscuit (why couldn't Thierry whip them up a batch of mouthwatering macarons?) and let out a long weary sigh.

Then she swiftly perked up, to the point where she was now sloshing hot liquid all over the bedspread, dammit.

But what was a girl to do? The man himself was outside her window once more – well, in the distance, anyway – and, once again, without his top on. Brooke could hardly contain herself. It was as if she'd magicked him up or something. His hair was another exquisite haystack, perfectly imperfect. His taut muscles positively rippled in the late afternoon sun. This time she noted the glut of green beans in his hands. It was enough to make any woman, or man, swoon. So Thierry grew his own veg, and everything! Aha, then that must be his kitchen garden stuck onto the property like a piece of Lego itself. In which case, tomorrow during the first of the morning's Introspection Breaks, when the coast was clear and he'd not yet clocked on, Brooke would just have to go down and take a wander around his Secret Garden.

As dusk fell and the group retreated to the dining-room for the main meal of the day, their dapper host was looking even more spellbinding, fully dressed now in a crisp white shirt, his sleeves rolled up to reveal a generous smattering of golden hair on tanned arms. Pristine despite the heat of the kitchen, and with that ever-encroaching tease of citrus and sandalwood cologne tickling the senses, *he* was good enough to plate up and eat. Forget the food.

"Jock and Jules asked me to let you know they 'ave gone away to buy craft supplies for their next retreat. Some kind of Tibetan sound bowl meets Tapestry week. It's a new course for them so there's much to arrange. They're sorry they didn't 'ave time to pop their 'eads in… but they will make every effort to see you Sunday before you leave. In the meantime, I am 'ere every afternoon – at least." Brooke's heart almost froze as Thierry's gaze met hers in a ritual that was fast becoming the norm, her lower abdomen fizzing in a most inappropriate way. "And I will be very 'appy to help with any reasonable requests."

"Thanks, Thierry. Most kind of you," said Ellie.

"*Oui, merci,*" Brooke found herself mumbling whilst averting her eyes from his, conscious that her cheeks were now the shade of last night's delicious rhubarb.

"*De rien,*" the human dish said to her, and her only, so she did, in fact, look to the left and the right to double check that she and Mr Delectable weren't the only people in the room. Dear God, she wasn't sure any man had ever left her so flustered, and not a smidgen of prudishness about him either.

Rubes would never be so frank in front of others. Whilst Barnaby would rather die than cramp his Ice Monsieur style.

"So what's on the menu tonight, oh Michelin-starred maestro of all things cordon bleugh?" Speaking of the devil himself, her brother couldn't resist quizzing Thierry petulantly.

How bloody uncouth. Barnaby seemed to think he owned everyone and everything.

"Ah yes. Tonight's menu is *parfait* for an almost midweek supper. We 'ave a starter of foie gras pâté on mini toasts."

"Oh, yuck. How revolting," Clemetine's pallor was alabaster this evening. "Some of us are veggies, here, you know? Plus," she tacked on with a shrug. "Poor force-fed birdies." How predictable that the ducks and geese' welfare should be the last thing on her younger sister's mind.

"Main is Burgundy Beef… since ze cat – *ze Jules* – is away," Thierry resumed his patter, completely unphased by the pair of them. "But do not worry, for you, mademoiselle," he waggled his finger roughly in Clementine's direction, "I 'ave made a Burgundy tofu version of this French classic." Clementine's face soured, and Brooke had to admit, it didn't sound like the most obvious foodie/drinkie pairing to her either. "And the crème de la crème of ze menoo is tonight's dessert: *croquembouche à la* Thierry."

Brooke let out an embarrassing squeal. She couldn't help it. She'd seen the spectacular edifice on a number of cookery programmes. This was going to be epic.

"Crock-what?" said Barnaby, nose wrinkled.

Honestly, despite his pricey education, you couldn't take her brother anywhere.

"A majestic tower of profiterole *balls*," Ellie informed him, a wicked glint in her eye that, now Brooke knew what she knew (and was trying very hard to forget/ignore/brush under the *gite*'s ethnically-patterned rugs, in the absence of any carpet) made her inwardly cringe, taking all remnants of her appetite with it. "Each filled with decadent whipped cream," Ellie licked her lips like the cat who'd damn well got hers. "Smothered in chocolate… and given, I should imagine, a little Thierry-esque *traitement*."

"Zat is right, Madame," he humoured her. Brooke couldn't deny the sparks of jealousy flaring in her stomach. "You will see for yourselves in a while, anyway," he winked and waltzed away.

When it came, the sugar-spun profiterole scaffolding was doused with luscious Cointreau. Even Ellie pecked at the pastry. Brooke nibbled the tower, Barnaby attacked it and Clementine devoured it. Then Thierry cleared the plates and bid them adieu. Brooke was slightly disappointed. She couldn't believe she was saying this, even contemplating it, but a part of her had totally expected him to pass her a 'meet me in ze kitchen for a tipple and a tea-towel flick' style note.

Pathetic! Rein. It. In. Lady.

Plus the rather significant fact: you are spoken for.

That was it. She vowed to keep the lust in check from this moment forth. How would she feel if the shoe were on the other foot?

Humiliated!

Oh, was that all?

Well, obviously what she really meant was *devastated*. She let herself off for her mental slip-up. Was it any wonder her inner world (endless chatterbox) and its words were playing games with her? Surely it was a given, cooped up with her siblings in such an inhumane way? In which case, it wouldn't really hurt to languish a little longer over a certain chef. Perhaps the kitchen scenarios that were already playing out in her imagination could lead her to spice things up with Ruben when she got home? That in turn could only fast track the fairy-tale finca wedding in Spain…

"We really ought to open them," Clementine's voice cut through the remnants of Brooke's self-indulgent Cinderella daydreams. "I mean, not just for me. You lot are the ones doing most of the drooling."

Brooke's palms went clammy, beads of perspiration gathered on her upper lip. She blew upward like one of those toilet hand dryers in a bid to get rid of them. With all eyes – including her own – locked on the decorative box, nobody noticed.

"She's right," said Ellie, pointedly avoiding eye contact with Brooke. "I think it's time."

Brooke closed her eyes momentarily, wishing she was anywhere but at the woodworm-encrusted table. Every expletive imaginable navigated her brain. Anything could happen. None of it was within her control.

Now she'd been given the green light, Clementine wasted no time drawing the box to her chest, stroking its intricate lid as if they were a pair of lovers entwined.

"Ahem," coughed Barnaby. "Share the wealth, sis."

Clementine gave him her best death stare and slowly untied the red satin bow to reveal – to herself first – the treasures that lay inside Pandora's box. She pulled out a piece of what looked to be handmade paper, front teeth biting into her padded (terribly over-filled this month) lower lip at the second protective concertina of paper guarding the hidden gems. But first she returned her attention to the beautiful handwritten note she'd extracted from the top of the chocolate box.

"Oh, how absolutely gorgeous! Squiggly, twisty gold calligraphy and everything. Look!" she cried, flashing the words briefly at the others, and then hogging the box and its paper to herself again.

Three pairs of eyes looked on, each of their owners having very different reasons for waiting with baited breath.

"*L'habit ne fait pas le moine*," Clementine read aloud, trying too hard to sound French. Thierry would have cringed, then wept into his pots and pans. "What's that supposed to mean?"

"Who cares? They're upmarket chocolates, let's divvy them up!" Barnaby made a grab for one and Clementine batted him off.

"I'd make an educated guess that it means, *don't judge a book by its cover*," a husky voice informed them.

But Ellie's revelation fell upon deaf ears. Clementine and Barnaby's noses were too deeply embedded in the delicacies' heady scents. Lord only knew what else the wannabe witch had done to these chocolates, but the perfume they were giving off was certainly Pied Piper overpowering. It unsettled Brooke. Even though she was in on the game. Then again, she didn't have to go through with this nonsense, she reminded herself. In fact, if she really wanted to, she could grass Ellie up right this minute, they could make their mini exodus, sprint to that bar in Pruneau – why couldn't she have had this inspiration twenty minutes earlier, before Thierry had vroomed off in his little Peugeot? – and order a cab for the nearest port.

But something about the *gîte*, the chocolates, and four more evenings with a sex-on-legs chef/waiter, had her rooted to the spot.

"*L'appel du vide*," Clementine read the next sentence aloud, inhaling deeply of the promises hiding beneath their protective layer. She bent the corner back to take a sneaky peek, her mouth forming a very round 'o'. Brooke repressed a giggle, vowing to keep control.

"*Ca veut dire*, hmm, let me see," said Ellie, pondering the words half in French, half in English; words Brooke suspected she knew all too damn well. She had probably asked for them to be inscribed by Honfleur's resident calligrapher. Again, not an eyelid flickered. Brooke's siblings remained eerily transfixed. "The urge to jump off the edge of a cliff... *I think*... well, something like that, anyway."

The hairs on the back of Brooke's neck stood ruler-straight, even as goosebumps prickled her arms beneath her oversized ballet cardigan. She wrapped it around herself tighter and folded her arms for extra – and quite pointless – protection. The translation and its implication washed over her brother and sister.

"*Qui vivra verra*," finished Clementine. She sang the final line aloud as if they were in a sweet little Disney movie.

"Let's see how this plays out," Clementine blurted in unison with Ellie, her French mysteriously improving by the minute, and they even exchanged the beginnings of a shared smile.

"Cute," said Clementine. "Whatever else this place has got wrong, they've definitely got one thing right."

Cute?

This showdown would be anything but that innocent sentiment, thought Brooke. As was fast becoming habit sitting around the table tonight, Ellie ignored her every attempt at non-verbal communication.

Brooke held her breath, mentally imploring her siblings to go easy on themselves; not to get hooked in. At least not yet, anyway.

Clementine finally pulled back the paper cover, as if she were head waitress at The Ritz removing a silver cloche on a platter of haute cuisine. Brooke quailed at the wows, ooohs and aaahs ringing out along the dining table like a row of water glasses being struck so they'd chime in varying pitch. Even Ellie joined in with her own spot of fakery so Brooke reluctantly had to follow suit.

"Am-a-zing!" she whooped.

To be fair, it wasn't hard. The array was spectacular to the point she could almost understand Ellie guarding it last night. Chocolate in every hue imaginable, from the darkest mud-brown and middle-of-the-road hazelnut, through to honey, fawn, snowdrop white and back again; a few colour pops breaking through on shapes and creations with exotic fillings, as if to give a hint of what was to come once ingested.

Predictably, it was Barnaby who dove in first. Brooke knew her brother would go for the expensive-looking gold-wrapped chocolate, its shiny envelope dazzling in the middle of the box. This was going to be very difficult to watch.

"Hang on a mo. Wait up, greedy guts. Where's the inlay card?" screeched Clementine.

"The... what's one of them?"

Barnaby looked genuinely perplexed and then pissed off at the interruption, his face going through myriad expressions as he cradled his treasure in the palm of his hand. Brooke winced again at the thought of the chocolate melting its poison into his skin.

"The information card with the pictures and descriptions, doofus. Surely you remember, after scoffing all the Godiva choccies last Christmas? I think it's only fair that we have the nutritional facts presented to us before we make our decisions. How am I not to know that you've got the best of the bunch there? It is the most bling, after all."

"They're artisan chocolates, guys," bleated Ellie. "The culinary equivalent of dining at... well... in the words of Thierry; a French trattoria. No menu, just go with the flow."

"Ladies first, then. I insist."

Barnaby's sudden chivalry almost had Brooke barfing. He relegated his selection back to the middle of the top tier of the box and she let herself breathe.

Clementine was a child on Christmas morning. Without a thought for another human being present, she did something weird with her lips, in contemplation of the decadent display of delights. Her index finger and her thumb danced over the chocolates and she bit down on her bee-stung pout again, eyes saucer-wide as she surveyed the goods on offer.

Just pick one already, so we can get this horror movie of a freak show over with and go to bed!

As if she could interpret Brooke's thoughts, Clementine made a claw-like pincer and extracted another square specimen, equal in size to Barnaby's original choice, and topped with a pale lavender bow.

"I guess that's all part of the fun, the unexpected," said Ellie with a grin that had the potential to grow to quite demonic proportions. Brooke arched her brow and their eyes finally met, Ellie willing Brooke to behave herself and play ball.

Perhaps she'd do that eventually. Give her a chance; let her see if her siblings didn't spontaneously combust first, Ellie the Evil Sanchez.

"Ja," *Barney actually said 'ja'.* Dear God. Sometimes, actually, make that always, she couldn't believe they were related. "Like those pesky jelly beans. The bogey flavour is always lurking. Ha, don't choose the poo one by mistake, Clementine," he sniggered.

"Oh, go to hell," she scowled. "I hope you get the earwax, dandruff and toenail fluff when it's your turn."

Clementine closed her eyes again and let the chocolate plop onto her long tongue in one deft move.

"Mmm. Ohhhhhh. Bliss," she muttered quite disgustingly with her mouth full. "That's... that's hit the... ooooh."

"All rightie. We don't want to hear the way you fake your orgasms. We're still at the dining table in case you hadn't noticed," tutted Barnaby.

"But what does it taste like? How is it?" Brooke asked her nervously.

Clementine halted Brooke's interruption to the food porn she was busy devouring, too busy sucking to speak.

"Bugger this for a game of soldiers, as Daddio would say. I'm digging deep," announced Barnaby. Was it Brooke's imagination, or did Ellie flinch a little just then? He lifted the first tray up and began to rummage around on the bottom layer for the gold.

"Nooooo!" Ellie shouted.

"That's right, nooooo!" Brooke found herself joining in – and in impressive megaphone style, too.

"Are you serious?" he stopped dead in his tracks, looking from one to the other. Brooke sensed this whole ridiculous plan could now unravel very swiftly before their eyes. "Why on earth not?"

"It's bad luck," Ellie spluttered. "And we don't need any more of that in the company."

"Too right it is," Brooke confirmed. "'Thou shalt never bypass the top layer unfinished unless thou wanteth trouble.' You might have got away with it at home when you were ten years old with the Family Circle tin at Christmas. But these are exquisite. Masterpieces every one of them. Definitely not for poking and prodding at. They're to be savoured, eaten in order... else... else karma really will wreak imminent havoc. Am I right, Ellie?"

"Absolutely."

"Pfft. What a crock of shit. Whatever, I can't be bothered to argue," Barnaby said, tilting his head as far back as it would go, and shaking his thimble glass to extract what little bounty he could. Brooke found it remarkable the way their female warning had been enough of a deterrent, stopping his foraging in his tracks.

Meanwhile, Clementine had cocoa-climaxed and decided to fill them in.

"Well, that was quite extraordinary," she gasped, licking

her lips unnecessarily. "I'm not even sure how to put it into words. Oh, okay: dark chocolate coating interspersed with the most delicately creamy lavender centre – so unusual … and then, I swear, it was like a layer of honey… followed by the kick of some kind of herb or aromatic… all rounded off again with another layer of lavender in reverse, the high quality, satiny choccy coating… and finally, that divine lavender chocolate bow on the top. You most definitely aren't worming your merry way into the next layer, Barnaby. Nobody could appreciate a duplicate of that chocolate like *moi*."

Geez. The Oscar speech was nice but quite what would happen next was anybody's guess. Brooke looked nervously at her wrist. The second hand ticked merrily on. Ellie fidgeted in her seat, flicked at the crystal around her neck, looked to the door as if something or someone might stampede through it.

Holy shit, no!

This wouldn't be like that freaky film, would it? What was it called again? It began with a J, she was sure of it, and the late Robin Williams was the sole reason Brooke had sat herself through the pure nineties cheese-fest it had been.

"All right. Keep your hair on," Barnaby piped up. "As long as there are no toffee pennies, I'm sure I can adhere to the rules." He looked from Brooke to Ellie. "Seeing as neither of you two are exactly champing at the bit…"

"Oh, I would be, of course," Ellie smiled politely. "But when have you ever seen me eating chocolate around the workplace? Food allergy. Brings me out in uncontrollable hives." Barnaby shrugged, for it wasn't as if he took a whole lot of notice of anybody other than himself, Saffron, and the latest female models hired to do a beach shoot.

"How very apt for the Queen Bee," he snickered. Now

Ellie's face was thunder and Brooke could only hope she wouldn't reinforce her hex at the table. "What about you?"

Brooke did a double take. Her brother was actually considering her! Or was he hoping to coax her toward said toffee penny? Hmm, undoubtedly this was some kind of obscure tactic. She could read him like a book. Or like a box of chocolates.

"I'm pretty full after eating so much of that *croquembouche,* actually…"

"Oh no you don't," said Ellie with a shake of her platinum head and an antsy laugh. "That's not going to help us build bridges now, is it? There's nothing I can do about my intolerance, but you can definitely indulge, so you should. I mean yes, we are on retreat, but we've also got to think of it as a little holiday," she winked. "Work hard, play hard, as they say."

"Well, er, I suppose I could take a small one back to my room for later." Brooke felt Ellie's eyes like drillbits. "I mean, I suppose I could eat one now at the erm, table."

Brooke really was a little full, as it happened. Plus her heart was all a-flutter, her stomach struggling to digest those intricate spheres of Thierry's theatrical *croquembouche*, which had seemed to whisper sweet and rather personal nothings the moment they touched her lips. But she resigned herself to her fate. Then her brother beat her to it. "Fair do's, I'll go first then. Give you time to build up an appetite."

Barnaby's hand was a metal detector in motion, zipping this way and that, his smooth skin and his manicured nails showing their true colours: that they'd never done a day's manual labour in their life.

Brooke gulped. She hadn't been giving her own fast-approaching decision much thought. Everything was working out so far, but what with Thierry's furtive glances earlier unleashing battalions of butterflies in her stomach, she was struggling to recall which chocolates she'd corralled beforehand as a (hopefully) safe bet.

"First things first: bagsy that gold one for later in the week," Barnaby announced, much as he would when he snapped up Park Lane in Monopoly before going in for the Mayfair kill.

He made a grab for the bottle-shaped confection now and Brooke tried to rein in a sigh of relief that threatened to echo around the room. Thank goodness for that. True to his tendency for a lunchtime tipple, he'd failed to surprise her too much there. He tossed it in the air and snapped it back with all the grace of a wolf, chomping away until – she guessed – the liquid centre of Bordeaux/Beaujolais/Burgundy oozed into his mouth. He'd clearly never contemplated the delicate fusion (read acquired taste) of cocoa bean and grape; his face rapidly soured like the latter. It really was too funny – for all of a few seconds, anyway.

And then again it quickly wasn't.

For how the hell would he be enticed to continue partaking as the week went on?

"Fuck me! That was verging on revolting!"

Ellie glared at him. Clementine let out a serves-you-right guffaw.

This was a disaster, the only saving grace that he'd swallowed instead of spitting. On the other hand, that was Barnaby on every wine tasting tour at every chateau, wine merchants, or friend's cheese and wine – actually, strike a line through the former – just WINE party.

What now, more to the point? Was his Fairy Godmother going to appear with a wand and a reprimand?

'That'll nip your liquid office lunches in the bud, lad. It was you thieving all that money and putting it aside for booze! From this day forth, remember that taste, cos it'll be fashioned into every drop of the devil's poison that passes your lips, boy. Gotcha. Mwahaha!'

And slightly more to the point, why in the hell hadn't anything happened to Clementine? She'd eaten her chocolate, what, ten minutes ago? Shouldn't this stuff be instantaneous?

It's not working. Why isn't it bloody working?

Maybe this whole charade was nothing more than an elaborate joke, and Ellie an award-winning actress? Brooke spontaneously made for the circular, layer-cake shaped chocolate; its succession of thin outer rings showcased every shade of the colour imaginable. She'd no idea what was inside it but she definitely remembered singling this one out as an unlikely contender for Tweedledum and Tweedledee. Somehow it just felt too avant-garde for her siblings.

She bit down quickly before she could change her mind, and nibbled her way through what looked to be layers of... yes, it flipping well was... *crêpe*. *Pancake* inside a chocolate? It was ingenious for sure.

"Interesting," she gave her verdict aloud for the group. "Never encountered anything quite like this unusual mix of textures before, not in all my cocoa-fuelled adventures... and there have been a few."

Which had mainly taken place without her gluttonous younger brother and sister; in other words, in times and places when, and where, she got first dibs.

"I vote we plough on and have another each, now we've cracked the box open," Clementine chanced, before Brooke had even digested her bizarre, but indisputably tasty gem. "Just for good luck. Really, it's only making up for the ones we never had last night."

"*Bonne idée*," said Ellie. Wouldn't she just?

Brooke supposed Clementine was unwittingly right, though. Double doses. That's what they needed. The magic couldn't fail to kick in after round two. Ellie had admitted she was a bit rusty. They obviously just needed another helping and BOOM. That was all it would take.

Like opponents sizing one another up before a poker game, everyone settled back in their seats for the encore. Barnaby flexed his hands dramatically, although the look on his face declared he'd probably rather be doing a rugby haka, ensuring he terrified his adversaries (women with intuition for good taste) and got his hands on the prize this time. Clementine cracked her knuckles, setting Brooke's teeth on edge, and Ellie's expression merely glazed over. Brooke sensed she had her emotions under the strictest control now, determined not to let her guard down.

"It only seems fair we go in the same order again. As if we're playing a board game. We can always switch things up tomorrow night."

"Oh yes, we'll definitely have to mix it up tomorrow."

Brooke's words came out in a panicked flurry. But it was imperative she gave herself the best odds at eating the untainted chocolates. In hindsight, she realised it would have been better if she'd laid claim to first dibs every time; maintained from the get-go that this was a box to be dismantled strictly by age order. Seniors first.

Clementine perused the remaining nine chocolates on offer in the top tray. It would be a tough decision for anyone, when they hadn't a clue as to what was inside.

"Good job none of us have nut allergies," she harrumphed as she dithered away.

"Can't help wishing you did, and you just happened to go for the peanut butter *surpriiiiise*," Barnaby sneered.

Brooke was riled now. She had friends with crippling nut allergies; life or death nut allergies. She could only thank humanity's lucky stars that her brother was a Sales Director for a company that manufactured whacky tourist shit, and not cupcakes. His joke hadn't been remotely funny.

He deserved what he had coming. All of it.

Finally Clementine squeaked with delight. She lifted a pear-shaped offering from the box, turning it this way and that, admiring it as if it were a jewel at Tiffany's. Once again, Brooke's gut instinct had served her well; Clementine was craving the fancy-pants stuff all right.

You could have heard a pin, or a crumb of *pain* drop, as all eyes now turned to Clementine.

"Well, c'mon then, what do you reckon, sis? Let's get your War and Peace description over and done with so I can have my chocolate and eat it."

Barnaby drummed his fingertips on the table, idling time away until he got another go. It was uncanny the way a box of chocolates could bring out the truculent and impatient ten-year-old Barnaby. Then again, had he ever really grown up?

"Su-ub-bliiime!" Clementine expelled a weird cackle and tipped her head back so that for a second or two, Brooke seriously worried she was choking and someone would have to attempt the Heimlich manoeuvre. "Out of this world *incroyable*," she continued, once she'd retraced the entire surface area of her pout with her tongue, moving it filthily, and at leisure, to her fingers. "Like, how do they do this? I mean... I've had the very best of Swiss..." Barnaby erupted into a fit of laughter at that announcement, but Clementine scowled and went on. "And I've tasted some of the finest chocolate in the boutiques of Bruges, but this is extraordinary in a can't-quite-put-my-finger-on-it way. Where were these made again, Ellie?"

"Oh, they're just from a little place in Honfleur. Nowhere special."

"Well, what was the filling? Pear... I'm guessing?" said Brooke as calmly as she could, when she knew full well the

Wicked Witch of the West had also infiltrated the chocolate's insides.

"Yes, that, of course… but it was like a deconstructed, oh, what's that dessert called again…? That's it: a Poire Bella Helen," Clementine smiled smugly as if she were a critic on Masterchef.

"*Poire Belle Hélène*," Ellie corrected her.

"Oh, whatevs!" Clementine scowled at Ellie.

Not her wisest move.

"So basically, you've had the best shit yet again," Barnaby huffed at the injustice.

"Not necessarily, because now it's your other sister's go," said Ellie, a hint sadistically.

Shit, shit, shit.

And now – a little late in the day, all things said and done – it occurred to Brooke that the other two could be in on this; that all three of them could be doing this to *her*, and her alone.

The thought was a knife to the stomach, those little beads of sweat making their highly unwelcome appearance on her upper lip once more. She balled her hands into fists, panicking blindly.

'*Get Brooke out of the company, do whatever we please, rule the world, retire early on the real-life equivalent of the rum cocktail Lego island she hilariously constructed for us earlier…*'

"I, er, I… thought we were mixing it up tomorrow, sticking to the same order tonight…?"

But Brooke's challenge was met with a stare from Ellie and she didn't dare repeat her question. Evidently, Ellie had done something 'extra' under the table cloth, which probably needed a few minutes to take shape before Barnaby went in for the kill. And now Brooke almost felt guilty for wondering if this wasn't just some elaborate ploy to take herself out.

Almost.

It was tempting to close her eyes and treat it all like a lucky dip. Something told Brooke she was safe as houses with the bottom left rectangle, though. She prised it out, following her inner voice, which hadn't exactly been the most reliable of narrators tonight, and bit tentatively at the thickly coated chocolate, until what looked like a strawberry nougat centre reared its quite beautiful head.

"Mmm, not bad at all," she informed her audience.

And it wasn't. Dark, velvety, luxurious chocolate with the merest hint of sugar gave way to a fruit burst of natural berry, the contrast stark and delicious, melding fabulously on the tongue.

"You sure you're still allergic?" Barnaby considered Ellie as he rubbed his hands together in anticipation. The fisherman about to cast off for the catch of the day. The very act was enough to make Brooke spit out her nougat. Nearly.

"Like I said before, when have you ever seen me eat chocolate? You lot don't know how lucky you are," Ellie purred. "Some of us have to make sacrifices."

Her last word crackled, reality hitting Brooke anew. Now her palms started sweating again.

Barnaby blew on his hands in readiness for his second go.

"Hygiene, you absolute toad!" screeched Clementine.

"Maybe there's method in my madness, though," he winked at everyone. "If I contaminate these little treasures, nobody else can get a look in."

Ellie's grin widened at that sentiment. It would surely get things sewn up a whole lot quicker.

Barnaby played out some lame rave moves with his hands, humming along in a world of his own. Just like he did when seizing the little silver car to whizz around the Monopoly board, leaving Brooke to trudge round with the iron. Finally he homed in on the least inspiring chocolate of them all, although it had to be said it was the perfect example of a sphere, and shiny with it. He plopped it into his mouth, sucked (bleugh) and chewed... and chewed... and chewed; his jaw working overtime to get through whatever lay within; his eyes incredulous that he'd been fooled yet again by outside appearances.

"Frigging doormat flavour!"

"What?" asked Brooke.

Oh, bollocks. It was coconut. It had to be. Her brother hated it. How had she forgotten to ask Ellie to itemise at least that flavour? Barnaby opened his mouth to protest again and Brooke clocked the tell-tale shreds of white poking out of his teeth.

"Of all the pathetic, time-wasters of a filling. Yuck!" he spat remnants into his napkin. Brooke looked to Ellie nervously. Once again nobody noticed, what with Clementine's snorts and chortles diluting everything else in the room.

Good job Saffy wasn't here, that's all Brooke could think. She'd be moving on to the next of his wealthy and uber-privileged friends if she knew her boyfriend had table manners like a warthog.

"Right, well, I'm guessing there's no cheese and biscuits to round things off," said Brooke, eager to change the subject. "How about I make us some dandelion coffee and we stay up a little longer. This has all been rather convivial, hasn't it? I wonder what it is about chocolate that makes the world a better place?" she waffled on desperately.

"Serotonin, allegedly." Barnaby slam-dunked the table in his attempt to get out of the chair. "And I'm done in from all this over-indulgence," he made air quotations which told everyone what he thought of Thierry's food and Ellie's alcohol rations.

Shit, shit, shit all over again. Brooke needed to distract him, divert him to the kitchen to help her. Anything! They couldn't fragment so soon. Maybe the chocolates would take another hour to work their wonders? Maybe things would only come to fruition if they were sitting at the table? How exactly would she know if anything had happened, if they retired to bed?

Thunder rumbled overhead, the curtains began to dance. Brooke knew they weren't due a storm. She'd checked the weather forecast. Clementine shrank in her seat, covering her ears with her hands. She hated the stuff.

Okay, brace yourselves all and sundry: this is obviously it.

But it's a sure-fire way for our physique to go to hell in a hand cart, for our will to dissolve.

Those models in their figure-hugging clothes are lying out their pert backsides. You can't have it all.

Love Mum X

JOCK, JULES AND JOURNALIST

**French Homes, Dream and Disasters magazine,
August 2020 edition:**

Jock: "I'd usually be fine with Jules going alone on a craft supplies trip. But this was more than an overnighter; a proper road trip of a mission, all the way down south to Marseilles to meet some geezers at the other end of their ferry from Corsica… all to secure fresh chestnut nougat for the other guys; the ones running our brand new for 2020 Tibetan Sound Bowls and Tapestry course. Oh yeah, some of our clients can take pernickety to the extreme."

Joanna: "Nougat? But surely they're not weaving with the stuff?"

Actually, I don't know why I asked that. Nothing about this place (well, what's left of it) and its owners – the garrulous, tangent-addicted Jock in particular – surprises me anymore.

Jules: "To be fair, though, they were paying us handsomely for doing this run."

The mind can't help but boggle at the subtext, when this mysterious nougat is taking us in the general direction of one of the world's largest drug smuggling routes. Don't worry, there's no way I'm opening up another can of worms for Jock to talk the hind legs off a donkey about. Oh, gawd, I'm starting to mimic his clichés now. This is the end of the road for my journalistic career as I know it. How did it come to this? Ha, I know how to answer that already: the svelte, leggy bitch of an office junior who replaced me as local reporter for one of Dover's finest local rags. It still smarts, readers. It still bloody smarts. How wrong I was, to think that a fresh start in the land of vin rouge *and* croissants *would change a thing.*

Jock: "Too right. The money had been put aside for building the rustic windmill at the bottom of the orchard. Anyway, that's all ancient history now, and what with the smaller than expected insurance pay-out – however long that rigmarole's gonna take – we'll have to shelve it to rebuild the *gîte*."

I make a discreet let's-wind-this-gig-up hand gesture, fortunately Jules clocks it. In fairness, this is not just because I can't take any more of Jock's inane wittering, but because I need a stiff Calvados. Next month's subscription numbers aren't so much zut alors *as a pile of* merde!

Jules: "We should have got home on Saturday, as we were saying… but then the bloody car broke down, didn't it? Thierry was there to look after the Westwoods and Ms. Sanchez, though, so we left the party in capable hands."

Joanna: "Hmm. Hands whose capabilities I intend finding out about for myself."

Shit! Did I say that bit aloud? Heaven help me, I'm losing my mind – and my sense of discretion.

Jock: "It's a Volkswagen estate." *These guys take the Breton biscuit, they didn't even notice!* "Picked it up in Honfleur a few years back. Kermit the Frog green when we bought it. Spray-painted it canary yellow. Much more zen."

Or really not.

Joanna: "I hate to state the obvious, but you two don't have a whole lot of luck, do you? Whatever did you do in a past life? One can't help but wonder!"

Silence.

Jock: "How did you know I was a priest who burned witches at the stake?"

More silence. Reading between the lines, dear reader, I am sure you can sympathise with my sudden desire to leg it... it was only ever a figure of speech...

Jules: "He was; he's not kidding you. We've both been through a number of past life regressions with different practitioners, just to spread the load... Always the same outcome, though. Every. Single. Time. Do you want to know what I was?"

Joanna: "I think we really... need to... wind up the inter-view... t...t...today. Y...yeah?"

ELLIE

*W*ere it not for the fact that Barney was so drop-dead freaking gorgeous, especially at dinner this evening, in preppy boating clothes with a sweater over his slightly unbuttoned shirt, Ellie might have been persuaded to re-cast that wretched spell right at the table itself.

He was looking as delectable and bewitching (ironic!) as if they were hauled up in Nice on a millionaire's yacht – something he'd undoubtedly had enough practice at.

Alas, they were still in the back of beyond at the flower power *gîte* she'd sought out especially for its vibe. Still a few more rolls of the di, before she got to enjoy fourth and fifth base; marital sex and that juicy divorce settlement.

Ellie might not have synaesthesia but Brooke's inner dialogue had flashed lurid neon tonight, a toxic cloud drifting over the table, tainting the empty Calvados bottles acting as Bohemian candlestick holders.

Give it time!

Ellie had tried to communicate with any number of eyelash flutters, but her best efforts were wasted on Brooke, who would look the other way just before the warning sign. It was beyond frustrating.

When there was a knock at her annexe door later, she thought it might be Barney or Clem. Maybe the spell was softening their demeanours already. Imagine her surprise, quickly turning to horror, when she found Brooke outside, hands welded to hips, aura poinsettia-red and burning ferociously.

"Well, this is becoming a bit of a habit," Ellie purred.

"And *well, this is a load of bollocks, if ever I saw—*"

But Ellie dragged Brooke inside, shut the door and caught hold of Brooke from behind before she could make sense of it all. She grabbed her by the waist with one hand, clamping the other over Brooke's mouth. Brooke kicked and scratched but Ellie refused to let any high-pitched Westwood screams escape. Once a minute or so had passed, Ellie released her captive. She did have a bit of a heart. The last thing she'd ever wanted was for things to come to brute force. She realised, with a giant sigh, that she'd now been and created herself one hell of a mountain to scale, to re-convince Brooke.

"Get your hands off me! Oh. My. God!" Brooke struggled to get her breath back. "Who do you think you are?" she gasped for air. "You were manhandling me... no," she gasped. "You were... you were *witch-handling me!*"

"Shh, keep your voice down," Ellie whispered. "And *you* didn't exactly give me a choice, with that carry-on." She held her hands aloft so casually you'd think Brooke had asked her if she wanted salt or vinegar with her chips, and she wasn't sure. "We've got a responsibility to our secret."

"Your *dirty* secret, you mean! None of this has anything to do with me," Brooke hissed. Ellie swallowed down a morsel of guilt; another emotion she didn't 'do' as a rule. "You can try and rope me in all you like, but you're on your own. And whilst we're on the subject, every last drop of that charade tonight at the table was bullshit. I should call you out. I should call *les gendarmes* out."

"Except you can't. Because you're in the shit as deep as I am, Brooke, and you know it. You grass me up, and I'm sorry to say I will get there first so that Daddy, Barney, Clem, and the local cops will have you out on your ear and in a cell. That's a promise, not a threat. You've no choice but to trust me now," she stopped and took a ragged breath. "We have to work together. We can do this the hard way, and that really would be unpleasant; something I wouldn't wish on anyone." Ellie marvelled at her acting skills, for the truth was she'd no idea how or what she'd do to back herself up; the only person the police would put behind bars, throwing away the key, would be hers truly. "Or we can do this the easy way. I'd heartily recommend you go for the latter. I just need to ramp up the intensity with the spell, that's all. In fact, it's what I was about to do just before you rudely interrupted, flying at me with your outrage. All you've done is slow down the whole process. So frustrating, so unnecessary."

"Me? Fly at you?" Brooke gave a Cruella de Vil laugh. "I don't have to do anything," she said defiantly. But it didn't matter because Ellie could go one better. She hadn't mastered the smoky eye make-up look for nothing.

"We are working together, as a team, and that's final." She glared at Brooke long and hard. "You won't be leaving this room before you've played witness to round two; you won't be leaving this room until we spit and shake on it." Ellie held out her hand to show she meant business, never taking her eyes from Brooke's face. How dare she try to derail Ellie's carefully constructed plans? She'd show her now, all right. She'd show the lot of them.

"Well? I'm not waiting here all night." Ellie motioned to her extended arm.

"Fine, whatever," Brooke snapped. "But there's no need for the saliva."

"You won't regret this," Ellie grinned triumphantly.

"I hope not," Brooke retorted, following Ellie reluctantly for the encore.

BROOKE

*B*rooke dragged herself out of bed, peeling back the curtains to reveal a sunrise to rival Monet, clouds like a stormy day on the Devonshire coast to match. It was beautiful and yet it made her sigh, and not in relief; she could just imagine Barnaby and her father capitalising on its magnitude with a spin-off special effect for a brand new merchandise range.

Brooke shuddered. She was determined not to let her life carry on like this, every precious moment being tainted by her family and their shiftiness. And that was before she even got onto the subject of Ellie Sanchez.

Succumbing to Mother Nature's paint box once more, she now knew why so many people harped on about the early hours being the best part of the day. She wanted to see more of their magic; unhurried, off the nine-to-five treadmill. It saddened her to think about all the sunrises and sets that she'd missed. Her only comfort was she was far from alone on that.

What she would do for some caffeine, though! Luckily she'd had the good sense to pack some Nescafe sachets from her last hotel stay. See, those Duke of Edinburgh expeditions and the grounding of her non-fancy pants education meant that when it came to the crunch, she was prepared for every eventuality.

Who was she trying to kid? No camping trip could have prepared her for being kidnapped last night, could it? And that's what it had been. Ellie might not have come at her with a handkerchief doused in whatever baddies used these days to knock their targets out. But she had covered her mouth! Talk about an infringement of human rights. Brooke had almost taken her last breath… during a week which was supposed to be about communication. Then that ungraceful shove into Ellie's annexe, the swift turn of the key. And she'd had the audacity to suggest a dirty handshake!

What a night. What a nightmare.

Ellie had redone the incantation like a woman possessed, her book in front of her this time. Brooke could barely bring herself to watch. She'd fixed her eyes on the wall. Brooke couldn't repeat the string of wails that had emanated from the woman's lips if she tried, but it was a sound she'd unfortunately never forget; something likely to haunt her sleep for ever more, a sort of cross between the painful *duende* part of a Spanish flamenco song and the scream of a banshee. And then, all had fallen deathly silent, until Ellie had taken a series of deep breaths, put the lid back on the remaining chocolates, extended her hand for Brooke's, and silently guided her to the front door of the annexe, closing it behind her. Brooke had remained there a while, dithering in the no woman's land of the corridor, unsure as to her next move. In the end, exhaustion had her inching her way back towards her own room, snuggling under her duvet and rocking herself to sleep.

She really couldn't believe she was going through with Round Two of this shit.

Brooke poured herself a strong black coffee: two sachets were essential. She was semi-relieved it was morning – and also not relieved at all. For last night hadn't been a bad dream… and who knew what this evening would bring?

She sprinkled the steaming liquid with a complimentary sugar sachet, also from her last hotel stay (it was clear that the dude and dudette who ran this place saw the white stuff as the nemesis of the twenty-first century) and swigged it back quickly, before she changed her mind. Perhaps a swift tot – or three – of her beloved vodka and Coke would have better psyched her up for this morning's mission. Alas, she hadn't been quite prepared enough to pack her hip flask.

She added a jumper to her PJs, slipped on her trainers and prayed that nobody would see her. But then again, why would they? It was 6 a.m. They, unlike her, could probably sleep.

Jock and Jules were on their craft supplies trip: check. Ellie would be exhausted after last night's shenanigans and the sheer amount of woo-woo energy she had surely expended; Barnaby and Clementine wouldn't move from their beds for all the tea in China. Maybe for all the coffee in Columbia, but that was off the agenda anyway. Check, check.

She took the back stairs, whose almost vertical drop gave the head a bit of a muzzy moment if you weren't one for heights, and tip-toed her way tentatively down their cast iron and moss-covered frame, crossing her fingers they wouldn't give way. The viewpoint from the second floor of the building was enough to let her know that no pert buttocks were airborne tending to carrots and their root veggie cousins at this hour, which after a short amount of deliberation, felt safer than chancing her luck during the Introspection Break. Phew. But then a sharp gust of wind attacked unexpectedly as she rounded the stairs' bend to level one, and Brooke's heart gave a nip of despair, fearing the weather would wake everyone and scupper her plans. She scurried faster down to the bottom, gripping hold extra tightly before things got gale force intense. The weather was definitely turning, after the delayed Indian summer at the start of their sojourn. Last night's thunder might have petered out as quickly as its arrival, but change was in the air. And not just of the meteorological kind.

Brooke was uber-conscious of the fact she was doing an ape walk over to the hedgerow marking out the border of the kitchen garden, but it was kind of necessary, given the circumstances. For all her checks, it wouldn't take much for a bedroom curtain to twitch. She reached the small wooden gate, straightened herself up to homo sapiens stature to unhitch it, smiling at the cute *'jardin de la cuisine'* sign tacked to its frame, and let herself in. What greeted her was breathtaking.

Serried rows of herbs in every hue of green from khaki to emerald to lime, the sad remains of sunflowers – although she could imagine they had looked golden and fabulous that summer – and more fruit and vegetables than you could shake a cherry picker at. The scale was vast and oddly misleading. Just how many tardises – or should that be tardi? – did this property have?

Brooke was in her element; touching leaves, breaking off small samples to smell and perhaps sneak back to her room for a *petit* Thierry memento. Suddenly an unfathomable feeling of loss swept over her, from nowhere. Today was Wednesday. Much as their cruddy attempts at corporate bonding had been a complete and utter flop, soon she'd only be able to commit the tasty chef's face to memory. The realisation almost floored her. Which was pathetic. Nothing had happened between them. They'd exchanged a couple of moments that could easily have been misinterpreted, Thierry could have thought she looked like an ex, for example. And on the girlfriend front, he undoubtedly had a current. How could he not?

Brooke let out a long sigh. She crossed her legs on a picnic blanket she'd found in the nook in the tumbledown wall next to the garden shed and admired the little collection of leafy and twiggy treasures in her lap, happy to see the sun again poking its warm rays through the vegetation. It had to be seven by now. Slumber would be breaking. Reluctantly she stood and began to amble her way back to the *gîte*.

"Come back *ce soir*," a male voice called across the greenery that trailed behind Brooke like the train of a woodland dress. Her heartbeat stopped, her mouth was the Sahara, her knees jelly. Nearby, a cockerel crowed from the farm down the road.

"I 'ave something incredible to show you in my hut," said Thierry.

Never in the history of time has a woman been able to have her cake and eat it. Even the Queen doesn't have it all. When have you ever seen her embrace the freedom of popping into Greggs for a sausage roll/browsing the frocks in Next/spooning out the caramelised pecan nuts in a Haagen Daz sundae beneath a parasol concurrently soaking up the rays of Londontown?

Exactly.

Neither can a modern-day female have her chocolate and devour it.

Don't shoot the messenger. I didn't make up the rules. I can only hope to spare you a repeat performance of my heartache...

Love Mum X

2 0

ELLIE

D-Day had come for Barney Westwood. Well, Ellie just knew he'd go for gold tonight, and it gave her great pleasure knowing what awaited him in the centre of said chocolate.

But there was no time to rest on her laurels. Brooke's unexpected visit had unnerved her, big time. Half of her wanted to trust the eldest of her future sister-in-laws – it was funny, but with so much of her focus on Clem, she constantly overlooked the fact she'd be gaining a pair – and the other half was smart enough to know she'd possibly created the quaint village of Pruneau's biggest shit storm.

What to do with her soldiers on Wednesday?

The truth was, she'd intended for everything to kick in by this point; they were almost halfway through the week.

In the end, she'd opted for a little video diary apiece *à la* Big Brother. It would be therapeutic for the siblings in one way, getting all their *nouveau riche* angst off their chests, but of course she hadn't bothered to play any of it back on her iPad. She couldn't give a toss about their cornucopia of complaints, each of which paled in comparison with her own.

Still, that couldn't possibly fill the entire day, and so she'd had them crafting *galette* savoury pancakes in the kitchen. Jock and Jules would be none-the-wiser, kilometres away, as they were... although Thierry might guess when he spotted his dwindling buckwheat flour supplies.

Maybe the incantation had inadvertently brainwashed them, too? Not a protest flew at her from anyone, not an argument unfurled between them. She smiled in the realisation that the magic was taking shape. Yes indeedy. For this was all part and parcel of it; blurring the edges, weakening their personas. Shame it wasn't working on Brooke. But she couldn't do it to her.

Okay, maybe she had a little bit; a notion which made her titter, since Brooke had been party to those very words last night without even knowing they were working their alchemy on her, too.

And, oh, how Ellie could have kissed those words.

Her stomach still fizzed and popped in excitement now, thinking back on it. As if her sheer determination, as if her refusal to give up had transmuted itself onto the very paper in that giant book, those words... well, those words; they'd only jumped, shifted and realigned themselves in a brand new order all over the page. Yes, at Ellie's will, they'd taken on a life of their own, numbering her instructions in a straightfor-ward and concise 1, 2, 3 bullet point list. Each line shining out at her, shimmering letters vying for her to read them aloud. Now she knew Gloria's secret. Evidently, Ellie hadn't shown that she'd wanted it enough, on her first attempt.

Dawn wended its way to dusk as reliably as ever and before they knew it, after another hearty yet high-end three course dinner courtesy of the suspiciously-smitten-with-

Brooke Thierry, the chocolate box was thrust upon them again. This time by Barney, who was keener than mustard to get going and, just as predicted, unable to resist saving the gold-wrapped specimen as *something for the weekend*. There was much to be said about rationing wine in thimbles. Ellie had been petrified that coffee and alcohol withdrawal would make a dragon of the boy, but she needn't have worried. His addiction was transferring itself beautifully from coffee bean and grape pip to the cocoa pod.

"Ah, I bloody LOVE this stuff," he gabbled, as he unwrapped the beautiful satin-smooth chocolate and threw it onto his outstretched tongue. Ellie had to look away, her head running rife with the things she'd much rather that body part were doing; the places she'd much rather it were going. He dabbed at the chocolate dribbles gathering at the corner of his mouth; inelegant, admittedly.

"Popping candy!" he yelled.

Ellie chewed back the giggle on the verge of bursting from her own mouth. Soon he'd know the true meaning of explosive… however that action chose to reveal itself.

"So much for going in the same order, Fat Arse. Still, the best things come to those who wait," Clem snubbed, reaching her hand across to commandeer the box and selecting the white and red speckled orb, as Ellie recalled Brooke had accurately predicted she would.

She placed the sphere in her palm and spun it with her other hand. Random. Ellie genuinely hadn't an inkling of what would happen after she'd eaten this one. All she knew was the intensity of Brooke's gaze, had it shifted from Ellie to Clem's chocolate, well, it would've melted it in seconds.

When would the girl ever learn to go with the flow? Not once had Ellie insinuated the results would be instantaneous. But then the magic happened:

"White chocolate and raspberry cheesecake, I do believe,"

Clem revealed, taking her first bite. "Unbelievably divine and as luxurious as last night's offerings. But, how very timely as well."

"What do you mean?" chanced Brooke.

"Today's Mum and Dad's anniversary, of course," said Barney.

"And what's that got to do with the price of fish?" asked Brooke. "Don't tell me: we'll make an old romantic of you yet. You're suddenly remembering the day they tied the knot when you can't even remember your sister's birthday… I suppose you've sent them a dozen red roses especially."

"*Birthdays*," scowled Clem.

"D'uh. They were cutting edge for their time, weren't they, Ma and Pa? They didn't have one of those stuffy, traditional wedding fruit cakes topped with marzipan and icing. See, Dad's always been a revolutionary. That's why he took my vision for the Really Bad Photo Company and dipped into his funds to help me get it started…"

"Now wait just a minute," snapped Brooke. "I think you'll find none of us would even be sitting here at this table if it wasn't for *my thumb* covering the Eiffel flipping Tower."

"All of which is totally irrelevant, when the pair of them are bedding other people," Clem snorted. She went to reach for the miniature wine carafe to fill her shot glass, but reached for her water instead.

Hang on. Rewind. What was that bombshell? Had Clem just said what Ellie thought she'd just…?

"Don't be so stupid," Brooke whispered, as if one or both of her parents might overhear. "Mum and Dad would never do such a thing. They're solid… in their quirky way. I'm sure their heads have sometimes been turned, especially Mum's. Dad punched above his weight when she said 'I do'. But they'd never entertain so much as a kiss on the lips from a significant other, let alone cheat…"

"You mean to say you didn't know?" Barney snickered. "Bloody hell. I've heard it all now. Naive to boot."

"W... well, of course I didn't know! There's nothing *to* know. You're making it up, every stitch of it."

"'Fraid not, Brookey," Clem said.

Brooke's head swivelled like something out of a horror movie; the look in her eyes pure shock.

"And how did you know? Wh... who are these significant others in their lives, the perpetrators you shifty idiots should have told me about? Am I, or am I not, their eldest daughter?" she shrieked, looking from one to the other of her siblings.

Clem shrugged.

"Some young trophy wife at the golf club for Dad, and er, sorry to break it to you... but Mum's been getting it on with Frank on and off for the past few years. She's not always out shopping."

"Enough!" Brooke stood up swiftly. "I think I'm going to spew." She slammed her fist down hard on the table instead. The wince across her face told Ellie the pain was excruciating.

"Sit back down," Ellie instructed her.

Brooke's thunderous face had Ellie's nerves on edge, until the non-verbal communication that passed between them was received, acknowledged and accepted. The eyes may be the window to the soul but they are also the gateway to the mind and its motivation. Ellie wrenched her palms together underneath the table, cracking her knuckles, begging Brooke to remember they were in this for the long haul; that each chocolate played its part in the game; that she should stop acting like a spoiled child, take her seat immediately and prepare herself for her turn. They could retreat to their rooms soon enough and pick the puzzle of tonight's revelation apart. And really, Brooke shouldn't be too surprised about it. She'd witnessed Ellie's work last night first hand. Fireworks were going to explode.

Besides, Frank had always come across as a player – and not just of golf. No wonder he'd stayed at the company so long, biding his time. Surely his daughter must have noticed? As for stuck-up Suzie, her extra-marital biz had been obvious to Ellie all along. The scant few times she'd decided her presence in the office was appropriate, a trail of heady *Angel* perfume hung in the air behind her, leading straight to Frank's office. Yuck.

Remarkably, Brooke did as she was told and sank back down.

"Take your turn, please, Brooke."

Brooke clenched her fists as if she were a toddler about to throw a hissy fit, drew them to her chin and propped her head on the table, eyes vacant. Ellie felt her patience levels begin to wane. She coughed a warning cough. They had much to accomplish between them. Now was not the time for rebellion.

Brooke turned her head in resignation and went in for the champagne bottle-shaped chocolate. Ellie couldn't help but admire her, knowing how close she herself was to the knife's edge; how very easy it would be for the woman sitting opposite her not only to turn her in, but to do so spectacu-larly, cutting her identity to shreds. Forget the sheer panic that comes from having a hefty flutter on the horses, or the adrenalin of betting the lot on a colour or a number in a casino; never had Ellie been so terrified of losing everything. All her hopes and dreams were at stake here on this rustic, woodworm-infested table. But she'd rather die than let it show. She arched her brows at Brooke to make her expecta-tions fully known. Mercifully, her co-conspirator obeyed, placing the second of the bottle-shaped chocolates from the top layer of the box in her mouth. Ellie felt her shoulders relax. It would be plainer sailing after tonight; each of the Westwoods absorbing yet more of the chocolate's energy, becoming ever more open to suggestions with the hours that followed.

Ellie knew Brooke was trying, but failing miserably, to disguise the fact that the chocolate was one of the most delicious things that'd ever graced her taste buds. And with good reason (according to the French food critic's magazine article she'd Google-translated on Robert's current choccie repertoire): apparently, it had the most exquisite centre of 1820 Juglar Cuvée champagne, suavely enveloped in the milkiest rippled chocolate; a contrast of textures and tastes. Simple yet so utterly complex.

"Well?" said Clem.

"Yes, well? How was it?" Barney joined in, adding a yawn. "If you make us wait any longer, I'm going to fall into a coma."

Brooke looked pointedly at Ellie. Ellie's shoulders stiffened.

Stop jumping to conclusions. I haven't given him a sleeping draught.

Although, now Ellie thought about it, that wouldn't have been a bad idea at all. A particularly great way to get him in the sack. Then she could easily convince him they'd enjoyed wild and passionate sex, when he finally came to. And came too, of course...

From that rather delicious moment of awakening, she could start the blackmail, claim she'd videoed the entire thing, coerce him into a relationship... and BINGO.

Get. Your. Head. Back. In. The. Room. You. Silly. Minx.

She pinched herself beneath the table, simultaneously blinking the dollar signs out of her eyes. This was no time for letting her imagination run riot. The spell was in charge now and the last thing she needed was for her thoughts to confuse it; making the energy shift and become the wrong kind of chaotic.

"Yes, well?" Ellie found herself inquiring, though she already knew the answer.

"Sinful," Brooke announced, her mouth twisting slightly.

"Sinful but oh, so very good," Ellie corrected her.

Another night, another rap on the door. Still, at least it had downgraded itself from yesterday's bang. Brooke was back.

"To what do I owe this pleasure, my dear?"

Ellie opened the door wide with a smile to match.

"Don't *my dear* me! How in the hell is that supposed to help? Revealing my parents are both knee-deep in the middle of extra-marital affairs?"

"Oh, don't shoot the messenger... who was technically, you may well remember, your sister. You aren't the first child to feel rocked by their parents' infidelity, or the last. Come, tell Auntie Ellie all about it."

"You heartless cow!" Brooke hissed. "They may not be perfect, but that's my mother and father you're talking about... besides which, you're the last person on the planet I'd choose to confide in."

"I'd so hoped we didn't need to re-enact last night's routine," Ellie shook her head. "But if you do insist," she lunged forward.

"Go to hell, Ellie. I'm off to bed," Brooke pre-empted, shouting over her shoulder as she spun on her heel and marched off. Interestingly, she was going in the opposite direction to her small bedroom, and in the general direction of somebody else's.

Ellie shut the door and let her get on with it. It was none of her business, after all, how her sis-in-law-to-be chose to conduct her love life. None of her business, but a jolly useful grenade which she'd keep to be thrown in the event of an emergency.

She poured herself a brandy and lit a cigar, luxuriating on her chaise longue; a pleased-as-punch smile on her lips at the thought of the others cramped in their pixie print armchairs. Those seats had sealed the deal when it came to booking the *gîte*; the image of Barney and Clem contorting limbs to fit on the little people-sized chairs tickled her pink. Literally. Her cheeks glowed at their downfall whilst she rolled around on velvet like Lady Muck.

The other slight detail that Ellie was about to mention to Brooke, before she'd slammed the door in her face (so now she'd have to do it tomorrow) was that she'd finally recalled Gloria's formula for requesting that extra calories be inserted into a recipe. Oh, yes. It was a thing in secret circles. She'd instructed the fat molecules to attach themselves to bodies pro-rata, over the coming weeks. It was sensible not to freak Barney and Clem out too much, otherwise everything would backfire, although the idea of clothes straining, buttons popping and zips misbehaving around the table had her in hysterics. Schadenfreude reigned supreme at the thought of her future sisters-in-law adding to their spare tyres. Well, one of them, anyway. She couldn't bring herself to do it to Brooke.

And then Ellie was brought back down to earth with a giant bump, although she promptly put a pin to her bubbling guilt. Had she been more rigorous the last time she'd experimented with foodie magic, she might well have spared the shops and females of Glastonbury from the antics of that elderly man from the caravan.

She lit up a final cigar and inhaled deeply, letting her eyelids droop.

Ellie woke with a start. The traces of a bang reverberated around the *gîte*.

Wonderful. Things had properly started now. And the echoes had even made it as far as her annexe. Well, that was impressive.

She glanced at the clock on the mantelpiece.

11.40 p.m.

She took her cigar from the ashtray and re-lit it. Waste not want not. Besides, she could hardly fall back to sleep now. She got into bed, puffing decadent smoke rings into the air, nervous excitement bubbling at her core. Now came the waiting game.

Her bedside phone rang five minutes later, just as she had suspected it would.

"Hello?" she answered, carefully stubbing out the cigar, knowing full well who was on the other end of the line.

"Els, it's me, Barnaby. Shit! Can you come over? Something really bad has gone down. You're a first aider, right? Please say you are... I'm sc-scared this is going to be a hospital job. I can't deal with that here, I don't speak the lingo."

Listening to his panic, Ellie's smile overtook her entire face, even her eyes beamed clear and bright. Wasn't it all so very cute, the things this jumped-up arse would admit to, once one whipped away his shiny veneer?

"Oh my God! Are you alright? Whatever's happened?" she feigned alarm.

"It's the sh-shower screen. It exploded. Luckily I wasn't in there at the time... just peeing nearby, but bloody hell. It's a mess. I've got a few cuts. Not sure how bad they are. I can't look without feeling nauseous. Just half an hour earlier I was inside that damn shower! I dread to think what could've..."

"Okay. Sounds pretty bad but try to stay calm. I'll be with you in a minute. I'll bring my box."

"Thanks, Ellie. Like, *so much*. Between you and me, it really shook me up and I could've di—"

"Shh, don't say it. I'll be with you soon."

She cleaned her teeth, doused herself in a little *Poison* – thanks, Yves Saint Laurent. She picked up the first aid kit sitting ready and waiting on the table, went to the small cleaning cupboard in her kitchen for the dustpan and brush, widened her eyes in an excitement she simply couldn't contain, and shook her hands in mid-air as if she'd won the lottery. Then she sped to her lover's aid. This was all going to turn out quite beautifully.

"The door's open," Barney whimpered.

And there he was, in cuteness overload, despite the worry etched across his face, and the way he was hunched down in the pixie print-festooned armchair. The temptation to turn dominatrix, to take him by the hand, leading him back to her palace, and the sumptuousness of the chaise longue, was almost too much to bear.

Play the game, Ellie. You're so close to victory now. Don't get dazed, fooled or overwhelmed.

In her most measured and collected manner, Ellie obeyed her ego. She put on her best nonplussed act, walked briskly toward Barney and knelt to observe the cuts: two on each arm, and even she breathed a sigh of relief that thankfully, they were nowhere near the main artery; three on his lower left leg.

In all honesty though, the boy was a sopping wet blanket. There was nothing much to write home about at all. She guessed that shock had embellished his interpretation of events, and she swiftly set about cleaning the small wounds with disinfectant and cotton wool, before applying gauze and plasters. Her nerve endings fizzed with a lust that she knew wouldn't remain unrequited for much longer, her fingers trembled with anticipation. It was essential she work quickly. The secret thrilled. She bit down hard on her lip and thankfully he didn't see that she'd drawn blood for him.

"There. All done and dusted. I'll sweep up the mess in the bathroom tomorrow morning." She gestured at the dustpan and brush sitting outside the bathroom door, cursing the warble in her voice. "Now get some rest. Another day of team building awaits."

She pivoted without a backward glance, marvelling at her discipline, as he croaked out his thanks. How easy it would have been to give in to her desires when he was at his weakest, unable to protest. Tonight had been one giant triumph. He was warming to her nicely, in just the way she'd hoped and predicted, but hadn't dared get too complacent about. Ellie Sanchez slept her very best sleep of the week in her opulent king-sized bed.

"Correct me if I'm wrong," said a refreshingly relaxed, reincarnated, and decidedly glowing version of Brooke the following morning when they met in the corridor, and Ellie checked for the umpteenth time that her intensive care lip balm had sufficiently patched up her own wound. "But the incidents seem to be building in intensity as the days go by. First that faraway rumble of thunder, like some kind of distant warning of all that's to come... then the foul secret about my folks, and the shattered shower screen."

"No, you're not imagining it." Ellie replied matter-of-factly, happy, at last, that Brooke was joining her on the same wavelength with this welcome olive branch of conversation. "But we need this to go incrementally. And we need everyone to stay safe. Shaken up so they change their ways is what we're after. There's a fine line. If you think I need to re-do the spell, slow things down a little, you will say, won't you?"

"Are you kidding? I've had time to think about it, to let the complexity of the situation sink in, and I'm sorry for ever doubting you, Ellie. I really cannot wait until we get to the crescendo," Brooke winked conspiratorially. "It's going to be epic."

Ellie couldn't help it. Lame or not, now was the time for a united fist bump. She was elated to see this change in Brooke, at long last, her fears abating now they were one hundred per cent in this together. She proffered both fists and Brooke grinned, slamming her tightly clenched hands into Ellie's.

"BOOM!"

BROOKE

"*J*didn't think you would come," said Thierry, peeping through the crack in the door of the garden shed and gesturing for Brooke to walk in.

He was topless (again), he held an outstretched bottle of champagne in one hand, two glasses in the other, and now her heart was properly out of control. She'd never been gladder that she wasn't one for those scary FitBit wrist contraptions, whose stats on the current state of her cardiovascular system would have probably finished her off, throwing her into immediate cardiac arrest.

She took a deep breath and inched a toe inside.

"My brother and sister have just revealed that my parents are both having it off with other people and I'm the last one to know, and now I feel like I've totally lost my identity, as if I didn't feel that way already, and… and… and my life is basically one gigantic and shitty mess with no hope of escape," said Brooke, without coming up for air.

She ran her fingers through her hair, like that might help her find the answer, still standing in the doorway. Inwardly, she berated herself for being so uncool.

"*Les chiens ne font pas des chats,*" said Thierry thoughtfully, beckoning her further inside with the bottle, cocking his head toward a large but slightly battered sofa. Brooke looked back at him blankly, making her way to the giant seat. "Like mozzer like daughter, I think you would say."

"Well, that quite doesn't work. *I'm* still my mother's daughter too, *aren't I*? Or are you going to be the one to reveal to me that actually, I was adopted at birth?" She shuddered. "Don't waste your breath. Nothing would surprise me this week."

Brooke grabbed at one of the blue striped cushions and let out a mammoth sigh, holding on for dear life until Thierry handed her a glass of bubbles. Suddenly her fingertips were as activated as the effervescent fizz that was just begging her to knock it back.

"It was your sister I was referring to."

He sat beside her, flipping his hair out of his eyes. He clinked her glass. It was a moment in time that could have come straight out of a Tatler spread; his godly figure artfully framed with the soft glow of the lantern behind him.

"And surely the saying extends to fathers and sons, too?"

Were they flirting... in a going off at tangents kind of a way? Batting debate to and fro?

"It surely does."

His eyes held hers with that intensity from the dining-room all over again.

They were.

"Good. *Bien.* It doesn't make me happy though." Whereas Thierry looking at her like *that* did. "I'm stuck in a quagmire of absolute despair, every which way I turn."

Brooke sighed again, momentarily breaking the spell.

"And what would make you 'appy?"

She sipped pensively on the champagne, unable to ignore the goosebumps decorating her arms and her scalp. Was the chocolate of all but an hour ago foreshadowing this current moment; this time and place?

Definitely, maybe.

A ridiculous idea flew into Brooke's head. Now it was dominating not only her thoughts but her movements, until she found her lips planted on a surprised, but not disappointed, Thierry – and more precisely, his utterly kissable lips. Her half-drunk glass of champagne remained outstretched in her arm for want of a resting place; an extraordinary portrait indeed, so much so that it probably wouldn't even have found its way onto the royalty-free image library section of Flickr.

Thierry accepted her proposal, his sweet, strong mouth letting out a thoroughly masculine moan that practically threw Brooke into instant orgasm. Instinctively, he reached for her glass as the kiss's intensity grew, expertly placing it on the small table before them, as if he'd found himself pinned down by an insatiable woman a hundred million times in the past and was thoroughly versed for such a spontaneous scenario.

Brooke's conscience ran rife with pictures of a distraught Ruben walking in on them at any moment, witnessing her hypocritical deceit; an act which had perversely come about because she felt betrayed by her cheating parents. But she was simply unable to break away from this rather delicious and unexpected intimacy, and when Thierry deepened their kiss, his hands roaming and fumbling at her zip to de-shell her from her passion-killing obstruction of a jacket, she knew she wanted as much of him as he was willing to offer; that she'd take it at the cost of her relationship because she'd never experienced this kind of dizzying and breathless attraction with anyone, and she'd happily die a sinner just to savour it in its entirety for one sweet evening.

ISABELLA MAY

"What are you doing here?" he dimmed the lamp and kissed her on the forehead as she curled further into the crook of his arm.

He smelt earthy, a little citrussy, and not remotely as if he'd recently been simmering garlic and onions. Which was a relief. And then she felt the sledgehammer of guilt hit her chest anew; how could she do this to poor Rubes? Why wasn't she running out of here, back to her room, locking the door, falling down on her knees, bargaining with heaven above for forgiveness?

"Team building. Apparently," she whispered into the dark, eyes now adjusting to take in the fact that there was a hole in the roof. She blinked several times to fully accustom herself to the night and saw it had glass over it; a makeshift porthole to the planets.

"That's one way of defining our activities tonight, *mademoiselle*," Thierry smirked, completely oblivious to the way his irresistible accent was turning Brooke on all over again, until she'd shrugged off what little remained of her dignity, straddled him without a further thought of her boyfriend, and they engaged in a thoroughly enjoyable encore.

"No, Brooke. What are you really doing here?" Thierry's tone was less playful half an hour later, more insistent now as she rolled off his delectable thighs and collapsed in an inelegant heap beside him.

"The truth is… I really don't know," she paused, turning to face him, taking in his high-chiselled cheekbones, revelling in the absolute flawlessness of the boy.

Did he have a girlfriend? He didn't act like he had a girlfriend. Maybe that was because he had a boyfriend? Brooke supposed all French men were like this; *charmant* and *insouciant.*

"I'll tell you what I think you might be doing here."

"Okaaaay," she replied, unsure that she really wanted to hear it, certain that some of his words would come loaded with an inevitable sting in their tail; now that the bubbles had worn off, and he'd realised this was all one gigantic mistake.

"Looking for a little adventure. Not necessarily with *moi,* although I would be more than ecstatic to have a woman like you by my side; to try to provide it." Her heart flipped, now that would be too good to be true. "I mean... I think you are looking for a little life adventure. You've looked trapped every night at that table, like somehow you just don't belong."

Was it really that obvious?

"*Il faut tourner sept fois sa langue dans sa bouche avant de parler.*"

Brooke's brain went into overdrive to translate Thierry's literary French nugget of wisdom... and came up with a blank. She threw him a confused look, cursing herself for not having paid more attention to her language teachers at school. Things might have been different, had she known she'd find herself in this man's bed!

"Most of the fault lies with your brother. He's your biggest problem. He needs to think before he opens his big mouth."

Brooke let out a mighty laugh.

"That would be extremely accurate. Is that why you invited me here, when you saw me checking out your garden this morning, to appraise my family?"

"I invited you to look at the stars."

"What... through that thing, the erm... cut-out circle, up there on the roof?"

"That *cut-out circle on the roof* goes with that thing over there in the corner."

Brooke sprang to her feet, covering what little was left of

her modesty with the sofa's throw. She walked the few paces to the corner of the hut Thierry had pointed out. A dusty-looking cover hung over a bulky object. Brooke peeled it back, to gasp at an enormous telescope, whose shiny features glinted back at her in the fairy-lit room.

"Oh, wow. This is a serious bit of kit. Do Jock and Jules know you have it here; that you come here?"

"Yes and no."

"That's a strange answer." Brooke furrowed her brow.

"I come and go as I please. I live 'ere during the busier months, and I live there when my cooking isn't in such demand; friends' sofas and outbuildings, cheap hotels, sometimes I camp a while. It's a long and boring story," he paused to reflect. "I lost my job, my very lucrative job, in Paris. Not that it was my true passion, but it paid very well, and supported my true passion."

"I want you to show me some stars, and then…" Brooke tiptoed back to her lover – at least she felt she could call him that for what remained of the night – and then she did something she would never usually entertain doing on a first date (not that she had EVER usually felt comfortable enough to go quite so far on the first date, such slapper behaviour). She ran her fingers along Thierry's cheeks with an inner knowing that spoke of lifelong bonds, babies and shared bank accounts; an inner knowing whose truth swashbuckled every protest raised by her ego:

"I want you to tell me your life story," she said.

"Only if you tell me yours." Thierry looked so deeply into her eyes that she swore he touched the edges of her soul. "*All* of yours. The unabridged version. That's the deal."

And so it was that she narrated her entire backstory, after he'd shown her Jupiter, The Plough and the iconic North Star – and okay, put on another rather good show of his own. From childhood to college to crap photography skills to conniving family members… to present day Pruneau and their desperate sojourn at the *gîte*, Brooke supplied him with the animated anecdotes to every milestone on her life's journey.

Except for the hexing. He really didn't want to know she was an unwilling accomplice to that.

Thierry listened patiently, only delivering his thoughts on her tale of woe after he'd furnished her with the details of his own modelling career in the capital; the way it had *almost* put him through one of Paris's top cookery schools; the way his agent had turned out to be a crook, running off with his earnings of 2017, leaving him penniless, unable to fund his last term at the prestigious culinary institution. Yes, he had family but he was too proud to run home for financial help, after most of them had nay-sayed his features being flashed across French *Vogue* and the rest. *Maman* and *Papa* were a doctor duo in the chic Bordeaux suburb he'd grown up in, and they were never going to be impressed with an errant foodie heir and his propensity to please the camera. From the day he'd made the decision to follow his heart, he'd been on his own; their only contact through postcards and thank-you notes. They still insisted on buying him medical journals for birthdays and Christmas. And once he'd even taken delivery of a skeleton. He wasn't kidding.

He sent them mementos from his European city food tours. Not that there had been many of those, since Jock and Jules had come to his salvation at the Gare du Nord station where he'd sat begging on the hard, cold pavement with his upturned beret, and a placard announcing his kitchen skills and willingness to work.

Brooke couldn't help but sob. It was a desperately sad story, and one which shone a spotlight on her many privileges, even if she and her family didn't exactly see eye to eye.

"I feel for you, Brooke," Thierry broke their silence. "You

are like ze middle child, no? Even though I can tell you are an old soul, not just the physical eldest of the three. Still, it's all about them: Clementine and Barnaby. So tell me: what is it that *you* want?"

"Oh, Thierry. I think we'd be here all night if I got started on that. How many countries are there in the world?"

"Well, let's see. Starting with A, there's Afghanistan, Albania, Algeria," he began to count them off on his fingers.

"Stop! I'll never get to all of those, although I am impressed you seem to know them alphabetically by heart."

"Perhaps we can start with Andorra… that's not so far… and neither are the Christmas holidays. We could go there together. Skiing, fondue, fun beneath the sheets."

Brooke's heart fluttered at the implications, rendering her speechless. Her teeth chattered. In a very good way.

"I plan to tread the soil of every one of those As through to Zs on my culinary adventures, by the time I'm old and grey. We must be kindred spirits, Brooke," he turned to wink at her and now her heart gave a jolt of pleasure that completely flooded her veins, willing the evening to last forever.

"Okaaay," she replied. "well, that's sort of answered *your* final question of the evening, and now you have to answer *mine*… why do you constantly have your top off?"

ELLIE

*E*llie paced the bedroom's wooden floorboards. Ben's call should have put her at ease, but something wasn't adding up about his story, or more to the (geographical) point, his co-ordinates. She couldn't get to the bottom of it, try as she might, and that crackly phone line; the yelling and screaming in the background, had done little to reassure. Something felt off kilter. Fishy even. Yes, very, *very* askew.

For the moment, though, she had more pressing issues to contend with. Thursday had arrived: what the hell was she going to do with her underlings?

She pulled back the curtains to glance out of the window for some inspiration. Hmm, leaves aplenty out there. A bit of autumnal collage could take up most of the morning – potentially. That would buy her a few hours to twiddle her thumbs and come up with something aptly mind-numbing for the afternoon. She was just about to turn from the window to finish preening herself in the bathroom, when a figure approaching the main house had her doing a double take.

Well… *somebody* was getting some last night, by the looks of it!

Sneaky.

Good job she hadn't agreed to other halves tagging along on this trip, she giggled, taking in the bedraggled form – and gait… Goodness, the mind boggled in that department, but Brooke definitely had a distinctive late eighties Tina Turner walk going on this morning as she strode across the lawn to the side entrance of the *gîte*.

Five minutes to go until breakfast. No way would Brooke make it today.

But Ellie would. She needed to be the first one up every morning, to ensure the chocolate box was still intact, locked away in the drawer beneath the dining table, courtesy of the key on the ribbon she'd found inside the hidey-hole at the entrance to the dining-room. Which was why she was also the last one to bed so she could tuck the box in at night, feigning a little late night note-taking with her peppermint tea. It was getting harder and harder to part with the chocolates, though. They'd feel safer lying by her side, on the spare pillows where Barney's head would soon be resting (she hoped he didn't snore like Carlos). But it was critical that she didn't over-expose the goodies to her will; things needed to go haywire in their own space and time. The chocolates literally had their own consciousness, now that she'd properly programmed them. They'd be the ones to decide everybody's fate.

She crossed the room to the hand-drawn paper that detailed the remains of the upper tray of the chocolate box: *mille feuille*, the Eiffel Tower, and *crème brûlée*. Who would take what? The power of the spell never ceased to amaze Ellie, for every chocolate would morph its potential based on the breakdown of good versus evil of each of its consumers. A lucky, or not-so-lucky dip!

Brooke wouldn't *really* go wrong when she took her pick... it just depended on the way the Universe chose to interpret last night's shenanigans. Ellie couldn't babysit the girl. It's not like Brooke would have listened if she'd tried.

From Ben to Brooke to the box of bombshells, so much of the end result now was way outside Ellie's remit. That was the hardest part, the excruciating wait. Ellie's life was about scheming and strategising. For the very first time in her adult life, she needed to let go of the reins, take her hands off the wheel and be completely still.

Only one thing was certain, tonight they'd be at halfway house; once shot of that first succulent tray, everyone would be scrabbling for the sensational gems lying in wait in the dark underbelly of the mystical box. Self-sabotage didn't get more delicious than that.

23

BROOKE

*H*ow would she face him tonight over dinner? How would she hide her guilt in front of the others? Yes, she was good at keeping a secret. Take the rather unconventional answer Thierry had given her, ref his seemingly constantly (not that she was complaining about it) naked torso: his parents made them all button their polo shirts up to the throat as children at the French Riviera's poshest beach clubs; it was a rebellion thing. But, when it came to her feelings for the man who'd be serving them dinner, well, their chemistry would be written across the *gîte*'s crumbling walls, *and* her face.

Brooke just had to hope that the excitement of the remaining chocolates would override everything else at dinner; that her duplicitous tryst would stay right with the tools and the twine in the garden shed. Although she'd be lying if she said she didn't fancy another *rendez-vous*.

After a pointless and tiring morning of foraging for leaves, twigs, and windfalls in the fruit orchards, as well as pilfering the herbs, veggie, and flower beds of Thierry's kitchen garden (luckily, Thursday was market day for him and a trip to a local vineyard kept him away until the after-noon), Brooke and co diligently returned to the dining-room to fashion together kindergarten pictures for Ellie, who had taken to an endless, and thoroughly annoying, pacing behind them, left hand on chin, supported by the right hand. Anyone would've thought they were Tracy Emin, Andy Warhol and Banksy, such was the undeserving attention she was giving their decidedly amateur creations. Art had never been Brooke's forte... except when it came to capturing money-making flaws on film, it seemed.

Reading between the lines (and the leaves), Brooke sensed Ellie's thoughts were on everything but their canvasses. The minutes and hours available for radical change were disap-pearing fast – as were the chocolates.

As was Brooke's time with Thierry.

He was just a fling. Just a stupid getting-it-out-of-her-system-before-settling-down indulgence. Nothing more, nothing less. He knew it. She knew it. Never more so, now that he had ignored her all throughout dinner and its service, spurning her polite smiles, turning his back on her and hiding in the confines of his kitchen for as long as was physi-cally possible, practically frisbeeing Brooke's food at her across the table so as to come nowhere near her.

Well, that was her head's version. Her heart wouldn't listen to a word of it. Last night had altered the course of her life forever, and her soul as good as knew it.

"I'll go first this evening," Brooke had made an executive decision. It felt right to snap up the magnificent and intri-cately crafted Eiffel Tower chocolate, and she was amazed that Clementine, with her penchant for all things Parisian *haute couture,* hadn't got there first.

"Fine. Go ahead."

Brooke sensed Ellie's antennae pricking at Clementine's unorthodox willingness to cooperate, accompanied by her *I-truly-insist-you-get-first-dibs* smile, but then she hadn't seen the way they'd bonded outside in nature; a phenomenon Brooke still hadn't quite wrapped her head around herself. Perhaps their day in the autumnal sunshine had transported them back to the simplicity of their early childhood, the pretences dropped, the competition almost non-existent. Even Barnaby had climbed trees for shrivelled fruit which they'd later cut, sharing its diminishing bounty for some interesting cross-sections to be layered and glued on their cardboard creations.

Hell, they'd even laughed, and not in their standard *at* each other way, either, but *with* each other! Clementine had welled up and cried at one point. Most importantly of all, they'd talked, each giving the other space to converse without interruption. Whilst it was a definite improvement, Brooke wasn't naive enough to think any of this made for a happy ever after, but it was a start; a pact to be civil, a covenant to get through the week and make amends, whatever the dent to their egos.

She smiled in anticipation of a velvet truffle filling, something nutty or fruity perhaps. Unlike most, Brooke was a big fan of a sweet jellied centre inside a chocolate. What passed her lips though, was the most unimaginable, the most inconceivable thing in the world.

A chocolate-enveloped croissant, in all its flaky and buttery manna, filled with thick and luscious strawberry jam and yet more silky butter. With all eyes upon her, Brooke found she couldn't speak. Meanwhile, Barnaby and Clementine couldn't stop laughing. She guessed her eyes were pretty much telling the story.

"Oh," she simply said. "Are there… would there any more of those, by any chance?"

Ellie shifted uncomfortably in her seat. Evidently she sensed the subtle way the siblings' relationships had changed – and she didn't like it one bit. Well, what had she expected, when she'd talked of personas softening? Brooke was loath to rev up her feelings of hurt and hatred towards her brother and sister, just to reassure Ellie. If their conviviality was a happy side-effect of the spell, she'd seize it with both hands for as long as it lasted. Redefining the state of the company was supposed to be their end goal, after all.

"I guess I'll be the gent for once. Clementine?" Barnaby smiled serenely, fluttering his eyelashes at his youngest sister. Oh, hell, no. That was going a bit overboard.

"Why not, then?" she replied. "Hmm, how do I choose between the last two?"

She closed her eyes and extracted the combed, thoroughly glossy royal icing of the *mille feuille*, complete with its Napoleon pastry. Ellie let out an unsteady sigh which Brooke thought she really ought to be keeping to herself. Thankfully, nobody else noticed.

Clementine took her time to work her way through the *petit four*-style chocolate; a confectionary version of the famous French patisserie.

Brooke's heart began to thud, remembering that everything would be ramping up with this next round. Damn today's country pursuits for making her forget, and tricking her into thinking this was some pretty little chocolate box. She looked to Ellie, who busied herself inspecting her nails.

"Gawjus," Clementine proclaimed. "So very clever, how they can recreate a work of art on such a miniature scale. Must have made the hands twitch, all that precision. And the taste is quite divine."

"Thrilled for you… you are all so *lucky, lucky, lucky*," Ellie began to sing as if she were going to break out into the Kylie Minogue hit – and really she shouldn't, for she wouldn't even make it into a cat's choir.

"Right then, Mr W," said Clementine, in a most unusually amicable fashion. "Off you go!"

But instead of lifting the patiently-waiting chocolate, Barnaby's hasty hand removed the whole upper tray, causing everyone to gasp. Ellie's face was a picture of shock. Brooke guessed hers wasn't much better. Instead of all eyes being drawn to the single deep circular caramel-hued treasure still waiting to be prised out of its mould, they were transfixed instead by the sacred jewels positively gleaming at them from the next layer.

Ellie began to shake. Big mistake. How dodgy this whole thing looked now. It was obvious she'd doctored the delights.

But then Brooke felt her own body start to tremble. Only slightly, and surely not enough for anyone else to notice. Cautiously, she panned the table from left to right and was certain her siblings, in their own imperceptible ways, were doing exactly the same. Everybody could feel it. Everybody refused to let on.

So tonight really was the calm before the storm. This was the warning. They'd thrown the dice, they'd taken their tokens, they'd signed themselves up. Now the game really began.

Barnaby slowly took the first chocolate from the lower tier.

"Looks like it might be crème brûlée," he whispered. "Mmm, tastes like crème brûlée," he added, after a wary bite. "Yum, cheers one and all: to The Really Bad Photo Company… and all who sail in her," he held his half-bitten chocolate in the air as if it were a wine glass.

Ellie turned ghostly white. Was it something he'd said?

24

ELLIE

$\mathcal{W}$ ell, of course she couldn't sleep. Was Barney in on this somehow? But no, Ben was on her side. How couldn't he be? She was overthinking it. That was all. Ellie snatched at her mobile resting on her bedside table, hands shaking as she scrolled through her contacts for Ben's number, finger hovering over the green button. She dithered a beat. Should she? Did she really want to know? She flung the phone down the length of the bedspread and slumped back against her pillow. This was ridiculous. She needed all the energy she could muster for tomorrow.

The surge of alchemy had been palpable. Every one of them had sensed it. Damn Barney for racing ahead like that. She tutted at herself for getting so complacent, for not standing guard better. She should have known what he would do.

Still, at least she had tomorrow's activities in place. A leisurely breakfast at 10am. They needed to tease the morning out with a lie-in, now her ideas were getting thinner on the ground. Then they'd play Chinese whispers at 11am, musical chairs at 12 noon, an early lunch (with a hidden agenda of getting them sleepy), pass the parcel at 2pm, followed by a three hour Introspection Break.

The schedule was childish, half-arsed and feeble, but why overtax her poor brain when they were going along with everything? She might as well retreat to her room and watch Netflix. Jock and Jules' sole TV set was in her fanciful annexe. She'd gotten rather hooked on *The Crown* since her stay. There was much to be gleaned from Princess Margret's rebellion, even if she hadn't any inkling of how lucky she'd been with her large and lustre-filled lot.

That just left Saturday and Sunday.

Slip of the tongue. She meant Saturday and *Fun*day.

BROOKE

*A*10am breakfast? Brooke would say Ellie had to be flagging, but she looked remarkably refreshed this morning. Meanwhile Brooke had played hide and seek with her bags, concealer working overtime to disguise the dark circles around her eyes, after a night of a different game – tug of war with the duvet. She'd been freezing and re-winding her recent past pursuits, her heart aching that soon she'd never see Thierry's beautiful face again.

She cringed at the way she'd lovingly, *possessively* run her fingers across his jawline, as if she'd ever really stood a chance. He'd used her for sex, set her up good and proper and in such a way that could never be claimed indecent, what with his believable sob story, and Brooke brazenly insti-gating things without the slightest encouragement. He'd even concocted a half-plausible excuse for never wearing a shirt.

Tidy, in the spirit of Ness from Gavin and Stacey.

And now Brooke had no choice but to give him an imagi-nary Ness-style high five, tacking on a 'fair play' while she was at it. For she'd loved and she'd lost him already. What else could she do but reacquaint herself with her relationship with Ruben, seeing where the tide took them, sitting it out on an imaginary pew for him to be ready to rock up in a suit to greet her at the end of a petal-strewn aisle? Somewhere and somehow. Actually, the latter wasn't a bad idea. Maybe he'd be more inclined to propose, more open to commitment, if she hinted at a low-key beach wedding in Spain. So that was what her entanglement with Thierry had been about. Self-confidence, go-getting, goal-grabbing. He'd unearthed something within that had forced her out of her comfort zone, made her take risks.

Then that's what she'd continue to do. Go home, count her blessings, make her wishes better known to her boyfriend, and thank God her path had at least crossed with Thierry's, that he'd graced her with an evening of his life.

She pasted on a smile for Barnaby, who finally joined her at the table, Ellie's encroaching clip-clops closing the distance on their peace. Thierry had already prepped their breakfast. There was little to do but enjoy the spread. Barnaby reached for the coffee pot, and the strange dandelion brew which still couldn't match the real deal if it tried. His free hand saluted the fast approaching Ellie. It was the strangest thing, witnessing him acknowledge the HR Manager like this, the obsequious grin on Ellie's lips lingering as she pulled out her seat to join them.

"Morning," Ellie crowed, eyes never leaving Barnaby's. Brooke's stomach turned, reminded again of the recent repulsive find which meant she couldn't bear to witness this kind of scene. She'd suddenly lost her appetite, and no, not just because the most exciting item on the table was linseed and apricot muesli all over again.

"Isn't it? Sun's shining, and TFIF," he replied, tilting the hot, muddy-brown liquid into his cup with one hand, reaching out for the clandestine sugar bowl with the other (at all other times Thierry hid the condiment in his hut), eyes fixed on Ellie, in return, the whole time.

"TFIF? Am I missing something?" she purred.

"I mean TGIF, where are my... *shiiiiit*," Barnaby howled, and Brooke's eyes widened in disbelief. He'd only gone and missed the cup, scorching his hand with a waterfall of dandelion coffee. "M... my manners?" he continued. Ellie continued to look baffled. She reached for the second coffee pot and began to pour her own, in a much more expert, and smug, fashion. Brooke wondered if she hadn't shapeshifted her serving into the infinitely more appetising Colombian caffeinated version.

"He means Thank God It's Friday." Brooke filled in the gaps, stretching across the table for a napkin as Ellie began to slice herself some suspiciously cardboard-looking rye bread.

"*Shiiiiit again*, it stings!" Barnaby hissed, lips pursed, embarrassment flecking his cheeks.

"Kitchen. Now," Brooke rose instinctively, grabbing her brother. "We'll need to run this under the cold tap before it scars."

Reluctantly, her brother did as he was told; it was the first time in years that he'd listened to anything Brooke had to say.

"I should let the air get to it," Ellie simpered, shaking her head. "Worst thing you can do is soak it in water."

"Have you completely lost the plot?" Brooke retorted.

Aha. And then she got it. She wanted him burned and scarred, didn't she? For that, in her warped little head, would presumably help him cave in all the quicker to whatever surprises she had in store regarding the New Ellie Sanchez Method of Business Management. Huh, and the rest. Brooke could see it now; the books she'd try to pen, the podcasts she'd line up to put out. The woman had a hidden agenda, all right. An agenda that ran deeper than any of the supposed cares and concerns about the RBPC. What a bitch to dress punishment up as advice. Brooke might not be a first aider like Ellie, but she was pretty sure her common sense instinct was right: take the heat out of the burn, like *yesterday*.

She dragged Barnaby all the more decisively to the kitchen door. Ellie stood, daring to challenge and defy her.

Which was the precise moment when Clementine finally decided to grace everyone with her presence. Brooke found herself forgetting all about her brother, rubberneck-staring at her sister instead. She looked like she'd been in a fight with a feather pillow, or ousted from a snow globe, or dusted with icing sugar. Scratch that. All three.

"C...can you deal with it yourself, little bro?" she asked him. "I... er... I think my assistance might be required elsewhere."

Wincing at his injury, Barnaby needed little encouragement to run to the kitchen sink to assuage his pain. Ellie was now glued to the spot, eyes transfixed by the same sight that had wrapped Brooke in its hideous grip.

"Clem? Your hair?" Ellie was doing the most abysmal job of hiding the delight in her voice.

"My hair is off limits. Do. Not. Even. Go. There."

"Well it's certainly diff—"

"I said don't."

A pair of razor-sharp eyes squinted, opening wider to glare at Ellie, before Clementine tried unsuccessfully to lose herself in her collar, like one of those terrible depictions of a man with no head, from the wooden films of yesteryear.

A deathly silence fell upon the room.

"What happened?" Brooke whispered, finally breaking all the rules.

"Giorgio at Toni & Guy will sort it. That's all I have to say. Now, does anyone have a baseball cap? Can we make an exception to the no-Internet rule, and express deliver me one?"

This was most unlike Brooke's sister. Clementine would never ask. More to the point, Clementine would never normally emerge from her room with her blonde locks in such a state. Why she hadn't thought to wrap them in a towel, or even in a pair of her knickers, Brooke had no idea.

"No can do, I'm afraid," said Ellie after thoughtfully gnawing on her cardboard bread. "We can't have one rule for one, and one for another. Giant dandruff flakes may not be fun but some poor souls have battled with them for years. Just switch from your designer shampoo to Head and Shoulders when you get back. All easily sorted... after a few months."

Bloody hell.

Brooke was being slower than slow this morning.

Crème brûlée chocolate... resulting in a burnt hand, then the flaky *mille feuille* confection with its many layers, and a sudden onslaught of avalanche-style dandruff; not forgetting a little sister whose vanity had mysteriously vanished in the morning mist.

What was in store for her?

Now she definitely didn't want to see Thierry again. It didn't bear thinking about. But on cue the dining-room door flew open as if it'd been hit by a gust of wind. In he marched, sporting a Made in Paris T-shirt, and a tray of freshly baked croissants, whose intense buttery smell perfumed the entire room. A large pot of homemade strawberry preserve sat beside them, a silver serving spoon peeping enticingly from it.

Where? When? How?

Weren't breakfasts here supposed to be clean-eating and wholesome and organic?

"Bakery delivery," said Thierry, actually bothering to

acknowledge her for the first time in getting on for forty-eight hours. "We always serve fresh croissants on a Friday. Organic, of course. I was too tired after ze market trip to get up and make them early this morning. The village next to Pruneau does ze next best thing."

"I bloody love this guy all of a sudden," Barnaby man-hugged him. He was now sporting a checked tea towel around his wrist. "He's patched me up a treat *and* he's brought us a proper breakfast!"

Hmm, for now, Humpty Dumpty.

Brooke clocked Ellie's floundering facade; her *merci beaucoup* of a smile was downgrading itself to a sour chew of her gum. But Brooke wouldn't let on that she'd spotted this significant chink in her armour, no. Shoulders back, chest puffed out, she successfully ignored the puzzled expression crossing Thierry's face, intercepted the tray and pranced about mollycoddling her siblings with this comfort blanket of a breakfast. The terrifying truth was, she'd no idea if all of Daddy's horses and all of Daddy's men would be powerful enough to put Barnaby back together again by the time Ellie Sanchez – who was now, incidentally, back to gloating, her expressions as wild and chaotic as the story of Brexit – had finished with him.

ELLIE

*E*llie could feel herself beginning to unravel, but frustratingly, she couldn't pinpoint the exact moment it had started. She forced a smile. It would all come good in the end.

It was law, after all.

She'd been relentless with her vision boards, she'd mentally rehearsed the proposal, the wedding, the keys, the blizzards of money. She'd put herself at the centre, catching those crisp banknotes like some diva on Egyptian cotton sheets with a one thousand thread count, rolling in her newfound wealth, engaged in a whole other kind of counting. Except she, unlike them, was entitled.

Law of attraction had processed it all, saving it neatly in its database.

She was made for the rest of her life.

She just had to trust in the universe's timing.

BROOKE

*T*he one small positive Brooke could take from last night was that Thierry was back on speaking terms with her. Finally.

She was far more spooked than she'd thought over the subtle results of their chocolate selections. A bad hair day would hardly kill Clementine, true. Quite the opposite; it'd probably ground her, help her see that others hadn't been gifted with her good looks, that surface flaws were an everyday occurrence, be they expanding waistlines, deeply etched crow's feet… or an unruly scalp. And yet it felt like things were getting too up-close and personal. Turning everything on its head again – gawd, that was apt – how else did Brooke think Ellie's enchantments were ever going to pan out?

Still, twice now Ellie had caused bodily harm to Barnaby. Actual injuries that required treatment.

Brooke had a mainstream mindset when it came to the intangible, and every branch of the mysterious world of the unseen. But she'd tap into the kindergarten-level access she had, in the only way she knew how.

Gut instinct and inspired action.

What choice did she have, when her siblings' lives were so clearly at stake?

ELLIE

*E*llie's elation threatened to deflate like a balloon. She just couldn't see how Barney would fall into her arms. Once again, she was forgetting to let the chocolates, and the spell, do their worst. This morning's evidence alone – after last night's eats – should have told her that the best was blatantly yet to come; she was simply being impatient *again*. As impatient as Brooke had been for instant gratification earlier in the week.

That made her see the funny side once more. For a moment.

She knew something had changed with Brooke. But whatever it was (probably just nerves now they were reaching the grand finale) it wouldn't be serious enough to interfere with Ellie's plans.

Now she'd re-evaluated, she couldn't deny the intricate beauty of the pattern. Neither could *mademoiselle,* with her unexpected gift of jammy croissants from the Hunk.

She needed to up her game on the activities front, though, she realised with a massive sigh. Yesterday's party shenanigans hadn't quite been what you'd call a runaway success.

Chinese whispers had proven that. Even with a handful of players, communication had become preposterously misconstrued. One potent case in point being the curious way that the simple question 'what's on telly?' rejigged itself to 'we've got something on Ellie'. Then again, it had done a dozen rounds.

Speaking of rounds, Clem was the first one out on every orbit of musical chairs; her customary cut-throat conduct, even when playing a simple party game, fading quicker than the daylight from a winter photoshoot in Scotland.

And pass-the-parcel had resulted in some puzzling behaviour from Barney, who insisted upon throwing the conkers she'd stuck between the layers of a 1990's Somerset newspaper (hint, hint) haphazardly into Thierry's garden. Even when he'd won back his Lyme Regis fossil, the star prize at the end of the game, he'd remained as clueless as ever.

"Great. What am I s'posed to do with this lump of crap? Office doorstop? I'll leave it here at the *gîte*. It'll blend in just perfectly with all the hippy-dippy crystals."

Ellie had had to swallow down hard on her frustration. It looked as if none of these props were ever going to jog his memory. Not even offering them on a plate. Bastard. It really bloody piqued. And though Jock's analogy and explanations, whilst sitting on her chaise longue mere days ago, certainly resonated, Ellie wanted the petulant teenage Barney whose spirit lay dormant (presumably *somewhere*) beneath that thick and ignorant skin, to know that she had become someone.

A sparkle.

A Meghan Markle.

Actually, no. That woman had no idea what she was playing at, turning her back on all those riches and entitlement.

Whatever. The point was, she was after recognition. An

admission that he'd been so wrong to pass her by back then as if she were nobody. Absolution from her wallflower status. Something more important than money.

And what she was after today on the team building front was something involving an air of mystique, an element of surprise – without over-stimulating her soldiers' increasingly delicate senses, of course.

What she needed was a miracle. What she needed was Ben. He hadn't returned her last call. She couldn't help but fret there might be a highly unwelcome reason.

A tap at the window distracted her, its sound oddly familiar. It was the African umbrella plant leaf that had interrupted Ellie's daydreams during her week of luxurious wallows in the roll-top bath. It must have somehow broken free from its stem in the bathroom, floated out the open window and swirled through the air, just for Ellie; its mini parachute gracefully gliding past her living-room window, toward the lawn below.

Two hours later and Ellie could barely keep a straight face as Thierry, and a couple of neighbouring farmers, whom she'd dragged away from their fields, held pegged bedsheets aloft to make a 'parachute'. Glastonbury's Arabella Churchill (yes, granddaughter of the one and only Sir Winston) used to come and visit St. Ed's, working with children with special needs in both special and mainstream schools; bringing kids together to play games under a billowing canopy of bold primary colours. Even Eleanor Finch had felt joyous and free in those rare moments, running from side to side; zigzagging, crawling, hopping, skipping; pretending to be a fairy or a troll, high-fiving her classmates when they met in the middle, getting ready to sprint like mad beneath the giant canvas arc should the charity's volunteers shout 'all those wearing spotty socks/sporting a ponytail/crazy for Elastica/mad about an unobtainable boy called Barney: GO NOW!'. Each and every one of her qualms ceased to exist under that magical material, which seemed to take every bad thought away, and make the world a better place.

Unfortunately, you needed a few more hands, and better quality fabric, to recreate the fun and games two decades down the line on the lawn of a tumbledown French *gite*. Ellie had hoped for revelations, swear words, accusations and denial beneath that umbrella of honesty. But not a single outburst greeted her eardrums. Her stubborn little puppets meandered from side to side; Barney with his hands in his chino pockets and a melancholy whistle, Clem dragging her decidedly shorter-than-usual heels, Brooke plodding in her baseball boots.

"Stop!" she'd shouted after half an excruciating hour (and a few crumpled notes to the farmers).

Thierry had teetered on his edge of the parachute to catch Brooke's eye but she was already long gone, and so Ellie too made her way back to her room for another Netflix marathon, with a giant sigh.

She had no idea what the others had been doing with themselves for the rest of the day, and she didn't have the energy to ask them when they gathered at the table a few hours later for a dinner of *coquilles Saint Jacques, marmite dieppoise* and *Teurgoule* (a rice pudding whose density made Ellie worry, with every mouthful her groupies sank, that their stomachs wouldn't handle after-dinner excess, quashing her carefully constructed plans). And then she mentally nudged herself. Self-preservation was paramount in these last few hours.

The back-to-back *Peaky Blinders* episodes she'd watched had been a revelation this afternoon; she had learned much from the Birmingham gang and their antics.

A melancholy Thierry cleared their plates without comment, and, as was now unchallenged ritual, Ellie lifted the makeshift ribbon pendant from beneath her shirt, opening the drawer with her key to pull out the box amidst a backdrop of bated breath.

Barney went first this evening, charmed by an ethereal Egyptian hieroglyphic chocolate; a milk chocolate slab etched with fine white chocolate symbols. Ellie had no idea what they meant, and now she hoped like hell that they wouldn't overpower or neutralise her incantation.

His wolfish appetite had curiously diminished to that of a sparrow, and he pecked at the edges like the bird at first. Finally, unable to resist the lure of the satin-finished chunk, he reverted to type and gulped the rest down in one go, without it even touching the sides.

Clem went next, not even waiting for his critique, teasing out a plump white chocolate tinged with a marmalade blush. She was about to go in for the kill when a knock at the door interrupted her.

"I am so sorry for my intrusion," said Thierry, hands behind his ruler-straight back, and rendering him almost penguin-like, thanks to today's black, white and yellow ensemble. "It's just I 'ave found this in ze post box. The stamp says it is from England." Slowly he pulled a letter out from behind him, as if he were a magician. Ellie did everything to avoid looking at Brooke, pulse racing at the implications. "It's for you, Monsieur Westwood." Wow to that, and wow to her skills. She should never have doubted herself. The speed of the spell had certainly picked up in the last twenty-four hours. Everything was going to plan.

Barney squirmed in his seat as Thierry handed him the mail. "Erm, thank you, I think."

"*De rien*," Thierry replied, turning on his heel and firmly shutting the adjoining kitchen door as Barney used the end of his dandelion coffee spoon to gingerly tear open the seal of the envelope.

"May I? Or would it be a *faux pas*?" Clem drawled to nobody in particular, clearly gagging to try the chocolate she was still holding centimetres away from her lips.

"*Mais oui*," Ellie smiled encouragingly, desperate to get this evening over, to find out what was in store now for Barney and the girls, so she could retreat for a much-needed smoke and a stiff drink on the chaise, decoding what all of this meant for the final day, and the final chocolates.

"Shit." Barney's voice sounded pained, his eyes becoming glassy. He gulped, then scanned the rest of the letter like a cartoon character, eyes pinging this way and that. Ellie bit her knuckle to hold back her laughter. "No way, man. This can't be true." He shook his head pitifully now. "Oh, my heart." Barney placed his right hand over the left side of his chest and exhaled deeply. "'*I've met someone else*,'" he read out loud. "'Which has regrettably led me to realise you're not the One, after all, Dearest Barnababy…'"

Mwahaha, that's because I am, thought Ellie, battling to mask her complacent grin, as Barnaby went on reading.

"'Deeply sorry for breaking it to you like this, but what with the social media ban…'"

"Oh, Barnaby," Brooke looked a strange blend of sad and petrified. "Surely you could have made some allowances, Ellie?" She addressed the latter to the middle of the table, not daring to meet Ellie's eyes.

"Rules are rules, Brooke," Ellie threw Good Cop her Bad Cop glare. "We all made sacrifices to be here. Anyway, whether she contacted him via WhatsApp, or a pigeon delivered the message, I'm sure it wouldn't read any differently."

But even as she said it, Ellie battled to keep her delight in check, forcing a sympathetic expression on her face.

"Just like that, Saffy decides it's over," Barney pined. "I don't get it. She seemed more attuned to me than all the rest. I... I genuinely thought we had a future together. The sex was great." He stared vacantly into space.

"Maybe it's for the best, if she called you 'Barnababy,' though? Just saying." Ellie knew she should butt out, but if that was honestly his pet name, well, how could she resist? Who in their right mind would entertain that, through fifty-odd years of marriage? Plus everybody could see the tart was only putting on a performance in the sack to get to his wallet. Ellie would show him some real moves.

Barney's face fell, and with the realisation this piece of news was hitting him harder than she'd expected, begrudgingly, so did Ellie's heart. Yeah, she did have one. On ice. Despite all the promises she had made herself that she wasn't head over heels in love with him.

"Shit.... this is *soooooooo* good that I feel utterly terrible the rest of you are missing out," said Clem, not even registering the dilemma, eyes harpooned on the remnants of the little nugget of luxury at her fingertips, adrift in a saccharine world of her own.

"I'm sorry, I'm being Mr. Selfish here, bringing everybody else down with me and totally spoiling your moment," Barney whispered.

What a flipping softie! Ellie had definitely been right to wait before she made her move. Going on his current rate of macho decline, tomorrow night would be the night, though! Why, she'd reel him in with not much more than a fake, but tasteful, eyelash flutter.

"Oh, that was so very uncouth of me." Clem buried her

head in her hands. "My poor just-a-bit-bigger-than-me bro," her lips quivered, and Ellie was convinced the daft mare would set Barney and Brooke off crying; that she'd have to dab at her own eyes with a tissue in moral support.

"Well," said Barney, "I think I might just take this to my room," he waved the letter solemnly, "and have an early night. It's all been a bit of a shock really. Last thing I'd expected. She told me she loved me last—"

Wait, what? Was that flatulence?

Ingenious!

And so fast... then that had to be a peaches and cream centre in Clem's chocolate? Ha, and super concentrated peaches, Ellie would bet. That bitch of a schoolgirl had really let rip.

"I wouldn't worry, Clem. Even the Queen farts, after all – just maybe not at the dinner table," said Ellie sarcastically.

Pop-pop-puff.

There she went again. Ellie turned to Brooke, this time with a pointed look she hoped would translate as make-your-selection-quickly-and-scoff-it-before-the-stench-puts-you-off-food-forever-this-could-get-gas-mask-bad.

Obediently, Brooke picked out the coffee bean, which Ellie was sure would be as safe as a bog standard cup of Nescafé. Brooke made short work of it, declaring its blend most harmonious on the tongue, trying her best to ignore the pollutant that was continuing to taint everybody's oxygen supply.

Damn it all though, thought Ellie. They still hadn't joined the dots. Not with regard to her identity – no, she'd long since given up hope there. But this series of outlandish events was instantaneous, in-the-moment stuff, for fuck's sake. It wasn't exactly rocket science to make the correlation. Their cluelessness was the most curious thing of all.

"Er, before I retire to my room, I have a small confession

to make," Barney announced. "It's going to sound random but Saffy's honesty has triggered something deep within me. Brooke," he turned to his sister, whose face had gone chalk-white. "It was me who wrecked your Pisa photoshoot five years ago."

An awkward and very lengthy silence enveloped the room. Clem was the first to break it with another loud and rather windy outbreak, fidgeting in her chair, biting her lip.

"You what?" Brooke spat, adding on a series of rapid blinks for good measure. "You mean to tell me it was *you* who rounded up those idiotic teens and their flash mob dance?" Barney hung his head sheepishly, genuine sorrow creasing his features. "You let those blithering idiots cost me, cost us – in case you'd forgotten this is a family business... the entire Tuscany travel range being pulled from a massive chain of souvenir shops?" She stopped then, staggered as the realisation hit home. "We're talking over one hundred thousand euros' worth of business down the drain, Barnaby! How could you? Well, I've heard it all now. Is it any wonder we're in this mess, holed up in this godforsaken place?"

Shit, evidently it had been a biggie. But wait, what (again)? There was no need to sound ungrateful, when an HR Heroine was doing her utmost to save the day. And how did this admission have anything to do with...? Aha, yes, Italia, home of the coffee bean. Nice one, Universe. Neatly played, not too harsh (in Ellie's humble opinion) and not too suspicious either.

"Care to fill those of us who weren't there in?" Ellie pushed.

"Not really," Brooke snapped. "But now we're on the subject which he's got the cheek to be so damned casual about, he can do the honours."

"I'm sorry..." Barnaby started.

Brooke raised her hand.

"Save your grovelling for whatever went pear-shaped between you and Saffy, and *tell her*," Brooke pointed a trembling finger in Ellie's direction, face now ruby-red with rage.

"Well, I, er... totally and utterly screwed up her, ahem photoshoot in Italy, that would be, at the leaning tower of Pisa to be precise," he said as if auditioning to play Hugh Grant in a rom com. "And on purpose, I hasten to add," he sighed. "I don't know why... I knew it was wrong... I just thought it'd be fun to get drunk, the day Brooke was giving me grief over the swear word merchandise, that's all." Ellie sensed she should already know about this particular company offshoot, had she bothered to read some of the things Brooke had written this week during their team building exercises. She also sensed Brooke's hackles rising to skyscraper height. "Then I, ahem," Barney stopped to clear his throat. "Then I called-up-my-friend-who-just-so-happens-to-run-a stage-school-in-Florence-and-he-got-a-bunch-of-bratty-teenagers-to-ruin-her-carefully-curated-plans-with-an-impromptu-flash-mob-dance," he blurted out.

Brooke glared. Evidently that analysis didn't cut it: "I can't believe you'd stoop so low! All the explanations to those businesses you watched me suffer through on my own, trying to protect our arses."

"I said I'm sorry, okay. I can't seem to do anything right." Barney stumbled to the hallway door as if inebriated all over again, gripping its frame. Brooke opened her mouth to volley another torrent of abuse, but he spoke first, arms thrust wide open, like Don Giovanni. "She's the first girl I felt like settling down with, if you must know. At this rate I'll be left on the shelf."

Not for much longer, chéri. The best things really do come to those who wait.

Ellie Sanchez licked her lips.

29

BROOKE

*B*rooke was still seething about last night but she was also smart enough to know she had to switch off now, stand back, and watch herself go through this ridiculous journey from afar, as if she were on a film reel. It was the only way, until Sunday. Once again she ignored the sinking feeling surrounding that one part sad, two parts shit-scary day of the week. Surely nothing could get worse than whatever Saturday night had up its sleeve? Pretty much all the chocolates would be eaten by then; it was unlikely that Ellie would want anything too theatrical playing out on Sunday. They had a ferry to catch at a faraway port, meaning everything just had to be neatly resolved so they could move on, literally and metaphorically.

Changing the subject briskly, though, why should she be surprised about Barnaby's foul play? She'd seriously let the improvements in their relationship cloud her vision. And yet she couldn't help but feel torn in two, just like she could see his heart was: he'd lost the potential love of his life, who had broken the news in such an insensitive way. Side note to that: Brooke couldn't help but wonder what would have happened if she herself had chosen the scroll chocolate? How would she have reacted to something similarly shocking penned by Ruben? Meanwhile, her brother had been so blasé about messing up her hard work. The Tuscan shoot had taken aeons to get right, thanks to the headache photographers – amateur and pro alike – are faced with when trying to come up with an avant-garde way of supporting the leaning tower via their subjects' anatomies.

Everybody had kept to their own devices on Saturday morning. That had definitely been for the best, with all the dust that needed to settle – and sweep itself under the carpet. And then on Saturday afternoon Ellie announced the very last team-building activity of the week; the one that would supposedly help her create her 'masterplan,' which she intended to implement the moment they set foot on English soil.

Pray tell, what was this brainiac task?

Apple bobbing.

Brooke only wished she were joking. Brooke only wished she hadn't rubbernecked, slack-jawed and astounded, when Ellie took a worryingly large amount of time passing a gargantuan cider apple beneath her chin to Barnaby. Giggling, flirting, fake eyelash-fluttering. Yes, her sharp cerulean eyes were adorned with Admiral butterflies today. Meanwhile, Barnaby had made a remarkable recovery from last night's heartache, and was positively egging the woman on in an unchecked display that made Brooke positively want to vomit.

She'd spotted Thierry watching her wistfully from afar, peering over the hedge before he went back to his hut. Just how many women from the *gîte*'s retreats had he wined and dined in there? That's what Brooke would like to know. Part of her would also like to march back up to his front door for a second helping, but no way would she give him the satisfaction. Those croissants might have felt like peace offerings from him, and admittedly, they had been very tasty, but all Brooke felt was a fool. Used and bruised. The latter figuratively, for a more tender lover she'd never had in her bed.

Apple bobbing preceded pin-the-tail-on-the-donkey. At which point, Brooke publicly declared Ellie unfit to host a children's tea party. She couldn't help it. The donkey looked more like a cow, the blindfolds were see-through, the pin was a rusty nail, and the targets all neatly hit the 'bull's eye' *à la* Michael van Gerwen, resulting in nothing but underwhelm.

Ridiculous didn't even do the scene justice. Brooke was beginning to lose her sense of reality, perspective and truth, all of which had to be a side effect of the spell. But when the same was evidently happening to those around her, it made for one confusing mix.

Then there was Thierry's oddball hot-and-cold behaviour toward her, which had warmed up several degrees by dinner time, and they were only on the starters – peach and goat's cheese tartine (poor old Clementine), which he had arranged in a sweet little heart shape. On Brooke's plate only. All right, then.

And by the time they'd reached dessert, Thierry'd seemingly reached the point of no return in the creativity stakes, somehow. She couldn't even imagine how painstaking or time-consuming his efforts had been, getting the fruit-puréed words *'retrouvez-moi chez moi ce soir'* to appear, once she'd cut into her serving of lemon and raspberry savarin. It was as if they'd been pulled through one of those machines used for making Blackpool rock. Swiftly, she'd hidden his request from potentially beady eyes, inelegantly mashing it up with her fork and gobbling the battered words down before anybody saw her dirty secret. Did she really have desperate written all over her face? The guy had ignored her for the past couple of days. He had probably hacked into the computer system to check out the profiles of next week's retreat guests, realised they were all male/over a certain age/more inclined to get excited over incense, crystals, and hemp than a hot chef, and decided to be grateful for this week's offerings while he could get some.

Well, he could bloody well forget it. She refused to play *pret à porter* again.

Brooke went first this evening, once Ellie was done with her lock and key rigamarole, placing the somewhat lighter box onto the table, a sea of expectation awaiting it. She was grateful for the small mercy of first dibs; couldn't deal with any more exposés of the you've-been-totally-and-utterly-duped kind. Brooke already knew she was naive, it was quite unnecessary for the chocolates to bring her another reminder. And so she chose the star, hoping its wisdom might point her due north – or wherever she was meant to be. Once she worked her way nimbly through the thick outer layer of white chocolate and lemon-infused bliss, she was rewarded with a taste of the richest, gooiest, custardy almond *petit four* cake. In other words, thank goodness she was a marzipan fan. In other words, she had no words to aptly describe it.

Mercifully, after she'd taken her last bite, there was nothing immediate to report. No shooting stars outside the window, no telescope hand-delivered by a starry-eyed Thierry.

Phew.

Clementine's antennae, reliably as ever, tuned into the heart chocolate. And it did look more than good enough to eat, but Brooke had left it. Something had told her it was too obvious a choice, especially after Thierry's culinary attempts to woo her so he could add another notch to his bedpost – well, battered sofa. She'd hoped Barnaby would have his heart miraculously healed if he went for it – an act that would have been miraculous in itself, no matter how in tune with his emotions he'd recently become.

Clementine closed her eyes in preparation for her first nibble, breaking the incessant chatter chasing its tail in Brooke's head. Well now, surely Archie would propose to her younger sister? Gosh, she would need to buy a hat. She didn't really suit hats.

Hold your horses, Brooke, and tether them to the gatepost while you're at it.

This was Ellie's game. Ellie's thoroughly wicked game. There wouldn't be any of those sort of happily-ever-afters, Brooke realised and her shoulders sagged further still when it dawned on her that she could always have opted for one of those elegant fascinators.

Speaking of horses, though, wasn't that the sound of an encroaching gallop?

"What's that?" Clementine asked, still, and rather rudely, sucking out the rich ganache centre of her chocolate. The noise, barely audible at first, continued to grow louder and louder in the background.

Thud-thud-thud-thud.

"Woooooo," simpered Ellie, in a rather cruddy attempt at something Halloween-y. "It must be the ghost of a horse from the days when the *gîte* was a farm."

"Okay, that's quite enough. I am totally freaked out now," Barnaby's eyes took on a wild and panicked look, he was even gripping the table, panning the vista from left to right. So freakishly out of character. Why, it was he who'd not long so long ago dragged them all to the London Dungeon when Ellie had suggested a sightseeing company reward trip to the Big Smoke... and then randomly left them all to it, heading off for lunch.

But this wasn't a horse, much less a ghost. Brooke had

already done the math. There was only one sound that replicated a filly and its rapid gallop. She looked to her sister but Clementine refused to hold Brooke's gaze, arms folded resolutely across her chest, head assessing the weird batik drape that adorned the wall. Pft, as if her younger sister would ever be interested in trading in her Marbella villa-themed interiors back home for one of those.

Puzzled, Barnaby stood and began to pace the dining-room, as if looking for a set of previously hidden speakers, and indeed, that's what had crossed Brooke's mind, too; perhaps some sound system was playing, magically rigged up by the meddling Ms. Sanchez. Gradually, the volume softened into nothingness and, apparently satisfied, Barnaby returned to his chair at the table, as if none of it had even happened.

"Looks like it's my go, then," he grinned.

"Sure is," Ellie massaged her knuckles in readiness. Why did Brooke get the feeling this wasn't exactly going to be the smartest move of her brother's life?

"Hmm," he rubbed at his chin. "This tree-shaped thing is calling me, for some inexplicable reason."

"Must have your name on it," Ellie smiled encouragingly, cocking her eyebrow.

Tentatively (for Barnaby), he grasped it between finger and thumb, easing it out of the tray.

"I do hope it's not a cherry tree," he stared at it, inspecting it every which way.

Brooke hoped not too, for the leaves from one of those would likely poison him, although she couldn't deny its outward appearance did make one think of an eighties Fisher Price toy tree house, so hopefully it was an oak. Before she could look to Ellie for a smidgen of reassurance, he'd shovelled the chocolate into his mouth, biting it off at the top of its little trunk.

Everyone braced themselves for Barnaby's verdict. Even Clementine was finally back in their presence, at least physically. There was still something remarkably faraway about her usually sparkly eyes.

"Best chocolate ever!" he finally declared, his face painted with a massive clown grin. "Like something from Willy Wonka's factory, actually." A succession of fidgets and bottom wriggles came from the direction of Ellie's seat. "Man, that is insane!" His eyes widened to such an extent that Brooke wondered if the centre had been injected with narcotics.

"It looked pink inside?" said Ellie. "From what I could see of it, anyway."

"That's because it was candy floss!" Barnaby laughed. "Melt in the mouth, moreish candy floss… inside a chocolate. Mind-blowing, right? I tell you what, Els, we really must visit this chocolatier on the way back, stock up on supplies for the office. Cadbury's will never have the same appeal again."

"Ah, bad luck, my friend. Tomorrow's Sunday. Chocolatiers France-wide will be *fermés*," she pulled a rather spiteful grin, but he failed to register, eyes closed, revelling in the aftertaste of bliss.

It was up there with one of the most unearthly and haunting moments of Brooke's life, but suddenly, as if they had been touch paper, waiting all along for a match, a pair of speakers finally made themselves known, descending gracefully through the ceiling from two air vents at opposite sides of the room.

Barnaby, now fully present, began to shake, bringing his hands to his mouth in the most curious way, putting Brooke in mind of an over-excitable hamster about to devour its haul. Brooke wrapped her arms tightly around herself, Clem sat open-mouthed, unable to process the hows and the whys. Ellie simply proffered a tiny beam, as if she'd seen this sort of thing so many times before in all her other HR guises. Brooke's foot was close enough to kick her hard in the shin; that soon induced a more likely reaction: another jaw scraping the floor in disbelief.

Mesmerised by the *gîte*'s hidden techie side, nobody stirred from the edge of their seats, all waiting for what would happen next. An outburst of piped, and very jolly, fairground music started to play, reminiscent of carousels and horses, toffee apples and more candy floss. Ohemgee, CANDY FLOSS. Dodgems and penny arcades, loop-the-looping roller coasters, coloured rock, and roaring waves.

Realisation flashed across Barnaby's face and he broke down in immediate and uncontrollable tears. Ugly tears. At which point, the music grew rowdier and faster.

"Nan?" he snivelled, peeping between the fingers he'd now plastered to his face.

"Wh… who are you talking to? Nan's not… course she's not here," Clementine's voice warbled, her breathing uneasy. "Barnaby, you're scaring me, you're scaring all of us. How can Nan be here?"

Brooke wasn't sure what she found the most hair-raising: Barnaby apparently talking to their grandmother's ghost, or that hideously frenetic music? She thought she might pass out. This was like something out of a Hitchcock movie. The music became tinny and warped now, playing faster and faster. She took some deep breaths and reached for her water glass with clammy hands in a bid to stop feeling like a spinning top. She didn't dare look at Ellie.

"It's a sign. She knows," Barnaby wailed.

"Knows wh… what, exactly?" Clementine was trying her best to stay level-headed. Brooke had to hand it to her. She herself couldn't string together a sentence. The shock of the surreal had turned everything, including her body and its reflexes, to the precise consistency of candy floss.

"It... w-w... was... it was the day she pissed me off on the pier." Oh, dear God, not yesterday's theme regurgitating itself all over again; the boy certainly had a penchant for recycling that tried and tested, masochistic bullshit. "I was happy as I was... in my element, and pl... playing on the penny slots," Brooke hated hearing him stutter like this, his teeth chattering away in a weird primeval sort of protection mechanism put to better use if one was being pursued by a woolly mammoth. "And she kept grabbing at me, trying to p...pick fl...fluff off my clothes. I got so fed up with it. Embarrassed me, she did. I was at that age when all I wanted to be was c... cool."

Brooke wasn't sure anything had really changed in that respect. She swallowed hard, unable to process what all of this was building up to.

"You... it wasn't... you couldn't possibly have," Brooke managed a whisper, fervently shaking her head. "You were only a child, Barnaby. Don't do this to yourself."

"How long have you been harbouring these thoughts, bro?" Clementine's concern cut through, eyes narrowed, as if Barnaby might be taking the blame for another, covering the real perpetrator's arse. Ha, in any normal situation, Clementine would have been the first to cling onto these little breadcrumbs of blackmail.

"Let him speak, girls! Let the guy bloody speak," trumpeted Ellie, the voice of authority.

"Ellie's right," said Barnaby. Brooke could feel the woman's self-satisfied smile light up the room at that. "I really do need to get this off my chest. Here and now. In this room."

Brooke gulped, heart pounding as she took in her mirror image via Clementine.

"Look, it wasn't exactly int... intentional, but I sort of b... b... budged her out of the way. *I'd had enough, Nan, what did you expect?*" Barnaby looked upward, eyes pleading for mercy, as if Rene Westwood's spirit were hovering along the wooden beams, awaiting this confession and overdue apology for her tragic and untimely death. It sent shivers down Brooke's spine.

"First she'd done it in the morning, *you'd done it in the morning, Nan,*" he added with a desperate shriek. "Pulling me along by the fricking hood when we were choosing pick 'n' mix sweets in Woolworths," he shook his head at the memory.

"That was her trump card, wasn't it? She had this thing about making me feel like I was in the way of the other shoppers. Huh, if she had her way, I'd still be a toddler on those reins. Well, I saw red when she was up to her tricks again on the pier as we walked back to the seafront, slowing me down again to attack the invisible fluff on my clothes... next thing I knew she'd top... she'd t...t... toppled," he closed his eyes as if to forget. "After I barged into her. She lost her balance. Literally fell into, and swung over, the railing. Nobody saw. I... I didn't tell anyone. I should have, I know. It was wrong. So very, very wrong. But I just kept running and running, never turning back, more concerned about playing with the other kids I'd bumped into from our holiday camp. You two girls were still in the arcade at that point, flirting with some tweenage loser or other. See, she'd leave you to your own devices!" he screeched. "Ridiculous, when Brooke was barely in double figures herself. But she was always making the beeline to fuss over me. *Sorry, Nan, but it's true... and you know it.*"

Now he placed his hands together as if about to pray. Brooke willed herself not to look back at the ceiling, although at least the vicious fanfare had calmed the heck down. "Later, when Mum and Dad returned to look for her, when they couldn't keep fobbing us worried kids off with saying she'd got side-tracked trying to win a cuddly toy with one of those grabber machines, Dad spotted her handbag. Unbelievable really, how it was still there, untouched, standing at the pier's edge. There was no CCTV back then."

Barnaby sunk his head in his hands and began to shake again. The music stopped abruptly.

"I killed her. I killed my nan," he mumbled between his sobs.

"No. There's no way. You'd have been all of seven or eight years old. I'm not buying it, Barnaby. Neither is Brooke... well?" Clementine insisted. "Are you, Brooke?"

"A... absolutely not. I'm sure you're er... it's probably just your memory trying to piece things together, fabricating st... stories to come up with a solution, just as you would in everyday business. A trait that's been ingrained in you since an early age. That's, er... all."

Brooke's tongue told him what he needed to hear, but she wasn't so sure her head was in agreement. She almost felt relief when there was an abrupt knock at the door.

Thierry. Great.

With any luck he only wanted to check what all the commotion was about.

But luck didn't seem to be on Brooke's side this week.

Thierry, looking hotter than ever tonight, crossed the room, walked around the back of the giant dining table, and presented Brooke with a strange little see-through bag; a strange little see-through bag, whose lacy contents couldn't have been more prominently displayed. The utter swine! Talk about the height of embarrassment. How could he do this to her? As if his ignoring her in recent days hadn't been torture enough.

"You left zees the other night," he winked, sauntering off before Brooke could form a syllable, let alone a word. She shoved the bag under her seat and twiddled her thumbs.

Clementine shot her a disgusted look; a bit rich coming from one so thoroughly versed in foul play. Barnaby barely noticed the commotion, lines of worry etched deep on his forehead, tears continuing to stream down his cheeks. Ellie smirked, knowingly.

But Brooke swore she'd completely dressed herself before leaving his hut the other morning! Why hadn't he returned her undies before? Oh, don't tell her... he would have, had she chosen the star-shaped chocolate yesterday, whose celestial body they were supposed to be studying through the telescope, instead of making shapes with bodies of their own. And now Ellie's hexing was having its wicked way with Thierry, too?

N'ah ah. Enough was enough.

As soon as Ellie gave them the go-ahead to leave the table, as soon as two sisters had supported their wilting brother, helping him make the long climb upstairs to his bed, Brooke locked herself in her room. She no longer believed Plan A was her (and their) only course of action. *Think D of E to get to B, Brooke. Think cubs, scouts, Girl Guides, and Brownies, all rolled into one. You need a back-up. Failsafe, ideally. Even if it does feel like the most off-the-wall Plan B in the world. A headtorch, Kendal mint cake, and a compass won't work this time.*

A small smile made its way lazily across her lips, until it morphed into a decisive nod. Letters were good, but they were even better when they formed words.

Better still when they came with pictures.

Yes, that was her answer.

All she needed was a little faith. Her intentions were pure enough to make it possible.

But first she needed to have some quite different words. And definitely not in person. Brooke picked up the phone, the welcome burst of confidence flooding her veins.

"You just couldn't resist, could you? Don't you think

you've wreaked enough havoc tonight? Thanks a bunch for ruining my relationship with Rubes, as well as, erm… making my little brother think he's a criminal worthy of Wormwood Scrubs."

"Whatever do you mean, Brooke?" Ellie replied on their crackly line, which failed to hide the woman's conceit. "I'm inadvertently doing you a favour. I should think a bit of gratitude is in order, *mon amie*! You'd never have had the gumption to end things yourself. Your relationship with Ruben, if that's how you'd describe it – he who has never been spotted in public with you – is headed down a dead end dirt track. Thierry, on the other hand, seems more than happy to let everyone know about your acquaintance…"

"Go to hell! I do not require your Tinder services."

"Ooh, mind what you say, now. There's power in words."

There it was. Carte blanche. *Merci beaucoup*. Brooke would take that as all the Plan B sign she needed.

"You're soulmates, Brooke. Absolutely made for one another, can't you see?"

No, she couldn't see that. She couldn't see it at all. The only thing she could see was that her life was one hundred times the disaster it had been at the start of the week, her brother was now framing himself as an under-age murderer, and there was no time to lose in setting about changing it all.

The only other things she could see were a pad of paper and a pencil. Calmly, she put down the phone on her unsolicited relationship counsellor and her relentless trail of advice, and began to sketch.

30

ELLIE

*E*llie was positively dazzled. "Would you just look at those results!" She voiced her thoughts aloud, hardly caring if she had nobody to share them with. Even the filing cabinet in her head was silent nowadays. How she wished Gloria could see her at this monumental turning point in her life. Damn, she'd be so proud. It really wouldn't be long now before jangling fancy-pants house and holiday villa keys entangled themselves in Ellie's handbag, and Louboutin became the new black.

But she couldn't get complacent. Yesterday's results might prove she was on track, yet still there remained six chocolates to go. She'd sensed Brooke's surprise that they hadn't been divvied up last night and chowed down in a Saturday night frenzy. Indeed, that had been her initial plan; to get them all high as kites on the curse, to knock on Barney's door, check on his various wounds, and then add another to his inventory – love sickness. It would be an affliction as sure as the sunrise, when they woke up wrapped in each other's arms, and he realised the true love of his life had been under his nose all this time.

Patience had been a learning curve and a half for Ellie these past few days, but the French country air had obviously done her some good, and she could only pat herself on the back for her stellar efforts.

Back to business, though. Who would choose what? And what, more to the point, would happen next? Certainly things would get wackier, and in such a way that the away-with-the-faeries Westwoods wouldn't question any of it; in such a way that the pathway to Ellie's fantastical future would illuminate itself loud and clear. Once again, she'd have to leave the intricacies to the universe, which was doing an admirable job so far.

Ellie screwed her eyes tightly shut and imagined the box was sitting in front of her.

First there was the salted caramel chocolate square. She knew from childhood memory, and her token nibble, that it was one of Monsieur Robert's signatures. The plain Jane design hadn't changed a bit, meaning it had Brooke's name written all over it.

Next Ellie hopped on a few more spaces in her mind's eye to the volcano-shaped offering. She had no idea what was inside that one but it spoke of fireworks. Dare she wager that it might be laced with a little chili pepper? Of course, the wonderful thing about being a chocolatier must be the artistic license it gave one to throw a surprise. Maybe a molten chocolate lava eruption of hot chocolate chili was too obvious an assumption to make? Perhaps this one oozed liquid honey, that made one frolic around the room *à la* Winnie The Pooh? Hehe, it wouldn't harm to make a little video clip of Barney or Clem doing that. The perfect ammunition for future blackmailing purposes.

The dagger, on the other hand, now that was contentious. Ellie would have to take a deep and steadying breath while they waited for the outcome of that chocolate and its lethal point – in both senses of the word.

The compass could be interesting though. All those directions. All those potential twists and turns. Would she be privy to another of Barney's confessions of corruption? Would Clem and Brooke turn on Ellie and Barney and walk out of the *gîte*, leaving them to their own devices? Now that was a notion to consider. Ellie would enjoy indulging in a montage of movie reels of her and Barney in cosy solitude as she slipped off to the land of nod tonight.

Reluctantly, she carried on with her assessment. She wasn't sure what she made of the random chocolate finger shape. It screamed ditchwater dullness, something thrown into the box as an afterthought to plug the gaps. Which meant Brooke was certain to opt for it.

And what to say about the feather? Its beauty was incontestable. It stood out from the rest of the box, as far as Ellie was concerned, something magical and ethereal that just couldn't be adequately expressed. In other words, it would probably be wasted on Clem who was going to want it.

Finally, her thoughts came to rest on the tempting letter T. A wolf in sheep's clothing, Ellie suspected. Somehow it sounded like the most trouble out of all of them put together. Somehow it sounded like the letter of her destiny.

BROOKE

*T*en and a half hours after bolting her door for the first time, opening and shutting it through clenched teeth and lack of options, and finally barricading it resolutely with a chair, Brooke emerged into the *gite*'s corridor to make her way downstairs for the last breakfast, tired but hopeful. Shock reverberated through her body when she realised she was the last to arrive. She had the hideous thought rewinding and replaying most unhelpfully in her head, that all this was an elaborate design to kick her out of the company. Until she took proper stock of the scene set before her.

Everybody looked plain weary, utterly frazzled and thoroughly distrustful of one another. Eyes were unable to settle, unwilling to focus, unprepared to engage in communication. Everybody's eyes, that was, except for Ellie Sanchez's gleaming sapphires, framed beneath an ever-lengthier pair of fake eyelashes, which would make the car sun visor's job redundant on their midday journey back to the port. Somehow, that made the air feel even thicker with suspicion.

Nobody had any idea what to think or how to react anymore, yet nobody had the strength to walk away either.

Breakfast dragged on for longer than was necessary, and Brooke began to panic all over again, mentally attempting to calculate the time it had taken them to drive from Calais to the *gîte* last weekend, building in time to finish packing – and scoffing Thierry's (it had to be said) decadent *pains aux chocolat*.

But then Clementine looked up, as if sensing her sister's concerns, and offered Brooke the merest hint of a smile, her eyes almost apologetic for what was to come, yet somehow full of something else Brooke couldn't quite put her finger on: promise, trust and resolution?

She felt her shoulders start to relax, but she wouldn't let it show. Too much was resting on the next couple of hours. Everything was.

Moments later and she was sure that Barnaby had foot-sied her beneath the table in a supposed act of solidarity, too. Yuck, but at the same time it was undeniably reassuring – at least until Ellie did the same, throwing Brooke back into a headspin of conflicting thoughts and theories. Once again, nothing and no-one made sense.

She exhaled deeply, treated herself to another pastry for sustenance and topped up her dandelion coffee cup. She was loath to say it, but it wasn't quite as bad as she'd made out at the beginning of the week. Nevertheless, the only romance she was hoping to rekindle after the shenanigans of this trip was with her Lavazza coffee machine – like the exact moment she re-entered her apartment; hugging it tightly and never letting go.

Ellie cleared her throat, forcing Brooke to emerge abruptly from her pleasant *hygge* daydream, back to the hideous predicament that lay ahead. Quite literally, now.

Ellie nudged the last six chocolates toward the centre of the table, pushing herself back into her seat in a move that might have worked slightly better in a chair with wheels. She folded her arms and a surly grin took over her face, once she was certain that Barnaby and Clementine were fully aware of the chocolates.

"It's a bit early, really," Brooke chanced, heart thudding. Not that she thought it would be a particularly smart idea to save the chocolates for the car journey, but maybe they could convince Ellie to keep them for the monotony of the ferry crossing, and then deftly throw them overboard. Poor seagulls, though. Maybe not.

"Rubbish. There couldn't be a more perfect way to start the day, Brooke; a little Sunday treat," Ellie countered, adding a wink. "Plus, all the calories will be burnt off by teatime. Breakfast like a king, as they say."

"Personally, I can't wait to get this party started," Barnaby rubbed his hands together in glee. "Now then, I've been wondering about this unassuming little square ever since we broke into the bottom layer – well, not for much longer," he chuckled, throwing the chocolate into the air as if it were a piece of popcorn, cowering slightly under its impact when the hard corner hit his tongue, and then scrabbling to regain some semblance of cool. He stuck up both thumbs and chewed appreciatively. Not for the first time, Brooke wondered how he could have moved so swiftly on from both his admission of murder, and his broken heart over Saffy. This wasn't normal. Sure, her brother had never been the definition of that. But his behaviour these past forty-eight hours was increasingly freaking her out.

"S'good," he managed to convey some dribbly words to his audience. "S'pretty good."

"Monsieur Robert's salted chocolate caramel square," said Ellie. "The very guilty pleasure he started out with. Award-winning, loved by the French nationwide, and allegedly inspired by a secret recipe that was a favourite of Marie Antoinette."

What utter bollocks. Ellie was so fabricating that last bit.

"I'm not surprised to hear any of that, Els," Brooke winced as her brother shortened the wicked woman's name. She could sense this was a sobriquet Ellie hated, and one that Barnaby had increasingly been taking liberties with.

The remaining chocolates glinted menacingly.

Yet Brooke felt a warm, buzzing sensation take over her body. It wasn't dissimilar to the feeling she got when she occasionally gave meditation a go, and it seemed to be coaxing her towards the feather. Its structure looked deceptively fragile. She was worried at first that she might break it before it made it to her mouth. Yet nothing ventured, nothing gained. Surely she was the right person to take it on? Particularly as none of the other shapes spoke to her. She looked to Clementine, silently berating herself that she was once again back to waiting for her younger sister's approval, but the girl was miles away. So, keen to wrap things up so she could put this hellish week and its temptations behind her, Brooke trusted her instinct, carefully toying with the chocolate and its wispy edges, until it was resting in the palm of her hand.

Here goes nothing.

She opened her mouth and immediately revelled in the sensation of satin rippling across her taste buds, as the milk chocolate melted in a pool of lusciousness. It flooded her senses with endorphins to rival even the most rambunctious romp beneath the sheets. This one didn't have a filling. With its hint of rum, it didn't need it.

"I take it you approve?" Ellie queried, putting the dampest of squibs on her momentary bliss.

"Pass me the sugar, sis," Barnaby was utterly nonchalant

as to Brooke's orgasmic state, more interested in sweetening his own irrefutably dour brew.

"Allow me," Ellie cut in. Clementine, to whom he'd directed his request, had not yet found her way back, in body or spirit, to the activity thrumming around the table.

Barnaby forced a smile of gratitude onto his face and took the shaker from Ellie. Brooke couldn't help but notice the fleeting stroke Ellie applied to his fingers as the object was transferred. From Barnaby's slight flinch, she knew he'd felt it too. The jumbled contents of her stomach protested. Meanwhile, Barnaby applied the condiment liberally to his drink. He took a hasty swig of his plant-based coffee and gagged violently, showering everyone – and the base of the mouthwatering mountain of *pains aux chocolat* – with his disgusting brown slather.

"Charming."

And now all of Clementine was back in the room.

"Salt!" His reflux barely let him get a word in edgeways. "So that little shit in the kitchen thought he'd have another pop at me, did he? Well, not on my watch," Barnaby rose in defiance, ready to take Thierry down, chest puffed out like a wannabe King Kong.

"Get your arse back on that seat at once," Ellie ordered, her voice shrill.

Remarkably, he did as he was told, shapeshifting back into the mellow male of the past couple of days. Brooke's head span, unable to keep up with the way things were chopping and changing so fast. And was it her imagination, or did that outcome seem a little tame for the finish line? She guessed her own meddling was hardly helping the spell know which way to weave its magic. A tug of war of the wills. She also guessed Ellie couldn't make her own designs over-obvious until they were down to the final couple of chocolates. Which meant she and Clementine needed to bloody well watch their backs. At least Brooke fervently hoped Plan B would take the hint, kicking in fast.

"Clem, eat up, you're letting the side down, there!" Ellie wailed, putting Brooke worryingly in mind of the Hansel and Gretel witch that she'd not so long ago accused her of portraying. Ellie dragged her fingers through her platinum hair, yanking at today's fire agate pendant, the one that was practically strangling her; the one that had put in its debut appearance this fine Sunday morning not just because of its pretty colour, but indisputably because of its propensity to protect, especially when worn by a female. Oh yes, Brooke's interest in crystals and their properties was paying off.

Brooke let out a deep breath, digging her fingers into her palms beneath the table to hide her anxiety. This was not boding well at all.

Clementine stirred from another sudden slumber, eyes glazed over. She shrugged and fingered the box for a closer view.

"Fine. I'm having this one."

She wasted no time at all in extracting the dagger, much to everyone's surprise. Brooke tried in vain to halt the widening of her eyes, but it was impossible. Things were going to get very dangerous now. No way would something so pointed leave them anything but wounded. Her heartbeat ratcheted up a notch. She feared she might have a coronary.

But there was no time to monitor her sister's reaction to whatever lay hidden in the foodie weapon's centre, much less to time her rapid pulse; Thierry burst into the dining-room, without even knocking. A fanfare of fast-paced Moulin Rouge style music suddenly blasted out of the hidden speakers, and the guy she was trying with all her might not to think about, embarked on some seriously impressive leg kicks, sending everybody's eyebrows into their hairlines. Well, all except Clementine, who was dedicated to the task of chomping her way through a chocolate dagger, as one does.

"You didn't show up last night, Brooke?" he shouted above the brassy music, panting slightly at the effort some of these moves must be taking, "I guess you ate my message before reading it, eh?"

"Erm, no," Brooke panicked. "Erm, yes, I mean…"

She tried not to giggle, because dammit, this whole mess was beyond serious, and she could do with the excuse to get some of it off her chest. But under the circumstances, faced with the proposition of some of Thierry's jump splits, not to mention the virility underpinning them – and then there were the ruffles of his shirt – Brooke just couldn't help herself.

Thierry took this as his cue to seize her by the hand, hauling the pair of them backwards to the kitchen door, which he opened wider mid-multitasking leg kick, to let in a patiently waiting throng of female *Can Can* dancers.

What in the HECK?

He deftly produced a skirt in the colours of the French flag, broke free from Brooke, held the garment up, and invited her to step into it. There was no time to think; the music increased in gusto whilst she let him wrap the bold-hued frills around her waist, and struggled to keep up with the frantic moves and the whirlwind of her dance partner and his newfound friends.

Don't look at Barnaby's tongue hitting the floor. Do not look at your brother if you want to retain your breakfast!

She did chance a glimpse at Ellie, though. She was quietly, but palpably, fuming.

"Did you know that ze final figure of the dance is officially known as the *quadrille?*" Thierry shouted over the infectious gaiety. All twelve of the ladies on the other side of his arm now went behind Ellie's side of the table for a magnificent display of cartwheels and *grand écarts*.

"Ah... that would be nope, Thierry... I, er, I can't say I did," she replied, amazed that she could find the words, or the volume, amidst the fast pace of the *après*-breakfast entertainment she'd unwittingly found herself a part of, let alone the fact she somehow intuitively knew the timing of the moves. This was like being in a West End show; the cast spontaneously bursting into a song and dance where everyone mysteriously knew the steps.

"One can best interpret it as a sign of rebellion," he shouted back, and Brooke tried her best to mouth an 'O'. "Did you also know that ze *Can Can* best translates as your English word 'scandal'?" Brooke attempted to shrug her response, heart fluttering at the sight of the ex-male model frolicking beside her, but not for long, because now the lead *Can Can* girl was weaving her troupe back around to the other side of the table (probably desperate to escape Barnaby's leering). "So let's give them one!" he continued, laughing as they were pulled along like a toy train. "Let's set your family's tongues wagging. Let's set you free, baby!"

Da-da-da-da-da-da-da-da-da-da-da-da-da-da-da-da-da-da-da... DA-DA-DA-DA-DA-DA-DA-

"Did you also know that ze *Can Can* actually originated as a dance for women and men... for couples... for lovers?" Thierry's eyes sparkled. "What I am trying to do is put my feelings about you into music and movement, Brooke," he shouted, but the music had grown softer now and, perhaps sensing their moment under the spotlight was over, the female dancers began to peel away through the kitchen door, leaving Thierry, Brooke, and their high kicks to it. "But perhaps I'm going a little too fast," he said, embarrassingly audibly; Ellie, Barnaby and Clementine were hanging on his every word too.

"So I won't say, 'run away with me', but I will ask you to fairy-step away with me instead, Brooke." She gulped. The giant batiks hanging around the room started to swim before her eyes. "You don't have to give me your answer right now," his voice became a drone, and her ears felt as if they were stuffed with cotton wool. "Just think about it. I can't promise you an 'appy ever after, any more than the next man. But I can promise you adventure ever after. And I do think a combination of that, and me, could make you very content, no?"

Okay then, no. She meant yes.

Yes, they probably could.

But on the no front, this was indisputably not her imagination at all. Because now the batik and the speakers and the comet-like tails of *tricolore* skirts running through the garden outside had all thoroughly meshed and merged into one.

"And I just thought you'd like to know that I'm pregnant with Ruben's baby," a voice sounding remarkably like Clementine's announced.

Brooke collapsed, mid-attempted *grand battement*, fully flaking into Thierry's arms.

Through her hazy vision and the whirring in her ears, she could just about make out Thierry's hand. It seemed to be waving a bunch of leaves about. Then she must still be dreaming. This was her mind's interpretation of the olive branch – and oh, so much more – that she wanted him to offer her after the constant cold shoulder. Except the smell was too overpowering for that, gradually spiralling its way up her nostrils, until the fragrance of mint was so intense, she attempted to sit bolt upright to escape it, and immediately felt several pairs of hands reaching out to steady her. Finally, she found the strength to bat the herbs away and her vision started to clear. She guessed it was the closest thing Thierry had had to hand in the kitchen. It definitely beat that hideous brain-blast of ammoniac smelling salts that her nan used to carry around like a trophy in her handbag.

Her poor, poor nan, though.

And she was back in the room, delayed reaction relief enveloping her in a hug. Then it all came whooshing back at her. Something terrible was about to happen. Scratch that. Something terrible had happened (well, aside from Thierry's declaration of a lust that might just turn into love, but there was no time to dwell on that just yet).

Clementine was pregnant.

Translation: Clementine had been sleeping with Ruben.

All this time.

All those double dates.

How could her sister betray her? How *could* she?

"Ouch," Clementine bit her lip, reacting to the cold, glassy-eyed glare of her older sister, as Thierry handed Brooke a sweet peppermint tea, which pepped her up within seconds. "Well, of course, I didn't mean to. You must know that. Nobody ever means to hurt anybody in these scenarios. It's just, Archie couldn't get over to visit as much as I needed. Well, then one evening, I had a meltdown over a spreadsheet that urgently needed updating on the laptop. Rubes," *she called him that? But only Brooke was allowed to call him that!* "Rubes had slipped me his biz card," *the bitch would use that suggestive verb.* "While you were powdering your nose that time when we ate at All Bar One… Incidentally, I don't know why you thought it was a good idea to take us there, it's hardly the Ivy," said the snobby mare. "And Archie must've been chatting to the waiter about the merits of Californian wine versus European... I couldn't exactly call any of the tech geeks from work on a Saturday night now, could I?" How bloody convenient. And how bloody nothing at all to do with the fact that the tech geeks would hardly weigh up in a Love Island audition. "It was he who made the first move. Two weekends later."

Huh, why did Brooke get the feeling all of this had conveniently taken place that weekend she was stranded in Stuttgart?

"I thought it only appropriate to repay him with dinner, and one thing regrettably led to another when he came over to mine and... and yet not so regrettably, Brookie, darling," Clementine rubbed her belly tenderly. "How can you begrudge your niece or nephew? You're going to be an auntie!"

Never mind a kick to the stomach, Clementine had delivered her a dagger, all right: straight to the heart. She couldn't bring herself to look at anybody else's show of pity, so her eyes fixed themselves resolutely to her baseball boots, and the frustrating knot in their laces which she really ought to adjust.

But then Thierry gently cupped Brooke's face in his hands and looked into her eyes with such conviction, that she knew the cold hard truth. Things with Ruben had been over before they'd started. Two years she'd spent, waiting for some kind of commitment. He'd never made as much as an offer, stringing her along, standing her up. And now here was this incredible burst of light who had zipped into her life and taken her breath away within moments. He couldn't make life promises, no. But he was clear about that from the get-go. Brooke respected his honesty already. Yet he could offer her the spontaneity she knew she desperately needed. Both of these factors were currently more than enough.

None of which was to say she forgave her sister on the spot. She didn't. No matter how much Brooke had tried to override that damned spell with good will, she was only human; emotions would have to be distilled over time. Today wasn't the day. She flat-out refused to grant Clementine the satisfaction of a quick answer. Thierry, on the other hand...

"*D'accord, oui*," Brooke replied to his question belatedly, breathlessly. "Are we really starting in Afghanistan, though?"

"Hmm. That is a bit far for our first stop," he laughed, as his face lit up with the realisation of her decision. "I thought perhaps we could slowly make our way to Andorra instead; get there for the snowy season," he arched his brow. "Like I was saying recently, the *après-ski* activities are rather epic."

"You're cheesier than a fondue," she cooed, allowing herself the indulgence of melting in the pools of his eyes.

"Puntastic as all of that is," Ellie cut through them all, trepidation edging her voice, making a sour line of her mouth. "There's a little unfinished business to attend to right here and now before any of us can be on our way anywhere," she tilted her head toward the last of the chocolates. "Assuming you are coming back with us, Brooke?"

Brooke's heart and her stomach tandem-somersaulted. She already knew the answer to that. But it wouldn't hurt to pause dramatically, keeping certain people in suspense. "Four chocolates left," she said, turning the subject on its head, and weighing Ellie up in a manner she knew the other woman couldn't quite decipher; a manner that totally threw her.

Meticulously, and without waiting for permission, Brooke gathered the goodies up, laid them on the table, and surprised herself, as well as her audience, at her sudden ability to shuffle them around at the speed of light. It was an unprecedented and proprietorial act of rebellion, and one that signalled Ellie's immediate abdication from the throne of alchemy. "Let's start with this one first, Ms.

Sanchez." Brooke stopped decisively to pick up the choco-late letter 'T'.

"What do you mean?" Ellie shrieked, hand clamping down hard on her pendant, and rubbing at it furiously. "Obviously they are for you three to enjoy... although I'm not quite sure who will get the fourth. You could always save it for Thierry. Gesture of goodwill for all the excellent cooking and that," she tacked on a nervous chortle. "Brooke? *Brooke?* I'm allergic, remember?" Ellie tugged at her pendant now and almost choked; for a moment Brooke thought she might stage a panic attack. "I made this clear to all of you at the beginning of the week. Anyway, you didn't answer the rest of my question, Brooke. Are you coming back…"

"Allergic – to the truth," said Barnaby, rising slowly out of his seat, arms folded matter-of-factly.

Ellie laughed again even more anxiously this time, wrin-kling her brow, spidery lashes shielding her eyes as they panned from right to left. "Wh... whatever do you mean?"

"Eat up, Els."

That was Clementine. Oh, sweet relief. They might all escape this alive.

Just.

"Afternoon *tea* just became the new breakfast," Brooke's younger sister continued decisively, and, in that split second in time, Brooke was prepared to overlook her fury, for the sake of everyone's future.

Clementine ceremoniously swiped at the remaining tea cup and saucer sitting in the middle of the table. Brooke saw this as her prompt to plop the letter T into the cup, and Barnaby assumed the role of waiter, delivering the refresh-ment to Ellie in the most dapper style. Thierry, completely clueless as to what any of this fiasco was about, retreated to the kitchen with the tray of unloved *pains aux chocolat*.

"I 'ave a new batch in ze freezer. I may as well bake them before the bosses come back zis afternoon, eh?"

"Great idea, mate," said Barnaby. "Erm, and sorry, once again for the er… mishap… as well as for doubting your culinary skills this week. You're not a bad *oeuf* at all. If my big sis thinks you're all the rage, then, well," he high-fived the air in the absence of Thierry's hand being within striking distance. "I'll happily make the effort… since we may well end up brothers-in—"

"Ahem," Brooke cleared her throat. "Now that you've finished your War and Peace speech, we have slightly more urgent things to deal with," she nodded at Ellie. "She's not exactly imbibing it, *mate*."

"She'll be ramming it down her neck in a matter of seconds if I have anything to do with it." Clementine pushed back her chair, statement-style, and let out a giant huff, fringe standing on end.

Ellie tensed as Clementine paced towards her.

"We've all played your game, sweetheart, but enough is…"

"H…hang on a minute, backtrack just a bit. Did you just say game?" Ellie looked to Brooke, genuine tears filling her eyes in the realisation that her trust had been spectacularly broken. "Well, of course there were *games*," Ellie snapped her head back to Clementine, unable to look Brooke in the eye for a moment longer, backpedalling furiously. "That's part and parcel of the corporate team building. There were always going to be games. We've been playing them all week, after all: consequences, *exercises in trust*," ooh, that was a dig. "Lego, and pin the tail on the donkey."

"Pin the tail on the witch," muttered Barnaby.

"Except this particular game was a little bit different, wasn't it Ellie?" Brooke knew she had to take control now. "Want to tell them about it… or shall I?"

"It's all right, sis, I've got this. No need to rake it all up again now, let's just do what we have to do, then get out of here," Barnaby was adamant. "Brooke filled us in a couple of days ago," he turned to Ellie with fire in his eyes – and sadly not of the yearning kind she'd spent her adult years longing to see reflected back at her. "Not that I owe you the specifics, but let's just say we rekindled our childhood bonds over a spot of foraging – for that much I thank you – after which, Brooke invited us all to her room for a blast from the past style sleepover last night, when she, oops a daisy, filled us in on the happenings of the present."

Hmm. More like her brother and sister had invited themselves.

Ellie tugged helplessly at her pendant again, but to no avail. Brooke may not have been an authority on lucid dreams, water divination or the newfound celeb fad of vaginal steaming, but as she was saying, she did know a little about crystals: this one would only ever protect its wearer to a certain degree.

Brooke knew it. Ellie knew it.

And so it was that the cogs in Ellie's brain began to perceptibly calculate: her options were extremely limited. She sprang to her feet and made to run out of the room. But Brooke had been ready for said scenario for what felt like a lifetime. She whistled to Thierry to guard the kitchen door, as she blocked Ellie at the table. Meanwhile, Barnaby flew at the hallway door, and Clementine took great joy in dragging Ellie back to her seat:

"It's teatime, my dear," she passed her the cup a little forcefully. "We've all mucked in and played our parts, now it's your turn to do the same."

Ellie pretended to comply, bringing the cup to her lips, the saucer trembling in her hand. But then in slow motion, Brooke watched them both fall, china skittering everywhere, the letter T smashed into four large pieces. All eyes turned to the debris, Ellie vaulted onto the table to cross it and make a fresh attempt for the exit, but skittered across its shiny surface, on legs so spindly she'd probably pass an audition to play Bambi. She flung herself off the side anyway, fell to the floor, scrabbled to get up, and made a last ditch attempt to throw herself at the door.

"I think not," Barnaby swiftly side-stepped, and blocked her path. "Game over, Ellie."

Ellie gawped, wriggled and writhed, finally surrendering to a sudden succession of unfetching snivels.

Clementine re-enacted her earlier role of chaperone, shunting Ellie back into her chair. Arms firmly folded, she hovered above her until Ellie had bent to retrieve every morsel of the broken chocolate.

"Eat!" she yelled.

Brooke couldn't watch any longer. She'd never intended for things to become inhumane. An eye for an eye had never been her style. Whilst she was glad they were all sort of singing from the same Westwood song sheet, for once in their lives when it truly mattered, her sister was already back to showing her true colours. She was bulldozing her way ahead with sheer entitlement. It wouldn't take long for Barnaby to join her.

"Clementine, I'll see to this." She raised her voice with the authority that was her elder sibling prerogative, and slowly walked toward Ellie, as if she were a wild animal she was hoping to coax into taking home as a pet. Which actually, once she'd got this over and done with, wasn't so far off the mark as an analogy.

"It's the only way out of this, Ellie. Nobody's going to die. But you do need to work with me."

"Me? Trust you?" Ellie emitted a deranged peel of laughter. "After you've stabbed me in the back?" she was virtually spitting now. "I'll let you into a secret: you're all the same, you lot. And you couldn't sound more unconvincing if you tried. *Unconvincing, Brooke!*"

"Very well then. Have it your way."

Brooke carefully picked up the remnants of the chocolate T and prised open Ellie's mouth with her fingers and thumb. Not up there with the most pleasant experiences of her life; she'd couldn't have cut it as a dentist.

Remarkably, Ellie gave up the fight, in a scene that was as messy as it was undignified. Brooke didn't like gluing herself to Ellie's side, yet she acted as a shield, of sorts, from the gawking Clementine. Barnaby, unsurprisingly, kept his eyes locked on the floor, visibly shirking all involvement now things had got catty. She couldn't blame him. None of this was exactly his fault… and yet, had he never been born, for certain none of this would have happened. For the first time in her life, Brooke felt a smidgen of sympathy for the guy, who still had no clue just how integral his existence was to this disaster zone.

"There. That wasn't so bad, was it?" said Brooke cheerily, ever mindful of the fact they needed to move on quickly to the next one. "How about we go for the compass now?"

"How about *no*. I've played along, as you've so quaintly put it, and tonight I'll probably be covered in fucking welts, clutching my stomach whilst simultaneously drafting all the necessary changes in RBPC teams, and then throwing up while the rest of you are tucked up in bed gorging on your missed Facebook and Insta notifications with a vat of coffee to make up for all your deprivation. It's bloody illegal to do this to someone with an allergy, you know. I could easily press charges!"

"You're not the only one," Barnaby thundered. "You've treated us like animals this week. Now, do as she says and eat the frigging compass before I…"

Ellie began to shake as she reluctantly took the small

chocolate, engraved with its N,E,S,W and brought it to her mouth.

"Don't drag it out, Ellie. It's not like we're making you eat snails… although I'm sure Thierry has some beauties he could put on the boil, with a generous helping of garlic."

"I do as it 'appens," Thierry shouted from the kitchen, "but, er, Brooke?"

"That won't be necessary," Brooke raised her voice for the second time in as many minutes so he didn't start whipping them up a gourmet, and thoroughly stomach-churning, *Escargots à la Bourguignonne.* "Clementine, that's enough." She turned her attention back to her deceitful sister. "And quite how you can be so macabre when you're a veggie, I don't know. Then again, it seems there are a lot of things I don't know about you."

"If you'd satisfied him in the first place, none of this would…"

Brooke shot her sister a deadly look. Were there really no limits to how badly she could behave? She was starting to make Ellie look angelic.

"Let me assure you zis has nothing to do with satisfaction."

Thierry shouted from the kitchen again, putting Clementine straight. Brooke flushed profusely, impressed at his ability to eavesdrop in another language.

"Why? *Why* did I get lumbered with a pair of bloody sisters?" Barnaby took a hiatus from studying the crevices of the floor to squint at the debacle playing out in front of him.

"You're nibbling, Ellie," Clementine sneered, changing the subject. "It doesn't work when you're a child being asked to clear a portion of peas, and it won't work now. Just eat the damned thing!"

"You're beyond cruel, Brooke Westwood," Ellie glared,

wedging the bulk of the chocolate between her stubborn lips so that, mercifully, Brooke didn't have to do it for her.

"So how long until these first two kick in?" Barnaby started to pace.

"That's like asking how long a piece of string is," said Clementine.

And then Brooke began to panic that nothing *had* happened just yet, until she reminded herself that she'd always suspected that if they reached this point, it would all happen at once – as long as they waited here. They categorically must not leave this room. What happened at the *gîte* stayed at the *gîte.* Taking this unfinished show onto the road, or the boat, didn't bear thinking about.

"You might as well let me go now," Ellie tried, mid-tremble, as if reading her mind. "We have to pack, else we'll miss our ferry. Might be an idea to take that into account, especially as I'm the only one insured to drive the car."

"Oh, who gives a flying fuck about insurance, Ellie?" Barnaby thundered. "The nerve of you making out you're so squeaky clean."

"She's right," said Brooke, springing into action, fear momentarily abating, "there's no time to waste; straight on to the next. Now, which order, hmm… let me see," Brooke inspected the last two chocolates closely, willing them to reveal a clue.

"Please, Brooke. I'm practically begging you," Ellie whimpered. "Just not the vol…" Ellie began in vain.

Brooke sighed deeply.

"Yes, Ellie. I'm afraid it does have to be the volcano. Something tells me it's too obvious for the finale; a red herring, if you will. But I get a gut feeling that this little nondescript oblong is going to be the key to resolution."

Ellie made a painful animal noise; a howl so guttural that it brought Thierry back to the door.

"Law of attraction's a damned hoax!" Ellie cried, shielding her head in her hands, rocking from side to side, and causing all four of her onlookers to exchange puzzled glances.

Brooke had always had her doubts about the triangular chocolate lying in wait on her palm, and, indeed, it was bizarre the way the others had instinctively shied away from it, too.

"I'm pleading with you, Brooke," Ellie said, one final time. "Not the chili pepper, please. I just know that's what's inside. I'll eat any of them except the chocolate chili. That combination is really going to cause a reaction."

"Then you should have joined in and helped feather the team-building *nest* like the rest of us," Clementine sing-songed. "But moreover, tweet tweet," she waited several beats, feasting upon her emerging smile, *"Eleanor the Fucking Fraud, Finch*, you should never have thought you could pull a fast one on a Westwood. There's a reason we've always been on our pedestal, way, and forever, out of your reach: we the golden eagles, you practically invisible and pecking at the seeds."

"Wh… what… did… you… just… say?"

"Brooke showed me your freaky portable shrine to my brother," a very smug Clementine announced. "Sorry to spring the surprise on you, Barnaby, but it's time the truth came out." She reached for the back pocket of her jeans and handed Barnaby her mobile phone.

"Clementine, no!" Brooke screeched.

"Clem… entine, no!" Ellie caterwauled her echo. "Please, no! It was nothing. Just an innocent laugh. I can explain…"

A tenterhooks silence engulfed the room, only punctuated by the ticking of the little hand slowly revolving around John Lennon's face on Jock and Jules' wall clock.

"Oh my God," Barnaby finally spoke, his fingers swiping quickly as he took in the colossal montage of pictures on the phone screen. Brooke studied her brother's freaked-out expression. He flinched, side-eyeing the images Brooke had captured, as if none of this could possibly be true.

"I think I am literally going to puke," Barnaby sank his head between his legs now, as if willing the floor to open up and swallow him whole.

"Who else has seen this, for fuck's sake?" he mumbled.

"Only us. Chill, dude." But Clementine's whiny voice did little to calm anyone. "Brooke had the pleasure of stumbling upon them at the start of the week on Ellie's phone. She sent them to me on WhatsApp last night after we'd... y'know.... made our pact ref. her attempting to you-know-what some good back into the chocolates. We didn't have the heart to tell you before."

"In other words, you've been having a right old laugh at my expense, saving this up for a public announcement," he moaned.

Brooke shifted her gait. Ellie's eyes were drilling red hot pokers into her side.

"Not at all. I'm totes disturbed!" Clementine protested. "For all I know she's got an altar to me in her bedroom at home, too."

"Don't flatter yourself," said Ellie with a sarcastic laugh.

"I should have trusted my better judgment the moment she floundered in that interview," Clementine raged. "But no, we were desperate; that candidate I had my eye on never showed up, and Brooke, you vouched for this excuse for a human being! How could you be so stupid?"

Oh, Brooke had been, all right. Stupid on so many levels, with so many people, in so many ways. Well, not for much longer.

"I just... I've been so naive," now Barnaby yelled. "I mean, I know I'm hot stuff. I've broken hearts far and wide... but this? I can't process it. It's just wrong. On so many..."

No modesty. Not an iota.

"I know, and I know what that's like. Our looks can be a blessing, and they can be a curse… ha, literally," Clementine nodded in agreement. "It was definitely enough to bring on my morning sickness when I saw all the hideous photographic evidence of Ellie's obsession for you," she added, as she plonked herself beside her brother on the floor, almost flooring Brooke in another sense of the word, and all over again, as Clementine's status as a mother-to-be sank in.

Bloody hell.

This super-warped scenario was so surreal it was almost laughable, but perhaps, maybe, just maybe, it had always been par for the course. This shit show of a company – well, the bitter shards that remained of it – was dubbed The Really Bad Photo Company, after all.

"You trespassed," Ellie raised her head slowly, blinking in disbelief at Brooke, wholly oblivious to the fact she was only further embarrassing herself. "I… I trusted you... and yet... you went into my room, you actually rifled through my belongings and onto my mobile phone!" Ellie yelled now.

Brooke was momentarily out of words. Clementine wasn't.

"Oh! Cut the crap, *Eleanor*. You've been stalking him for years, you hideous freak! He's our brother. We all had a right to know what you were playing at. Brooke only did what she had to, and you'd better be glad it wasn't me who'd discovered your dirty secret. Well, you're out on your ear with immediate effect, and I can assure you, I'll be doing everything in my power to ensure Saffy sees what a mistake she's made so I can do my bit to help my brother rebuild things with *the love of his life*," she shouted, cradling Barnaby's slumped head in her arms.

They might be Brooke's family, her flesh and her blood. Yet it was Ellie Sanchez who Brooke would always side with in that moment, and from that moment forth. Controversial, contrary and more than a little crazy – until one fully understood, as Brooke did in that moment, how they would put their vanity before their values. Every. Single. Time

Brooke realised now that she should have kept Ellie's freak show and her own pathetic attempt at the counter-curse to herself. She couldn't even say it was a decision she'd made lightly. No. She'd wrestled with herself, as anyone in her oddball predicament would have. Alas, just as quickly as Ellie had managed to convince her that her chocolate spell was a good thing, the magic had worn off.

"See yourself out, Brooke," Ellie had said after their handshake (the one where Brooke had screwed her eyes shut to imagine another, more sensible version of herself, crossing her fingers behind her back – well, it was as close as she could get to neutralising the current version of herself that had unwittingly got embroiled in all this hubble, bubble, toil and fricking trouble.). "I'll just blow these out and tidy everything up," Ellie had then gestured at the candles and shut the kitchen door on her.

That was precisely when the glow of another object had caught Brooke's eye. The silent but vibrant vibration of Ellie's mobile phone. Ellie's very unattended mobile phone. A mobile phone which seemed to be calling to Brooke, as it happened – and not in the literal sense of the word. Brooke bid a hasty farewell to her unsought partner in crime, following the illuminating lead to the hallway, and, once she was sure Ellie's attention was very much elsewhere in the kitchen, and that she wasn't about to burst back onto the scene, she'd tiptoed gingerly into the HR Manager's bedroom, which was conveniently en route, waiting patiently by the bedside table for the phone to stop doing its thing so she could have a little snoop.

WhatsApp and Facebook Messenger quickly revealed

nothing more than a list of blank conversations, only high-lighting Ellie's indisputable admin efficiency when it came to tidying up. Brooke deftly set the phone back in its original position – but then something told her to have the sneakiest of peeks in Ellie's image gallery. If for no other reason than she was sure there must be a couple of random snaps of the guys she'd most recently dated, but frustratingly never shared any titbits about. Brooke checked the coast was still clear behind her, retrieved the phone, and let her nimble thumbs investigate.

Oh!

Brooke had only made it to the final image on Ellie's camera roll when the phone slipped from her (hand), merci-fully onto the soft cover of the bed. She let out a massive gasp and briskly covered her mouth for fear of expelling a high-pitched shriek. Mindful of the imminent threat of Ellie creeping up on her from behind, of one hand clamping down on her shoulder and the other covering her mouth in a deja-vu, she quickened her trawling to investigate further.

The hideous extent of the scene that unfolded before her became more and more screwed up with every scroll and every picture.

Her brother.

No, not in the flesh, but in forms large and small; old and new; black and white, and in high resolution colour pops; a portable duplicate of the many pictures Brooke could only guess were scattered around Ellie's bedroom back in Blighty.

Every image of Barnaby was encased in a frame and then shrouded with tiny fairy lights.

There were printouts Brooke recognised from his ever-changing Facebook profile. There were cuttings taken and blown-up from newspapers. In some images Barnaby was shaking hands, receiving awards for innovation – huh... all the awards that Brooke herself should have been collecting.

In others he was part of the furniture (beautiful crowd) at a socialite party. And then there were others where Ellie had superimposed her own image into the scene. One twist on that artform, in particular, had Brooke gagging and running. Ellie Sanchez receiving a spanking, wearing next to nothing, exhibiting the widest grin.

So that was what all of this was really about.

ELLIE

*T*hey say that pride comes before a fall.

On that score *they* are right.

All the feeble little mishaps that life had thrown at Eleanor Finch paled in comparison with the sheer humiliation of what happened at the *gîte*.

All Ellie's attempts to keep the volcano chocolate out of her mouth were in pitiful vain. In the end, Clem prised her jaw open with her nail file. Bitch. Meanwhile, Brooke deftly plugged the triangular object into Ellie's mouth, and what ensued was a tableau of disgusting brown dribble, and yet more snivels and whimpering protests that brought an increasingly concerned Thierry back to the door.

"I 'ope I can 'elp you all make up! *Ce n'est ce pas bon.* We never let things finish on a rainy note at *Les Nuages.*"

She heard his attempts at peacemaking try to punctuate the desperate scene. Perhaps she was imagining it, but a string of token but distant clucks seemed to embellish his every other word.

"I don't know much about team building, or ze corporate world, but I 'ave an idea. Just stay where you are, don't come into the kitchen. I want it to be the best surprise ever. Never underestimate the power of food to bring people together... in ze... er, right way around the table. Hold on. I've just got to... *Tiens*, don't go anywhere, okay?"

But Ellie needed more milk than even the dairy down the road could provide, after those two Westwood wenches had force-fed her the chocolate chili, and Barnaby had meekly looked on. Huh, she wasn't so invisible to him now.

Despite the searing heat that scorched her throat and tongue, coiling its way menacingly down her windpipe, this true-life vision of the utter hopelessness of him had been cathartic. Oh, it might still have been the spell muting his humanity, but not even Carlos would have sat there watching a woman being tortured like that.

Barney Beauteous Westwood was more than a little pathetic.

But before she could formulate a plan to lull them all into a false sense of security, sprinting past the lot of them into the kitchen for a gallon of ice cold milk, Brooke was inching toward her with the last chocolate, an incongruous look of compassion on her face. Well she could shove that up her backside where it belonged. It didn't fool Ellie.

Curiously, though, that was when the sweet relief of Eureka enveloped her in its invisible balm: what if this was just a case of one (rather giant, admittedly) step backwards (into apparent doom-filled failure) in order to take five steps forward (to success)?

It had to be.

She'd crossed all the i's and she'd dotted all the t's.

Ellie Sanchez had been meticulous.

Ellie Sanchez was sorry for insulting the magical, mysterious Law of Attraction; she took it all back. Every scrap of it.

Ellie Sanchez was a survivor; outwitting them all. And

once she'd digested this sinful elongated chocolate, they'd witness exactly that, in all its spectacular glory.

And so she accepted the rectangular confection between finger and thumb, whilst all three Westwoods looked on, and she ate the entire thing without as much as putting up a fight.

Ha – just as she'd suspected: Brooke, Barney and Clem, whether already sitting, standing or staring vacantly, devoid of heart and soul, curled up in exhausted heaps on the floor.

Cinq, quatre, trois, deux, un: ALLEZ!

Ellie pelted toward the kitchen door, crossing her fingers behind her back that there'd be a lock on the other side of it... *voila* and haha, yes there flipping well was. And, even sweeter still, there wasn't an interfering Thierry in sight! She opened her mouth to let out a victory guffaw, only to find, to her enormous alarm, her teeth had completely cemented themselves together. Then that last chocolate... oh, she got it... toffee, the absolute arseholes; Clem had always been destined for anything that prevented communication! This was so unfair. So very, very wrong.

Mired in this new twist, Ellie swivelled, lost her balance, and stumbled backwards into something hot and bright. Four twinkling sparklers topping a farewell cake; the stupid surprise that Thierry had hinted he was preparing.

It tumbled in slow motion, and in a multitude of directions; one lit sparkler catching on a pile of baking parchment, which in turn caught on a pile of carelessly discarded, and bone dry, tea towels, which in turn were not so strategically placed next to a mountain of Jules' hippy-dippy tea bags, which in turn caught on the wooden worktops and proceeded to spark up a succession of mini fires, which, even if she hadn't been rendered mute, would have left Ellie spellbound, speechless and in an unshakeable trance.

The domino rally of combustion raged on; eating up everything in its path, no time or regard for Ellie's quandary.

Only half of her registered Thierry's fast-approaching foot-steps crunching on the gravel toward the kitchen's back door, racing back toward the cake he'd so carelessly left unattended.

"*Toujours les poules!*"

She heard his words ringing out, evidently the hens had escaped again and he'd had to abandon the lit cake, clumsily trading one potential disaster for another.

Now he took stock of the orange flames, licking up at the curtains, heading for the ceiling. "*Merd, nooooooon!*" she heard him cry, as he entered the room and held his breath in preparation for the onslaught of smoke.

He took in the sight of the strewn cake and its debris, but Ellie, who'd skilfully hidden herself behind the kitchen island, charged at him with a strength she never knew she had and, letting the adrenalin continue to fuel her, taking advantage of Thierry's puzzled reflexes, she found she could push him, with little effort, out of the back door, bolting that too.

The Law of Attraction was evidently a steaming hot pile of misleading poo, so Ellie Sanchez, and what remained of her inner child; the Nothing; the invisible wallflower; Eleanor Finch, might as well go up in flames while they were at it.

Ellie fully intended to end her days *à la* Joan of Arc, regardless of the fact Thierry had bolted over to the *gîte*'s front door, frantically banging on it for help. The others hadn't even detected the smoke, much less run after Ellie (well, the chocolates had been eaten now, and even if she was attempting to purge herself, no doubt it was too little too late), their weary huddle interrupted by an earlier knock on the door.

So much could happen in the space of mere minutes.

Not only had the sticky toffee stalactites and stalagmites

mercifully dissolved into nothingness in her mouth, Thierry had also kicked down the front door – he'd also swiftly been followed by a woman named Gloria; a character who'd seemingly emerged from the Avalonian mists. She quickly caught up on the drama, wrapped her cloak around her solid frame to muck in with the action plan, and flung herself into the kitchen first, to drag Ellie out. The slightly more casually dressed Connie hovered behind her.

All four resurfaced from the deadly plumes in record time, coughing and spluttering, Thierry patching the door back up as best he could with a couple of chairs and a rolled up batik that had once graced the dining-room wall.

Ellie's face was partially covered with speckles of soot and ash.

"Wh… what are *you* doing here? I thought I'd never see you again!" she mumbled at Gloria, not before taking in Connie's dithering form in the background, and toppling backwards again. Part of Ellie was furious with Gloria. Part of her was relieved. Clearly today wasn't the day that Ellie would sink to the depths of hell for her scumbag earthly behaviour – although she might have relished the good old-fashioned slanging match with her father there.

"Ironic. I was going to ask you the same… but there's no time to explain any of that just yet," Gloria chided. "Side note: did you bother to brush your teeth this morning, my child, they're looking a bit brown?" Ellie glared. If it wasn't for her juju friend and her inadvertent teaching methods, none of this carry-on would have happened in the first place!

"We need to get out of here and fast. All of us," Gloria stated the obvious. "Your friend Brooke's calling the fire brigade." Huh, the sentiment was nice but Ellie doubted Brooke would ever talk to her again, let alone consider her as one of those. "There isn't even an extinguisher here to help give those muscle-clad firemen a head start." God, Gloria could be so extra when it suited. "That's certainly taught me a valuable lesson to check up on health and safety when I book a future retreat." Gloria pointed her finger in the air, momentarily lost in her thoughts. "Being unconventional is all well and good," she motioned for Connie to take Ellie by her opposite 'wing' so that the pair of them could forcefully remove her from the smouldering building if need be. "And of course I've indulged in any number of fire rituals over the years, but only outside, mind you, and only within striking distance of a river or lake. This is categorically not what I had in mind when I signed up for a Tibetan Sound Bowls and Tapestry holiday in Northern France."

"Me neither." Connie's demure reply told Ellie her school friend was still the tranquil character she'd known and loved. Even in the face of looming disaster.

"They're on their way," Brooke yelled, running from the hallway where the old-fashioned rotary phone was fixed to the wall, ushering everyone out the front of the *gîte* to gather on the lawn, where Barney and Clem were careful to keep their distance from Ellie and her re-found friends. Then again, Gloria was in her fabulously individualistic Dairy Milk purple cape, which she'd paired with her non-matching, star-strewn, racing green Doc Martins, all finished off with an interesting mix of half-blue, half-grey dreadlocked hair.

"Now, I know it's madness, and pretty much the last thing any of us should do under the circumstances, but I'm going back in for our passports, and don't anyone try to stop me."

"Brooke, no!" Thierry and Ellie cried out together.

"I'm with them," Gloria frowned, and Connie opened her mouth to agree. "It's a very bad idea. Even if the flames are semi-contained in the kitchen, it won't take much for them to break through to the first floor... plus smoke inhalation, hello!"

Barnaby shrugged and let his sister get on with it. Clementine cuddled the tiny curve of her stomach.

Like it hadn't already occurred to Ellie, the guy she'd spent most of her life pining for was just a tad tragic.

"It's fine. I've got this," Brooke shook her head.

"Correction. *We've* got this," Thierry announced. "No way are you going back in that building alone."

"Our bedrooms are all at the farthest end of the property from the fire. We'll run fast. We've got strong lungs," Ellie didn't doubt that after Brooke and Thierry's activities this week. "And I have no intention of missing out on all the future travel opportunities a certain French chef and I have planned. Just tell me where your passport is, Ellie? Luckily I took charge of Barnaby and Clementine's when we got here, so I've only got to leg it to the safe in my room."

"In the bedside table drawer," Ellie paused to cough on the remnants of toffee coating her throat. "Oh, and if you wouldn't mind bringing my phone?"

Brooke gave her a weak smile. Ellie flushed with a thousand sins, well, one-hundred-and-sixty-five to be precise; the exact number of images of her former love that would soon go up in flames if Brooke didn't agree to snatch Ellie's mobile while she was at it. The nearest fire station was fifteen kilometres away, and it was a small one at that. She wrestled in her pocket for the key to her luxury room, hoping that Brooke wouldn't get waylaid again by those photos.

"We've got this, babe. I know it. But we'll need to be quick." Thierry reconfirmed Brooke's view, doing that weird face-cup thing again like he had her head in a vice. "I'm calling the neighbours for 'elp with the chickens as soon as we get out," he could be heard to shout as they ran toward the *gîte*. "Then I 'ave my bag 'andy and ready to go by the hut door. I 'ave always kept it packed since my squatting days. You never know when you'll be on the move." He sprinted on into the distance, before shouting back. "Zis is all my fault… if only I'd secured the birds in their coop… if only I 'adn't baked ze farewell cake. Knowing Jock, he'll 'ave forgotten to renew ze insurance, too. *Merde, encore une fois!*"

"*Non, Thierry. C'est à cause de moi et je vais leur dire.*" But Ellie's protests went unheard by Thierry or Brooke. "The only one going down for this is me," she whispered sadly.

"Not if I have anything to do with it," Gloria let out a long breath. "Seems we have a mountain of catching up to do, young lady."

Ellie had never heard Gloria call her that. Seems Gloria had finally acknowledged Ellie's transition from teen to grown woman, though once she'd got the gist of the destruction she'd single-handedly caused, Ellie doubted Gloria would be quite as happy at the coincidence of their paths crossing again.

"Right, now; it might be a little bit cosy, but I'm going to ask you all to hop into my van." Gloria gestured at her daisy-themed VW contraption in the distance. "That's right; even you two toffs, who are no doubt accustomed to higher-brow transportation." Gloria motioned at Barney and Clem. Clem scowled. "Well, you are thoroughly stuck up your own backsides, no point denying it," Gloria continued. "I'll deposit you all in that macho café in the village; the one which could definitely do with a spot of goddess TLC to liven it up. But first," she paused to reflect, sticking her finger in the air again, as if receiving some kind of inner and invisible wisdom on the breeze. "Let's just say I'll come back when I've briefed the firemen… an unexpected perk of retreat plans going tits up."

Ellie was too tired to know what any of that meant, or to correct Gloria for being un-PC and failing to refer to the people in question as firefighters. She relinquished herself to the guidance of her two childhood friends, letting Gloria strap her into the back seat next to Connie, who patted her continuously, and reassuringly, on the knee. Warily, Clem and Barney climbed into the front passenger seat (which was infinitely closer to a leather settee from the eighties), while Gloria lolloped to the driver's side, thoroughly squashing them and beaming with way too much enthusiasm.

Ellie's conscious mind told her Brooke and Thierry would be fine, and indeed, they were, emerging within minutes from the house, a fan of passports and Ellie's phone in their hands. They headed straight for Gloria's eye-catching van, just as the window above the kitchen, shit, Ellie could only guess that was Jock and Jules' private quarters, went up in a marmalade rage of light.

———

The silence was practically deafening at the café. Everybody trying their damnedest to process the astonishing turn of events.

Where to even start?

Ellie guessed that depended on the individual, and frankly she was too tired of this mess she'd single-handedly created, to spare a thought for anyone else. She could only hope the fire brigade would arrive fast, and with them, the police and her punishment. There was no doubt in her own mind she'd set off the ultimate disaster. Too many 'if only I hadn't done that's' were circumnavigating her brain.

Meanwhile, Thierry filled the owner in on the hideous state of play, and the short bearded man shook his head in dismay.

Mutters of *"quel horreur"* echoed around the counter as the village men necked the remains of their coffee, and bounded outside to mount Napoleonic bikes (and have a good old gawp at the scene of devastation on the village's outskirts, three kilometres away).

The café owner turned on the TV, like a Brit might switch on the kettle, and Ellie couldn't be gladder to have the sound in her ear, even if it was a boring French political talk show. That was when perhaps the most unpredictable thing of all happened. Barney, miffed at his inability to understand any of the fancy-sounding Indo-European chit-chat bandying back and forth between the glamorous female presenter and her guest, stretched across his bar stool and swiped at the remote control, hitting the buttons like the piggy bank character out of Toy Story, until he reached an English news channel.

"*Connard*," said the café owner under his breath, flipping his cloth over his shoulder and disappearing into the kitchen.

The remote Norwegian Lofoten islands beamed up on the TV's giant screen. Nothing so very exciting about that, although the puffin-fringed cliffs and the jewel-green grass at the edge of those rough China-blue waves did look atmospheric.

And then came the next frame; an image whose impact took a couple of seconds to fully wire up to Ellie's brain. But once she'd seen it, she couldn't unsee it.

"Ben!"

At least Ellie tried to shout his name out in disbelief. A muffled grunt was the best she could do.

"Ruben?" Brooke was incredulous.

"*Putain!*" Thierry eyed up his love rival, hands planted firmly on hips.

"*Ru?*"

That was Clementine. A few seconds late to the party.

Three women danced like dervishes, even whilst pinned to their seats. Spinning tops whose worlds were rapidly falling apart at the seams, they somehow remained rooted at isosceles triangle distance apart. But not an iota of oneness was to be obtained here between them, in a scene that was anything but serene.

"But h… how do you know him?" Clem and Brooke blurted in unison, Brooke adding:

"Oh, of course," and then she laughed sadistically. "He's been having his cake, eating it, and going back for a third helping. Bloody hell, I am naive."

But there was no time for Ellie to reveal she was innocent for a change.

"This is a message. A message for Ellie," the male at the centre of their attention snapped them back to the screen, which panned quickly now to reveal a late middle-aged man being released from a rather compromising position. Normally, Ellie would question any broadcasting company's right to air this. But, of course, nothing about the merry and thoroughly muddled mindset of these chocolates was 'normal', and she released a gasp (a mercifully, non-adhesive one) as she made the connection: so that was where the compass came into play.

"Dad!" yelled Clem, before flopping into Barney's open arms. Geez, if marrying one's sister was a thing, Ellie realised, at last and after all these years, these two were truly, madly and deeply made for each other,

"No shit!" Brooke bit at her nails.

Meanwhile, Barney simply moved his head slowly from side to side, struggling for everyday compos mentis.

It wasn't that Ellie didn't know Ben had some sailing pals; that they'd infiltrated Harry's yachting team, taking him hostage to help her behind the scenes; a little pressure in exchange for the answers and figures that explained the missing mounds of cash. But tying him up inside a boating shed on a remote Norwegian island? Hell, no. Things were never meant to go to quite those extremes!

ISABELLA MAY

It might have looked idyllic, if it hadn't been for Daddy Westwood's tortured face.

"Ellie, if you're out there and somehow listening... I'm sorry," Ben began. "I'm so very, very sorry. I didn't mean for things to get so out of hand. I couldn't get close enough to the system. Not at first. Not through Brooke, anyway."

Brooke tried to gasp as Ellie had, but her mouth froze with a contortion that was going nowhere.

"No, no, no, no. This cannot be happening," screeched Ellie, partially relieved at her newfound freedom of speech.

"Lovely girl, Brooke." Ben continued. "And I feel terrible for using her the way I did. I'm a scumbag through and through." Ellie saw Thierry's mad pacing from the corner of her eye. "I tried for two years... I mean I really tried, but every time I thought I'd come up with the perfect excuse for us to visit the office; every time I suggested she bring home her laptop so I could have a tinker when she wasn't looking... well, let's just say she didn't exactly take the hint. That's when I got desperate and moved onto Clementine. That's off the record, though..."

"Why did you take it so far, you utter bloody idiotic numpty?" Ellie hissed at the TV as if he might hear her. "I told you to calm things down!"

"You total bastard of a buffoon! Didn't it occur to you I might be listening?" Clem peeped at the TV before rubbing her head further into the crook of her brother's arm and bawling.

Bloody hell. For one so smart, Ben really lacked any common sense.

"H...how dare he... when he's fathering my child!" Clem sobbed into Barney's chest, half an eye still peeping at the TV.

"Never mind all that," said Barney. Clem looked askance

308

at her brother. "I mean, not that my sweet nephew isn't important," he quickly added.

"Or niece," Clem snivelled.

"What I mean is, aren't we all slightly forgetting Dad, there? On live T.V. and in grave danger, and... and... and, well, who in the hell will do business with us again, who will invest in us again after seeing this?" Barney yelped.

As if he'd somehow heard Ellie, and Ellie only – in a severely stunted and time-delayed flurry of words – Ben put his head in his hands. The camera was still rolling. Ellie guessed, sitting half the world away in this sluggish Norman noshery, that whoever was behind the camera would let this play out, it might well record them some compelling evidence. She also guessed correctly that everyone was so busy computing Harry's predicament, so busy computing Ben's identity (something she could kick herself for not having worked out before now), that they'd completely overlooked the fact he'd just made the grand reveal about her own involvement in Harry's kidnapping.

Not that it mattered. French law would never set her free, once they'd heard her version of events at the *gite.*

"But don't you see? There's a very good reason I've gone to these lengths. I owe you everything."

Ellie's eyes almost popped out of her head.

"Don't you also see half of yourself when you look at me, Els?" Ben pleaded. "I've hoped and prayed you would for so many years. All those sushi bar lunches I've stomached, all in the name of putting wrongs right. I don't even like freaking fish – let alone when it's raw!"

Ellie tugged at her hair, then her pendant, then her hair again; anxiety entwining her inside like invisible ivy. What the hell was he on about?

Ben looked earnestly into the camera, as if only the two of them existed in all the world.

"I'm your half-brother, and you, you're my half-sis... through Keith, of course. I mean, you'd probably have realised if I'd come about via your mum."

Jesus Christ.

And then, within mere seconds, it all quickly made sense. So that was why 'Ben' had started visiting her at the university library, borrowing ever-more-towering piles of books, asking for advice on tracking them down, chatting her up about literature, non-fiction and general nonsense. He was only her father's love child. Her entire life had only been one gigantic and ludicrous lie!

"Keith had an affair with my mum when she was briefly working at the sheepskin factory. Times were hard for her back then; my step-dad up and leaving. My real name is... well, it's Ruben. Actually."

No shit. Except yeah, she'd probably sussed the last part out as of very recently.

No words. Ellie couldn't extract a blasphemy, much less a curse.

The Scandi police looked through the lens, as if trying to communicate with whoever was filming, and Ellie, all at the very same time. But Ruben was on a roll now, his voice warbling on in the distance.

"It all started when I turned thirteen. I was earmarked as a maths and computer whizz kid. That's when mum asked Keith to stump up the money to send me to private school, to make sure I got the best of the best, education-wise. I can't blame her. State school was stunting my growth – what with the mixed ability classes." Wow, what an entitled and self-important git. Get the violins out. Ellie couldn't see a single similarity in their features, although if she were honest, she'd already traced the identical dimpling in their chins, the cerulean shade of their eyes, the slight crinkle between the eyebrows... the attitude. "But Keith... Dad. Well, he couldn't afford to keep you there too. Evidently, he saw my talents as being worthier of the investment. One in, one out."

The bastard. Ellie's eyes welled up, anger and sadness battling it out for her undivided attention.

"I feel guilty as hell for that. How can I not, sis? I've got a fab job and you... well, you're doing okay, I suppose." Yeah, cheers for the vote of confidence. And here was Ellie, snubbing Ben and his 'misguided bravado ref. his chances with her' all this time; she honestly didn't know whether to laugh or cry. "But you've totally missed out on the golden opportunities I've had showered upon me; you've inadvertently been my sacrifice! That's why I'll do anything to help you; to make up for Dad's unfair treatment of us," he continued.

She cast her mind back then to when all this had started. Initially, she'd refused Ben's incessant busy-bodying and interference. He wasn't her bag, she wanted nothing to do with him, especially when romance with Carlos was on the cards. The last thing she needed was some little boy sniffing around and putting the Prof off her scent. Besides, when had anyone truly helped her anyway? She prided herself on self-sufficiency. And then, once she had Carlos, well, she could stand on their own four feet.

All right, she had let him take her out for a few token lunches (mainly when she was broke and waiting for the settlement to ping its way into her bank account), and Ben had certainly come in handy for the HR homework.

But once she started at the RBPC; once she realised Barney (and Saffy's) power to stymie her every attempt to woo her prey, well then, she hadn't been able to resist taking Ben up on his offer.

"I took the computers, too," he shrugged as best he could in handcuffs. "It helped round things up to the exact amount Dad had spent on me instead of you," Ben added as the camera panned the boat's deck, and he and his friends were led away in the direction of the patiently waiting police boat.

Ellie mouthed her apology on Ben's behalf to Brooke, and Brooke only. But Brooke had now adopted the Westwood staring-through-a-pane-of-glass habit. Ellie really couldn't blame her.

"All I was ever doing was giving karma a helping hand," Ben added, as he was frogmarched several steps down a small metal ladder, and onto a neighbouring boat.

Then came a jumble of confusion; Ben's body thrashing against the police officer, thrusting himself and his minder in front of him into the icy blue depths of the waters below. What the heck was he playing at? Did he honestly think he was some kind of merman Great Houdini?

The entire café held its breath. Ellie felt herself going down like a pack of cards, despite the reassuring grip of Connie's hands on her own shoulders.

Thierry's bunch of herbs trick (courtesy of the grumpy café dude reluctantly obeying commands to clip his rosemary bush) brought Ellie back to consciousness, along with a restorative hug from Connie. Okay, and the three chocolate eclairs had also helped (Ellie had already decided she now had carte blanche to devote the rest of the day to the culinary dark side). Just as well. There was so much backcombing required to even try to make sense of the ridiculous complexity of the morning's events.

"I have just one question: why my brother?" Brooke asked. "You might want to cover your ears for this bit, Barna-by," she added.

"Never mind any of that," Barney was back to yelping again. "How can you all just sweep Dad under the table like this? Every one of us has witnessed the absolute shitshow Ellie's managed to get him caught up in. What's wrong with you?"

"C'mon, Dad's no angel," retorted Brooke.

"Well he flat-out did not deserve this," Barney quipped.

"Oh, Barnaby! He always had his comeuppance awaiting him, no matter how it was engineered," Brooke protested. "Dad's strong enough to deal with it anyway. It's not like he hasn't got help. He'll be back on his feet in no time."

"You're a fucking disgrace to the family," Barney's eyes were shot through with tangles of glowing red capillaries now. "The dictionary definition of traitor."

"Hear, hear," Clem wailed. "And what about my darling Ben? The father of this princess?" she traced a heart around her stomach. "He's only gone and thrown himself in the icy Norwegian waters because of that gold-digging cow," she looked pointedly at Ellie as if she were something off the bottom of her Louboutins. "And you," she sneered at Brooke while she was at it.

"Erm, hang on just a minute," said a formerly unregistered voice; the voice of a wonderful wallflower called Connie who'd, unbeknownst to Ellie, grown to be a bit of an omnivert poppy over the years, able to break out into theatrical colour when circumstance dictated. "Perhaps the stupid twat just realised what a giant mistake he'd made, letting either of these ladies down in two very different and two very unacceptable ways... and yes, you heard me right, biyatch... I did refer to them as ladies... something you couldn't hope to pull off in a billion laps of the sun, you stuck-up mare."

Oh. Em. Gee.

Go, Connie Hsu!

And what a pity Connie hadn't displayed, or taught, Ellie

that unique brand of sass and sprinkled it liberally all over Monty's when they'd had the chance.

Brooke rolled her arm out in Connie's direction and granted her a demure (ish) curtsy-stroke-bow. Ellie tried in vain to mask her grin, whilst Clem gritted her teeth, a pampered and severely pissed-off lapdog.

"I learnt everything about how not to behave from the pair of you, actually. Be proud of yourselves," Brooke snubbed her siblings and turned to Ellie so they could pick up from where they'd left off.

But Ellie remained unusually mute. Astoundingly, or perhaps not, because he probably really didn't wish to know the juicy details, Barney did as he was not so long ago instructed, hands morphing into earmuffs.

"Ellie, listen to me, for once, and for the love of God. He's a nobody, beneath that rich chocolate hair-do, which is even looking a little helmet-like of late."

Clem scoffed. Ellie chewed on both cheeks, because although she agreed; although his hair bloody well was looking as rigid and glossy as something out of a toy box, she wasn't used to laughing at the former love of her life's expense.

"Oh, don't give him more gravitational pull than he deserves. He's not the moon," Brooke paused to let that sink in. "It was lust, Ellie. Teenage hormones. Something you should have relegated to the attic along with the Smash Hits mags and Impulse body spray years ago. And whilst, as the guy's sister, said lust isn't something I can even begin to wrap my head around, what I do know for sure, is that you deserved better then and you deserve better now. When has he ever given you the time of day, past or present? I'll let you into a secret; it ain't gonna happen in your future either."

"And how can you forgive *him* so quickly? Where's your dignity?" Ellie motioned at the television screen, desperate to change the subject, to make somebody else the centre of attention. Thierry moved tentatively closer. Ha, it had worked.

"Well, of course I haven't forgiven either of them yet," Brooke rolled her eyes towards her sister. "But I will." A small smile illuminated her face. "I've got you to thank for that." She walked slowly toward Thierry in an action that bridged her own past, present and future.

Lucky bitch.

"And I have you to thank for that too." Brooke returned her focus to Ellie now. Great. "Well, you're my reflection, aren't you? Visual proof of how desperate things can get when we don't take the hint and move on."

Poetic, Brooke. Thanks a bloody lot for so publicly putting it like that.

Ellie remained silent. She knew Brooke was right. Over the course of the past few hours, she'd already reached this decision herself. But change was hard. She'd unwittingly made Barney her comfort zone. Nobody else could measure up to him – for better or for worse. So how would she ever find the man she was really supposed to be with? No wonder Carlos had looked for a new dance partner beneath the sheets, when she put it like that.

"Look, it's not you, it's him. It's how he treats us all, to different degrees, in different ways."

Brooke would be hoping something was registering at last, but Ellie was aware that they had an audience, thrumming in anticipation of her reaction, and this was a conversation she was only ever willing to have with Brooke. Alone.

Not that she'd ever get that now. Well, unless Brooke came to visit her in her cell. Shit, French prison didn't exactly sound like a fairy-tale.

"Oh, maybe it's not entirely Barnaby's fault. That much I'll concede. He's hardly had the best role models when it comes to parenting. Huh, neither has she," Brooke inferred Clem with a tilt of her head, "but we're never bound to those destructive genetic patterns. Reading between the lines, I'm sensing your childhood was hardly a bed of roses either." Gloria (who was back now from fussing over the fire brigade with the leftover hemp-infused chocolate supplies from her journey) and Connie nodded sagely.

"Fire's out, by the way, and only three quarters of the *gîte* was destroyed in the end, so, you know, every cloud and that. Erm," Gloria put her hand to her mouth, evidently recalling the former property's French name. "Excuse the very poor pun," she continued, taking in the astounded faces of the small gathering before retreating to a corner table and fanning herself down with a Le Pere Jules cider coaster.

"But you're no more destined to repeat history than Barnaby is," Brooke picked up the threads of her crusade. "Everyone has a choice."

"Don't be so naive, big sis. This was all about the money. Can't you see?" Clem looked exasperated, it clearly pained her that not everybody saw the world through a pair of cartoonish dollar-sign eyes.

"Don't listen to her, Ellie," said Brooke, and Clem gawked at the nerve of her sister. "If money was the be-all and end-all of life, then why in the hell do you think I'm walking away from it?"

A flurry of the inquisitive regulars piled back in then, hot on Gloria's cape tails. The moment was lost… until a new one was created, and Ellie found herself not only eating the previous words that had billowed through what was left of her brain, but regurgitating and sharing them, spectacularly with the entire cafe.

Thoroughly unnecessarily.

"B… but I was invisible then, and now I'm not." That was one way of putting it. So much so that a sudden stillness fell upon the place and even Michel the owner's severe and squeaky buffing of his cider glasses, the cafe's constant background theme tune, could be heard, until he, too, stopped in his tracks to listen. "And I... I... don't really want to go back to being a nobody, you see?"

The old men gabbled quietly among themselves as Ellie checked them out individually for a response. Bloody hell, what had it come to? Asking retired French cider drinkers for their life advice! Well, when in Normandy, and all that.

"I can't go back to being a nobody."

She got into her stride, a makeshift stage opening up now as everyone – with the exception of Barney, who had scuttled to the village's *pétanque* court at the end of the road to sit on a bench and stare at a tree, wondering where it had all gone so wrong – gathered around her, street-performer style.

"I just can't do it." She paused to laugh at how pathetic her life had become.

"No such word," heckled Gloria, cheeks glowing profusely from so much action on a Sunday morning.

"The finishing line was always marrying him, having her as a sister-in-law... well, and you, which would have been infinitesimally nicer," Ellie tipped her head towards Brooke (and Thierry, since they'd already morphed into one being), and yeah, all right, I'll admit it, the money would have been cushy too."

"Oh, my God. I've heard it all now," said Brooke, and the crowd murmured their agreement.

"Ellie, that's nothing to aspire to," Connie set foot on the 'stage' and looked beseechingly into her former school friend's eyes. "You don't need any of that shit to complete you, or to feel that you've arrived at your destination, and deep down you know it!"

And just like that, as if she were a comedienne at the end

of her live performance, bouquets falling at her feet, the crowd broke out into euphoric cheer (well, all except Clem, who'd slunk off to look for her brother) and first Gloria, then Brooke and Thierry, came to envelop her in a giant and much-needed group hug. It was up there with the slightly more bizarre moments of her life, and granted, only one per cent of Ellie believed she deserved a second chance, but maybe, just maybe, when all was said and done, somehow she wasn't quite as wicked as she had always feared. Connie was wise, and Connie knew her of old. She'd hang on to the threads of that hope for dear life, now she really had been given another shot.

Well, after however long she was destined to spend inside, that was. Speaking of which, why in the hell weren't the police here questioning her, or questioning any of them?

"I want you to have some therapy," said Brooke, half an hour later, once Michel had seen some settlement of their initial bar bill and, semi-satisfied, agreed to bring them yet more coffee and chocolate éclairs. "Will you do that for me, Ellie? Will you do it for you? Despite this gargantuan mess, I'm actually thankful for what you've done; the way you've shaken everything up and made me see the light. And there's a job waiting for you, if you'll have it. A partnership, actually. I want us to run a company together."

Ellie almost spat out her coffee at that.

"God knows what we'll even do," said Brooke. "But I'm sure we'd come up with something better than my family's gimmick. We could even be their rivals." Her eyes glinted now and Ellie was sure she was in some kind of freakish shapeshifting state between nightmare and dream. "We can spend the next few months thinking about it. Let's meet up half a year from now to the day." Brooke pulled out a business card from the back pocket of her jeans and she scribbled a faraway date in 2021 on the back of it. "But therapy first," she added.

Ellie took the card, hands trembling. She rotated it between her fingers under the table. Its promise of a better future was tempting. But why would anyone be this forgiving, after all she had done, all she had put them through?

"We had a responsibility, too," said Connie, as if reading her mind.

Ellie tried to find the words to protest but now Gloria, it seemed, had X-ray vision into the frontal lobe of her brain, and beat her to it:

"In the words of a certain Larkin, they bleep you up, your mother and father… you're not cut out for prison life, honey. Look what freedom has done to you."

"I… I need to pay for this. Don't you dare take my glory away," Ellie countered weakly.

"I rather think it's me who should be saying that to you. It's me who needs to foot the bill, Ellie: G.L.O.R.I.A, the clue's in the name… as much as in the boots." Gloria chuckled away to herself before biting eagerly into a chocolate éclair, relishing the crack of its dark, glossy icing, as if she were at her Last Supper. "Quite simply, you were the wrong apprentice, sweetheart."

"Hey? What?"

Goosebumps prickled Ellie's arms. But that just couldn't be.

Gloria nodded and sank her teeth into the whipped cream. Ellie (and Brooke, Thierry, and Connie) averted their gaze, busying themselves playing with cutlery, thumb-twiddling, and generally anything they could think of, until Gloria resumed her patter, signalling it was safe to re-establish face contact.

"Later I met the right one, when my travels took me to Avebury and the stones," she continued perkily. "Of course I prayed that word would never wend its way back to me that you were in trouble, and I even asked my deity for extra help, that she'd edge you firmly back towards mainstream life. But then Connie came to me for a tea-leaf reading while she was back in England on a business trip, and that was that."

Connie flashed the table a wan smile and the final clue to the chocolate box puzzle slotted into place. "It was certainly what you might call revealing," she added.

"Aha, I did wonder," said Brooke, as if she were Velma summarising a Scooby Doo mystery. "So that's the significance of the letter T, then."

"Thank Mother Earth for Connie's intuition," Gloria confirmed it. "And well, no such thing as a coincidence that we should just happen to be here, to start our Tibetan Sound Bowl and Tapestry retreat, as you lot are leaving. Not that there will be a retreat anymore. Not in the traditional sense, anyhow. Yes, a bit of French prison will suit me fine. Some meditation time to reflect on acting too quickly on my many impulses. A diet of bread and water won't harm me too much, either," she patted down her rotund frame.

"But you can't. That's not justice. You didn't start the fire," Ellie hissed. "I'm the most wanted at this table, followed swiftly by him." She pointed at Thierry, who looked mortified. Brooke looked like she'd had her heart torn out.

"Okay, then. I'm the one and only wanted," Ellie corrected herself.

"This isn't Denmark! You'd die in there, Ms. Sanchez. There's no need to be a martyr. I won't allow it. Here's where I step in to mend the error of my ways. In fact, I already have. The firefighters have been given a full report. The police will be here any minute now. Besides, if I plead guilty, they might reduce the sentence. Depends how the *gîte*'s owners want to take it, of course, but I do hear they're fairly laid back."

"Er," Ellie couldn't help but picture Jock on the beautiful

ice-blue chaise longue, so laid back he was, indeed, horizontal. However, seeing his life's work go up in flames, she doubted he'd be inclined to fully recline, and take all of this on the chin.

"But it was still me who started it," she pleaded again in vain, as Gloria's hand fell proprietorially upon the plate for second helpings. Just then a trio of male, and searingly hot, *gendarmes* burst through the door.

Hmm. All right. Now Ellie got it. She could only hope Gloria had the same enthusiasm for prison officers, and their slightly more drab attire.

Because it turns out that while you're having your chocolate, and eating it, on the day you've miscarried your baby, nursing your heartache in the way half your kindred spirit sex tend to do, whilst the other half shun the very notion of comfort food's nourishment and sink straight into that deep, dark hole... on that very same day, you discover something else that destroys your world as you thought you knew it.

Mum X

You find out that fifteen years ago your husband was having an affair; an affair that resulted in his lovechild. An affair that resulted in your daughter's half-brother.

Mum X

That's why I can't be with you, Eleanor, my darling. I can't even look at you. I let you down. I failed to stop my husband's eyes wandering.

I ate the chocolate.

I got fat.

Mum X

33

ELLIE

*O*f course, confidential information should always be handled appropriately, and never divulged to any unauthorized person. Pamela had managed to hold back her final pearls of chocolate-based aversion therapy, tucking them in the book jacket of a dusty old Jilly Cooper romp.

And Ellie had successfully mastered that much herself. Which is why she never shared the notes from her mother with anyone. Not even the shrink.

Words are a powerful thing.

They can transcend space, time and logic.

They wend their way down through the blood, half, step, royal and blood-brother veins, in one of two ways; Chinese whisper-style so their message becomes antiquated and diluted, often highlighting the progress we have made in the modern-day; old wives' tales whose punch is no more. And then there's the way they've been handed across and down in the Finch family.

Pamela sought refuge in chocolates after a bad day at work; the kind of bad day that is only magnified by a bad marriage. Keith came home drenched in a December rain-

325

storm, caught her in the act after his own equally bad day at work – redundancy rumours had begun – and proceeded to spout at her:

"Well, there'll be no need to put the heating on this month, now you've demolished all those guilty pleasures and added an extra fat later to your middle. What do they call it nowadays…? Oh yeah, that's right," Keith had smirked. "The muffin top."

Pamela never touched a chocolate from that day forth.

Yes, words are a very powerful thing. Never more so than on the day you have a miscarriage… a day which just happens to coincide with discovering your husband has been having an affair.

If there's one thing Pamela thought she was doing for her daughter, it was warning her about chocolates. She loved Ellie very much in her own screwed up way; her daughter whose looks, particularly in her teenage years, were the spit of her polygamous father. That had led Pamela to feel she had no choice but to run to sunny Spain and its healthy Mediterranean diet when she'd met Fabien at his yoga-fused-with-parkour classes in Glastonbury. Ellie Sanchez lay on her recently-acquired ice-blue chaise longue – she had the six-month salary Brooke insisted upon paying her to thank for that – sifting through memories to satisfy Dr. Holly's homework. For the millionth time, she recalled her parting conversation with Brooke before driving herself and Connie back to the port.

"You've done me the biggest of favours… in a roundabout and tangential kind of way. A *very* roundabout way," Brooke had told her.

"If you insist. I still don't understand how."

Guilt had crept around Ellie's gills, to the point she wasn't sure she could retain the contents of her stomach. If she stopped to list all the terrible crimes she'd committed, the ferry would have docked in Dover by now.

"Okay, I'm going to level with you, like you want me to," Brooke's face became momentarily harsh, her brows knitting together. "You are a bitch. You are a cow. And you are undeniably and dangerously evil... all rolled into one." That felt better, every word of it resonating. "And yet beneath that exterior, you're made of light; a sort of legendary guru in your own right – both as Ellie Sanchez and as Eleanor Finch. You've helped me reset my inner compass, you've made me reassess everything in my life, and if it wasn't for you, well, I definitely wouldn't have met you-know-who." Starry-eyed, Brooke looked at Thierry, who was settling the final, and rather excessive bill at the cafe counter. "Neither would I be taking a much-needed few months out to travel."

Was Ellie still that unintentional 'guru' person now? And, more to the point, perhaps, was half of her still the angry victim who'd stop at nothing to settle scores? The number of times she'd started to key Brooke's number into her phone... but then she'd stopped, telling herself that Brooke and Thierry might be scuba diving in the Red Sea at that moment, or bungee jumping off a bridge in New Zealand, or indulging in mind blowing sex in a yurt in Mongolia.

The only thing she knew for certain was that the filing cabinet in her head felt more like a small A4 folder nowadays. And that had to be good.

It would take Ellie Sanchez precisely ninety-nine days into her time away from Brooke to realise how lucky she was. The Universe had come up trumps in many ways, gifting her with a second chance. It would take her another fifty days to get over Barney (all right, Barnaby, if that's what he wanted to be called now), to understand the way her teenage emotions had clung to someone who had never really grown up. A boy who may or may not have killed off his flipping nan. It would take her another twenty-four hours more to finally call the greatest Westwood of all time; to catch Brooke at just the right moment in a cafe in Paris, sipping pink champagne with Thierry, brainstorming business ideas for a food, photography and travel retreat, whose pins in the map would soon span from Andorra to Zanzibar.

Oh! Go on then.

34

BROOKE

*J*n the end, Brooke had reasoned with herself, what difference could there possibly be between her ability to chant at chocolates, and Ellie's? Especially when her own words were steeped, rooted, and gold-tipped in good.

And she'd used her mainstream powers, fused them with logic, and went for it. Love had to banish fear, and since Ellie's bitter and angst-ridden hexing had yielded increasingly uncomfortable results to date, any remotely positive diatribe directed at what remained of the chocolates had to be a vast improvement, by the law of averages alone.

She memorised the assortment that remained in the box, put pencil to paper and sketched a none-too-shabby repro to aid her next step.

"Transform the curse for everyone's highest good."

Seven simple words. But she believed in their potential to resolve, and their sprinkle of happily-ever-after, with all her might. Counter-curses could be just as powerful as their opposites, as far as Brooke was concerned. And, well, her results sort of spoke for themselves.

Clementine flew to Lofoten to bail out Ruben/Ben/Whatever-His-Actual-Name-Was. It had to be the first time she'd spent a significant sum of money on anything other than haute couture, signifying at least a catwalk-style strut in a new direction: compassion. The last Brooke had heard, Archie'd offered Clementine, R/B/W and their baby boy (yep, her sister had also come to learn that not everything could be pre-ordered to match her specific requirements) a penthouse in New York. Pretty compassionate of Archibald himself, all things considered. A fresh start for them all, and a chance for R/B/W to impress Wall Street with his, ahem, *skills*.

And how ironic, hey? Ellie had inadvertently got what she thought she wanted, after all: an extended family link to the dynasty that was the Westwood clan. Quite literally, too. Shortly after which, the RBPC went into liquidation.

Barnaby – where to start? Saffy speedily moved on from him, and married his best friend. Yep, one of the backstabbers from Monty's. Heartbroken and distraught, her brother 'did an Ellie' and became consumed with lust for Amelia Garland, who had, unbeknownst to even Clementine, apparently always been the real love of his life. Conveniently, Amelia lived across the pond too in her native Canada, putting the neat wedge of the Atlantic between the alleged event on Brighton pier, and the guilt-ridden git.

Daddy Westwood came home in the end, and in need of a bloody good shave. Daddy also caught Mummy having sex with Frank. But not in the office, erm, nope… in the Westwood marital four poster bed.

Mummy breathed a sigh of relief that everything was out in the open, and went shopping.

Brooke also knew Gloria was right. Prison would have destroyed Ellie, and if she had made it through, she'd only be back out to reoffend. Things had gotten catastrophic enough this time, her next cry for help didn't bear thinking about. No. What the girl needed was a healthy dose of the right kind of counselling; definitely no more woo-woo witchcraft.

What the girl needed was the same kind of second-but-last chance that she'd sought to achieve for the Really Bad Photo Company. All right, admittedly, failing spectacularly.

And what the girl needed more than any of that was an even healthier dose of love. The right kind of love: a strictly unromantic and rooted-to-the-earth endearment this time.

35

JOCK, JULES AND JOURNALIST

French Homes, Dreams and Disasters magazine, August 2020 edition:

Reluctantly, I return to Pruneau to ask Jock and Jules my final question. At their insistence, this is face to face and not via the shield of Skype, which would have felt infinitely safer after Jock's previous declaration about his past career. At ***my*** *insistence we meet in the café where the village's male boules brigade kindly agree to clutch their balls (of the sporting variety) in their laps, should I give them the nod for their heavy duty ammunition.*

P.S. Bless their cotton socks, they've all subscribed to the magazine, despite the fact it's in English with a focus on ex-pats buying up all their quaint local properties and getting their Laurence Llewelyn-Bowen on. You can't ask for better community spirit than that.

Joanna: "Any final words on the extraordinary revelations of the strange month of September, and the arrest of one Gloria van Gaia?"

Jock: "None of this would ever have happened if Ellie Sanchez had gone for Jules' raw cacao truffles."

Jules: "We don't harbour grudges, though. Forgive and forget. Brooke Westwood came up trumps with the bail money. Human kindness isn't dead quite yet… although she could've subbed us a few euros while she was at it. Anyway, all of that's by the by now. Jock is a man with a plan."

Heaven help us…

Jules taps his knee excitedly, before turning her attention back to perusing the menu for anything gluten, lactose and sugar-free, and plumping for a glass of water instead. Waste not want not; I order the award-winning apricot tart that very same Brooke Westwood recommended as we chatted most cordially at the counter while I waited for my interviewees to show up. Apparently she's turned the experience into a positive and is starting some sort of retreat business of her own. She was just passing through on her way back from Paris. Aw, I do love a happily ever after.

But phoar, I wouldn't have minded a side of that male dish she was standing there arm in arm with. Which reminds me… I must pilfer the elusive Thierry Faubourg's deets from Jules before we go our separate ways today. Perhaps I'll coax Tweedledum and Tweedledee to sit outside on the pavement at one of those rusty cafe tables with the wonky legs. She can indulge in her waccy baccy out there at her leisure, and I can casually pop the question once she's suitably pie-eyed: 'New feature for the magazine; French Homes, Dreams and Disasters' Spotlight on Rural Properties and their Chefs… wouldn't it be wonderful to kick 2021 off with a triple spread special on yours? Help him get a bit of extra work while you rebuild the ark?

Jock: "It's early days and I'd rather this was off the record…

you never know who might be reading, can't risk having my idea poached. If I pull this one…"

Jules: "Not if, my love. When."

Jock: "I bloody love you. Just you wait till I get *you* home tonight." *Jock's voice goes up an octave and he throws Jules an elongated wink. The café's white poodle begins to yap behind the counter. Even the card-playing grandads in the far corner of the room are about to spit out their Pays d'Auge.*

Joanna: "Your secret's safe with me, Jock," *and my approximately 1,000 readers. Actually, make that 1010. I forgot to include the old farts in this bar.*

Jock: "I was riffing some ideas with an old school mate the other day, as you do. We're only making a bloody pilot! Forget every reality TV concept you have ever seen. This is going to be epic. We're going to spin the lot of them on their heads."

Jules: "The world won't know what's hit it."

Joanna: *The mind boggles. I have no words.*

Jock rubs his hands together so fiercely, I swear Bear Grylls and Ray Mears are going to jump out in tandem from hidey holes beneath the tables and congratulate him on creating fire with the mere friction of his anatomy. God, what am I saying? My poor brain's alight after the trials and tribulations of this interview feature. I can't wait to start writing about shabby chic upcycling again, and the dilemmas of the French bricolage store.

Jock: "It's a six-season fly on the wall style documentary called... wait for it... drum roll... *Bubblegum and Blazers.* We gather up a load of forty-somethings, shove them in a properly kosher, reconstructed early nineties classroom, complete with blackboard and chalk, detentions and disillusioned teachers; throw in a tuck shop for authenticity purposes. We'll have to, Jules, please don't eyeball me, I know you don't do bubblegum, or sherbet dips, and chocolate mice are sacrilege... but it's all for the greater good."

Joanna: "I suppose that will cover the *gîte*'s reconstruction and the quintessential barn conversion, allowing you to welcome even greater numbers of arty-farty folk, whose ripples will extend to help the world."

Jock: "Exactly. Bingo, m'lady! You got me at last. Sometimes in this blessed roller coaster called life, we have to do something a little bit sweet and sour, be cruel to be kind, lead the way for the lost souls of this strange, somnambulant world. I actually couldn't have put it better myself."

FIN

ABOUT THE AUTHOR

Isabella May lives in (mostly) sunny Andalusia, Spain with her husband, daughter and son, creatively inspired by the mountains and the sea. Having grown up on Glastonbury's ley lines however, she's unable to completely shake off her spiritual inner child, and is a Law of Attraction fanatic, and a Pranic Healer.

Cake, cocktail, churros, gelato, and travel obsessed; she also loves nothing more than to (quietly) break life's rules.

The Chocolate Box is her sixth novel.

You can keep up-to-date with all Isabella's bookish news here:
Twitter - @IsabellaMayBks
Instagram - @isabella_may_author
Facebook - https://www.facebook.com/IsabellaMayAuthor/
Website – www.isabellamayauthor.com

Also published by Isabella May:
Oh! What a Pavlova
The Cocktail Bar
Costa del Churros
The Ice Cream Parlour
The Cake Fairies

Coming soon... Bubblegum and Blazers

Reviews Matter!

Whether this book made you snort out loud laughing... or cry (the latter hopefully in a good way), please, please, please (x a gazillion) consider leaving an Amazon and/or Goodreads review.

Authors LOVE reviews as much as they love rainbows and unicorns, and, when you give out good karma and spread the word about their book, not only do you help other readers discover an author who doesn't have the marketing budget of a big name on the NYT bestseller list, but something good is sure to happen to YOU...

Thank you,
Isabella XX

Printed in Great Britain
by Amazon